To a … -)
and …

IN THE COMPANY OF JACKDAWS

Tony Jackson,

by

Tony Jackson

GHP
Grosvenor House
Publishing Limited

This book is published by
Grosvenor House Publishing Ltd
28-30 High Street, Guildford, Surrey, GU1 3EL.
www.grosvenorhousepublishing.co.uk

A CIP record for this book
is available from the British Library

ISBN 978-1-78148-844-7

Acknowledgements

I would like to acknowledge the following people for the help they have given me in the making of this book.

Alan Strong
Ken & Val Graham

Who helped me with editing the book
And who also helped in the design of the book cover

Not forgetting
My wife Pat

Who put up with me during the months I sat at the computer writing this novel

Foreword

"In the Company of Jackdaws"

This is the second book to feature DS Bene Douglas of the Levensbridge Police Force.

In 1944 an astonishing secret is discovered by German soldiers in Northern France. The secret is never revealed and goes to the grave with them.

In 2010 two bodies are exhumed from the woods and a deadly chase begins to find the secret.

Suspicious deaths, attempted murder, robbery and a missing young boy all threaten to overwhelm our hero and his new colleague.

The investment club are being wooed, the bowls club members are running scared, and a crime from the past is re-opened.

Chapter 1

Etaples – Northern France January 1944

The Horrors of War

Dark clouds hung like a deathly shroud over the German coastal defences which stretched along the northern coastline of France: this was part of the Atlantic Wall which stretched from the Netherlands all the way down to Spain.

The rain which had been falling incessantly for the past eighteen hours had slowly turned into a cold and miserable icy drizzle. The wretched weather was reflected in the faces of the three German guards who stood uneasily in the cold night air continually shuffling their feet and tugging up the collars of their sodden grey overcoats. Their thoughts were focused solely on the end of their shift when they could return to the newly constructed concrete bunker. Once in there they could look forward to a hot drink and a change into dry clothes; if there was any wood left for the fire they could put some warmth back into their shivering bodies.

This was not what the three friends from the small town of Maierhofen in southern Germany had joined the army for back in 1939. Otto Bauer, Lukas Kohler and Dieter Hoffmann, along with many others of a similar age had enlisted in the ever expanding German armed forces. They had been swept along on the rising tide of nationalistic passion which had engulfed not only Maierhofen but the whole of the German nation.

The three friends had borne witness to many crimes against the local community during their time in northern France. Every man, woman and child in that part of France hated them, some actively taking part in obstructing the Germans in any way possible. If caught they were dealt with in the severest possible way. The local townspeople would be rounded up in the public square with family members placed at the front; here they were forced to watch the slaughter at close quarters. A single shot to the back of the head was the preferred method and the body left where it fell for the family to take away and bury. If they were lucky it was a straight forward execution, if not they would have to endure some form of torture first, before finally begging for a bullet to put an end to their suffering.

The worst single atrocity had taken place the previous day, and for the friends it was the final straw. It was this particular action that had determined them to plan their escape from this horrible place and the appalling life they had been forced to live there. If this was an example of the way of life the German people wanted for their future and for that of their children, then the three friends wanted no part of it.

The day before had started much the same as any other day but around midday everything started to change.

The three men had been summoned to accompany the two Huber brothers to a farm. The intention for this visit was not clear at first, but it became apparent as soon as they arrived at the farmhouse. The farmer's daughter had stupidly rejected the advances of Karl Huber the previous day, so together with his brother Franz they had returned to the farm to exact revenge on her and her family to atone for the humiliation he had suffered.

The daughter and her father were dragged from the farmhouse and taken over to a barn where they were shut in with the brothers. Once inside the farmer was tied to a post where he was to forcibly watch as his daughter was raped by the two thugs. The three friends waited outside feeling guilty but too frightened to intervene; they were powerless to prevent the forthcoming degradation of the farmer and his daughter. Standing by their vehicle and trembling with shame they waited for the screams to begin. When none came they began to wonder what was happening in the barn, but still none of them dared to go over and look.

After almost ten minutes of silence, the brothers together with the farmer came out from the barn and headed back to the vehicle where the friends were waiting. All six climbed into the truck, and under the direction of the farmer they drove out of the farmyard on a rough unmade road away from the farm. Nothing was said but the Huber brothers were looking smug. After about a kilometre they stopped and the six on board alighted from the vehicle to continue the journey on foot. The three friends had no idea what was happening or where they were going, but they would soon learn the reason for this unexpected journey, and the secret they would discover at the end of it would remain with them forever.

Four hours later the group returned to the vehicle; the brothers appeared satisfied with what they had seen and the six drove back in silence to the farmhouse. On their return the farmer was noticeably more relieved, he was hoping that the secret he had shown them would save his family from any further attention from the soldiers. He walked over towards the barn with the intention of releasing his daughter, unaware that Franz and Karl were close behind.

Reaching the door he pushed it open and entered the barn, as he stepped inside he felt a huge hand on his back which propelled him into the centre of the barn where he stumbled and fell forward onto his knees. A shot rang out and the farmer slumped forward onto the floor with a gaping hole in the back of his head. The brothers entered the barn completely unmoved by the high pitched screams of the terrified daughter. The poor girl had to endure almost half an hour of physical and sexual abuse before her ordeal was finally ended by another single shot. The brothers though were not yet finished with the family; their thirst for revenge would not be quenched until it was final and absolute.

Walking back to the truck they took out a can of petrol and returned to the barn where they poured the fuel onto the wooden walls and door, then likewise with the farmhouse. Karl calmly lit a cigarette then threw the match to the door. Standing back the brothers watched as the flames shot up the walls of the house. When a face appeared at an upstairs window Franz calmly pulled out a revolver, he fired successive shots up towards the window where the farmer's wife and her young son were looking for an escape from the fire. The shots drove them back inside; there was to be no escape for them. When the flames reached the rooms above more screams could be heard from the two people trapped inside. These had no effect on the Huber brothers who were in their element, laughing raucously as the screams shrieked out from the farmhouse. At last the heartrending cries died down as the two remaining family members succumbed to the flames. In the truck the three friends sat weeping at the horrific scene that had been played out before them. The Huber brothers remained until the entire farm had been razed to the ground, then suddenly and without any sign of emotion they climbed into the truck and drove back to base.

Chapter 2

September 1939 – January 1944

An opportunity presents itself

In late 1939 the three friends had enlisted into the newly formed local regiment in Maierhofen, and very soon they would find themselves to be part of the huge force that would invade France. In early May following on behind the main German thrust across the border into France they met with little resistance to impede their progress, the French forces were continually falling back towards the capital keeping distance between themselves and the invading army. The invasion had been planned well, it was efficient and disciplined and moved forward with a concerted urgency. In no time at all they found themselves on the outskirts of Paris itself. As the regiment arrived on the outskirts of the unguarded city it was held there waiting while negotiations between the two sides came to an agreement on armistice. The regiment from Maierhofen was part of a much larger German Army and would remain in Paris for the next three months. Then it was to go north to join up with the Army again and defend the northern coast against a possible Allied invasion.

The three young men had been schooled together and had remained close friends throughout their teenage years. More studious than aggressive by nature, they had only enlisted as their duty to the Fatherland, not through any personal choice or ambition. Not to have volunteered would certainly have incurred a good deal of anger from their fellow citizens in the staunchly pro-Nazi town of their birth.

Otto and Lukas had been close neighbours in their home town, and until the start of the war both had been studying at medical school. Otto stood tall and slim, well over six feet, in fact in his uniform he had the appearance more of an officer than an infantryman. He was a quiet, sensitive man, an only child of whom his parents had high hopes of fulfilling his and their ambition of becoming a surgeon. He wore small rounded spectacles which suited his long narrow, rather serious looking face with its sharp features. His pale almost unhealthy looking complexion gave the impression he would always be ailing something, but on the contrary he rarely ailed from anything at all. He had sleek black hair which was swept well back from his forehead.

Lukas was a little shorter but still around six feet tall; he also had the same pale complexion but lacked the sharp features of Otto. His face bore a slightly pained blank expression, almost as if a little confused by his surroundings and the people around him. This was a misconception as anyone taking him at face value would soon discover, the brain behind this plain exterior was sharp and he was in full control of himself and his actions. His hair was similar to Otto's, black and swept back.

Dieter on the other hand was the perfect example of the Arian race, tall and blonde with a powerful athletic body; a well formed slightly ruddy face with sparkling blue eyes. His body language oozed confidence and demanded respect. He possessed a ready smile and had a sense of humour with which to charm any lady. He had worked as an apprentice in his father's antique shop and it was his father's wish that Dieter would take over the business when he retired.

At the other end of the spectrum were the two Huber brothers Franz and Karl. They were part of a large family of notorious bullies who were feared for their renowned violence and reprisals against anyone who dared to cross them. Although they were not twins the appearance of both was chillingly similar, huge men with large round heads. Their deep red faces sported large thick ginger moustaches that matched their closely cropped ginger hair. The flared nostrils and small eyes set well back in their heads completed the features that stood them apart from all others. Unfortunately for the three friends the Huber brothers had enlisted in the same regiment.

2

It was now 1944 and they had been in France for almost four years. The war which had started out so well and had promised to be a short and decisive one now seemed to be turning against them. With the British and

American armies now gathered only a few miles away across the channel, going home anytime soon was looking very remote indeed. Even more worrying was the fact that with the German forces so stretched, would they be able to keep an increasingly expanding and well-equipped Allied army from landing in France. If they were to get a foothold in Europe they would surely not stop there, but drive the German army right back into the fatherland, and then what? How would they exact their revenge on the German nation. Knowing how they had steamrollered across Europe and Russia destroying everything and everyone in their path, this was too frightening to even think about.

3

The events of the previous day still consumed the minds and thoughts of the three men who were coming to the end of their guard duty. The last few years had taking its toll; they had witnessed and experienced things that no one in this world should ever have to do. For Otto there was nothing to look forward to except changing out of his wet clothes and getting some hot liquid into his frozen body, maybe some coffee if he was lucky. He should have followed his two friends back to the bunker but instead he made his way over to a point overlooking the little harbour where he thought he had seen something that was not quite as it should have been.

Moving quietly forward to get a better view he spotted what he thought was part of the ground that looked as if it was moving on its own accord. He continued to watch, and as his eyes adjusted to the conditions he saw what looked like a small fishing boat being dragged out from under cover. Screwing up his eyes he could just make out the outline of someone who was pulling it down to the edge of the water. He moved closer and as he approached the man suddenly became aware of his presence. The man turned and waved to someone Otto could not quite see, but when he shone his torch over in that direction he picked out a woman and two small children standing by the harbour. All four froze not knowing what to expect from the German.

Otto found himself temporarily unable to move, he was just as astonished as they were. After a short silence and no movement from the four people Otto approached the man and asked what he was thinking about, putting a boat out to sea at this hour of darkness. The man who was a local fisherman realised that there was no reason or excuse he could give to account for what he was doing prepared himself for the inevitable. He spoke quietly, but his voice was shaking so much that Otto had difficulty in taking in much of what he was trying to say. After what seemed an age Otto finally came to understand that all the man wanted to do was take his wife and children over to England, to take them away from this horrible war where they would be able to live in safety with friends. The man went down on his knees and wept openly, begging the German not to report them. A long silence followed and both men seemed reluctant to break it. The fisherman was confused by the German's lack of reaction and his continued silence, knowing fine well that others who had defied the occupying army had paid dearly with their lives.

Otto was tired of war, he had seen too many atrocities carried out against these people. He didn't want to see the fisherman or his family punished for trying to escape the war, in the same situation he was sure he would be doing exactly the same. His mind was still numb and he was taking his time deciding what to do for the best. If he allowed the family to go to sea he might be found out himself and punished, if not, then punishment for the fisherman and his family would be certain death.

It was as well that he took time to decide for slowly a solution began to form in his mind, a solution which could benefit them all. He spoke quietly to the fisherman explaining first what would happen to them if they were reported, the frightened fisherman listened intently. After a short silence Otto suggested the alternative. He would not report the fisherman but he would have to take Otto and his two friends with him to England. The fisherman agreed at once but said they would have to leave immediately as the conditions that night were perfect for a night crossing of the channel. If they didn't leave tonight there may not be another chance for weeks.

As a precaution Otto took a small but essential part of the boat's engine with him and quickly made his way back to the bunker. Once there he motioned his friends over to a quiet corner and explained to them what he had agreed with the fisherman. The two were taken completely by surprise and it took a minute or two for the information to sink in. What they were about to do was desert, nothing less, and punishable by a firing squad if caught. All three went silent as they considered the enormity of what they may be about to do.

Thankfully there was not enough time to think it through properly as the boat would soon have to leave if it was to have any chance of getting away unnoticed. With the events of the day before weighing heavily on their minds the decision was made. All three were in agreement, this would be their only chance to escape the horrors they had been living through. Whichever way the war ended Germany would never be the same again, not for them or their families. They collected dry overcoats and stepped outside.

The rain had all but stopped and if they hurried there was a good chance they would get away unnoticed before the next change of guards had reached and taken up their positions. Going as fast as they dared they sped down towards the coast and climbed into the waiting boat. The fisherman urgently held out his hand for the missing engine part, Otto went into shock as he realised the part was still in his wet overcoat which had been left in the bunker. He jumped out of the boat and hurried back up the hill to the bunker almost knocking Karl Huber over as he rushed inside. "What the hell you doing man," Karl shouted.

Speechless and fuming at his own carelessness Otto went over to his coat, with his back to Karl he took out the engine part and put it in his pocket. He turned to leave but saw Karl barring his exit. "Well," he said "What's the bloody hurry, don't you have time to sit down and have a nice hot drink with us?"

"Sorry but I've got a girl waiting for me, its bloody cold out there and she won't wait forever." it was all he could think of saying, "I've got to rush."

Karl roared with laughter

"About bloody time as well, I thought there must be something wrong with you three, let me have her when you're finished and we'll say no more about it." With that he let Otto pass; he was still enjoying the joke as Otto rejoined the party on the boat, the engine part was quickly installed and the little boat slipped quietly away from the French coast and headed off across the channel to England.

Chapter 3

Lower Hutton P O W Camp –
Levensbridge, England – June 1944

An unhappy reunion

The three friends had been in England for almost six months and had settled easily into life in the POW camp. Close to the river Leven it was only a couple of miles from the northern market town of Levensbridge, which nestled in a naturally formed valley near the southern end of the Lake District.

Back in January it had been dark when they had stepped ashore from the boat on the south coast of England. The three men had helped the fisherman to haul the small vessel out of the water and pull it a little way up the beach where it could be secured. Luckily they had not been spotted, if the boat had been seen they would surely have been fired on and possibly killed before they had been given the chance to surrender themselves. Once on land they split up from the fisherman and his family and set off for the nearest town where they could surrender. When this had been accomplished they were sent under escort to the camp at Lower Hutton which had been specifically set up for Germans who had surrendered. The camp was separate from other camps which housed German soldiers who had been captured.

For the first time in years Otto, Lukas and Dieter felt safe and secure. The war which was still raging in Europe seemed a million miles away. They had adjusted to a different way of life and were settling in quite happily. At first they were unsure about how they would be accepted at the camp, but soon found that the officers were friendly and treated them with respect. With the help of an interpreter they were encouraged to learn the language so they could be sent out to work on the local farms. After a few short weeks they were allocated a farm each where they would work throughout the day, and return to the camp in the evening.

The work was hard as some of the local farmhands had been enlisted into the army and labour was in short supply, but there were no complaints from the three men. Time passed quickly and soon the bad memories they had brought over with them began to dwell less and less on their minds. They tried not to think about what was happening in France, but were worried about how Germany and Maierhofen in particular were faring. They received no news at all from their home town, the only information about the war came from the guards at the camp and the farms where they worked. The camp was a pleasant place to be and if it was not possible to return to Maierhofen they would remain in England and make this their home.

There had been no more talk of the trip they had taken with the Huber brothers and the French farmer, or the secret they had discovered in France. As far as they were concerned the secret could remain there forever, and if the Huber brothers wanted to return they were quite welcome to whatever rewards awaited them.

The camp guards were not really guards at all in the sense of the word as no one in the camp wanted to, or even thought about escaping. As time went on the guards and prisoners would often sit together in the evenings. Friendships were formed and developed which would last long after the war was over, until now everything had been going smoothly. The farmers fed their workers well in reward for their efforts, and in the evenings the atmosphere was warm and amiable with a good mix of interests between the prisoners and their guards. Although the prisoners were not allowed out at night the guards would sometimes bring in a few drinks to share with the inmates.

Then came the news of the invasion by the Allied forces, many prisoners had been taken in northern France and the camp at Lower Hutton would have to accept some of the new prisoners. The officers in charge of the camp didn't want any discord between the prisoners already in the camp and the new ones coming in, so they agreed to say nothing about the inmates who had surrendered.

There were to be around twenty new POWs coming to the camp and the inmates waited anxiously for their arrival. The following day the new batch arrived. It was a sorry looking bunch of men who trudged slowly into the camp, their unshaven faces grey and drawn. What clothes they had on were dirty and ragged and the footwear was an odd collection of boots and wellingtons; one man wore a boot on one foot and a shoe on the other, another only had one boot. The three friends scanned over the new arrivals and their hearts sank when they saw the familiar forms of the two Huber brothers approaching.

This was the worst possible news. They couldn't believe that of all the men who had been captured it was their bad luck to be thrown together again in the same camp as these two men. To be fair the Huber brothers didn't seem remotely interested in any of the inmates already in situ in the camp. The war had not been kind to them, but nevertheless the mere sight of them sent shivers down the backs of the three friends, were they never to be rid of them. It would not be long before they were discovered and the brothers would know instantly of their desertion. The three friends went to bed that night with sunken hearts.

On their return to camp the following evening they found the new arrivals had settled in; it had been a warm sunny day and they were sitting outside talking quietly amongst themselves. The guards were wary and on edge as these new prisoners were real prisoners and would need to be watched carefully. It was Karl who first spotted the three friends; he jumped to his feet immediately and snarling obscenities made to rush over and confront them. One of the guards raised his rifle and quickly positioned himself in front of Otto, Lukas and Dieter. Karl stopped short of the guard but continued to shout loudly and gesticulate towards the three men he had been prevented from getting his hands on.

Other guards quickly came onto the scene and forced Karl back to his quarters. Franz had also seen the commotion and after making a gesture as if drawing a knife across his throat he followed Karl inside. There was no mistaking what the two brothers would like to do to the three men if given the chance. The guards had been unaware of the history between the two parties and were visibly shocked and frightened at the reaction of the two new inmates.

From that day on, the atmosphere in the camp became almost unbearable. The guards had to be on duty in the evenings and throughout the night, there were to be no more pleasant evenings in which to sit outside socialising with the inmates. During the day it was a little more relaxed as the inmates who worked on the farms were away for most of the time, but on their return there was an atmosphere of bad feeling between the two groups. Three weeks later the situation if anything had got worse. Franz and Karl had stirred up a lot of trouble and were a continual worry for the guards and the camp officers. On one occasion the pair had managed to gain entry into another block and had attacked two of the men who were sleeping there. As for the three friends, they had to be guarded all the time they were in the camp as they were the prime targets for the brothers.

The following week and with no improvement in the circumstances, the camp Commander Edwin Ferguson called the guards into his office for a meeting; the inmates had been separated and were having their lunch. It was obvious that something had to be done, the situation had got so bad that unless action was taken soon, someone was going to be killed. During the conversation between the men it became clear that all the trouble in the camp was caused by just two of the prisoners, the Huber brothers. The original inmates were no problem at all, and from the recent arrivals all but the two brothers had settled in fairly well and were reasonably happy there. The only time they needed to be guarded was when urged on by the brothers who wanted to stir up as much hatred and unrest in the camp as they could.

The Commander had listened to his men and stood up to address them. "It would appear that these two people are the sole cause of all the problems here." and after a short pause "It's a pity we can't send them to another camp but to do that we would need a good reason. All the other camps will have their share of trouble makers just as we have, so that alone is not sufficient to transfer them." Still standing he bowed his head in silence looking vaguely at the table in front of him and drumming his fingers on it. None of the men wanted to break the silence, they knew that the Commander hadn't finished addressing them. Finally, lifting his head he continued. "I know we're on a knife edge here, before the last prisoners came we had enough staff to function efficiently, but now we're stretched to the limit and I'm fully aware that none of you have been able to take any leave. You've all supported me and I appreciate the work that you're doing here, but it's too much to ask you to carry on like this indefinitely. I wish I could bring in more officers to help but it's no good even asking."

He took another short break before continuing. "Just tell me what the position would be if those two men were not here?" Several of the officers volunteered the answer, but it was left to one guard to express the view of all of the men.

"All the prisoners except those two are no problem at all, even the new ones. If they were not being bullied they would happily join the original inmates and go out to work, there would be no more trouble it's as simple as that." The meeting closed and the Commander had his solution.

The following day the brothers were marched out of the camp to work in the woods, escorted by two guards who stood over them while they carried out the work. The same procedure took place each day for the remainder of the week. It kept them away from the camp during the day, but as soon as they came back into the camp the trouble flared up again.

On Friday when they returned to camp they were led into the Commander's office. He closed the door and put a suggestion to them. "The work you have been doing through the week has been appreciated but there is still a lot to do, we're well behind in our schedule for wood clearance and we need to catch up. What I would like is for both of you to do an extra shift tomorrow." The brothers made it clear that they had no intention of doing any such thing.

"Weekends were not worked at the camp." they stressed. The Commander ignored this comment and continued.

"You will have realised that we are understaffed at the moment and my men are working long hours, they deserve some time off. If you'll agree to work this shift tomorrow a guard will take you out to the woods and leave you there. He'll come back later and bring you back to the camp, but during the day you'll be allowed to work unsupervised. The point is can I trust you to work unsupervised?" He waited for their response which was not long in coming.

Both men made it perfectly clear they would be only too happy to work on the Saturday, and of course they could be trusted. Where could they go to, they didn't want to leave the camp and all their friends. The Commander had the answer he had been looking for.

The brothers left the Commander's office with huge smirks on their faces, thinking of the following day when they could make good their escape. As they disappeared into their quarters, the Commander sent for the three friends. Closing the door behind them he told them they were free the following day if they wished to leave the camp. The three were a little surprised but would enjoy a little time out of the camp when they didn't have to work. Then came the crunch. The Commander explained the reason he was granting them some free time.

The three listened in silence with serious faces. He spoke to them quietly but clearly, giving exact details of what he wanted them to do. The three remained silent as they listened to what he was suggesting; they had been given an opportunity and it was up to them if they wanted to take that opportunity or not. The Commander continued. "I don't care if one, two, or all three of you carry it out. But it could be the only chance you'll have to rid yourselves of these bullies once and for all, and return the camp to what is was like before they came.

I can't stress strongly enough how the situation here has deteriorated and it could get even worse. The guards here are stretched to the limit and they can't be everywhere at all times. I'm sure that before long those two will find a way to get to you, and when they do I may not be able to guarantee your safety."

The following day came and the two brothers left the camp with their guard, shortly afterwards the three friends also left the camp. It was a good half an hour later when gunshots were heard back in the camp. "That will be the farmers shooting rabbits I expect," said the Commander to no one in particular, but making sure that the guards and at least some of the inmates could hear him. Strolling around the yard he made the same remark a little later although no one else could recall hearing further shots. His job for the time being done he returned to his office.

Later that afternoon the three friends returned to camp. Their faces were not showing any signs of the pleasure that should have been there, after all it wasn't everyday that free time was granted to inmates. They should also have been hungry, but instead of joining the others for the evening meal they went straight to their quarters and stayed there for the remainder of the day.

The guard was sent out to bring back the two brothers, but to the surprise of all but a few in the camp he came back alone. Almost out of breath he rushed into the Commander's office blurting out that the brothers were nowhere to be found. "They must have run off sir," he gasped. "Maybe it wasn't a good idea to leave them on their own." Strangely enough the Commander didn't seem too concerned.

"Not to worry they won't have gone far, they'll soon be found and brought back here again. It'll be dark soon but I'll send out a search party first thing in the morning." The guard left the office to tell his comrades of the escape.

The Commander was looking more stress-free now as he gazed over to the three empty spaces in the gun cabinet. "I'll have to make sure they're back in place before morning," he mused. Settling back in his easy chair he reached over to the cabinet and produced half a bottle of whisky, pouring out a large measure into a tumbler he sat back and relaxed. "Ah that's much better." he said.

2

Over the next two weeks the camp slowly returned to the peaceful state it had been in prior to the arrival of the Huber brothers. Their disappearance had been the main topic of conversation between the inmates for much of the first week, but gradually the men began to notice that the atmosphere in the camp had changed and had been steadily improving since their disappearance. The camp was a much better place without them, and it wasn't long before memories of the two men had faded altogether.

When the war finally ended many of the inmates wanted to return home to Germany to be re-united with their families, but although the fighting had stopped there was still a concern for the POWs. The government didn't favour the idea of sending all these people back to Germany so soon after the war. They wanted to ensure a period of lasting peace so the POWs would be returned to their homeland slowly over a period of time. The camp at Lower Hutton continued to function until the Autumn of 1946 when the last of the inmates were finally sent back for repatriation. There were a few who didn't want to return to their own country and these included the three friends. They wanted to stay in England, to live there and make careers for themselves.

When at last the camp closed the Commander gathered together what remained of the camp records, the majority of which had already been sent to head-quarters. Only a few remained and as well as these there were some personal items which had been kept. Looking through these he discovered some letters which had been given to him to post by the inmates. Memories of the two brothers came back to him. "Yes" he thought, "With all that trouble going on back then I must have forgotten about these." The letters had been checked to make sure they contained no information which may have been useful to the enemy, but for whatever reason the letters hadn't been posted. Two of them were addressed to Herr A Huber, that must be their father I suppose, it's a bit late now but I've got a couple of stamps that should do for one of them, I'll post it off tonight. The other ones I'll keep until I can get some more stamps in the morning."

Before the war Edwin had been head librarian at the central library in Levensbridge and he had been looking forward to taking up his position again as soon as the war ended. He had left his assistant in charge during his absence as the library had only been open two days a week during the war years. The two were good friends as well as colleagues and were keen to re-establish their close working relationship. Edwin called at the library first before going home taking all the items from the camp with him in a large tin box. "I'll put it in the storeroom until morning," he thought, "Then I'll make arrangements for it to be collected by the authorities." He dragged the heavy box down the steep stairway into the basement. The room was kept at a constant temperature which was needed to preserve the more valuable books and records kept by the library. He placed it alongside similar boxes and trunks which contained numerous miscellaneous items of historical value. Climbing slowly back up the stairs he found himself a little out of breath. "Well I'm not as young as I used to be," he reflected. "I'll have to be more careful and not overdo it from now on." He cast a swift eye over the library before leaving, then locked the outer door and went home.

Once home he made himself a quick meal and then poured out a good measure of his favourite whisky. Sitting back in his much-loved armchair he recalled how he had had to adjust to life on his own when his wife had suddenly been taken from him some years ago. Sylvia had always taken care of his needs. They had not been blessed with children, but had lived a contented and comfortable life together, just the two of them each dependant on the other. Then when Sylvia was diagnosed with leukaemia it was only a matter of a few short weeks before she gave in to the inevitable.

"Well thank goodness that's all done with." he sighed, the war now finally over he could look forward to his work back in the library. He raised himself wearily out of the chair, spread his arms and yawned. "My God that box must have been damned heavy it's quite worn me out, a good night's rest is what I need." Edwin went upstairs and climbed into his bed where he fell asleep almost immediately.

Morning came and the sunlight began to drift in through the bedroom window, over the next hour or so it crept slowly around the room until it rested on Edwin's face. The sunlight was strong but it didn't waken Edwin. Gradually the temperature in the room was getting warmer but the body in the bed was now cold. The tin box with all its records and letters would have to stay where it was, locked away in the storeroom at the library.

Chapter 4

Levensbridge – July 2010

Retirement Party

The party in the Fox and Pheasant public house was well underway and most of the staff from Levensbridge Police station were present. Following a successful career in the Metropolitan Police and latterly Levensbridge Police Force, Adam Firth had been looking forward to this moment. He could now put his feet up and start to enjoy his well earned retirement. Also leaving the force were Detective Sergeant Steve Mitchell who was retiring through ill health, and Detective Constable Mike Ostler who was being transferred to the North Lancashire Force.

The tall, rather rangy figure of Chief Inspector Sowerby with his distinctive sharp angular features was preparing to make his speech. He had nothing but praise and good luck messages to pass on to the three who were leaving the station, but it was also his duty to pass on news which would disappoint another member of his team.

DS Benedict (Bene) Douglas had proved to be a first class officer under Adam's guidance, and with Adam's retirement both he and Chief Inspector Sowerby had assumed that Bene would be promoted to Detective Inspector. Earlier in the day the Chief had received news of the proposed budget cuts for the forthcoming year; he was feeling uneasy and a little guilty about having to break the news to Bene. But it had to be done and now was as good a time as any. If he left it any longer Bene might find out from another source and that wouldn't do at all. Pulling Bene over to one side he began to explain the cuts which had just been announced. Bene listened intently.

He was slightly shorter than the Chief Inspector, but still an inch over six foot, he had put a pound or two on recently but was not overweight. His slightly weather beaten face with its rustic features was topped off with a mop of thick curly brown hair set a little back from his broad forehead, his big friendly brown eyes were fixed firmly on the face of his superior. There was to be no replacement for Adam and neither would the vacancy left by Steve Mitchell be filled. Bene was stunned; he had been planning his wedding and was looking forward to buying a new house for Alex and himself. The promotion he had been expecting would have gone a long way to securing a mortgage for the newlyweds.

"I'm sorry Bene I feel partially responsible for this myself. You passed all the exams and you deserve the promotion. I fully expected you to get it and I honestly didn't think this new round of cuts would be so drastic." The news had completely floored Bene and it took a little while for it to sink in. The Chief continued to try and console him but could offer little in the way of comfort.

He would appeal against the decision of course and hope to have the grade of Detective Inspector reinstated, but by the tone of his voice he didn't seem very confident of getting the decision overturned.

There followed a short silence which gave Bene a little time to take it all in and compose himself. "Well I can't say that I'm not disappointed, but if these cuts have to be made I suppose I have to be thankful that I still have a job. I mean if the cuts are carried out across the force then I expect quite a lot of people will actually lose theirs."

The Chief was relieved that Bene had taken the news this way. He wanted to remind him how well he had managed when working on his own, using his own devices he had singlehandedly solved two cases earlier in the year.

"Remember a few months back when Adam was off with a heart attack, Steve was on long term sick leave and Mike was spending most of his time in the office?"

"Yes" said Bene "But that was different, and it was only for a couple of months or so, I couldn't do it all the time."

"No of course not," said the Chief. "But in those few months you grew up and you proved yourself to me and everyone else in the station, and look at the results you got."

Bene listened to the praise he was getting from the Chief but a sudden thought threw him into a state of panic. "If they're not replacing Adam, Steve and Mike that means I'm going to be on my own again, I don't think I can manage without any support at all." The Chief was quick to calm him down.

"Well there is a bit of good news Bene because I've no intention of letting you struggle on by yourself." Bene looked quizzically at the Chief wondering what was coming. "Granted, Adam and Steve won't be replaced, but starting on Monday we'll have a new Detective Constable at Levensbridge and he'll be working directly under you." This news cheered Bene up a bit. For although Mike had been in CID he had never really been much help to Adam or to him. Most of his time had been spent in the office working for the Chief, he had utilised him to free up a uniform officer for duty on the beat. And of course Steve had been off sick for quite a long time as well.

"Oh well" he thought "At least now I'll have some proper help, and I'm sure Adam will still be around to lend an ear if I'm really stuck even though he is retired. Yes maybe it won't be too bad."

Bene and the Chief separated and went off to join their colleagues who were now well into the party spirit. The only thing bothering Bene now was how he would break the news to his girlfriend Alex and her mother Dot with whom he was living.

At the far side of the room he spotted the pretty young PC Jenny Stephenson who had been cornered by Mike and Steve. They were plainly trying it on with her, and although he was sure she could handle them without any assistance she beckoned him over with a friendly wave. "Hiya Bene!" she shouted. Bene began to make his way over towards the group; he was barely half-way there when her raised voice got his attention again. "You'll never guess what these two have been suggesting." She was clearly more amused than upset, and laughingly told not only Bene but everyone else within earshot what the two men would like to do with her. They should have known better, but obviously the alcohol had taken over their senses and given their confidence too big a boost. Wittingly Jenny brought them down with a wallop when she related their suggestions to the large audience she now held. The colleagues who were gathered around were having a good laugh at the expense of the two men.

Alone with Jenny the disappointment of his conversation with Sowerby was fading into the back of his mind. Jenny was a stunner, she had an hour glass figure, legs that went on forever and long curly black hair that swept around her well formed pale face, she had large sparkling blue eyes that would seduce you and drag you in under her spell. "Well" she said "It's certainly going to be different at the station from now on isn't it. I mean we'll all miss Steve 'cos he's a great guy, but Mike's always been a bit of a wet fish hasn't he; you and him never really got on that well did you?" Bene had to agree.

"No I suppose not, we did have our differences I know, but this last month or so he's been a lot more friendly and helpful. Still we'll have a new face at the station on Monday I've just heard it from Sowerby."

"So will you be made up then?" She asked. Bene had to admit that with the proposed cuts it was now very unlikely.

"Oh I'm sorry Bene, because you've worked so hard for it and you really deserve it, anyway who's this new guy that we're getting?"

With the disappointment of missing out on his promotion Bene hadn't thought to ask the Chief who it was that was coming in.

"I haven't a clue you know, Sowerby never told me. I'll ask him later on if I get the chance."

But the chance never came, every time he looked over towards Sowerby he was deep in conversation with someone. In the end Bene decided to forget all about it and concentrate on enjoying the evening; he would find out on Monday, that would be soon enough.

Bene looked around for Adam Firth his boss for the past three years and who had just completed his last day of service in the police force. During their time together Adam had been as much a friend to him as his superior. It was Adam who had taken him under his wing, had looked after him and guided him throughout his career in CID. Many times Bene had wondered if he would ever be able to hack it on his own after Adam retired. He had been lazy and far too reliant on Adam, but for some reason Adam had seen hidden qualities in Bene that even Bene himself didn't know he possessed.

The change had come when Adam had suffered a heart attack and Bene had been left on his own with two difficult cases to crack. He had just met his girlfriend Alex at that time, and in a few weeks from now they were to be married. With her support and Adam's he had shed his old lifestyle and become a more responsible and dedicated person, someone who could now be relied on, not like the Bene of old. He had worked tirelessly on the two cases, and despite several setbacks he had stuck firmly to his task and finally brought the culprits to justice.

They say a crook can spot a policeman a mile away whether he's in uniform or not. But at least one copper could confidently allege to dispute that claim, for Adam Firth looked anything but a Policeman. He preferred his country casuals, the checked jacket he had worn faithfully for a number of years now sported new patches sewn on top of the original ones. He had a kindly face, which together with his attire would easily pass him off for a Solicitor, or maybe an old fashioned doctor. At the moment he was looking rather glum and Bene wondered what it was that was troubling him. "Hey come on Adam, you should be enjoying this more than anyone."

"Oh it's you Bene don't worry about me, I'm just taking a minute or two thinking about all those years I've spent looking forward to this day."

"Well it's here at last boss, Ellen will have been waiting for this day to come just as much as you have. She'll have you all to herself now and I bet she's got lots of jobs lined up for you." "Yes you're right there I think that's what I'm afraid of you know. I mean here in the police I could always use that as an excuse, but now I'm finished there's no escape."

"Well," said Bene "I suppose it'll take a little time to adjust, but it won't be long before you start feeling the benefits. It's been fairly quiet here recently, maybe a bit too quiet. I think we both needed something to get our teeth into this last month or so to keep us occupied. I don't know about you but I get the feeling that this quiet spell isn't going to last much longer."

Adam thought about it. "Yes maybe you're right, I've had the same feeling but I can't think what on earth it is that could be brewing up. The only odd thing that's happened recently is the discovery of those two bodies that were unearthed in the woods near that old POW camp. But they've been in the ground for over sixty years, and anyway division have claimed them so it can't be anything to do with that."

"Yes I know" said Bene. "It's strange though isn't it, because they seem to have been German POW's. Do you know any more about them Adam?"

"Not much more, the only thing they're sure about is that they were brothers, DNA has confirmed that fact. Oh and I believe they had identical gold bracelets which were obviously gifts from the family. There is one problem though, both of them had been shot more than once and the bullets they found in what was left of the bodies were British army issue. I believe their details have been given to the press in Germany to see if anyone over there can identify them and maybe want to reclaim the bodies."

"Well whoever gets that case is on a loser isn't he," said Bene. "I mean how the hell can you find out what happened out there in the woods after all this time; it's an impossible job."

"Yes" agreed Adam, "Just think yourself lucky that division have claimed it." Bene certainly was pleased that it was division that had taken it over and not him. But he still had that uneasy feeling, something was waiting for him out there but he had no idea what it was.

It wouldn't be too long before he found out.

Chapter 5

Disturbing news

Levensbridge police station was situated a little way from the town centre on a narrow street with parking on one side only; it sat rather unobtrusively at the end of a row of small terraced houses. It had been built in the Victorian era and had retained its outward frontal appearance although the rear of the building had been extended. Inside, the building had undergone several alterations, and was now fully equipped and fit for purpose for a modern police force.

Bene arrived early at the police station on Monday morning. Not that he had any reason to do so for there had been little for him or Adam to do during the last few weeks. It might have been because he was a feeling a little apprehensive. Adam had always been there to guide him, but now he was on his own and feeling rather exposed and vulnerable, like a rabbit caught in the headlights of a car. His mentor had now retired and the support that he had always relied on had gone with him. He knew that both Adam and Chief Inspector Sowerby had confidence in him to do the job alright, but just the thought of not having that father figure to turn to made him jittery. If only he had something tangible to get his teeth into it would help, just sitting at his desk with little to do but check his emails and deal with a mass of meaningless paperwork was not helping him one bit. "Damn," he thought "If only that telephone would ring, anything at all however trivial just to get me out of here."

It was a sign of his nervousness that when the phone did ring Bene almost jumped out of his chair. He picked up the receiver and gave his name to the caller. As he listened a frown began to form across his large forehead. The call was from Mrs Janes the manageress of Greenacres residential home which was on the southern outskirts of the town. When the call ended he picked up his jacket and left the office, telling Val the civilian administrator as he left to take any calls and that he should be back in an hour or so. "It might be something, it might not," he muttered to himself, "let's just hope she's not being paranoid."

He had passed the home several times before in his car but had never had any reason to call there, until now that was. He was let into the building by one of the carers who took him along the wide featureless corridor to the manageress's office.

"Thanks for coming over so quickly sergeant," welcomed Mrs Janes. "I hope I haven't got you out on a wild goose chase."

"Well" said Bene "Just tell me again and in more detail exactly what's been happening here." Smiling broadly he added. "I'm not too keen on sergeant, just call me Bene it's much better."

The manageress seemed more at ease with this. "Well Bene it may be nothing at all, but last week we had a death in the home. That in itself shouldn't be too surprising you might think as all the people we have staying here are quite old. Very few of them leave here to live elsewhere and most of them stay with us for the remainder of their days. Over their time here we notice all the little changes in them; that's natural of course it's aging and it happens to us all. But then comes a major change and when we see that, we know that it won't be too long before we lose them. So you see most of the deaths here are not totally unexpected. But when someone is old but in good health and spirit and they suddenly die, then that comes as a bit of a shock."

"So the death of one of your patients last week was not expected then?" asked Bene.

"It was a shock I admit," said the manageress, "But it does happen and it shouldn't have given much cause for alarm. It was the events leading up to it, and what happened last night that got me worried."

"Right" said Bene. "Start with last week first."

The manageress began to relate the events that had taken place over the past week. "The man who died was Dr. Lukas Kohler and he had been with us for a number of years. As I say he had been in good health and was still very active for his age so we had no concerns about him at all. He had regular visits from his family and friends and we got to know most of them fairly well. But then a week ago someone we hadn't seen before came to see him; we thought little about it at the time and the visitor only stayed with him for a short while. But when this man left his room Dr. Kohler became quite upset. I asked him if there had been a problem but he declined to say anything about the visit. The next day he wouldn't leave his room at all which was most unlike him and when one of the carers took in his meal he was shaking and mumbling something she couldn't understand. The doctor came from Germany originally and she thinks he may have reverted to speaking in his native tongue. Later in the evening when the carer went in to check on him again he seemed a little more relaxed. He told her he would not be able to leave his room again though, and then he said the strangest thing to her."

Bene had been busy taking all this down and was keen to know what the doctor had said to the carer. The manageress continued with her story. "He told her that he had a secret which he had kept since the war, but now someone else wanted to know his secret. He told her that he wanted the secret to die with him but was afraid of an old enemy who might get to him first and force him to give the secret away."

"Did he tell her what the secret was then?" said Bene.

"No he seemed to recover a little at that point and he reached out and took her hand; quietly and calmly he spoke to her." He said.

"I've been very happy here, and I'm lucky that you and all the other girls have looked after me so well; I'll always be grateful and I just want you to remember that."

"And with that he waved her away. The next day when one of the girls went in with his breakfast she found him still in his bed. He had died sometime during the night."

"Was it natural causes then, or was there something suspicious about it?" asked Bene.

"The doctor could find nothing to suggest it was anything other than natural causes. He said he had probably suffered a mild heart attack and at his age his heart had just given up. He came back later and wrote out a death certificate. But when the carer told me about what had happened and what doctor Kohler had said to her the day before I felt uneasy about it."

"And you said that something else happened last night as well," said Bene. "Was this connected to the death of the doctor last week?"

The manageress was keen to unburden herself of all the strange events of the last few days. "Well I don't know for sure, but there are certain coincidences that I can't ignore."

"OK then, just tell me everything." invited Bene.

"Well we have another patient staying with us, Dieter Hoffmann. He is much the same age as Dr. Kohler and like Dr. Kohler he is also German. Dieter has been with us for some considerable time. He and the doctor had been good friends and Dieter was as shocked and surprised as we were at the death of his friend. Well two days ago Dieter also had a visit from someone we didn't know; unfortunately we can't tell if he was the same man as the one who came to see the doctor last week. The handwriting in the visitors' book was the same but the name he signed in with was different. Anyway yesterday when Dieter didn't come down for his meal one of the girls went to check on him. Like the doctor he seemed afraid of something or someone, and she thought he had been crying. The girl couldn't get anything out of him but made a point of looking in on him every time she passed his room. Later last night he took a funny turn and I had to send in the nurse to attend to him. She gave him something to settle him down and before long he seemed to return to his normal self again. But this morning when one of the girls took in his breakfast she found him sitting up in bed with his hands around his knees. He was in a dreadful state shaking and sweating profusely. She was the same carer whom the doctor had confided in last week. She immediately called for the nurse. Then while she was waiting for the nurse to come she remembered what the doctor had told her, so she asked Dieter.

"You haven't got a secret from the war as well have you?"

"Well," said Mrs Janes, "The poor man just cracked up."

"What do you know about my secret he shouted at her, you're not to say anything about that."

"Thankfully the nurse came in then and gave him something to calm him down."

"So how is he now?" asked Bene.

"He seems to have relaxed a little, but it's just like last week all over again. It's got to be something to do with these visits and some dreadful secret they both share. It's all too much of a coincidence and I'm really worried about Dieter. If he were to go the same way it would be dreadful."

"I don't suppose I'll be able to see Dieter will I?" asked Bene "I'd like to ask him a few questions if I could," he added cautiously.

"I can't let you see him just yet Bene, he's still under sedation; it's better for him if he stays that way for a while. I think tomorrow will be soon enough for any questions, if you can call back tomorrow we'll see how he is then, and if he's up to it you might be able to find out what's behind it all."

"Yes I think that should be good enough; just keep an eye on him in the meantime, we don't want anything to happen to him or we'll never find out what it is." With that Bene left to make his way back to the station, deep in thought. "Yes it's a puzzler alright, I wonder if this is what's been lying in wait for me."

Chapter 6

An ideal investment

Monday night in the Fox and Pheasant was darts night, and when you combine a couple of highly competitive local teams together with all their pals then it's liable to be a bit lively. It's much quieter on Tuesday nights and that's when the reading club choose to have their weekly meetings. Wednesday is curry night which is always popular with the locals and on Thursday night it's the turn of the investment club.

This Thursday night's meeting began in much the same way as any other. Drinks were on the table and greetings had been exchanged. There were the usual latecomers but eventually the meeting got underway. The chairman of the group was Andrew Rawlings, a tall and slim grey haired bespectacled man, a little fragile now as he was approaching his eighties. An ex-headmaster who was quietly spoken and well respected by the group and in the community as a whole.

Then there was the treasurer Patricia Latham, head librarian in the towns only library. She was sixty two years old and a stickler for order and cleanliness.

Standing about five foot five she had kept her figure well, blessed by nature with a rather small rounded face which required little in the way of makeup. She was a staunch supporter and admirer of the chairman, and as she had never married herself some would say there was more to it than that. In fact it was pretty obvious to most people that she was besotted with him.

Joe Templeton was a local farmer who looked every inch a man of that profession in his tweed jacket and cap. He was not a happy man and tended to treat these meetings more like a forum where he could complain about milk prices, how the poor weather had affected his crops and how he was losing money every year. It was probably the only place he went to thinking he might get some sympathy, but he was wrong of course. Although no one actually told him to his face he was regarded as a complete bore who tended to spoil the evening for the rest of the group. If only he would accept the group's offer to take out his share of the investment they could get rid of him. But the farmer was not to be moved, somehow the group would have to find another solution.

Another member was Jamal Shastri. Jamal was of Indian origin but had been born in Levensbridge as his parents had before him. Together with his father they had entered the property market and been very successful so far with their acquisitions. Their portfolio was made up of fourteen houses and flats in the town which were all occupied and providing them with a good return on their investments.

Robert Ellwood owned his own painting and decorating business in Levensbridge. A man in his late forties he had many good contacts in the town, and in particular on the council where he had gained some regular and profitable contracts. He never advertised his business as the majority of his work was obtained via word of mouth. He was a tradesman who could be trusted and who charged fair prices for his work, and generally started and completed the work on time. Over the years he had trained and built up a good quality workforce so he was in a position now where he could relax a little more, leaving the day to day running of the business to his foreman. Robert was a jovial man and liked a night out with his pals having a few drinks and a good laugh. A few years earlier he had been a member of the local jet set, a lifestyle that had left him with receding hair, the addition of a few extra pounds around the waist and a number of discarded females along the way. All that was behind him now and he had finally settled down with his partner Jennifer of the last five years, she was probably the pick of the bunch and she knew exactly just how to handle him.

Sylvia Parrish was the most recent member of the club. She had joined with the sole purpose of taking her mind off her personal life which had suffered a serious setback recently. Her corrupt husband Ray had been part of a gang who were caught printing and circulating forged currency. He was now serving a prison sentence for this offence. Sylvia had been fortunate not to be jailed herself as she had also been involved in an illegal operation. Often over the last few months she had come to realise just how lucky she'd been, it was only by chance that she had narrowly avoided a custodial sentence herself. Sylvia was in her late thirties, a good looking brunette with a cracking figure to match. She was the owner of Fellside Fashions on the High Street in Levensbridge which catered for the more affluent ladies in the town.

The two remaining members of the group were Agnes and Harriet Bowes who could easily have been modelled on the TV adverts for wonga.com. Two spinster sisters, both in their seventies who loved the thrill of being involved in the rise and fall of the money markets. Whilst not being big investors themselves they were hugely excited by the small risks they were taking. None of the members were going to make a fortune from the stock market as most of their investments were modest and widely spread over several companies.

With the group now fully assembled Mr Rawlings raised himself from his chair and opened the meeting. "Well it looks as though we have everyone here now so let's get on with the business. Patricia will start by giving us the latest figures and then we'll see if there's anything we need to change. I know one or two of you are not happy with some of the shares we hold so I've asked Patricia to produce a chart which will show how they compare, one against another. Then when we've agreed which ones to hold on to and which ones to sell, I'll go round the table and ask for suggestions for new investments."

Pat handed out the weekly balance sheets and explained to the group how their portfolio had performed over the last week. The value of their investments had gone down slightly, not by much but it did draw gasps from the two sisters. After a short discussion it was decided to cash in some of their less profitable shares and replace them with others which looked more promising. One by one the items on the agenda were discussed and agreed on. Then came the last item on the agenda, any other business. The chairman glanced around the group for input but no-one had anything to add. The members started to get ready to leave the meeting but were held back by the chairman who motioned them to take their seats again. The group sat down and waited for him to speak.

"I've had a request from a fellow investor who would like us to hear a proposal which he thinks might be of interest to us." The group were eager to find out who this person was and what they had to say. The chairman looked over to the far side of the room towards a man who had been sitting alone. Catching the man's attention the chairman invited him over. "Ladies and Gentlemen I would like to introduce you to Mr Alastair McKay."

The man who had been unobserved by the group during their meeting now approached them. He moved effortlessly and stood before them without seeming to have moved at all. He was a man of small stature and quite nondescript in appearance. He was aged about fifty, reasonably well dressed and smart without being flashy. He didn't appear to have any noticeable or distinguishable features, and that made him difficult to describe or even to remember. It probably explained why his presence in the pub so far had gone unnoticed. Although the man's physical presence was not one to command an audience he nevertheless had the full attention of the group. He was quietly spoken and appeared a little coy. "Good evening everyone, I'm delighted to have this opportunity to meet you all. I'm a newcomer to

Levensbridge and haven't had much of a chance to meet many people here or to explore your lovely town." There was a slight pause before he continued. "Like yourselves I am a keen investor and I only found out about your club through a chance meeting a few days ago. I don't know how your club operates or what your interests are, and obviously I don't know what you invest in or what the level of investment is."

Patricia Latham held up her hand. "Perhaps you are thinking of joining our little group Mr McKay. If so perhaps you would like to attend our meeting next week, you'll be able to see how we operate and judge for yourself if we have similar interests."

The newcomer appeared to welcome this approach.

"It's kind of you to invite me but I'm not sure that I'm looking for any long term investments at the moment. What I do have is a rather attractive proposition that I would like to put forward to your members. I'd be interested to see if any of them would like to join me in an enterprise which I guarantee will generate a substantial return on their investment, and with no risk to the initial outlay."

He looked around the table to try and judge how his proposal had been received so far. The group remained silent but attentive so he took this as an invitation to press further. "I must stress that this is not a cheap venture and anyone who is interested would have to be in a position to put up at least a hundred thousand pounds." This brought gasps from not only the two sisters but some other members as well. Mr McKay gave them a little time to digest this before speaking again.

"If this figure puts any of you off the idea then it's maybe not a good idea for you to stay and listen to the full proposal. I only want to offer this opportunity to the really serious investors in your group."

The sisters got up to leave. "We're sorry Mr Rawlings but this is far too much for us."

"Too much for me as well." said Patricia.

Mr Rawlings had to admit that it was not for him either. He rose to say that the meeting was closed but the remaining four members were welcome to stay and listen to the proposal from Mr McKay.

Of the four remaining members it was Sylvia who spoke. "Well how about another drink first and then we can carry on and hear it in full?" This seemed a sensible idea so a round of drinks was ordered from the bar. When the glasses had been refilled the four members sat back to listen to the proposal in more detail.

Alastair McKay took a sip from his glass and smiled at the people around him. "Well that certainly took the wind out of their sails didn't it. I hope I don't frighten the rest of you off as well or we're all in for an early night." It wasn't clear if it was the fear of admitting they were not wealthy enough to invest at this level, just plain curiosity, or greed that kept them at the table. Whatever it was they all wanted to hear what the man had to say, and he didn't keep them waiting long.

He checked that there was no-one sitting close to them who would be able to overhear the conversation then pulled his chair a little closer to the group. "I expect that like me you all read the local papers. If you do you will have seen letters to the editor concerning a section of land on the Eastern outskirts of the town. According to rumours this land could be a suitable site to build on." Nods of agreement came from the four, two of whom never even bought the paper. Leaning further forward he kept his voice deliberately quiet. "Well this information is confidential so don't spread it around, but I happen to know that planning permission would almost certainly be granted if the right plans were to be submitted."

This was getting interesting. Robert was not too sure and queried this last remark. "I've heard nothing about this and I see and speak to council people on a regular basis."

"Don't worry about that," replied Alastair "only one or two people in the know have any knowledge of it, it won't become public for a little while yet."

"OK then," said Robert "So how come you know about it? I mean by your own admission you're a newcomer here."

"You're right of course," said Alastair "And I'm pleased you picked up on that because it shows that you're no fool, you wouldn't be taken in easily that's for sure. I think you'll be a very shrewd investor indeed," and with an expansive sweep of his arm to include the group as a whole, "As I'm sure you all are."

Joe and Jamal had remained silent throughout the presentation so far, but Sylvia was keen to hear more and said so. "Right then, so let's hear how you're so knowledgeable about this scheme and why you're so keen to include us in it." This was what all the others needed to know but hadn't wanted to ask. They were pleased when Sylvia had come right out and said it. Alastair took the hint and began to explain.

"The letters in the paper are genuine enough and written by people with concerns about building a housing estate on that land. You would see that there was no denial from the council in the paper or even a response, so why are they trying to keep this quiet? Because they expect to make a lot of money out of it themselves that's why." The group seemed to accept this and were waiting for the follow up.

"The point is, that at the moment, although the land is available to buy it hasn't yet been acquired by the council. They've signed up with a national house builder and have provisionally granted them permission to build there. But the owner isn't keen to sell to them and hasn't yet accepted their offer; he's holding out on them and hoping for another offer to come in. He wants to sell the land to someone who would agree to let his cousin's company build on it. That way it would keep all the work in the town, more local men would be taken on to build the houses and the materials would all be supplied by local trades people. The thing is, I know he will sell at a much reduced price if the buyer agrees to the deal, and he won't lose out himself because he has an interest in his cousin's company."

"So how do you know all this?" enquired Robert.

"Because" said Alastair "I happen to know the builder, the owner's cousin. He knows that at a push I can put up half a million to buy the land but there's no way I can raise sufficient funds to buy it all myself. That's why I thought that local investors like yourselves would not only make up the difference but also have a vested interest in the building of the new estate. The owner would be delighted if we could raise the capital locally to buy the land. He was a councillor in the town himself until a few years ago, but other members ganged up against him and forced him out when he opposed their plans to sell off the school playing fields. They wanted to steamroller the sale through before anyone got wind of it and started to raise objections, they even had a builder lined up standing by ready to build on the fields."

"So this is his way of getting his own back on them is it?" said Robert.

"That's exactly it Robert, Jack's off to Florida to live and this deal will be his revenge on them. So for obvious reasons we won't be able to tell anyone about it until the deal is done. But when the news does get out about who bought the land it will be the four of you who get all the credit. It would put one over on the council and scupper their plans to give all the work to outside agencies, people who have no connections with the town and no interest in the people in it."

Jamal spoke for the first time. "I would have to talk it over with my father first of course because we're partners, but I'm sure he would be interested. If we are talking figures, how much do we need to raise?"

"Yes of course," said Alastair "that's always the bottom line isn't it, OK then this is the deal. The council will pay two million two hundred thousand for it." The four went very quiet, this was big very big. Alistair could see the disappointment in the faces of the members and was quick to try and get them back on board again.

"Don't let that figure put you off though, as I said he would take less than that if the party agreed to his deal. The lowest he would take would be one million eight hundred thousand pounds. I would put in five hundred thousand myself so that leaves one point three million to be raised to clinch the deal."

It was still a huge amount of money and all four were apprehensive about committing to such a large sum. "Yes I know it's still a large amount" said Alastair, "But think of the returns, I haven't mentioned them yet but believe me they're going to be massive. I'll give you an idea of the potential. I reckon the land will accommodate in excess of a hundred houses, these will be a mixture of detached houses and bungalows with a few semis for the cheaper end of the market. Well you know better than I do what house prices are like here, and these are high quality houses with top of the range fittings, and of course we'll be sharing the profits with the builder. I'll leave you to work it out for yourselves how much is involved here. When you do you'll see that the initial outlay I'm asking you for to be part of this venture is going to seem very small indeed compared to the high returns you'll get. I guarantee they will far exceed anything you ever dreamed about."

"Then what you're offering us is the chance to come into this scheme for one million three hundred thousand pounds, it's as simple as that isn't it?" said Sylvia. "Well I'm still interested how about you three?" Jamal said that he was up for it as well, Robert was still not one hundred percent convinced but admitted that he was very tempted.

Joe had listened to the offer but however small the risk involved he couldn't bring himself to commit to the scheme.

"I'm sorry folks but I'm not going to get involved, I wish you all well with it and you have my word I'll not breathe a word to anyone else." With that he took his leave and only Alastair, Sylvia, Robert and Jamal were left.

"Well that changes things a bit." said Jamal.

"Yes," said Sylvia "But just think, fair enough we'll have to stump up a bit more ourselves but the returns will be even greater."

Alastair suggested that they meet again after the club meeting the same night the following week to check that sufficient funds could be found to clinch the deal.

"We can't leave it any longer than a couple of weeks because the owner needs to complete the deal before the council come back to him with another offer."

With that the four left the pub and went their separate ways home. Three of them with minds intoxicated, partly with alcohol but mostly with dizzy thoughts of the fortune they were about to make.

Chapter 7

Two new recruits

Bene arrived back at the station with his mind still full of the events that had taken place at the residential home. He sat staring at his desk deep in thought a worried frown etched across his forehead. "Well" he thought. "I didn't have to wait long did I, I mean Adam only left on Friday, I wish he could have stayed on a bit longer. Anyway he's not here and he's not coming back either so I'll just have to get on with it, now let me think. These two at the home, they're both German, they were friends and they've been here for years. Both of them seem to have a secret of some sort which they don't want anyone to know about, or are too frightened to tell anyone, I wonder what the hell that is? Then there's this stranger who visited them both and put the fear of God into them. Who is he and what's the connection. One is already dead and the other is scared witless. I hope they keep a eye on him at the home because I don't want to lose him before he's well enough to talk to me. Maybe I'll find out something tomorrow, I hope so. Oh Adam! I wish you hadn't retired."

He gave a long weary sigh and slowly lifted his head. The man standing in front of his desk had not dared to interrupt Bene's thought process but now he thought the moment had come to introduce himself. A shocked Bene couldn't at first find the words he wanted to use, but after treating the visitor to his impression of a guppy fish looking for food he finally managed to blurt out. "Who the hell are you? How did you get in here past the front desk? This is a police station you know."

The man held up both hands and took a step back. Speaking in his distinctive Welsh accent he introduced himself.

"I'm the new detective constable sir."

"But you're Welsh!" said a surprised Bene.

"Yes I'm sorry about that sir, but it's not a crime is it?" Bene was still in shock and trying hard to regain some composure, he had forgotten all about the new DC who was joining the station.

The man facing him was about three inches shorter than Bene but much broader. Bene figured he would almost certainly be a rugby man. His face showed all the classic signs of being involved in such an unforgiving sport, the squat nose, deep set eyes under a broad forehead and ears that appeared to be welded to the side of his head. His hair was cut very short which only helped to accentuate his facial characteristics. Generally though Bene seemed pleased with what he saw. Behind the mask he thought he could sense a man who was hard working, honest and intelligent. First impressions only though, time would tell whether he would be proved right or wrong; he hoped he would be right.

Eventually Bene stood up and offered his hand to the newcomer. "Well I'm Bene Douglas and I'm detective sergeant here. Sorry about the confusion, I'd forgotten you were coming today and it wasn't the way I wanted to welcome you on your first day. Tell you what let's go and grab a coffee and we'll introduce ourselves properly and you can tell me all about yourself." The two men left the office and found a table in the canteen where they could sit down and talk.

"OK then," said Bene "You know who I am so tell me who you are and how you came to be transferred up here."

The newcomer proceeded to introduce himself.

"I'm Emlyn Thomas and as you can easily tell from my accent I come from Wales. Both my dad and I were in the force down there. He started and finished his service in Swansea, but for a few years in between he worked for the Met in London and when he was there he had the privilege of working alongside Adam Firth. Well I was a bit fed up in Swansea, so when dad saw the vacancy advertised up here in Levensbridge he said that if Adam Firth was working here it would be a good place for me to get some valuable experience. I didn't realise Adam was retiring, but by then it was too late to change my mind as I had already accepted the post. So here I am."

More pleasantries were being exchanged as Chief Inspector Sowerby came in. "Ah, good to see you two have met up. Have we got anything for him Bene?"

"Well I've been over to Greenacres residential home this morning and there's been some strange happenings there over the last week." Bene proceeded to fill the Chief in with the details he had been given at the home.

"Yes it sounds a bit odd I must admit," said the Chief. "See what that chap can tell you tomorrow, it might be something it might not. Take err.......," the Chief hesitated and looked sheepishly at his new recruit "It's Emlyn isn't it?"

"Yes sir, Emlyn Thomas."

The Chief smiled, something was amusing him. "I've been speaking to your old superintendant down in Swansea and he told me what name you were known by down there, you'll probably find that you'll get the same here."

"Yes, I expect so sir, down in Swansea I was known as ET and I was half expecting it would follow me here as well. But it's OK sir I don't mind, in fact I've got rather used to it and I quite like it."

The Chief and Bene both agreed. "It's ET then."

Bene arranged a desk and a laptop for him and together they spent the next hour or so settling into what they hoped would be a good working partnership. When five o'clock came the two men left the office for home. Emlyn to his new flat, and Bene to his girlfriend Alex's house where the two of them lived together with Alex's mother, Dot.

Bene could smell dinner as he walked down the drive towards the house. Dot was a wonderful cook and she never ceased to surprise him with her culinary skills. Alex rarely got a look in at the kitchen, but Bene hoped that when they had their own house she would inherit her mother's talent in that department. Just as he arrived at the front door he caught a glimpse of a small face peering at him through the hedge, but before he could focus on who it was the face quickly withdrew from sight. Catching sight of Alex who had opened the door to greet him he promptly forgot the little face.

Alex had only just arrived home from the village school a few miles away where she had been teaching. A delightful looking girl, not what you would call drop dead gorgeous but certainly very pretty. She was a few inches shorter than Bene and had a good figure that suited her height, her short dark hair surrounded her naturally pretty freckled face and sparkling blue eyes which exuded mischief. She greeted Bene in the usual way "Hiya Sherlock how's your day been, are all the bad boys locked away for the night so we can sleep soundly in our beds?" Her laughter carried all the way through into the kitchen where her mother was putting the dinner out on plates.

"Honestly Bene I don't know how you put up with her, are you sure you still want to marry her?" Bene wanted nothing more than that, and joking aside all three knew it as well.

During the meal Bene told them about the events at the retirement home. He knew that anything he told them would go no further, he had unwittingly involved them in a serious case once before and they had helped him then. To be truthful he doubted if he would have been able to bring the case to a successful conclusion without their help. Alex's mother Dot was a natural blonde with her hair done up and curled around the top of her head, she was quite slim and had a pleasant face which belied her age, for some reason she always wore a housecoat when at home.

"Maybe the man you're going to see tomorrow will be able to tell you what's going on, it does sound strange though doesn't it."

"Oh well," said Bene, "There's nothing we can do about it until the morning, I must say though it's a bit intriguing isn't it? I wonder what it's all about." He went on to tell them about the new addition to the force and they were keen for Bene to invite Emlyn over so they could meet him.

After the meal the three settled down to an evening of television. Alex and Dot were avid viewers of the early evening soaps but Bene had no interest in them at all, he would pick up the evening paper and concentrate on that until they had finished watching. It was then that he suddenly remembered the small face he had seen earlier and asked if either of them knew who it was. Dot had the answer. "Oh don't worry about him, he's Ken and Maggie's boy next door. I think he sees you as a bit of a hero you know, after those two big cases you were involved in a few months ago. He was telling me he wants to be a secret agent or a detective like you. Maybe you should talk to him, I think he's a bit shy and wouldn't dare ask you himself, but if you had a chat with him he'd love it."

The next morning Bene left the house to go to the station, walking down the drive towards his car he was instantly aware of the young boy's watchful eyes. It hadn't occurred to him before but maybe the boy had been watching him for a while. At the end of the drive he turned and peered into the drive of the adjoining house, he saw the crouching form of a young boy who appeared to be about ten years old. "Hallo then," he said smiling at the small figure "What's your name?" The boy stood up tentatively and walked a few paces towards him. He was quite chubby for a boy of that age, he had short trousers, a mop of unruly dark hair and a pair of small round spectacles which unfortunately likened him to Billy Bunter of Greyfriar's fame. Bene could well imagine he would come in for a bit of ribbing from his school friends.

"I'm Ethan, and I'm a secret agent," the boy said. "Wow that's great," said the admiring Bene "And what case are you on today?" The boy seemed a little less shy now that Bene had shown an interest.

"I'm on the trail of a gang of inter-thingy crooks whose been robbing banks and stuff."

Benny was beginning to enjoy his chat with the little secret agent. "OK then tell me how you get on, if you need any help let me know and maybe I could be your deputy."

The boy's mother appeared at the door and told Ethan not to be late for school. "I've got to go now but I'll be back later and I'll probably capture them then." Bene was amused but he tried not to let his face betray the fact. Suddenly, just as the boy was about to pass him he stopped and held Bene with an intense stare, and in a voice which was very serious for a boy of his age he said. "You're a policeman aren't you, I could hand them over to you and you could lock them up?"

"Good idea," agreed Bene.

"Then" the boy said "I can help you with your cases, what case are you working on now?"

Bene indulged the boy a little.

"Oh it's top secret just like yours, I have to catch a murderer who's murdering old people in this nice home they've been living in." That should keep him friendly Bene thought, I hope I haven't gone too far. The young boy looked up at him.

"Yea that would be good fun, you can help me with my cases an' I'll help you with yours." The youngster seemed pleased with this new arrangement and went off to school whistling happily.

On his arrival at the station Bene signed the book at the front desk and entered the office, he was greeted by ET who had just finished taking a phone call. He motioned to Bene not to bother sitting down. "That home you visited yesterday?" He looked quizzically at Bene. Bene nodded. "Well they've just been on the phone Mrs Janes it was, she wants you to go up there right away, she sounded upset it seems there's been some sort of accident."

Chapter 8

A mysterious death

Waiting at the front door of the home Mrs Janes invited Bene and ET into her office, she offered a chair to both men before taking her own seat behind an old fashioned desk. A desk that seemed to reflect the image of the person seated behind it for it seemed to have aged along with her. There were no signs on it to show that any modern methods had been used to give it that distressed look which is so popular nowadays, all the stains and scratches were the result of many years of loyal use to its owner.

Mrs Janes was looking tired, she was making no effort to conceal the fact that she was deeply troubled by the events of the last week. Bene could only sit there and wait for the news which he knew wouldn't be good. Mrs Janes began to tell them what had happened. "I'm sorry you never got the chance to talk to Dieter yesterday, but to be honest I don't think he would have been able to tell you anything coherently, he was in such a bad way and none of us had any idea why. We had hoped that by this morning he would have settled himself down again and maybe we could have found out what it was that was upsetting him, but I'm afraid it's too late now. One of the girls had been looking in on him throughout the night, and although he was a bit uneasy he did seem to sleep. At four o'clock this morning he was a lot quieter and he looked more comfortable, but when she went in again at six o'clock he had passed away."

Mrs Janes was clearly disturbed by the death as she continued to unburden her fears to the two officers. "I could understand him dying if his condition had deteriorated or changed, because he had been in a pretty bad way, and of course he was quite old. But the carer said she could definitely see an improvement in him each time she looked in, that's why she saw no reason to continue checking on him after four o'clock." Bene looked over to ET to check that he was taking down notes on her statement. Mrs Janes continued. "When I heard the news this morning I began to think about the sudden death of his friend last week in similar circumstances. I could see too many coincidences which were hard to ignore." She paused for a moment before continuing. "I can't think how or why, but I get the feeling that there's something sinister behind it all Bene. I hope you can find out what it is that's happening here because the staff and myself are getting worried. It's beginning to turn into some sort of horrible nightmare."

Bene had listened attentively to Mrs Janes and hadn't wanted to interrupt her, but now he had some questions he needed to ask. "Did he have any more visitors after I left here yesterday?" Mrs Janes could think of only one.

"Yes, his son Peter came in after lunch and spent about half an hour with him. He came in to see me before he left and he was worried about him. He couldn't understand what had happened that had got his father into such a state, he was babbling and Peter couldn't make out what it was he was trying to tell him, the more it went on the more excitable his father became. He thought it best to leave in case he had a seizure or something even worse. He intended to come back today when hopefully his father was more relaxed, but of course I had to phone him this morning and tell him that his father had passed away. I don't know if he can tell you anything that would help but if you want to see him he'll be at his shop in the town." Mrs Janes gave ET an address where they would be able to find him. Bene continued to question her.

"And both these men died sometime during the night, and after someone had been to see them, someone that you or your staff didn't know or recognise?" The manageress nodded in agreement. "And in both cases the doctor could find nothing suspicious about the deaths. Were post mortems carried out, I mean that would be natural under the circumstances wouldn't it?" Mrs Janes nodded.

"Yes that's usual when the death isn't expected, according to the pathologist the post mortem on Dr Kohler didn't show up anything, he's going to be cremated tomorrow. Then this morning a private ambulance came and took Dieter's body away, it left here just before you arrived. I expect it will be in the morgue now awaiting a post mortem, maybe you should call there and have a word with the pathologist."

Bene confirmed that he'd be going there. "Yes I'll make that my next call after I leave here. Now because of what you've told me I have to cover all aspects of the two deaths. Firstly, if the deaths are connected or suspicious in any way. Is it possible that someone from outside could have gained entry into the home during the night? The doors and windows for instance are they all locked at night? Can you think of any way that someone could get into the building unnoticed?" Mrs Janes was horrified.

"Oh no Bene that's not possible, all the doors are locked at six o'clock at night, after that the only door that's used is the front entrance door. It's only opened when the staff arrive for the night shift, and the late shift staff leave the same way shortly afterwards. After that it's all secure until six in the morning when the shifts change again."

"And the windows, are they secure?" asked Bene. "Well they're not all shut of course, some of our residents like a bit of fresh air in their rooms, but the windows can only be opened a few inches from the inside it's not possible to open them any further from the outside." "Hmm," said Bene. "So the only way that anyone could get in unnoticed is if one of the night staff, or one of the residents themselves were to let them in is that it?"

"That's about it Bene, but most of the staff have been with me for several years. I can't see any of them giving access to anyone at that time of night, certainly not to anyone who didn't work here. I mean I'm sure I can trust them."

"How about keys?" suggested Bene. "Do the staff have their own or are all the keys kept here?"

"There again Bene, only myself and one of the girls on each shift has keys, and when we're here the keys are kept in that cupboard up there." She pointed over to a cupboard behind her desk. Bene went round and tried the cupboard door which he found was unlocked.

"I expect it's possible for one of the staff to take a key, have a replica cut and then replace the key again before it's missed?" Mrs Janes had to admit that it was possible.

"Yes I suppose it could be done, but I can't believe any of my girls would do it."

There didn't seem to be any further questions Bene could think of, he needed information from other sources before talking to Mrs Janes again. "Right, well I don't think there's anything else for the moment. I'll drop in at the path lab first then call at the shop and see if the son can throw any light on it. I'll probably be back tomorrow but if there's anything else that you or any of the staff can remember then give me a call." With that he gave Mrs Janes his card, and together the two detectives left the home and headed for the pathology laboratory.

The pathologist had nothing to tell them as he hadn't even started his examination of the body. "I'm not saying there's anything suspicious about the death," said Bene "But if you come across anything unusual at all I want you to call me right away. I just have an uneasy feeling that the two deaths in the home are connected in some way." The pathologist was the same man who had carried out the post mortem on Dr. Kohler but he was positive there had been no sign of foul practice. He assured them that he'd be thorough in his examination and if he did find anything suspicious he would let them know immediately.

The next call was to Peter Hoffmann. Peter was looking after his antique shop which Bene found in one of the narrow lanes which led directly off the main street in Levensbridge. The lane housed a variety of small locally owned shops, a Methodist chapel, and a little further down there was a row of small terraced houses which had been renovated by a local developer and were now rented out. The antique shop had only a modest frontage but was blessed with an attractive rather quaint bow fronted window, it allowed the goods displayed inside to be viewed easily by any prospective customers who may be passing by on the narrow pavement outside. There were no customers in the shop when the two detectives arrived so Peter pulled over the closed sign so they would be able to talk without being disturbed. He led them to the back of the shop which had broadened out a little, but was still quite small in relation to the nature of business that was conducted there.

Peter was very much his father's son and had all the features and characteristics his father had when he was that age; a photo displayed in the shop confirmed it. Peter was obviously still very upset over the death of his father earlier in the day and it took him a little while before he was ready for Bene's questions. Bene began with an apology for their intrusion into his grief, but was hoping for some answers which could maybe explain the state his father was in the previous day. "I believe you visited your father yesterday afternoon is that right Peter?" Peter acknowledged the fact. "How did you find him when you went into his room? I understand he was upset about something, do you think it was the man who came to see him the day before?" Peter thought it must have been the visit which had upset him. "Have you any idea who it was?" asked Bene.

"No, no idea at all. But it was someone either from his past or connected to it in some way I'm sure of that. I couldn't understand what it was that my father was trying to tell me, he was in such a state that all I could get out of him was a lot of babbling. I was afraid he would do himself some harm if I stayed much longer so I thought it best to leave him and hope that he would be better today when I called again. Then this morning I got a call from Mrs Janes to tell me he had passed away a few hours earlier."

Bene pushed further. "What do you know about your father's past Peter. Was there anything, or anyone in it that he was afraid of?"

Peter told him about his father being in France during the war then later in the POW camp at Lower Hutton.

"There were three of them who went through the war together, one was my father, another was a man called Otto Bauer who died about a year ago, and Dr Kohler who was fathers best friend and who lived in the home until his death last week."

"Did he ever confide in you a secret that he had kept from his war days, because it seems there was something that both your father and Dr Kohler knew but didn't want anyone else to know about."

Peter thought about this for a while, there was something but he wasn't sure if he should mention it or not, eventually he decided to tell the detectives what little he knew about it.

"One night last week when I visited my father he didn't look too good. Dr Kohler had just died the day before and of course he was depressed about that. It was only natural and to be expected of course as they had been the best of friends since childhood. Anyway that night he told me a little about his early life and his time in the army during the war. In all the time I can remember he never spoke about his life before he met my mother, whether he told her or not I don't know. In any case he never spoke about it to me and I never asked him, maybe I should have done I don't know. However that night he wanted to tell me something about himself."

He took a deep breath before continuing. "He was only eighteen when he joined the army and up until the start of the war his young life had been a very happy one with a promising future in his father's business. As he was telling me I could imagine him as a young man living happily with his parents in Maierhofen, a normal family with dreams of a bright future for themselves in a resurgent Germany. Then of course all that changed when the war came. Father spent most of it in Northern France guarding the coast against a possible allied invasion. He hated everything about the war. My father and his two friends were peaceful men who didn't want to go to war, but like many others in Germany at that time they had no choice. In the same regiment there were two brothers also from Maierhofen. They were bullies and the war seemed to give them licence to carry out all sorts of violence and atrocities against the local people. Well my father and his two friends were witness to most of these acts and were appalled by them. One incidence in particular shocked them so much that when the chance came they deserted and fled over here to escape from it."

He took another breather before continuing. "Eventually they arrived at the POW camp here at Lower Hutton and they spent the rest of the war there in virtual peace. Apart from a short period when the two brothers arrived at the same camp, my father recalls there was a lot of trouble at that time. Then one day the brothers managed to escape from the camp and were never seen or heard of again."

"Did he mention anything about this secret then, or anything about the man who came to see him?" asked Bene.

"No not exactly, but he did give me something that he wanted me to keep for him."

"What was it?" asked Bene.

"He gave me a briefcase from his wardrobe and asked me to look after it, he said that inside I would find a diary he had kept all those years ago, and a rough sketch map of somewhere he had been to in France. Along with these items were papers listing names of his comrades in the camp. He said the diary and the maps would explain everything but I was not to use them until he was no longer with us. He went on to say that after he'd gone it would be up to me to decide whether I did anything about it or not. I haven't had time to look into the briefcase yet so I've no idea what he meant by that."

"Did he say anything about the man who came to see him?" asked ET.

"No, as far as I know he had no-one to be afraid of, those two brothers were the only ones he feared but they're probably dead now, anyway it was a younger man who visited him, not someone his own age."

"Could you let us have a look at the briefcase Peter, it could help us to find out what it was that your father was frightened of. There might be something in there that could explain what led to his death and that of his friend Dr Kohler."

ET looked hopefully at Peter. "Yes of course," said Peter. "I don't have it here with me though it's at my home in Preston. I only open the shop here two days through the week as business has dropped off a bit with the recession, there's no need for me to be here all week. I look after this place part of the week and the other days I'm in the shop we have in Preston. My wife also has a small shop in Preston where she sells materials and bits of things for quilting. If you think the briefcase could be important you're welcome to come down and collect it. It's about forty miles away, much better and cheaper by train I find, and from the station its only a short walk to my house." The two detectives left the shop after agreeing to call at Peter's house the next day and collect the briefcase.

Chapter 9

An unwelcome reunion

Chief Inspector Sowerby beckoned Bene into his office. "I hope this isn't going to become a problem in Levensbridge like it has in Preston and Lancaster, Bene. But we've just received a report of a burglary up on Beech Drive. The owners have just returned from a holiday in Greece and found their home has been stripped of some rather expensive items." "I'll go up there and see what's missing," said Bene. "Do they know when it was burgled sir?" "No it could have been any time during the last two weeks. I don't know if they've spoken to their neighbours yet, but anyhow you'll have to find out if any of them saw or heard anything that could help us."

"Right I'm on my way now sir," Bene was already half way to the door. "Those are pretty expensive properties up there, someone must have known the place was going to be empty and they must have had a vehicle ready to take the stuff away."

"OK," said the chief. "From the little I know it could well be the same people who have been operating in the north west this last month or so, expensive properties being targeted and always when the owners have been away on holiday. There are quite a few wealthy families living around here, and with the summer season coming up we won't have the resources to keep an eye on all of them when they're left unoccupied."

"Want me to come with you?" asked ET.

"Yes it's better if there are two of us," said Bene. "We don't get a lot of burglaries around here and this one seems to have been premeditated which is a bit worrying. Then this afternoon I want you to go to Preston and get that briefcase from Peter Hoffmann. I'd like to know what's inside it and maybe it'll clear up some of the mystery around those two deaths at the home."

Bene and ET arrived at the house to find the irate house owner waiting outside for them. "About bloody time some of your lot showed up," be bellowed out, "I'll bet there's never been a policeman round here in all the time we've been away, fat lot of good you are. You should spend some of your time trying to catch criminals rather than sit on your fat arse's in your nice cosy offices." Bene was surprised but not shocked by the man's ranting, he was probably right in some of what he had said. The force had come in for quite a bit of criticism lately in the local press for not being visible enough in the town. The stretched resources didn't allow for much visible policing especially on the estates on the outskirts of the town. It was bad enough through the week but even worse at the weekends. All available staff were concentrated in the town centre then as this was where the trouble would flare up, usually late at night when the town's lads and lasses were doing the rounds of the pubs and clubs.

"Maybe it's best if we go inside sir and you can tell me what it is that's been taken." suggested Bene. The two officers and the owner went into the large detached house and met the owners wife who showed them into the lounge. The owner was Mr Taylor and he hadn't calmed down at all, he threw his arms open and spun around in the centre of a completely empty room.

"Taken the bloody lot they have, the bastards." he boomed. The man looked to be around seventy, his face was purple and he was shaking with rage.

"OK," said Bene "Try and calm down a bit sir or you'll make yourself ill and that won't help anyone. See if you can find a chair for Mr Taylor, ET." A chair was brought through from the kitchen, the owner sat down and gradually Bene began to find out how the thieves had gained entry to the property and what exactly had been stolen.

Mr Taylor told them what he knew which really wasn't much at all. "We came back this morning from a holiday in Greece. As we drove up to the house everything seemed quite normal, it was only when we came into the house that we found out we'd been burgled. They've taken all our furniture from this room and some from the next one. It was good stuff as well, none of your modern rubbish. We had a lovely Old Charm dining table with six chairs in here and a dresser to match, all in solid oak. They've also taken two new leather sofas, a matching reclining chair and a large flat screen TV and other electrics from the room next door."

Bene had been looking around the downstairs rooms as the owner had been speaking and was a little puzzled. "Any jewellery, money or other valuables missing?"

"No," said Mr Taylor "My wife doesn't like expensive jewellery and we never leave any cash lying around. Surprisingly they don't seem to have bothered with anything else, just the furniture."

"There doesn't appear to be any damage done," said Bene. "It looks as though they've just taken what they wanted and left it at that." Mr Taylor had calmed down a little now. He left his chair and walked around the room.

"Well the furniture was expensive, but it was insured of course so it can be replaced, I suppose we should be thankful that they haven't wrecked the place while they were taking the stuff out."

"Yes," agreed Bene "It seems as if they knew exactly what they wanted, broke in, took it and left as soon as they had what they had come for. So how did they get in?"

"The back kitchen door," said the owner rising from his chair, "Over here, see, the lock has been smashed in." Everyone followed the owner into the kitchen. "The alarm was set and it would have gone off, but they must have found it quickly and silenced it. Unfortunately it's on the wall in the hallway so they would have seen it as soon as they came in and been able to disable it right away."

"Have you spoken to any of your neighbours yet to see if they can shed any light on what's happened?" Bene was hoping that someone would be able to tell them they had seen something suspicious but the owner shook his head.

"Our neighbours on the far side hadn't seen or heard anything at all and they're good friends of ours, they would have been looking out for us while we were away. The house on this side has been empty for a while and the new owners are only just in the process of moving in. It could have happened at any time during the last two weeks I suppose." Bene was concerned about the lack of information from the neighbours.

"I mean whoever it was who broke in here clearly came and left in a hurry, but to be able to take such a lot of heavy furniture they must have had a large vehicle, surely someone would have noticed a vehicle that size."

Just then an officer arrived to take photos of the break-in and dust the surfaces for any traces of fingerprints. "I don't think there's anything else we can do here at the moment sir," said Bene, "I'll go round and see the neighbours myself and see if I can stir up their memories a bit in the hope they can remember something that might help us. In the meantime I think you should see about having that door repaired and make the place secure again. Oh, and give your insurers a call too, they'll want to come and get a list of everything that's been taken." With that the two detectives left.

"Well what do you think of that ET? It looks to me as though whoever it was knew the property would be empty and exactly what they wanted to take from it. I suppose it's what they call stealing to order, it looks that way to me anyway." ET could only agree.

"Yes we had a bout of it down in Swansea a couple of years ago, we did catch the culprits in the end but we never recovered any of the stolen items, I expect it all went overseas. There are plenty of customers over there who would pay a fortune for genuine antique furniture, and not be too particular about where it comes from, or how it was obtained."

"Right," said Bene. "You get off to Preston and pick up that briefcase and I'll go round the houses here and see if I can find out anything. I'll see you back at the station later this afternoon." It was only a short walk to the railway station so Bene kept the car with him. As the owner had told him earlier the neighbours immediately next door could tell him nothing. They had been keeping an eye on the property during the last two weeks but hadn't seen or heard anything unusual.

"I mean we're not here twenty four hours a day you know," the man said, "Maybe whoever it was had been parked up somewhere near and waited for us to go out, I don't know but we never heard the alarm go off and we're both light sleepers."

No success there then. Bene moved to the house on the far side of Mr Taylor's property and knocked on the door there. A large Volvo estate was parked outside and Bene could hear the sound of someone moving things around inside. "Must be arranging the furniture," he thought "I wonder if it's the same stuff that was taken from next door. Don't be daft Bene" he muttered to himself. Then there was a loud bang followed by some rather choice language. "Now where do I know that voice from?" He knocked again and this time the door opened. It was difficult to tell which of the two men was the more surprised.

The man who answered Bene's knock was a well built man of generous proportions all round. He had light blue eyes set in a round face with a ruddy complexion, and all this topped off with a shock of pure white hair, every inch of him a ladies' man. Bene found his voice first. "Paul Hanbury! When did you get back in Levensbridge?" Paul had also recovered and now laughed out loudly.

"Well get this, it's me old mate Bene, what the hell are you doing up here, not looking for a house on Beech Drive on your wages are you?" he scoffed. Bene was slow to recover, Paul had always been much sharper and quicker with his tongue than he had.

The two men were certainly not mates, in fact it was one of Bene's main ambitions to nail Paul for crimes which he was sure he had committed but couldn't prove. Paul had covered his tracks well, he hadn't left any incriminating evidence behind when he had suddenly sold up his business and left Levensbridge months earlier. "So what brings you up here?" asked Paul. Bene explained the burglary which had taken place next door and asked if Paul had seen or heard anything suspicious. "Sorry mate, I'm afraid I can't help you with that one, Nicola and I have only been back in the country a couple of days and this is our first day up here. This is our new house and we're busy trying to move in. You'd better have a look inside, just to check that the furniture here is ours and we haven't nicked it from next door."

Bene could easily see into both the large downstairs rooms and it was obvious that the furniture there was new and in the process of being unpacked. Nicola was busy along with another woman putting it all into place. "No I'm sure it's all OK, and you only came up here today then, so you won't have noticed anything happening next door."

"No, we'd only been here an hour ourselves this morning when the guy next door came flying round asking if we had seen anything, somebody's nicked all his good furniture, I hope he's insured. Hey Bene, I hope you're going to catch this lot, we're moving here 'cos it's a good area, we don't want a spate of burglaries breaking out; You lot had better get your arses into gear and get the buggers caught."

Bene checked on several other householders in the neighbourhood but none of them could give him any information. No-one had heard or seen anything out of the ordinary, there had been vans in the area but none of them arousing suspicion. Bene gave up in the end, disheartened and disillusioned he made his way back to the station. He had nothing to go on, not the slightest clue as to when or how the burglary had taken place. The chief would not be happy when he reported back, surely someone must have noticed something. Then to top it all that bloody sod Paul Hanbury was back in town again and Bene knew he would be seeing a lot more of him. It was Bene who had been responsible for arresting Paul's friend Ray Parrish who was now in prison serving a sentence for his crimes.

Bene was determined to find some incriminating evidence which he could link to Paul. He had certainly been involved along with Ray and the Polish fellow in the foreign currency scam. But he had not been as greedy as Ray and had got out in time just before the other two were arrested. Bene was also sure that Paul had something to do with the deaths of Matt and Cathy Renwick, but again there was no evidence or proof to link him to that either. "Yes, he's a clever dick alright," thought Bene "But somehow or other I'm going to find something that I can nail him to the cross with. Like most criminals he'll get a bit too cocky, and sooner or later he'll slip up and then I'll have him."

His thoughts were being overshadowed by the events which were taking place around him and were seriously threatening to overwhelm him completely. Up until a few days ago Adam and he had been experiencing the quietest spell either of them could remember in their time together in the force. But since Adam retired last weekend he now had two suspicious deaths to look into, a burglary which may just be the start of a spate of burglaries, and Paul Hanbury thrown in for good measure. "I wish Adam could have stayed another week or so to help me out. Still I suppose I've got ET and he seems OK, maybe together we'll be able to sort it all out."

Chapter 10

Incident on platform 4

It was only a short walk to the railway station and ET was in plenty of time to catch the train to Preston. The weather was warm and he had enjoyed his walk, it had given him a little time to reflect on his move to Levensbridge. He hadn't been entirely sure whether the decision to move north would turn out to be a good one or not, but the people he had met so far had been friendly enough and had made him feel welcome. He hadn't had much time to get to know Bene as yet, but in the short time they had spent together he'd felt quite comfortable working alongside him. He hoped that the promising start they had made would blossom into an effective and successful working relationship.

Peter Hoffmann had been right. The train journey was much better than using the car. In no time at all he was in Preston and on his way to the house. Peter was waiting for him and had the briefcase ready for him to take back to Levensbridge. "Would you like to come in and have a coffee before you go back," he asked.

"Yes thank you, that would be good, the train back doesn't leave for another hour." ET followed Peter into the kitchen and took the seat offered at the breakfast bar. He was introduced to Peter's wife Claire who was busy with the laundry. A small slim woman with mousey brown hair and a rather sad looking face. ET thought she had been crying.

"I expect it's too early yet to know when the funeral will be," ET asked.

"Yes, I'm going to see about the arrangements shortly so I'm afraid I'll have to leave you in a minute, no need to rush your coffee though you may as well stay here a little longer. Preston station isn't the nicest place to spend your time in. There's a draught that blows right through it, even in the summer it's quite cold, it's a natural wind tunnel. Anyway I'll have to go now, don't forget the briefcase will you. I haven't had time to go through it myself, father's death has rather knocked me sideways I still can't believe it. Let me have it back when you've finished with it I'll be interested to see what's in it myself." Peter picked up his coat and made for the door.

Once he had gone ET found himself alone with Peter's wife who hadn't spoken at all when her husband had been in the house. "Had she been crying before I came in," he wondered. "If she had then what had caused it, she seems a bit younger than Peter so maybe that's the problem, Peter doesn't look like a wife beater though. Oh well, it's none of my business maybe they've just had a row." Claire finished the laundry and came over and sat next to him at the breakfast bar.

Pulling herself up onto the high stool ET didn't know if what she did next was deliberate or not, but somehow getting up on the stool had resulted in her skirt creeping well up onto her thighs and the loose top she wore had now drooped to reveal rather too much cleavage. The serious face he had noticed earlier had changed dramatically to one which looked both inviting and seductive, in a seemingly innocent way if that's possible. "You're not local then are you?" she smiled at him. ET was a little flustered as he tried to explain his Welsh origin to her. The coffee was only half drunk and he was aware that her eyes were holding his without wavering. She laughed at his embarrassment and placed a small delicate hand just above his knee. "Are you married then?" she said smiling, her head leaning over at a slight angle but without once taking her eyes from his. ET was feeling very uncomfortable and reached up to run his finger around his collar. "Cat got your tongue then?" she teased, her voice was very childlike and this added to the effect she was having on him.

"Boy but she's hot," thought ET, "Peter will have a job holding on to her alright."

"Have you and Peter lived here long then?" was all he could think of to say.

"Hmm, Peter, remind me now who's Peter?" she laughed, teasing him again and at the same time moving her hand a little further up his thigh.

"Got to get out of here quick," thought ET "Or she's going to gobble me up, bloody hell she's rampant." "Oh, I've just remembered," he said getting up from the bar stool. "I need to get some train times for a trip to London next week I'd better get a move on, I should just about have time to do that before my train comes in." Leaving his empty cup in the sink he made a beeline for the door and his escape out of the house. "It's been nice meeting you and thanks for the coffee, tell Peter I'll let him have the briefcase back as soon as we've finished with it." Claire had left her seat and got to the door just before he did, she put her arm across to block his exit.

"You're not married are you, I can tell, come back again when Peter's busy in his shop and maybe we can have some fun together." Then still laughing she dropped her arm and let him leave. Heaving a huge sigh of relief he closed the door behind him and started the short walk back to the railway station.

"Good God," he thought "She's too much for Peter to handle, he must have caught her at it or at least suspected her and they've had a blazing row or something, that must be why she was crying." Walking back to the railway station in the sunshine he thought about his lucky escape from the clutches of Peter's wife. "No Claire, I don't think I'll be back there again, you can find someone else to hook your talons into."

Once in the station he prepared for a long wait until his train back to Levensbridge arrived. Peter was right about the wind, although it was sunny outside it was damned cold in the railway station. He walked the length of platform four before he found a bench seat which was sheltered from most of the wind, he settled down there to await the train back. Glancing at the briefcase on the seat beside him he wondered what the contents would be able to tell them. He could have a peek inside of course and he did, but only a casual glance at some of the papers as he flicked through them, a couple of other things caught his attention and he saw the diary was there. His conscience wouldn't permit him to take anything out of the case. He would have to wait until he got back to the police station where Benc and he could open it together, they would find out soon enough if it contained anything of value or not.

At last the train was announced and ET left the bench and made his way to where the second class coaches would pull up. There was quite a crowd of people waiting for the train, some of them had just finished work and were eager to get home. Along with these were a group of visitors who he assumed were on their way to the Lake District, most of them lugging large haversacks, they surged forward and joined the melee of people determined to claim a seat on the crowded train. ET had no intention of getting involved in the fight for a seat, if there was one available then that was OK, if not he wouldn't have long to stand. It appeared that he had picked the right place on the platform as the rest of the travellers came rushing over to where he was standing.

The second class coaches were at the rear of the train so it was still moving quite fast as it approached platform four. ET was standing at the front of the crowd of people near the edge of the platform, his thoughts were on the briefcase and what it would reveal when he got it back to the station and they could examine it thoroughly. He was totally relaxed and unprepared for what happened in the next few seconds. The same moment that he felt the briefcase being snatched out of his hand a sharp object stabbed him in the middle of his lower back. The excruciating pain from the force of the impact and the suddenness of the attack propelled him over the edge of the platform, he landed awkwardly on the track below right in front of the oncoming train.

Chapter 11

Things begin to turn nasty

Bene arrived back at the police station and was anxiously waiting for ET to return with the briefcase. The more he thought about it the more he wanted to find out what was in it. Surely among its contents they would find some sort of evidence to tell them what lay behind the deaths of the two residents, and the stranger who had visited them. Whatever this person had done or said to them had to all intents and purposes scared them to death. "Jeez, it's like something out of an Agatha Christie story." he said out aloud.

"Anyway that train should be in by now, I'll call his mobile and see where he is." He tried several times over the next half hour or so to contact ET but each time he called there was no answer. "This is too bloody much," he said, throwing his phone down on the desk, he was not only frustrated but rapidly working himself up into a real temper. "He knows he should always be available on his mobile so we can contact him, what the hell is he playing at? I honestly thought he was going to be OK, he seemed competent enough and he gave me the impression he was keen but now I'm not so sure.

I'll suppose I'll have to warn him about his conduct, it's not good enough."

On platform four at Preston railway station several passengers were standing around waiting for their train to arrive. Most of them could hear the mobile phone ringing quite clearly, but none of them wanted to go down onto the track to pick it up.

Bene finally gave up waiting and left the station to go home, cursing himself for not having the address where ET was staying. He should have got it from him earlier in the day because the Chief wouldn't be happy if he found out. "Never mind I'll get it tomorrow when he comes in with the briefcase so there'll be no need for Sowerby to hear about it." The only contact details Bene had for ET was his mobile number, and that was now useless.

As he pulled up at Dot's house Ethan the little secret agent was waiting for him, keen to tell Bene of his latest success. "I got them crooks for you mister," he spouted. "Well done agent Ethan so what have you done with them?" asked Bene now in a slightly better mood. The little fellow cheered Bene up and he was looking forward to hearing all about Ethan's exploits. "I locked them up in the shed at the back, and they'll have to stay there till they stop being bad people."

"That's good," agreed Bene "So what are you going to do now?"

"I thought I'd give you a hand in catching them murderers." Bene didn't think he should go too far down the road with the little boy on such a serious subject so he decided to ward him off. He told Ethan he had solved the case.

"I've got them locked up now so that case is finished. But now I'm looking for burglars who have been stealing antiques from rich people's houses, maybe you could help me with that one?" Ethan seemed pleased to be able to lend Bene his expertise in solving cases and quickly agreed.

"OK mister, I'll soon have them caught for you, so if you want to go off and do something different I'll hand them over to you when I got them locked up in the shed." Bene thanked the little agent and left, smiling to himself as he went into the house for his meal.

Alex and Dot were waiting with a hot meal ready. They had seen him talking to the little boy and Alex wanted to know what Bene had said to him. "What have you been telling him, nothing that will get him into trouble with his parents I hope. He's very impressionable you know you don't want to lead him on too much."

"Well actually I think I handled it pretty well." said Bene. "He's going to solve my burglary for me, so according to him I can forget all about that and concentrate on something else." All three had a good chuckle at Bene and his new found associate.

"Fancy going out for a drink tonight?" Alex asked.

"Yes, why not," said Bene "We haven't been out for ages, we'll go down to the Fox and Pheasant and see Kris and Ebony."

An hour and a half later they were seated in the pub, it wasn't too busy as there were no darts or quiz teams in. The pub was set back in its own grounds not far from the main street, it had changed little since the day it opened to the public almost a hundred years ago. The Virginia creeper which over the years had been allowed to spread wildly in all directions, fully covered the front and sides of the building, only the windows and the main entrance remained uncovered by this beautiful foliage. Nothing could be seen of the solid red sandstone of which the building had been constructed.

The landlord and his wife, Kris and Ebony had come to Levensbridge several years ago when in their mid-twenties. The couple were well liked by the customers and the natives of Levensbridge and business had boomed during their tenure. They had brought up two children during their time at the pub. Kris was a man of medium height, and a figure that suggested more than a few pints had passed through his lips over the years. He had a pale rounded face with a permanent smile etched upon it, and a good head of thick sandy coloured hair. Ebony by contrast, was a few inched shorter than her husband, but where he had let his figure spread outward, she had retained hers, and was proud of it. Her reddish auburn hair was swept up into a bun, and this allowed her face to be shown to its best advantage, a happy face, with nice clear rounded lines which required only the minimum of make-up.

Kris joined them at the table and said Ebony would be over once she was sure the new barmaid could manage by herself. Kris leaned over the table to face Bene and spoke quietly with a little apprehension in his voice. "Did you know that Paul and Nicola are back over here?"

"Yes" said Bene "Funnily enough I bumped into him this morning. I had to go up to Beech Drive and check out a burglary, and when I went next door to see if anyone had seen anything, blow me if Paul didn't come to the door. It gave me quite a shock when I saw him, I thought we'd seen the last of him when he left Levensbridge after his wedding."

Kris was also thinking about the time Paul had left Levensbridge a few months earlier. He had given him a mobile phone number to keep, with instructions to call him if and when something happened. At the time Kris had no idea what Paul had meant by this statement but he kept the number anyway. He didn't have long to wait before he found out. Almost immediately after Paul had left for his honeymoon his best friend Ray Parrish and another colleague had been arrested for printing forged currency. Both men were now in prison. Kris had phoned Paul to tell him the news and Paul hadn't seemed too surprised when he heard it. Kris was sure that Paul had been expecting the call and had known well in advance what the news would be. He had grave suspicions himself that Paul had been mixed up in the scam but had somehow managed to escape in time, leaving nothing behind that could implicate him in it.

Ebony came over to the table and joined them. They were settling down and looking forward to a fine session of drinking and general banter when Bene's phone rang and interrupted the flow of conversation. His face turned serious as he listened intently for a full minute without speaking, then with a pained expression on his face and in slow motion he quietly withdrew the phone from his ear and switched it off. "What is it?" asked Alex, concerned at Bene's reaction to the call.

"It's ET, he's been taken to the hospital in Preston, there's been some sort of accident at the railway station. I'll have to leave you and get over there as quickly as I can and see how bad he is."

"Want me to come with you?" asked Alex.

"No you stay here and maybe Kris can run you home later. I'll have to take the car, it's lucky I've only had a pint. Is that OK with you Kris?"

"Yes of course mate you get off and see to your colleague, either Ebony or me will get Alex back home."

"You'll let us know what's happened as soon as you can," said Alex "I hope he's OK and the injuries aren't serious."

Bene got onto the motorway as quickly as he could and sped off down the road to Preston Infirmary, he couldn't get ET out of his mind. Only a short while ago he had been cursing the man, accusing him of being negligent in his work. The more he thought about it the more he thought that if anyone was to blame it was probably him. If he had not been neglectful in his duty by not even knowing where his DC was lodging he would have been able to check out the address, and when he found that he hadn't returned from Preston he could have taken steps to find out what had happened to him. He had remembered to inform Sowerby of the news as he was leaving the pub and fully expected an earful on his return to the office the next morning.

On his arrival at the ward where ET had been admitted he was directed to the nurse's base. Here he had to wait patiently for the nurse on duty to finish her phone call before he could get any information from her about ET's whereabouts and condition. She told Bene that they had found his phone number in ET's note book. They had also found a contact number for his parents down in Swansea and notified them as well, his father was travelling up to Preston and should be there within the next two hours or so. She said that ET's condition was not physically serious, mainly a few cuts and bruises and a strange puncture mark in his back. They were more concerned about his mental state as he was still in shock and finding it difficult to communicate with them. "He was very lucky you know." said the nurse "He had fallen off the station platform right in front of an incoming train. Fortunately for him there was a gang of workmen checking over a train on the next line, they heard the commotion and one of them rushed over and pulled him off the line."

Eventually he was shown into a single room where he found ET sitting up in bed but looking a bit confused. "I can let you stay with him for a while but don't press him too hard. " said the nurse. "We don't want to tire him out so don't ask him too many questions you can see the state he's in. He is improving but we don't want him to have a setback and risk long term damage."

"OK I'll keep him company for a while but I won't stay too long." agreed Bene. The nurse left him alone with ET and he pulled up a chair to be near the bed. "Well, look at you," he said smiling at ET, secretly relieved that there didn't appear to be any serious physical damage sustained in the accident, none that he could see anyway. "I wondered where you had gone skiving off to." He looked around the single ward and was impressed by how clean it was, and nicely decorated too. But as his eyes travelled around the room he could see no sign of the briefcase ET should have brought back with him.

"Well you've got a nice room here and the nurses seem to be looking after you, you'll be in no rush to get back to work that's for sure." ET had looked to be in a bit of a state when he had first entered the room, his eyes had remained transfixed on Bene and it was clear that he was still a little disorientated. Bene sat there quietly in order to give ET time to survey his surroundings and get accustomed to them. Maybe if he waited patiently it might give ET the chance to recover some memory of what had happened. Presently the vacant look began to fade as ET began to regain a little composure. Bene continued to stay silent, partially for fear of holding back ET's recovery and partly because he hadn't yet decided what questions he could ask which wouldn't scare him off. Clearly ET had been shaken by what had happened to him at the railway station.

It was ET who finally broke the silence "It wasn't an accident boss, I was deliberately pushed off that platform and my back's as sore as hell. Have a look for me will you I can't see it myself but it hurts like mad." He turned over and pulled up the hospital night shirt so that Bene could see the area around the wound which was now covered with a dressing. Bene couldn't make out the puncture mark in the small of ET's back, but could see the remains of dried blood showing through the bandaging and the nasty bruising that had developed around it.

"Good God man no wonder you ended up on the line, whatever instrument they used for this could very easily have killed you, never mind the train." As the recollection of the attack returned ET was anxious to tell Bene all he could remember about the incident.

"I was standing along with other passengers waiting for the train to pull in when I felt this sharp object stabbing me in the back. The force behind it and the agonizing pain thrust me forward and over the edge, then it all went black. I can't remember anything after that."

Bene thought ET might be up to a little questioning and he was keen to find out if he had possession of the briefcase when he was attacked. "Did you manage to get up to Peter Hoffmann's house then?"

"Oh yes that was no problem," The memory of the visit came flooding back to him. "When I first went into the house I think his wife had been crying, maybe Peter beats her or something. He's got a really sexy wife you know she certainly likes the company of men, I think she's a nymphomaniac. When Peter left the house and I was alone with her she kept trying it on with me. It was really embarrassing, I made up an excuse and got out of there as soon as I could."

"And the briefcase" asked Bene, "Do you remember whether you had it with you or not?" ET had to think for a minute.

"Yes, Peter gave it to me and I took it with me when I left."

"So what happened to it can you remember, maybe you dropped it or something."

ET thought about it and then suddenly recalled exactly what had happened, his face lit up. "Of course I do remember now I had it with me on the platform, and just a split second before I was stabbed in the back someone snatched it away from me, yes that's what happened. Bloody hell boss someone was desperate enough to try and kill me for it."

"Good God," exclaimed Bene loudly "It must have contained something valuable. It looks as though whoever it was has gone to great lengths to prevent us from finding out what was inside it. We'll have to get hold of any CCTV footage from the station and see if we can find out who it was."

ET was starting to feel guilty about losing the briefcase.

"I'm sorry boss it's my fault, I should have been more aware, it's obviously very important and I've lost it and let you down."

"Don't be silly man, you had it with you and it was secure, you weren't to know that someone would try to kill you to get it. Did you by any chance have a look inside while it was in your possession?" ET thought hard again.

"Yes, I did actually. I was sitting on one of the benches waiting for the train and I opened it just to check what sort of contents were in there, to see if it was just papers or maybe other items as well."

"So" said Bene, "What was in there?"

"There were quite a lot of papers, records of some description I think, a large diary and a variety of letters, oh and a couple of rough sketches of something that may have been a map or directions to somewhere maybe, I didn't look too closely at any of them."

"Did you notice anything in there that might give us a clue?" Bene didn't really expect anything more from ET, if there had been anything he had probably forgotten about it. But ET perked up, he sat up in bed, smiled a little and waved his finger in the air.

"Yes there was something that caught my attention, a name that was shown on some of the papers, the same name appeared on several sheets." Bene jumped up from the chair as if an electric current had just shot through it.

"So what name was it?" ET thought hard again, then he had it.

"HUBER, yes that was it, definitely HUBER."

Chapter 12

This time next year we'll be millionaires

It was Thursday night in the Fox and Pheasant and Andrew Rawlings was bringing the investment club meeting to a close. It had been a short meeting as nothing much had changed since the last time they had met, it had been a relatively quiet week in the financial markets. Sylvia, Robert and Jamal were guilty of not giving their full attention to the meeting as their minds were elsewhere.

Now the meeting was closed they could invite Alastair McKay over to join them. He had been waiting at a separate table ready to step in when the remaining members of the group had left. "So was it a successful meeting then?" he enquired. Sylvia spoke for the three members.

"Pretty boring actually. We could have cancelled it and left it over until next week. But it's Andrew and Pat's little pet and they like to go through the motions even if there's nothing to discuss. I don't know what they'd do if they didn't have the club, I think their lives revolve around it. I mean last year we each made about a hundred and fifty pounds so we're never going to be millionaires are we?" This was not offered as a question, just a plain statement of fact.

"Right then, any more thoughts about what we discussed last week?" asked Alastair.

The three members had been thinking of nothing else all week, it was Robert who spoke first. "I've got to admit that I've thought long and hard about it and I've been sorely tempted. But to tell you the truth I'm a bit of a coward that way. I've got everything in life that I need and in two or three years time I'd like to hand over the business to my son. If I were to lose a lot of money on this deal it would put in jeopardy everything I've worked hard for. So I'm afraid I'm going to back out, sorry and all that but it's too big a risk for me. And like the other members who decided not to be involved I'll not speak to anyone else about it, you have my best wishes and I hope it goes well for you all." Robert took his coat and walked away, now there were just the three of them.

Jamal was also getting cold feet, as members were backing out of the deal the price of staying in it was going up and up. "It's getting too big for me as well I'm afraid, I talked it over with my dad and he isn't keen on getting involved in anything other than houses that are already built and available. Land deals don't appeal to him, and without his backing I can't go it alone. I'm sorry and I'd love to be part of it but there's no way I can come up with that sort of money on my own." Jamal left the room after wishing the remaining two people good luck. A long silence followed Jamal's departure, the only people left in the pub were Alastair, Sylvia and the barmaid.

The deal was dead in the water as there was no way that the two of them could finance the deal on their own. Any thoughts they had entertained over the last few days of becoming millionaires had been cruelly snatched away from them in the last few minutes. "I don't suppose the barmaid could cough up half a million or so." said Alastair, trying to brighten up the atmosphere a bit. Sylvia smiled, she could just about see the funny side of it. "What we need is a fairy godmother, someone who would trust us with their money, someone who has no honourable principles and is greedy to the point of obscenity. But most of all someone with loads of spare cash to invest." They both had a good laugh at this.

"Yes if only." said Alastair, "It's not asking too much is it." he chuckled.

The door opened and Paul Hanbury walked into the room and headed straight for the barmaid at the far end of the long bar. "Bit quiet in here isn't it, give me a pint of your best beer love." Unaware at first that there was anyone else in the room he stayed at the bar taking the first few sips of his drink before starting up a conversation with the barmaid. "You're new here aren't you, It was always a busy place when I was here last, what's happened Kris is still here isn't he?" The barmaid leaned over the bar.

"It's just tonight really, Kris and Ebony have stopped doing meals on Thursdays it wasn't worth it, but most nights we're still busy, weekends especially. Tonight's the night the investment club meet here, but the meeting's finished and most of them have gone home. There are only two of them left on that table over there, and yourself of course." Paul looked around to the table in the far corner. He didn't recognise the man who was facing him but he recognised the woman instantly.

He picked up his drink and walked over to their table, a little unsure about what kind of a reception he would get but smiling anyway. "Sylvia long time no see, are you going to introduce me to your friend?" It was the first time they had met since he had left for his honeymoon in France and Sylvia's husband and his best friend Ray had been sent to prison. He wasn't sure how she was going to react to meeting him again. "Does she blame me for Ray's imprisonment." he wondered. "Yeah sure I was involved in the scam with him alright but I got out in time. Ray had been too greedy and it was his fault entirely that he had been caught, he should have given it up and got out when I did, she can't blame me for that. Anyway she was just as greedy herself with that fake fashion stuff she was bringing into that shop of hers, she must have made a packet out of it. If it hadn't been for the fact she'd sold all the phony stuff she had in the shop and couldn't get any more, she would have been locked up as well."

"Paul what a nice surprise." Sylvia stood up to greet him with a broad smile on her face. "Let me introduce you to Alastair, funnily enough we might just have been talking about you." Alastair rose from his chair and offered Paul his hand, the two men shook hands warmly.

"I'm pleased to meet you Paul, obviously Sylvia and you are good friends."

"Yes" agreed Paul, "We go back a long way don't we Sylvia?"

Sylvia smiled in agreement.

"Good friends indeed," she thought. "This bastard is the reason my Ray's in prison and he bloody well knows it. I'll not have to let him see what I really think until we can find out if we can get him interested in the scheme, it should be right up his street. I'll hate myself of course but we could really do with having him in with us, he's got plenty of spare cash. I'll let Alastair handle it he's good and very convincing, Paul will believe him rather than me. I can see he's a bit nervous about meeting me again, I'll keep smiling and that should allay any suspicions he may have."

"So you're in an investment club now Sylvia," and looking over to Alastair. "And you're part of it as well are you Alastair?" Alastair explained that he was not actually a member of the club but had made a proposal to the members which required quite a substantial investment from them to be part of it.

"Unfortunately I seem to have frightened most of them off." he laughed. "Not too many real investors here I'm afraid. I thought there might have been since it's a project which will have huge benefits for anyone who has a sound business brain and not afraid to invest in the future development of their own town. Not to mention the financial rewards that come with it of course. Sylvia and myself seem to be the only ones with that foresight. Of course the benefits to the town and local economy are not to be overlooked either. Never mind, Sylvia is still with me and we'll take it down to Preston and Manchester and get some real investors on board. It's a pity we couldn't have kept it in Levensbridge, but I'm sure we'll have no problem finding some lucky punters down in the bigger towns and cities."

Paul had been listening to Alastair carefully and he liked what he was hearing. He had plenty of money to invest and had been thinking about what to do with it when he returned to Levensbridge. He didn't want to have his money tied up in banks or boring old blue chip companies with little or no risk, he much preferred something a little more unconventional, something that carried a few risks. "I'm not getting into anything like we were doing before though, that was too bloody risky. But I've got plenty to invest and this guy seems to know what he's talking about, Sylvia's in on it and I know she's no fool. I think I'd like to hear a bit more about it but I don't want to give this fellow the impression I'm too keen, I'll flatly reject whatever it is at first then maybe come back to him later."

"It sounds interesting what you've said so far and I'm sure you'll both do well out of it." Paul was looking over to Alastair trying not to give the impression he was greatly interested. "But you're right of course there aren't many people here who have the courage to invest at that level. I agree with you, you'd probably be better off taking it elsewhere." Whatever else Alastair was he was certainly no fool, he could see that Paul was interested even though it was not showing in his face, speech or body language. He got up ready to leave.

"Right Sylvia I'll have to get going but I'll be in touch soon. It's a bit too late to do anything about it this week because it's Friday tomorrow, and the people we need to speak to will be thinking more about how they're going to spend the weekend, it's not a good time to be talking money. I'll give you a call on Monday, by then I should have some contacts for us to meet around midweek.

With a bit of luck we should have it all sown up by next weekend." He offered Paul his hand again. "Nice meeting you Paul. I don't expect we'll meet again but good luck with whatever you're doing."

Paul had to relent, he wasn't going to let this opportunity slip away as easily as that. "Do you have to rush off right away?" he asked.

"Well I think I'm done here Paul I thought I might go for a bite to eat first before going home."

"Well to be honest," said Paul "I think I would like to hear a bit more about what Sylvia and you have in mind. It's just possible I might be interested, and if it's something I could help you with it would save you having to go looking any further. I'll just nip over to the bar and get some more drinks in." Alastair sat down again and looked over at Sylvia, no words were spoken but there was a brief exchange of knowing smiles.

"Right now tell me all about it." said Paul as he placed the freshly filled glasses on the table and sat down to join them. Alastair talked through the same proposal as he had given the previous week to the investment club. When he had finished Paul had all the facts he needed. "So you'll put up half a million yourself Alastair, and what about you Sylvia how much are you putting in?"

"Well originally I was looking at a hundred thousand with two hundred thousand as my limit. But to make it up to a round figure for you, if you're interested of course, I'm prepared to push that up to three hundred thousand because it's just too good an opportunity to miss. That would leave a straight million pounds which we would need to complete the deal. As Alastair says we should have no problem raising that next week, but if you're interested then you'll have to be quick, we can't wait too long or we'll miss out on it all together."

Paul had been put on the spot, he hadn't wanted to commit to such a large amount of money on the spur of the moment. He had already been offered partnership in another possible deal and this had been the real reason for his return to Levensbridge. On the other hand he didn't want to miss out on this one either. Neither did he want to give them the impression he didn't have the money or that he was frightened to use it. If he didn't join in the venture and it proved to be as good as they said it would be, he would never forgive himself, and Sylvia wouldn't let him forget it either. He couldn't afford to let that happen so the decision was made.

"I'm in." was all he said. Alastair smiled.

"That's great Paul, how much do you want to put up?"

"The lot." replied Paul.

"What the whole million pounds, are you sure Paul?" Paul was feeling good now, he hadn't felt this good for a long time. He was back and very soon everyone would know it.

"I have to admit that I'm already involved in another possible deal in the town but yes I'm sure alright, count me in for the full million. There's no need to look any further now, it's just the three of us."

All three shook hands on the deal, each one of them delighted with the outcome but for very different reasons. The smiles of all three belied their true thoughts.

Paul was ecstatic, he thought happily to himself. "Did you ever doubt I'd pass up this chance, I'm the main player in this deal and the two of you had better believe it."

Sylvia was giving Paul her most gracious smile, but her thoughts like his were less congenial.

"OK, so I'm pleased the deal's done but I'll get you somewhere along the line you bastard."

Alastair smiled broadly at his two new partners. "Gotcha suckers!!"

Chapter 13

Bene declares war

Bene's heart sank as soon as he walked into the police station. He had deliberately gone in early that morning with the intention of settling in before Sowerby arrived, it would give him time to prepare for what he was going to tell the Chief about the accident. Should he admit that he had failed in his duty by not having ET's contact details? With a bit of luck the Chief wouldn't pick up on it, maybe he'd just be interested in finding out ET's condition and what Bene had been able to discover. He was soon to find out because the Chief was already in his office and waiting for him.

"You've been to see him then?" he asked Bene, stern faced.

"Yes sir, he was still a bit shaken and confused when I went in but not badly injured thank goodness. He was recovering all the time I was with him and I don't think he'll let them keep him in there for much longer, he's itching to get out and back to work. It was no accident though he's absolutely certain of that. He says he was deliberately pushed off the platform just as the train was coming in. Thankfully a workman on the track pulled him clear just in time."

"And the briefcase Bene, what about that?"

"He remembers that it was snatched from his hand just before he was pushed, we're certain it was an attempt on his life, there's no doubt about it."

The Chief took his time thinking this through. "So whatever was in the case was important enough for someone to risk trying to kill a policeman in order to get it. Any idea what it was supposed to contain? You spoke to the son didn't you did he give you any idea?"

"He did tell us a little when we met him in his shop, but not enough to give us any significant information." said Bene. "His father told him there was a diary in there and a map of somewhere he had been to in France during the war, there were also records showing the names of the other inmates at the camp. But it was the diary and maps which would explain everything. But Peter hadn't the time to examine it himself. His father told him he shouldn't do anything about it until after he was dead, then the decision was up to him. But what he meant by that is a mystery. I think it goes back to the last war when his father was in France, that's where the secret lies but what it is or where is anyone's guess. We'll probably never find out now."

"And that's all we know?" asked the Chief. Bene suddenly remembered the name that ET had seen in the briefcase.

"The one clue we do have is the name Huber. ET had a quick look into the case when he was at the station and he saw several papers with that name on, but that's all I'm afraid."

"Right" said the Chief. "You've got plenty to get your teeth into now. Two deaths up at the home which are certainly suspicious and now look more likely to be murder, and both somehow linked to that missing briefcase. You'll have to look at the attempt on ET's life as well, that's certainly connected to it. Then there's the burglary to look into. Oh, and by the way you'll be getting a phone call shortly, there was another one last night. I don't want a spate of those starting up here. It's a pity Adam's retired, but hopefully ET won't be off too long because you're going to need him to help you. OK then, get out there and let's see some progress."

The Chief had given his orders and went straight back to his laptop, Bene had been dismissed. He remained in his chair a few seconds longer before taking the hint then rose to leave. The Chief didn't raise his head but just as Bene reached the door he spoke. "And Bene, next time don't rely on the hospital or anyone else to tell you where your DC is, it's up to you to know where he is twenty four seven.

Bene went over to his desk and slumped down in the chair. "What a bloody mess, where do I start. I mean who the hell is this damned stranger, and how am I going to find that blasted briefcase. If it's still in Preston I'll have to get help from the police there, but then if it's that important it could be anywhere in the country by now. Then there's the incident at the railway station, I wonder if the fellow who snatched the briefcase and pushed ET off the platform is the same one who visited the home, I bet it was."

He was feeling sorry for himself and the heavy sighs emanating from his corner of the office drew the attention of Val the female administrator.

"Come on Bene it can't be that bad, you were a bit like this a few months ago remember, and look how well that turned out." Bene looked over to her and smiled. Val was a great comfort to him, when he was down she could always find something to say to cheer him up. She was a constant, always there and always supportive. She was almost sixty years old now but the wispy grey hair, the frumpy baggy clothes she wore and the old fashioned speckled framed glasses belied the razor sharp brain that lay behind them. She could complete the large daily crosswords in less than fifteen minutes.

"Yes I suppose you're right Val, it's just that everything seems to have come at once. The last few months were so quiet that Adam and me were longing for something to happen, then as soon as he retires this lot comes down on me like a bloody great avalanche."

The phone on his desk rang. "Maybe this is some good news." he thought picking up the receiver.

"Bene is that you?" the voice on the other end was all too familiar.

"That you Paul what can I do for you, have you remembered something about the burglary next door?"

"No I bloody well haven't," shouted Paul. "I've been bloody well burgled myself, someone broke in last night and nicked my roll top desk which was in the hallway."

"Is that all that was taken or was there more?" asked Bene

"No just the desk, we don't have an alarm fitted yet, I've got one ordered but they can't come to fit it until next week. I heard a noise about eleven o'clock and got down just in time to stop them taking anything else. They must have just got the desk into the van when they saw the lights come on and me coming down the stairs, when I got to the hallway they shot off in the van as quick as you like."

"Did you get a chance to see what kind of van it was?" Bene hoped that Paul could give him a description of it.

"Yeah, I'm not certain but I think it was one of those delivery vans, it was definitely white and it had writing on the side but I couldn't make out what it was. It was like the ones you see around the town all the time, that's maybe not too helpful they're pretty common I know."

"Didn't catch the registration did you?" Bene asked.

"No," said Paul. "I didn't get the number but it was short, maybe a couple of numbers and two or three letters, it looked like a personalised plate, you know the sort that's made up from someone's initials."

"OK," said Bene "I'll have to come up and get a proper statement, will you be in later this afternoon?"

"Yeah we'll be here all day, come up anytime but don't make it too late. And Bene, you'd better get that desk back for me quickly, there are things in there that are very important to me personally. The desk is valuable in its own right but the stuff inside is worth a whole lot more to me than the desk. So much more that there's a personal reward in it for you if you can get it back to me with the contents intact." Bene was thankful he was sitting down when Paul told him exactly how grateful he would be. "But that's just for your ears mind, don't go spreading it around. I'll lend a hand myself if you think it would help to catch whoever did it, I'll start by asking around a bit, I still have a few friends in the right places."

"If it hadn't been so serious it would be funny." Bene thought. If anyone was going to be robbed then he would love it to be Paul, but now of course he realised that the burglary at the Taylor's house was not a one off, it could be the start of something much bigger. It was up to him to catch whoever was responsible for everyone's sake, for Paul's sake, for the sake of the Taylors and the Chief, but most of all for himself.

"This is turning into another war." he said to himself. "Murders, attempted murders and burglaries, and just like before I'm all on my own." Ten minutes ago he had been feeling down and pretty much washed out. But in the last few minutes all that had changed, it was as if all his latent energy had been suddenly switched on to full blast, once again he was up for it. "Right you bastards, I'll not rest until I've solved all these bloody mysteries and got the lot of you locked up. - But maybe not in Ethan's shed." he added with a chuckle.

Bene pulled up outside the home of Adam Firth. "He's round the back in the garden," said Ellen. "He'll be pleased to see you, he's been a bit lost without his work to go to." Adam appeared around the side of the house smiling.

"Bene my boy am I glad to see you I thought it was your voice I could hear, is it still that quiet at the station you've got time to come round here to see me?" Bene was quick to reply "My God, but you got out at the right time." He was anxious to tell Adam how things had built up at the station since he had retired. They walked around the house and into the rear garden, Bene noticed it was looking much tidier and more pleasant than when he had last visited. Adam had plenty of time now to nurture his plants and keep the lawn tidy. Two chairs were set up on the decking which was still in the process of construction and the men sat down. Bene took time to look over the garden before complementing Adam on it, then proceeded to tell him all that had happened since he had left the force.

Adam listened attentively until Bene had finished relating all the events to him. “Well I wish all this had come up a few weeks earlier when we were really quiet. I was itching to get stuck into one last case before I retired, but there you are it’s come up just too late for me.”

“I’ve nothing much to go on either,” said Bene. “No clues at all on the deaths at the home, or on the attempt on ET’s life. The only clue I have on anything is a vague description of the van used in the burglaries.”

Although he was now retired Adam was keen to offer Bene all the help he could, he was sorely missing his involvement in the police force. It had always taken up a large part of his life and now he had left it behind there was a vacuum that he was finding difficult to deal with. The garden alone didn’t fill up much of the spare time he now found himself with, it was going to take some time to adjust to this new way of life. His mind had always been active and imaginative before, and planting a few flowers, pulling up weeds and cutting the grass did little for him in the way of stimulating his little grey cells."Have you checked the CCTV footage from the railway station yet?"

"Not yet Adam, I'm expecting copies of them to arrive shortly and I'll have a look as soon as they get here."

"While you're at it get the CCTV from the town centre as well. You never know the van might show up on one of them, either just before or just after eleven o'clock last night when Paul's house was broken into, it could have passed through the town on its way there or on the way out."

"Yes that's an idea, there could be something in that."

"And Bene you need to find out who this guy was that visited the home, have a word with some of the girls there, one of them must have spoken to him when he visited. If the two men who died were German and you think the visit was connected to something that happened in the past then he may have been German as well, there can't be many of them about in Levensbridge."

Bene's mobile rang. The CCTV footage had arrived from Preston and was at the police station. "Right I'll have to go Adam and thanks a lot for your help, I hope Ellen doesn't mind me bothering you with my troubles, I mean it's nothing to do with you now and she might not want you getting involved again. Anyway I'd better get off it's been great seeing you again."

"OK Bene and don't leave it too long before you come back again, you know we're always pleased to see you, and bring Alex with you the next time, right? Oh and let me know how you get on. If I can be any help at all it'll be good to get my brain working again, I know Ellen won't mind she knows I've not fully adjusted to retirement yet."

Bene noticed a broad grin which had spread across Adam's face. Adam waved a finger at him.

"Don't you dare tell anyone, but I've joined the local bowls club up in the town. I'm hoping that I'll like it and it will help to take up some of my spare time." Bene grinned back at him. "Maybe you should get Ellen to join as well."

Back in the office again Bene sat watching the camera footage on his laptop, he started the recording about half an hour before the attack on ET and was watching as all the people were moving around platform four. He couldn't see anything unusual or anyone acting suspiciously. A minute or so before the train arrived he spotted ET together with the briefcase walking towards the camera, he stopped at a point where he could still be seen, but only just in view of the camera, not in full view. Now he could see the train approaching the platform and bent his head nearer the monitor to watch closely. People were milling around now, but because of the angle the camera was set it was difficult to get a clear view of anyone standing behind ET. The train was almost there now and Bene had a clear view of ET as he was pushed over the edge of the platform. The waiting passengers backed away hurriedly from the edge of the platform in disbelief and horror. Bene was looking closely for any sign of who had attacked ET. It had all happened far too fast, he would have to slow the recording down. He ran it back a little then ran it again at a much lower speed. This was much better, this time he saw a hand pull away the briefcase from ET's hand, and as ET was pushed forward and the crowd moved back he spotted the instrument that had been used to stab him with.

"There! did you see that!" a voice yelled in his ear. Bene nearly wet himself, spinning around he saw ET standing over him his eyes glued to the screen.

"Bloody hell man, are you trying to give me a heart attack." he cried. "What the hell are you doing here anyway you should be in hospital.

"Oh I've had enough of that place I signed myself out, anyway there's nothing wrong with me apart from this back injury. Can you believe it was an umbrella that did it, I didn't think they could be so bloody dangerous."

When Bene had recovered a little self-control the two men went back to watching the screen again. Bene had to rewind the film a bit, as when ET had crept up behind and shocked him the film had continued to run, showing the events that immediately followed the attack. It was an umbrella alright but the man wielding it couldn't be identified. The only sight they had of the assailant was what looked to be a man in an old type raincoat with a hood which covered his head. The film was in black and white so the colour couldn't be recognized, only that it was dark. Bene saw something on the coat but couldn't quite make out what it was. He froze the film at that point and enlarged that part of the frame. Now he could make out exactly what it was, for on the sleeve of the coat was an elbow patch which was of a much lighter colour than the coat itself, probably white. The film gave them no further clues even though they watched several parts of it over and over again. Whoever the man in the raincoat was he was never seen again.

"Right then" said Bene. "What are you doing for dinner?"

"Oh I don't know, I'll probably get something on the way home." Bene got out his mobile and made a call, a couple of minutes later ET's dinner was sorted.

"That's fixed then you're coming back with me, a hotpot OK?"

"Hey that's great boss I've never had a real homemade hotpot for ages, are you sure she doesn't mind?"

"No of course not they've both been looking forward to meeting you, but first you'd better let me have your address in Levensbridge or I'll be in trouble again for not getting it from you." Bene made a note of ET's address as they left the station together and made for Dot's house.

Bene left the car on the road outside the house and the two men began to walk down the drive. "These robberies" asked ET, "What about that Peter Hoffmann he's got an antique shop hasn't he?"

"Yes but you can see he's only small time, his premises aren't large enough to get much in there. If there had been anything to see we would have seen it. No I think we can rule him out."

"Maybe he's got somewhere at the back or another place somewhere in town, you never know." said ET.

"No I can't see it myself, the people we want are down in the Manchester or Preston area that's where it all started, we'll get some addresses from down there and make a start on it."

The two men arrived at the front door of the house and went in. On the other side of the hedge the little secret agent had also been walking down his driveway, he reached the front door of his house at the same time as the two detectives reached theirs, Ethan opened the door and went inside for his tea.

Chapter 14

A plan of action

Dot was the first to greet ET as he came into the house. "I'm pleased you could join us for dinner Emlyn come on through to the lounge and make yourself comfortable, dinner won't be long." Dot followed the two men into the lounge and introduced ET to Alex. "Alex this is Emlyn, Bene's colleague, he's having dinner with us tonight so get up and make him feel welcome." Alex jumped up

"Yes of course Mama." She turned to face Emlyn and curtseyed demurely with her head bowed. "It's too kind of you to grace us with your presence your majesty, I hope you will not be disappointed with our simple fare." Eyes still glued to the floor she backed slowly away, and with a generous sweep of her arm offered up her seat to him.

ET was gobsmacked he couldn't think of a response which would have been adequate, he hadn't been prepared for this form of greeting and had no idea how to reply to her. "God," he thought, "I've only been here a few days and this is the second crazy woman I've met, poor Bene I hope he knows what he's getting into."

Shyly he averted his eyes from Alex and took the seat offered to him. Bene was rarely surprised at Alex's strange behaviour but this just about took the biscuit. All he could do was shake his head in disbelief and apologise to ET.

"Take no notice of her she's as mad as a box of frogs. Alex how could you, you've scared the life out of the poor fellow now get up and apologise." Alex laughed uncontrollably.

"Sorry about that Emlyn I just couldn't help myself, these silly urges come over me and I just have to go with them." She went over and sat beside him on the sofa. "Now tell us all about yourself, obviously you come from Wales but why on earth come all the way up here, are you on the run or something." She leaned closer and dropped her voice to a whisper "If you are your secrets safe with me, but don't tell Sherlock over there."

ET was feeling a bit more relaxed. "Thank God for that she is quite normal after all." He proceeded to tell Alex the reason he had asked for a transfer, that he had wanted to work under Adam but hadn't realised that he was retiring.

"Never mind" said Alex. "I'm sure Sherlock will look after you just as well." For the second time ET looked a little lost for words.

"Oh, she means me ET, that's her pet name for me, but don't go spreading that around the station I don't think I could stand the ragging."

"What's all this ET business anyway, is it a nick-name or something?" asked Alex. ET had to explain how it had been given him by his colleagues down in Swansea.

After the meal in which ET had been grilled thoroughly by the two women the men went back to the lounge with coffees. Bene was worried about ET's injuries.

"Do you think you're fit enough to come back to work then?" ET confirmed his intention of returning right away.

"My back's still a bit sore but apart from that everything's fine, I couldn't face staying in that small flat on my own for too long it would drive me nuts. No, I'll be OK." Bene was thinking about the following day and which of the crimes they should concentrate their efforts on. There were two possible murders, one attempted murder, and now two burglaries as well.

"OK then," Bene was trying to form a plan of action in his mind. "The burglaries will have to take a back seat for the moment, we'll have to concentrate on the two deaths at the home and the attack on you, they're the most important ones. I'll get a print out of that figure in the raincoat and take it to Preston with me tomorrow afternoon. Some of the passengers for that train will be the same ones that were there when you were attacked, one of them might have seen him and be able to give me a description, it's worth a try anyway. While I'm there I'll call at the police station and see if they've managed to find out anything about those two bodies that were dug up recently, I've a funny feeling they're connected to this in some way."

"So what do we do in the morning?" asked ET.

"In the morning" said Bene. "We can have a look at more CCTV film. I've got films from all the cameras around the railway station and maybe they'll show more of this figure in the raincoat, where he came from and where he went afterwards. While we're looking at films we can also have a look at the ones from the cameras in the town centre here in Levensbridge, maybe we'll catch sight of the van that was used in the burglaries."

"Blimey" said ET "We'll be bog-eyed by lunchtime.".

"Yes I know," said Bene. "It's a ball aching job alright but it has to be done so we may as well do it tomorrow and get it over with. I just hope we get something out of it, if not I'm not sure where we go next."

The following morning found the two men with their heads down examining footage from the CCTV cameras. Chief Inspector Sowerby was keen to see some progress on the case so he gave Bene one of his uniformed officers to help look at the films. "And you can have Val as well. If there's anything to find on them she'll be the one to find it." Bene showed them the picture of the man in the raincoat and told them to examine the films closely to see if they could pick him up entering or leaving the station. It was a long boring morning and by lunchtime all four were weary with the tedious task.

It was time for Bene to leave for Preston and they still hadn't finished going through the films. "I didn't realise there were so many damned cameras in use at the station. Some of them are bloody useless, the quality is so poor you can hardly make out anything or anyone on them, they're all blurred. Anyway I've got to go now so I'll leave it with you, but for heaven's sake take a break or two and give your eyes a bit of a rest, I don't want you to lose concentration. We've got to be thorough and make sure we don't miss anything. If you do find anything useful run off a copy and keep the film OK? If you finish the films from the station have a look at the ones from the town centre here and see if you can spot that white van. I should be back later this afternoon."

2

Bene had arranged his meeting with DI Selby for 1.30 at Police HQ in Preston. The police there also had copies of film from the railway station, and just like Levensbridge they were having difficulty getting any decent images from the cameras at the entrance and outside the station.

"The problem is," said the DI. "We have trouble with the kids down there. They chuck mud up onto the cameras to blot out the vision, then a day or two later they come back and if the cameras haven't been cleaned they get up to all kinds of mischief. Then of course they run off before we can get there to catch them, and with the cameras being obscured we've no means of identifying them."

Bene could understand now the reason why his own people were having problems with the films. It wasn't a fault with the cameras, it was vandalism.

"Yes, I can see now why it's making it difficult. We probably won't get as much as we'd hoped for but there's still a chance we could catch a glimpse of the guy in the raincoat, hopefully with the hood down this time."

Bene got down to the real reason for his visit. "Have you had any success with the two bodies that were found in the woods over at our place yet?" The DI was able to tell him quite a lot about the case.

"Yes, we've actually made quite a bit of progress on one aspect of the case. We did think it would be a waste of time at first. I mean sixty odd years is a long time you know. I don't think anyone would have been too bothered about it if it hadn't been for the way in which they died, shot with British Army bullets!"

Bene wondered if that was all he was going to find out, but the DI continued.

"I don't know if we'll ever know who shot them or why, because there's not many left alive who were at the camp at that time and would remember. The chap in charge there died shortly after the war ended. We did manage to track down two of the guards who were at the camp, but both are in their nineties now and they couldn't tell us anything about any shooting there. It was by all accounts quite a relaxed camp with little security needed, the POWs seemed happy to sit out the rest of the war there in peace." The DI paused for a moment, not sure if he should continue talking about a case which was still active. He didn't want to give out any information which might interfere or endanger the ongoing enquiry.

"Well I suppose it will soon be made public so I can't see a problem" he thought, and continued. "They did both remember a spell of trouble towards the end of the war. Two brothers arrived at the camp along with a batch of new prisoners and they were the cause of a lot of friction between the inmates. But they were only there a matter of weeks and then they managed to escape. Neither of the men heard anymore about them, whether they were re-captured and sent to another camp, or maybe they had managed to get back to Germany. Whatever happened they were soon forgotten."

"Is there any chance that the two bodies we found could be those two men?" asked Bene.

"More than a chance," said the DI smiling, "The bodies have been identified and we know now exactly who they are, or who they were anyway."

"Come on then," said Bene "Give me some names."

"Well we sent all the details we had on them to the German police. We asked if they could give this information to the press over there and see if anyone knew of, or were related to two brothers who were POWs over here in the last war. We also sent a photo of the identical gold bracelets which were found on the bodies that were obviously presents from the family."

"So someone knew who they were and contacted you?" said Bene.

"Yes, well the German police contacted us anyway, it was the gold bracelets that clinched it. Someone recognised the photo of them and even took in to the police station a bracelet of their own which matched exactly. This person agreed to a DNA test and the sample was identical to the DNA from the two brothers, it was proof that this person was a blood relation."

"So what happens now?" asked Bene.

"Well because we still haven't completed our investigation into the deaths we can't release the bodies for repatriation just yet. I think our lot will eventually have to admit that we'll never be able to find out who shot them. Then of course we'll have to satisfy the relative in Germany that we've done everything possible to try and identify the person or persons responsible for their deaths. But there's no-one left living who can tell us anything, and the only evidence we have is the bullets which were found with the bodies. There's nothing we can get from them after all this time and the rifles have long been destroyed. It shouldn't take too long now to wrap it up and that will be the end of it."

"The names then," asked Bene. "Who were they?"

"Oh yes, I nearly forgot Bene, they were Franz and Karl Huber."

Huber! Bene nearly went on to tell the DI about the name Huber appearing in papers in the briefcase but then thought better of it.

"No not just yet" he thought, "Maybe later. I'll keep that quiet for the time being I don't want to hand everything over to division, especially if it has anything to do with the attempt on ET's life." His thoughts were interrupted by his mobile ringing. Bene took the call and when he had finished gave DI Selby his thanks and left HQ.

"So the team have found something on film, I hope it's something that will give us a name."

Before he left Preston he called into the railway station and asked the people who were waiting for the train on platform four if they could remember seeing the person in the raincoat. None of the ones he spoke to could help him, only a few had been there the previous day and their view had been blocked by the ramblers with their bulky rucksacks.

Chapter 15

Concern at the bowls club

It was late when Bene finally got back to Levensbridge, it had been a long day for everyone. The last thing he expected to see as he entered the office was any of the team he had left behind earlier. Hours spent looking at blurred images on their monitors must have drained them all. But one of them had spotted something worthwhile and none of the team wanted to leave until Bene had returned and looked at it himself.

"You'll not be getting overtime for this you know." he joked as he entered the office. Nevertheless he was secretly pleased that they had stayed on and waited for him. He knew that none of them had any intention of claiming the overtime, they had found something they hoped would be useful to him and wanted to be there when he saw it. Bene remembered a session he had attended at his training college where they were asked what it was that motivated people and how they liked to be rewarded. The top answer not surprisingly was money, the second was personal recognition, a simple thank you for a job well done was usually sufficient. He would make sure that they would all be acknowledged for the effort they had put in.

"Right then let's see what you've come up with." Bene was directed over to Val's desk where there were some blown up photos from the films she had been watching. She picked them up and showed the first one to Bene. It was still a bit blurred but there was no doubt that the figure in the photo was the same man in the raincoat with the white patches on the sleeves. "Which camera has this come from Val?" Bene asked.

"It's from the camera at the front entrance to the station." replied Val "From the camera angle it looks like the man is leaving the station and heading towards the covered market. If he goes in there we've lost him because there aren't any cameras in there. We'd have to get footage from the cameras in the town centre and try and pick him up again when he comes out. It could take some time to trawl through all those mind. Do you think it would be worthwhile me getting them?"

"Yes I do," said Bene, "It's the only clue we have and we really need to find out who it is. It's late now so can you get them first thing in the morning and make a start as soon as you can. I'll square it with the chief when I get in."

Bene reached over and picked up the rest of the photos. "Are these the photos taken from the cameras in town?"

"Yes, there were just a few vans but no obvious ones, none with personalised number plates or anything like that. We looked at all the films from eight o'clock at night until two in the morning but none of the vans really matched the description we were given. We've also checked film from the cameras on the three major roads out of the town but nothing showed up there. There was very little traffic moving that night."

"Ok" said Bene, "That's enough for today, get yourselves away home and I'll see you all tomorrow. And by the way thanks to all of you for your efforts today. I know it's not much but you've done a good job and I appreciate it."

Bene left to go home but wanted to call and see Adam on the way, he needed to talk to someone, although he knew that he shouldn't trouble Adam with his problems, the last thing he wanted was for Adam to think he couldn't manage without him. "I should talk to ET about it," he thought. "But I shouldn't have to admit to him that I'm a bit lost on this, he should be looking to me for guidance, not me looking to him for it."

Ellen invited Bene into the house and took him through to the lounge. Bene was surprised to see the room was empty. He had expected to find Adam in his favourite chair. "He'll be back in a couple of minutes" said Ellen, "He's been at his bowls today but he'll be back any time now."

"I'm pleased Ellen how's he getting on with it?"

"Oh he seems to like it, he's had one or two lessons and I think it's helping him. He says the members there are lovely people and there's such a lot going on. What with all the competitions, league games and so on its keeping him busy, not to mention the social side of it, he's even got me involved in that."

"Well that's good Ellen, he certainly needed something apart from the garden to keep him active."

"Yes the only thing he doesn't quite like about it is that he seems to be one of the youngest members there, some of them are getting on a bit you know. But then that's the reason they're pushing him into the team. A lot of the older ones have been there, done it and got the Tee-shirt, so they're quite happy to let some of the younger ones take their place."

Adam arrived home just then, and after seeing Bene's car sitting outside he went straight through to the lounge to join him. Bene got up to greet him. "Well you certainly look the part in all those whiter than white clothes, is that the uniform then?"

"Yes" said Adam, "But only for matches and competitions you know, otherwise you can wear anything you want, within reason of course. So how have you been getting on, have you made any progress yet?"

Bene had to admit that in all the cases he was now looking into he was really no further forward with any of them. He told Adam about the man in the raincoat and that he hoped they would be able to get further pictures of him from other cameras in the town. "But apart from that I'm stumped Adam. I wish I knew what was in that briefcase, I feel that it holds the key to the whole damned thing."

"Have you spoken to any of the girls up at the home yet?" asked Adam.

"No not yet thanks for reminding me, I'll go up there in the morning and speak to them. Maybe they'll be able to tell me something. God I hope so, I'm desperate for a lead."

"Don't worry too much Bene it will come, just keep at it. Have you thought about putting out a TV appeal for information on the man in the raincoat, it might be worth a try."

"I'll have a word with Sowerby about it, it would have to be his decision of course. He doesn't like to admit to the media that we can't manage on our own, but he might want to do it."

"Anyway how's the bowling going Ellen tells me you're enjoying it."

"It's not bad Bene, I wasn't sure at first but I seem to be slowly getting the hang of it, I just hope it continues."

"Why" said Bene, "You're not thinking about giving it up already are you?"

"Heavens no, but there's some doubt about the club itself. Evidently it's a private club owned outright by four of the members, and that's where the doubt lies. I mean the land it occupies is prime location in the town. One of the owners who doesn't play much anymore would like to sell it for a nice fat profit, but he can only do that with agreement from the other owners and they don't want to sell, they want to keep it as it is."

"So where's the problem?" asked Bene. "If only one of them wants to sell and the other three don't, then it won't happen will it?"

"No, but where there were three other owners now there are only two, one of them died recently in a nasty road accident. That leaves only two against selling the land, and one of those was taken to hospital this morning with severe food poisoning. If he were to die then that leaves only one against the sale." Bene was curious.

"So when one of them dies, who gets his share? his wife or family I suppose, and surely they would want their husband's wishes to be carried out."

"No it doesn't work like that Bene. If one of them dies his share is split up and given to the remaining owners. So you see, if the owner who is in hospital dies there will only be two of them left, and the one who is dead against the sale is not a young man, he must be well into his seventies if he's a day, so how much longer will he be with us? The members are all a bit worried about it. The club was originally owned by the council but they were going to close it back in the sixties so a group of members bought it from them. It's an old club though, it's been there for almost a hundred and fifty years and we were looking forward to celebrating that with a host of events which are being planned for next year."

"Hmm I can see now why you're worried, but there's nothing suspicious in it is there?" asked Bene.

"Well nothing on the surface of it, but you know as well as I do that coincidental deaths always look a bit suspicious even when the people concerned are old, just like your two up at the home. I mean in this case, if the accident wasn't an accident and the food poisoning was deliberate then there may be a case to answer. And if there is something going on behind the scenes, a third party with an ulterior motive maybe, then that person has been going to great lengths to create this situation."

There was a short silence in which both men paused to take in the implications of what Adam had said.

"I mean the guy who is intent on selling has only just changed his mind. According to the members I've spoken to they said that all four owners were of like minds only a month or so ago. Something must have happened to change his mind, it looks like he's been got at by somebody."

"Right" said Bene, "I'll be interested to know how this fellow in hospital gets on, I hope he recovers and everything gets back to normal again, but if not you must let me know."

Bene left the house even more worried than when he had arrived there barely half an hour earlier. He knew his old boss far too well, and if Adam had doubts about anything then you could be sure they were well founded and not to be ignored. "I'll have to keep any eye on this one, I hope the guy in hospital doesn't die, the last thing I want at the moment is another case. Adam is worried though and that makes me worried, bugger I hope there's something good for dinner tonight."

Chapter 16

A lead at last

Next morning Bene and ET left the station and made their way to Greenacres residential home for the third time. They were let in and shown along to Mrs Janes' office by the senior care worker on the day shift. As they entered the office they couldn't fail to notice that Mrs Janes was looking more troubled than ever. She had been badly affected by the recent deaths of two of her residents, and the failure to reveal or understand the circumstances surrounding the deaths had visibly unnerved her.

"I was hoping you were coming here to give me some answers Bene." she said. "But you said in your call that you only wanted to talk to the girls, is that right? I have asked them myself of course but none of them have been able to shed any light on who the person was who called here to see the two men. But you can speak to them yourself if you want to, two of them are out doing the rounds of medication, and you'll find the others either in the staff room or in the kitchen preparing the lunch. One of them, Susan, is just back from holiday, it's possible she may be able to tell you something, I haven't had time to speak to her since she came back to work."

The two men left the office to speak to the carers. "Right ET, you have a look around and see if you can catch the two girls dishing out the tablets, see if you can get anything out of them. I'll try and find this Susan and have a word with her."

ET soon found his two girls and straight away asked them if they could remember seeing the stranger who had visited the home, but neither of the girls could tell him anything. They hadn't been aware that anyone had called to see either of the two men, at least not until after the deaths and they had been interviewed about it by Mrs Janes. He left them to continue their round and moved on to the staff room. He had the same result from the girls in there as well. "Somebody must have seen the guy, even if it was just to let him into the building," he thought, "And he must have been asked to sign the visitors book surely. I'll have a look at that shortly."

His last call was to the kitchen where two of the girls were busy with the cook preparing the residents' lunch. At last, one of them remembered the man who had called.

"It was me who let him in to see Dieter," said the younger of the two girls, "But there was nothing strange about it, or him. I mean he seemed alright, polite and everything you know, he told me he was a relative. He certainly wasn't English although he did speak the language quite well, I would say he was German the same as Dieter."

"So he told you he was a relative?" asked ET.

"Yes and he seemed to know all about Dieter. I thought he was genuine, a distant relative maybe who had found out that Dieter was staying with us and came over here to see him."

"Can you describe him?" asked ET.

"Well there was nothing much out of the ordinary about him, apart from being a foreigner of course." she replied. "He was a smart looking man, well dressed in what looked to be an expensive suit, he was no more than medium height and rather slim as well which suited him. The only thing I thought a bit unusual about him was his hair, it was ginger and for some reason I didn't think Germans had ginger hair, but there you are." She looked hard at ET and spoke deliberately as if what she was about to say was very important. "But this is what I thought was a bit funny about him even though he was a foreigner. I mean the first thing that most men do when they come in from outside would be to take off their hat but this man didn't. I don't know why, maybe he kept it on because he didn't like people to see his hair I don't know, but it was ginger all right and that's about all I can tell you about him."

"So, how long did he stay with Dieter?" asked ET.

"Not long, about half an hour maybe, forty minutes at the most, he did sign in and out again so you can easily check."

It didn't look as if there was anything more to be gained from the conversation so ET put away his notebook and left the girls to carry on with their work. He went first to check the visitors book before meeting up with his boss again. The book was lying open on a side table in the entrance hallway. ET flicked through the pages until he came to the one which showed the entry of Dr Kohler's visitor. He looked quizzically for some time at the name which appeared beside the time the stranger had visited the home. Then he turned over two more pages to the date and time of the second visit which was to Dieter Hoffmann. Here again he stared at the name for several seconds, then with a look of annoyance on his face he slammed the book shut and walked away.

"Smith! bloody Smith! how many flaming Germans are called Smith!. I don't believe it."

Then with the speed of an express train a sudden thought shot into his brain. "Smith, ah no, no, no, never mind about Smith, how about SCHMIDT, I bet that's what his name is, I'm pretty sure Schmidt is the German equivalent of Smith. Ha-ha, maybe now we're getting somewhere."

In the meantime Bene had tracked down Susan who was busy cleaning one of the residents rooms. He wasn't making much progress, and when ET caught up with him Susan was in full flow. She had just returned from a holiday in Italy, and when Bene told her that he had also been there and had enjoyed it she wanted nothing more than to talk about Italy and how fantastic it was. Every time Bene tried to cut into her excited prattle he found that she had no intention of allowing herself to be sidetracked from telling him all about her wonderful holiday. It was obviously the first time she had been abroad and she just had to tell everyone about every single minute of it. Bene soon realised that the reason he had found her on her own was because she had bored the pants off everyone else in the home with her holiday. There didn't seem to be anything else for it, he would just have to sit back and wait until she had finished. He needed to have her full attention, and there was no way he was going to get that until she was satisfied she had told him every single detail about the holiday.

ET could see how exasperated Bene was becoming and he was finding it hard to keep a smile from his face. The babbling continued unabated for the next five minutes until Susan had completely exhausted her subject. Then even she had to admit to herself that she had left nothing out. The dialogue eventually dried up but Bene continued to remain silent for a few seconds longer for fear that she would suddenly start up again.

Finally, feeling that it was now safe to bring up the reason why he needed to speak to her he bent forward in his chair and looked intently into her eyes. "Susan I want you to tell me anything you can remember about the man who came to visit the two gentlemen who died here recently. The visits to both men were made the day before each of them died and it's important for us to find out who this person is. I know you've been away for the last few days but I want you to concentrate hard now and tell me everything you can remember about him."

Bene wasn't even sure that Susan had seen the man, and a less than friendly thought entered his head. "Christ, If I've had to endure all that bloody wittering over the last fifteen minutes and in the end she didn't even see the guy, I'll bloody well strangle her."

Susan surprised him though, she had calmed down now and had realised just how much of his valuable time she had taken up. She hadn't meant to be so garrulous, it was just that once she started she found she couldn't stop herself.

"I was away when this last visit was made so I don't know if the man I saw was the same one who called then." Bene heaved a sigh of relief, he thanked his lucky stars that at least this girl would be allowed to live.

"Well if you can give me a description of him we'll be able to find out Susan." The girl went on to give Bene the same description of the man that matched the one given to ET by the girl in the kitchen.

"Is there anything else you can tell us about him Susan?"

"Yes" she said. "As a matter of fact there is, because it's the second time I've seen him." "What you've seen him here before?" asked Bene.

"No not here I saw him in town, he was in the library."

"When was this?" asked Bene.

"It was just before I went to Italy, you see my auntie Pat works in the library and I called in there to see her before I left. When I went in I had to wait for a while before I could speak to her. She was busy showing this same man some records that had been stored in a box in the library, he was looking through them and seemed very interested. There were also some letters in the box and my auntie handed one of them to him. He seemed pleased with the letter and thanked my auntie for it, he took it with him when he left." This was news to Bene, he needed to track this man down and find out how he was involved. A visit to the library would be their next move. There was no more the girl could tell them, so after checking out with Mrs Janes the two detectives left for the town's library.

"Fancy a coffee first?" asked Bene.

"Yes that would be good. Just being in that place depresses me," said ET "I hope we've finished there, it's the smell of disinfectant and medicine that gets me down, and however they try to disguise it there always seems to be a whiff of urine about the place. I'm sure they look after the residents alright but I hope I never have to go into one of those places."

They went into the small coffee shop and took a table beside the window. ET insisted he would pay and went over to the counter to order the coffees. Bene watched him curiously for a minute or so and then smiled quietly to himself as he realised the purpose behind the offer. ET returned to the table carrying a tray with two coffees and some cakes.

"Well you haven't taken long to make yourself known around here have you?" joked Bene. "She's a good looking girl isn't she?" said a beaming ET. "I came in here on my first day and she was serving then, there weren't many people in so I had the chance to get to know her a bit."

"Fancy your chances then?" said Bene.

"Yeah course I do boss I've just asked her out. I thought I might have jumped the gun a bit and I was a bit worried she might say no, but then it was too late to hold back, I'd already asked her." Bene waited for him to continue

"Go on then what did she say?" ET smiled smugly

"Couldn't resist my natural Welsh charm could she, I've got a date for tonight."

"Well done you ET, but I hope she doesn't call you that on your first date."

Bene took up the conversation again but this time on a more serious note.

"According to two different sources the man appears to have been the same one who visited both the men."

"Yes" agreed ET, "But using two different names. Now why would he do that if not to hide his real identity? I thought Smith was the name he used instead of Schmidt but maybe it was just a guise, the other name you couldn't make out, it was more of a scribble but it was nothing like Smith, more like Brown or Braun, and both those names have English and German parallels." The two men finished off their coffees and rose to leave. Bene left the premises first and waited outside, ET just couldn't leave without re-affirming his date for the weekend.

It was late afternoon in the library and Pat was getting ready to close the premises for the day. The library closed at five o'clock on most weekdays, the exception being Wednesday when it stayed open until seven in the evening. But as it was Thursday she was looking forward to the weekly meeting of the investment club. She had certain things to prepare for that meeting and she wanted everything to be ready and on hand for the chairman. There was the weekly update on the shares held by the club, a forecast she had produced based on the steady gains the FTSE had been making over the last two weeks, and one or two other bits of information she had prepared in case he should need them. "Yes Andrew can always rely on me." she thought. "None of the others could be relied upon to contribute much to the club. All they want to do is hand over a few pounds every now and then and expect Andrew and me to provide them with a nice fat profit. Well it would be much better if it were only Andrew and me, yes" she sighed "just the two of us."

She was still dreaming when Bene and ET came into the library. There had been a window left open to bring a bit of fresh air into the room, and when the draught caused the door to slam shut behind them, it brought her back into the real world rather sharply.

"Sorry about that," winced ET, apologising as he had been the last one to come in. Patricia quickly pulled herself together and walked over to meet them.

"I've been expecting you. My niece rang me and told me you would be coming over. It's about the two German people who came here recently isn't it?" Bene was confused.

"There were two of them you said, we only heard of one man but you say there were two of them."

"Oh yes" said Patricia "There were two of them alright. It was only the man spoke to me but his wife was with him, yes there was definitely two of them."

"And they were looking through some old records and letters is that right?" asked Bene.

"Yes that's right, they came over from Germany to find out about two of their ancestors, you know the two bodies that were found in the woods, well this man was a grandson of one of the men, he had been a POW in the camp at Lower Hutton during the last war."

Bene remembered that the DCI at Preston had told him the bodies had been identified by someone in Germany, but he didn't know that someone had actually come over here to enquire about them. "So what were the records they were looking at?" asked Bene.

"Well it's a bit of a coincidence really," said Patricia. "We were clearing out the basement to make room for some records coming over from Appleby. One of their council offices is being renovated and they wanted somewhere secure to keep them. We knew we would have room for them here so we were pleased to be able to help them out, and it keeps them within the county." Bene waited patiently for Patricia to come to the point.

"And the records the Germans were interested in were in the cellar were they?"

"Until recently anyway, we found them in a large box which must have been left down there years ago. Most of the things down in the cellar have been there for a long time, most of them are recorded in our files up here so we know what they are or what they relate to. But for some reason this box seems to have been unrecorded and gone completely unnoticed since it was put here. I can't even remember having to go down to look for anything in the cellar for a long time, it must be months when I was last down there."

Both Bene and ET were curious to find out what the records were and they were getting rather impatient with Patricia, would she never get around to telling them. Finally she remembered the work she still had to do for the evening's meeting in the Fox and Pheasant. A quick glance at the clock told her it was almost five o'clock, she needed to get these two men out pretty quickly so she could lock up the library and get off home.

"The records were from the last few weeks of the Lower Hutton POW camp. Mr Ferguson was the Camp Commander and the records were written in his hand. There was nothing much of any value or importance, just the day to day running of the camp itself. There were a few personal items as well and a few letters which hadn't been posted. It was one of those letters that the gentleman was interested in. It was from his grandfather and written to his father back in Germany. I don't know why it hadn't been posted, just forgotten about I suppose. Maybe the Commander thought that with the war over the man would be repatriated and the letter wouldn't matter anymore."

Bene wondered if Patricia knew the contents of the letter so he asked her.

"No I didn't open it. The gentleman showed me proof that he was a genuine relative so I gave it to him to take back to Germany. He did open it while he was here though and he seemed pleased with what was inside. He didn't say anything mind, but I expect he was probably a bit too emotional and overcome with reading his grandfather's last known letter home."

"He showed you proof of who he was then?" said ET "What identification did he have with him?"

"He showed me his passport which had his name in, Alois Huber."

"And his wife's name, what was that?" Patricia thought for a moment.

"I didn't ask for hers because there was no need, her husband's ID was sufficient. But he spoke to her just as they were leaving, he held up the letter and said.

"This is good Sabine we can get much from this, we'll take it back home with us." Then he thanked me and they both left looking very pleased with themselves."

"Any idea where they're staying in Levensbridge?" asked ET.

"No idea I'm afraid, I never thought to ask and he never said."

Bene asked. "There were other letters in the box as well as the one he took with him, could we take those with us to see if there's anything we can do with them, maybe arrange for them to be sent back to Germany to someone else's relatives."

"Yes of course, there are only two others and you can have them certainly, maybe you can make someone else happy as well."

"If you do happen to see this man or his wife again can you let me know immediately, we really do need to speak to them urgently." Bene passed her his card. Patricia handed over the two letters and as there was nothing further to gain by staying any longer the two men left.

Patricia quickly shut the open window and turned off the lights, she locked the door behind her and was soon scuttling home along the pavement as quickly as her ancient legs could carry her. Her thoughts again turned to the evening and her beloved chairman "Don't worry Andrew I'll soon have everything ready for tonight."

Bene and ET went back to the police station with plenty to think about. "Well ET I don't know about you but I'm about done in for today. Dot's doing a barbeque tonight fancy coming along? It'll be better than having to start making a meal for yourself?"

"Yeah that would be brilliant, what time should I come?"

"Oh just when you've changed into something more casual, We'll expect you about seven."

Chapter 17

Lambs to the slaughter

The investment club meeting had just finished. Sylvia was bored and hadn't been showing much interest in the proceedings. Looking frequently over to where Alastair and Paul were sitting she was anxiously waiting for the group to disband and leave her to concentrate on something much more interesting. A meeting and a deal which would dwarf anything that had been discussed earlier with the investment club. One by one the members collected their belongings and began to leave the pub. Joe, Robert and Jamal quietly wishing Sylvia success in the venture that they had been invited to take part in but had declined.

Once the members had left, Alastair and Paul brought their drinks over to Sylvia's table and settled down to discuss the way forward with their plans. As usual it was Alastair who opened the meeting. "Well there's not much to talk about so we'll get it over quickly before the pub starts filling up again." Then looking over to Sylvia he addressed her directly "While Paul and I were waiting for your earlier meeting to finish we more or less agreed between ourselves to press on with this as quickly as possible." and before Sylvia could object, which she had been very close to doing, Alastair held up his hand to stop her. "But we haven't made any decisions without your knowledge Sylvia. The only thing the three of us need to be sure of is that we all have the agreed funds ready and available for an immediate transfer."

Sylvia settled herself again and confirmed that the sum she had agreed to invest was ready to be paid out. "All I have to do is make out the cheque," she said. Alastair looked to Paul for confirmation that his funds were in place.

"Yes I've transferred mine to an account which can be drawn on at any time, no problem there."

"Right" said Alastair, "I've arranged a meeting for tomorrow morning with the solicitor who is handling the sale on behalf of the owner, it's at eleven o'clock, I hope that's convenient for you both?"

"Whereabouts is the meeting?" asked Paul.

"It's in Preston, I would have preferred it if we could have used the solicitors here but the owner insists that we use his own solicitor and his office is in Preston. I know where it is so I'll pick you both up here at.... say ten o'clock and we'll go down together in my car, is that OK?" Sylvia and Paul agreed although Sylvia wasn't looking forward to travelling down in the same car as Paul. But as she didn't know where the solicitor's office was in Preston it would have been rather childish to refuse. "Just one thing before we close," added Alastair, "Make sure you both bring your cheque books along with you. As long as the solicitor is satisfied that we have the agreed amount of finance to complete the purchase the deal will definitely be concluded tomorrow."

The following morning the three drove down to Preston and walked the short distance from the car park to the solicitor's office. The office was on the first floor above a retail unit and had its own separate entrance door leading directly from the street. The door displayed the number 28C and had a brass plate attached to it which stated that the premises were occupied by Samuels, Gordon & Ogilvy - Solicitors.

Alastair went up first and knocked on the door at the top of the stairs, after receiving an invitation to enter he led Sylvia and Paul into the small office. Mr Ogilvy rose from the chair behind his desk and walked around to greet them. He was every man's idea of what a solicitor should look like, aged somewhere in his late fifties of medium height and slim. He had a long narrow face with a pale complexion, his long straggly grey hair was in dire need of a decent barber and he had a pair of narrow rectangular spectacles which hung down his front on a long strap. He was dressed in an old tweed jacket which must have been his favourite for many years and a badly faded multicoloured pullover.

The office appeared quite sparse, there was Mr Ogilvy's desk of course, another one sitting further back where a middle aged woman was seated staring at an open file and two large metal filing cabinets. There were a number of shelves along one wall and they held a selection of box files alongside several volumes of books.

"Sorry about the small office," he apologised spreading his arms around the room, "It's not really adequate for the nature of the business we carry out, but we have to make do with it for a short time until our main office in the town centre has undergone some underpinning. Apparently the whole block has been subject to subsidence over the years and the council has decided that the work must be carried out now before there's any lasting structural damage to the building."

Sylvia and Paul were not really interested in Mr Ogilvy or his subsidence problem they were there merely to hand over their cheques and get their hands on the deeds to the parcel of land they were buying. Mr Ogilvy seemed to sense their lack of interest and decided to forgo any further attempt to engage in anything other than the business in hand. He returned to his chair and from one of the drawers in his desk he brought out the deeds to the land together with attached maps.

"Right ladies and gentlemen I believe these are what you have come here for, the deeds to land on the Eastern side of Levensbridge, known locally as French's Field. The owner instructed me to have them brought here today from the vaults in our main branch and has asked me to conduct the sale on his behalf." Then lifting his head to address each of the three in turn. "You have the agreed sum of money with you for the purchase, one million eight hundred thousand pounds I believe is the agreed fee, is that correct?" All three were in agreement with Mr Ogilvy's statement and the fee he had quoted. "So if you can let me have the cheque then we can proceed to the next part of the sale." Alastair explained that there were three separate cheques which together came to the asking price.

"That is quite satisfactory," said Mr Ogilvy, "As long as they are payable to Mr D J Graham I can take them to his bank tomorrow." The solicitor took the three cheques and looked them over carefully before placing them in the top drawer of his desk. "Now we can move to the next phase of the sale where the deeds are submitted to the land registry office. They will transfer the ownership of the land over to you and once that's done you will be the new owners."

"How long will that take?" asked Paul, who had thought that once the money was handed over they would automatically be able to take the deeds with them.

"The cheques should clear tomorrow or Monday at the latest and as soon as they do I can send the deeds away, in the meantime they will have to remain here with me. It's usual for this part of the process to take between a week and two weeks, certainly no longer than that. In the meantime I can let you have a copy of the deeds and the maps which you can give to an architect to draw up his plans. You can also use them for the initial application for planning permission as long as you submit the originals when they come back from the land registry office. I can let you have them on Monday if you care to come back then."

Mr Ogilvy bent forward on his desk and looked expectantly at the three individuals from over the top of his glasses, he was looking at three slightly disappointed faces "You must understand that the cheques have to be cleared first before any handover of the deeds can take place, the owner would never allow them to be transferred without that happening. Apart from that it's against all the ethics of our profession, and illegal in terms of the law. My word, we would be struck off from practicing if we were to allow it." The three had to be content with this and arranged to meet with the solicitor again on Monday afternoon.

Leaving Preston on their return trip to Levensbridge the three were still a little subdued, the sale was taking place alright but it was going to take a little longer than they had anticipated. "I don't suppose there's anything we can do now but wait." said Paul. Alastair was quick to agree with him.

"Yes I should have warned you about registering the land, but there's no problem it just means we'll have to wait another week maybe. It's a formality that's all, don't worry about it the land is ours alright. Let's be happy, we have much to look forward to."

That seemed to cheer them up. Of course it was all still going according to plan, it would take just a little longer than they had bargained for, but in a few days time they would be able to take possession of the deeds. Then they could set about having plans drawn up for developing the land, and wouldn't the council be infuriated when they found out it would be them who were building houses on the site and not them. Yes things were looking very rosy indeed.

Sylvia was pleased with how things were panning out. "Well I'm just a woman, I think I'll let them get on with it, I'll be happy to take a back seat and just wait for the money to come rolling in."

Paul sitting beside her in the back seat was also happy with the progress they were making. "Well I'm a bit disappointed that we didn't actually get our hands on the deeds today, but I suppose there is a process that has to be followed to ensure it's all legal and above board. Anyway whoever we get to draw up the plans will have to be aware that we need to maximise the potential of the site to give us the best possible returns on our investment."

Alastair was humming along to a tune on the radio as he drove them back to Levensbridge. "Yes, you excelled yourself there Donald you almost had me convinced, and it was a good idea to get Grace to sit in as your secretary. Silly buggers they're too damned greedy by far. They never even bothered to check anything out or ask any of the questions they should have been asking. I'm afraid they're in for a bit of a shock when the truth jumps out and bites them on the bum." His thoughts turned pleasantly to the huge profit he was expecting to make. "One point three million eh just like that, what a nice little reward for Donald and me." He was enjoying the song being played on the radio at that moment and raised his voice to express his happiness.

"Lah de da de da, Lah de da de da. All good friends and jolly good company."

Chapter 18

Barbeque with a difference

There was quite a group gathered in Dot's garden, Dot was there of course with Alex. Bene and ET had just arrived and were pleased to see that Adam and Ellen had been invited as well. "Just as well you went to the butchers, mum," said Alex, "Otherwise we would only be getting a sausage and a drumstick each and that would be no good for you would it Sherlock?" She laughed as she gave Bene's stomach a gentle prod. "Look at that mum I nearly lost my finger in that lot. You're feeding him too well." She moved swiftly away before he could grab hold of her.

She went over to Adam and whispered something to him which made him laugh.

"Is that right Bene, you used to be a thirty four waist and now its thirty eight." Alex giggled at Bene's embarrassment.

"It makes him nice and cuddly though," she said "I've got plenty to hold on to." Bene decided he had had enough and ran over and picked her up, he turned her upside down and carried her over to the fish pond.

"What should we do with her Dot put her in with the fish?" Alex screamed and tried to wriggle out of his hold.

"Don't you dare you beast, help me mum." The whole party were enjoying the antics of the two love-birds which was not unusual as they made fun and played tricks on each other all the time.

Dot had made sure there was plenty food for everyone to eat and enjoy, as well as the chicken, sausages, steaks and kebabs, she had put together a large tossed salad to compliment the meal. The wine was flowing freely and the evening was speeding by far too quickly. It seemed only natural that the three men would sit down together and give the ladies the opportunity to catch up on all the local gossip. They moved their chairs away from the barbeque and settled a little closer to the large privet hedge, it gave them some respite from the setting sun which was getting ever lower in the evening sky.

Adam was curious to know how the two detectives were getting on with the cases they were investigating. He wished he could have been working with them as he was still missing the involvement. "Have you been able to make any progress on the deaths up at the home yet, and are you anywhere nearer identifying who it was that pushed poor ET here off the platform?"

"One thing at a time Adam," said Bene. "We now know who it was that visited the two men shortly before their deaths. He was a relative of those men whose bodies were found in the woods recently. His name is Huber, the same as the two men. Evidently he saw the notice in the German press and came over here with his wife to claim the bodies. I'm only guessing but I suppose he would like to find out what really happened to them."

"Well that seems natural enough Bene, so what's the problem. Is it the fact that they were shot with British bullets. Surely after all this time he can't expect you to find out who actually shot them."

"Well we haven't been able to track him down yet so we don't know what he expects. But the strange thing is that when he visited the home he signed in with a different name each time and neither name was his real one, now why would he do that if not to disguise who he really was."

"Yes I see your point," said Adam. "But the fact that he visited the men shortly before they died doesn't actually prove that he was the one responsible for their deaths. But it does seem to suggest that whatever he did say to them was probably the reason for the changes in their medical condition immediately after he left. Did you get anything back from the post mortem?"

"Yes we've had the results but there was nothing unusual about either of them. Both deaths were put down purely to heart failure, but there was nothing to show what had caused the heart to fail. The pathologist didn't find any traces of unusual substances, poison or anything like that. Judging by what Mrs Janes told us about the changes in the men immediately after this man's visit it seems they were just plain scared to death, if there is such a thing of course. But no doctor would put that down on a death certificate."

"How about you ET," asked Adam, "What do you make of it?"

"Well, we've got to find this fellow first and bring him in for some questioning, only then will we be able to find out what's behind it. He's contacted Preston police about the bodies and proved to them he was a genuine relation so they should have a contact address for him. My fear is that even if we bring him in he might not tell us anything. Although we know his name and should be able to find out where he's staying he did go to some lengths to conceal his real name from the home, so there must be a reason for that. I think there's a lot more to this, a lot that we don't know about. I think something very sinister is going on and I'm sure its connected in some way to the last war and the old POW camp up here."

Adam was impressed but decided not to say so, not yet anyway. "And the incident at the railway station, that must have a bearing on the case as well don't you think?" Adam posed this question again directly to ET.

"Yes for sure, that briefcase probably holds the key to the whole investigation, if only we had that I'm sure we'd soon be able to find out what's behind it all. There's something else as well, there's a connection with France somewhere in all this and that seems to go back to the last war as well. I'd say that's where this secret is, somewhere in France. But without the briefcase we'll never be able to make the connection, or to find out what or where this damned secret is."

"This cloaked figure that pushed you off the platform then," asked Adam, "Could that have been this German chap do you think?"

"I think it's got to be him, although how he knew about the briefcase or that I had it is beyond me.

The only people who knew anything at all about it were Bene, myself and Peter Hoffmann. Well it wasn't Bene and it couldn't have been Peter because it was him who told us about it in the first place. I think someone up at the home is involved in this somehow. Dieter Hoffmann kept the briefcase in his wardrobe and it must have been there all the time he's been in the home. Don't tell me that at some time or other one or more of the staff haven't been a bit curious and had a look inside it."

Without thinking about it ET was showing why he had been successful in his transfer up to Levensbridge. He must have really impressed the panel, a panel which would have included Chief Inspector Sowerby. "Yes" thought Adam " Sowerby is no fool, this lad is good. Bene and him together will make a good team."

ET continued. "We did suspect that one of the staff might have let someone into the building at night, it might have been the German fellow coming back to finish the men off. I know there was nothing in the post mortem to show foul practice but I honestly think those two men were killed, they didn't just die naturally. It's also possible someone at the home is working with this fellow and they could have killed them" Bene had been impressed too "Well it's probably the best theory we have to go on so far and I admit it is plausible. And if that's the case then one of the staff at the home is in collusion with this German fellow, we'll need to go back and speak to some of the girls again, that's a job for you ET."

Bene turned to ET, he wanted to move on to another aspect of the case. "You remember when you looked into the briefcase when you were at the station you said there was a map or something like a map in there as well."

"Well not a proper map as such," said ET. "It was a sort of map, I mean it had things drawn on it, symbols maybe or markers, but it was all done by hand. There were directions on it because north was shown, and it had distances marked on as well but I can't remember what they were or where they started from or where they went to. There was definitely a wood shown on it and some buildings which may have been two or three houses or a farm maybe. And there was writing along the bottom but I didn't have time to read it, it looked like French to me. The train was coming in then so I thought I'd leave it until I got back to the station and we could have a good look at it together."

"And that's all you can remember about it?" asked Adam.

"Yes, that's all about that one, but there was another sketch in there as well, it was the same size as the first one but it didn't have much detail on, it seemed to be an enlarged drawing of a wood, and that was all that was on it. There was some writing below which could have been the name of the wood, but again it looked to be French. Something was drawn in the middle of the wood but I've no idea what it was and that's all I can remember about that one. I wish now that I'd looked at it a bit earlier and taken more notice of what was there but I felt a bit guilty about doing it, I didn't want to overstep the mark by snooping through it before you'd had a chance to look at it." This with an apologetic look across at Bene. Bene waved it aside.

"Anything you can remember about the papers in there apart from the name Huber?"

"Not really there seemed to be lists of names, German names mostly. The name Huber just seemed to crop up a lot and mostly in fairly large writing so it stood out more than the others. The diary was there as Peter had said it was but I didn't look at it, and that's about all I can tell you."

There followed a minute or two's silence as the three men sat back and digested the information. They were all trying to make something out of it all but nothing much was coming. They had two lines to follow, one was the German who had come over to discover the fate of his ancestors, but even if they found him it was doubtful if he would be willing to help them unravel the mystery. The other was the home, did this man have a colleague working there. One thing was sure, there would be many hours of hard police work to be done before they could relax in Dot's garden like this again.

Adam pressed on. "I haven't heard of any more robberies this last day or so Bene, has anything turned up on that score yet?"

"No, I've had a couple of the lads looking at them but apart from the white van we haven't been able to come up with any other clues."

"Any description of the van then, size, model or number plate?"

Bene was about to tell Adam what little he knew of the vehicle but was drowned out by a raucous laugh from the garden next door.

The barbeque in Dot's garden wasn't the only one taking place in the road that night. Next door at the Teasdale's house Ken and Maggie were enjoying the little party they had organised for their friends, here also the wine was beginning to have an effect. Ethan had been running around the garden until he had tired himself out. It was nearly his bedtime but he didn't want to go to bed just yet. He took one of the rugs and plonked himself down on it beside the hedge. "Poor little thing," said his mother, "Look at him he's completely exhausted."

"He should be in bed." said his dad.

"Oh he's no trouble just leave him there he's doing no harm." Ken and Maggie turned back to the circle of friends and re-joined the conversation.

Ethan was tired but not too sleepy. He was fed up with all these people in his garden, all they wanted to do was eat all his mam's food, get drunk and do daft things that weren't even funny. "What do they know about robbers and murderers and them things, nothing, that's what they know nothing. They couldn't catch criminals like I can and lock them up in the shed 'cos they're useless."

He was starting to feel a bit drowsy, there was still some heat in the evening sun and he thought he might just go to sleep there on the rug. With a bit of luck they would forget all about him and he could sleep out there in the garden under the hedge. It was Adam Firth's voice he could hear and it was that which was preventing him from going to sleep. Something Adam was saying caught his attention and suddenly he was no longer tired. The conversation which was taking place on the other side of the hedge was beginning to sound far more interesting than the one in his garden, the little secret agent listened intently to what was being said on the other side of the hedge.

Bene told Adam the little information he had regarding the robberies, which wasn't much at all. "All we really know is that a white van was used, about the same size as a Ford transit or Mercedes sprinter maybe, something in that class anyway. Paul Hanbury got a quick look at it when it shot off from his house but he couldn't see exactly what it was. He did say something about the registration number though, he thought it might be a personalised one you know two numbers and three letters or something similar but he couldn't make them out. Oh and it had writing on the side, but he couldn't make that out either except it started with a large S."

"Well there's no shortage of those vans around," said Adam, "Most firms are using that type of vehicle now for their deliveries. You could be looking for a needle in a haystack."

ET entered the conversation.

"Well we checked the cameras on roads leading out of the town and couldn't pick it up, also the cameras in the town centre and we drew a blank there as well. It looks as though it might be local, we might have to check them all out."

Bene wasn't convinced it was local. "The burglaries started much further south and only seem to have moved up here in the last week, I still think the people we are looking for are based down there, not here in Levensbridge."Adam wasn't sure about it either.

"How about storage for these items, if you haven't picked up the van leaving the town it could be that they're using premises somewhere in Levensbridge to store the stolen items. Maybe they move from town to town and use premises in that town to store the stuff, then when they have enough they move the whole lot in a large wagon or container maybe."

"Yeah that's possible," agreed Bene, "The problem is we don't have much resource for all this. What with suspicious deaths, attempted murders and robberies as well we can't be everywhere at all times, we'll have to prioritise. Sowerby won't give me any extra bodies to cover all this and I know I'm going to have Paul on my back because he's desperate to get his desk back, but we just haven't the time to go around checking all the places which may or may not be used for this crime."

The little secret agent was very sleepy now, but he had heard all he wanted to hear. "I told you I'll get them for you Bene, I'll be on the job tomorrow and I expect I'll soon catch them for you, then we'll go and get them murderers as well."

"Come on you lot" shouted Alex, "Don't think by sitting over there talking a load of rubbish will get you out of doing the washing up. Come on Sherlock here's a dish cloth for you, and a towel for you ET, he can wash you can dry." With that she tossed the tea towel to ET and slapped the wet dish cloth across Bene's face. Bene jumped up and chased her around the garden. "Mum help me I think he means it this time he's going to put me in with the fishes." Dot shook her head and looked at her guests.

"They're mad you know, both of them completely bonkers."

Chapter 19

Visiting time

It was the weekend and Ken and Maggie were going off to a wedding in York. They had all been up late the night before including Ethan who had fallen asleep on the rug in the garden. The wedding was not until three o'clock so there was no rush, Ethan could have a lie in. As long as he was up and away to his aunties before ten o'clock that would still allow them time to get ready for the big day. It would be late before they got back home again so it was as well that Ethan stayed with his auntie until the following day.

Upstairs Ethan was wide awake and instantly he remembered what had happened the night before. Lying there by the hedge he recalled the conversation he had overheard between the men in the garden next door. Usually on a Saturday morning he would lie in bed until about ten o'clock, but today was his big day and he wasn't going to waste any of it by lying in bed any longer.

"At last a real case to solve, and boy will everybody be pleased with me when I come back with all the robbers. I'll have a look in the phone book first so I'll know where the shops are, there can't be many places in town where the stuff's hidden. I expect I'll find it pretty soon then I'll arrest them and bring them back to the shed and lock them in, they won't be able to get out of there. Then when I got them locked up I'll go round and tell Bene and get the reward. I'd better take these handcuffs with me. It's a good job I've got two of them, they're just plastic but they're really strong. I expect they'll be strong enough, I mean Jimmy couldn't get out of them when I put them on him." Then a frown came over his face as he thought about how he was going to arrest them. "I'm not sure what I'll say to the robbers, I think I'll just say your arrested, and then they'll put their hands out an I'll put the handcuffs on, yea that's what I'll do." He seemed entirely satisfied that it would happen just like that.

Ken laughed when he saw little Ethan running down the stairs. "What's this then, can't wait to get away from us quickly enough?"

"I got lot's to do today dad and I have to get started right away." he replied, then suddenly panicked. "I shouldn't have said that, I'll have to think of a good excuse."

"And what's so important that gets you up out of bed so soon on a Saturday morning," said his dad "I usually have to come up and drag you out of it." The little secret agent had to think quickly.

"I got to help auntie, I think she wants me to cut the grass for her." He was pleased with his answer. "Yeah that sounds good enough, he'll believe that." Ken laughed again

"Did you hear that Maggie, Ethan's going to help his auntie in the garden, he must be after some pocket money, I've never known him to be so generous with his time."

Ethan gobbled down his breakfast as fast as he could and when neither of his parents were looking he quietly sneaked out the phone book and took it upstairs with him. Shutting the bedroom door behind him he silently flicked through the pages. Using his pencil he circled the shops and warehouses where he thought he might find the stolen goods, and when he had done that he wrote down all the names in his secret agent's notebook.

"I've got to go now." he called out as he came rushing down the stairs.

"My but I've never known him to be as keen as this, he must suddenly have developed a great love for gardening." said his dad. "I hope it's not a passing fancy, if he's as keen tomorrow he can cut the lawn for us." Maggie had to laugh now.

"You'll have to be prepared to pay him then, I can't see him doing it for nothing can you." Ethan was heading for the door. "You have a nice time at auntie's now and tell her she can ring us anytime tomorrow and we'll come over for you OK." his mother reached down to give him a kiss."If you're having a good time you can stay until teatime if you like, but if we don't hear from you before that we'll come over and pick you up then." Finally the little secret agent left the house rubbing his sleeve over his cheek.

"Only girls should have to be kissed 'cos their soppy, secret agents aren't soppy."

He took his bike out from the shed and rode off down the driveway. As he reached the road he almost bumped into

Bene who had just left the house next door. “Whoa Ethan where are you off to in such a hurry?” he asked, smartly stepping aside to avoid colliding with the little lad. Ethan didn’t want to give the game away, it was him who was going to catch the robbers not Bene, he wouldn’t tell Bene anything about it until he had them locked up in his shed.

“Oh I’m just off on a case, I can’t tell you what it is yet but when I got them caught I’ll come and tell you and you can take them away and send them to prison.” Bene was trying to hide his amusement. This little fellow had to be humoured and he didn’t want him to think he wasn’t being taken seriously so he kept a straight face.

“Good man Ethan but if you get stuck or need any help you just call round and see me right.” Ethan told him he could manage on his own and promptly threw his leg over the crossbar and headed off towards the estate where his auntie lived. “I suppose I’ll have to go and see her first before I go and catch the robbers, I’ll tell her I’ve to get some things at the shops for mam and I might not be back till tea time.”

Pedalling through the town he was approaching ET’s flat just as the detective was about to get into his car, Ethan braked sharply and almost collided with him. “Hey, steady on little fellow what’s the rush?”

“Your Bene’s friend ET aren’t you? Ethan said.

“That’s right sonny, and don’t tell me but you’re the little lad who lives next door to him aren’t you?” Ethan nodded in agreement, he was looking at ET curiously.

“Why are you called ET, that’s not a proper name is it, it’s a daft name.” Just then a sudden thought came to him, “You’re not an alien are you?”

ET had to explain that ET was just his initials and his real name was Emlyn Thomas. Ethan looked long and hard at ET and slowly a smile crept over his face.

"Well in that case I could be ET as well."

"No you couldn't," replied ET who was starting to get a little irritated by the little boy. "You've got to have a name with the initials ET to be called that, you'll have to be called something else. Use the first letter of your first name and the first letter of your surname and that's what you'll be called OK."

"That'll get rid of him" he thought and promptly opened the car door, jumped inside and started the engine. Ethan was not to be put off quite so easily though and pulled up his bike beside the driver's window grinning broadly into the car. Now ET was getting annoyed, winding down the window he looked out crossly at the little boy.

"OK then let's have it." he wanted to get away from here quickly but realised he would have to show some interest in the little lad first. "What's your name then?"

"Ethan Teasdale" replied the boy proudly, "So you see I'm ET as well as you mister clever clogs." ET was gobsmacked and it showed in his face, he wasn't usually stuck for words but the little lad had stumped him good and proper. He sat back in his seat and shook his head in disbelief and then started to laugh, Ethan laughed as well. "Well you're a detective like Bene aren't you and I'm a secret agent see, and I'm helping him to catch robbers and murderers and other things."

ET couldn't help but admire the boy, and smiling he offered his hand out of the window. "Right then if you're helping Bene then you're helping me as well so shake on it partner and together we'll catch the lot of them and lock them all up."

"Well I suppose you'll always be ET but I can be little ET yeah?"

"Yeah course you can I think we'll make a good team the three of us." ET finally escaped the attention of little ET and chuckled loudly to himself as he drove away and up to the home.

"I Hope I haven't led him on too much, but then again it's all in his head he'll soon forget all about it." But little ET had no intention of forgetting all about it. He was a full partner now and great things would be expected of him. "They'll soon be pleased they've got me on their side, I'm as good as them any day, and just wait till I catch them, I'll be famous and they'll want me to be a detective same as them, then after a bit I'll be an inspector."

2

It was the weekend but that didn't mean Bene or ET could relax, there was a lot to do and there would be no let up in their efforts to track down the German visitor, the hooded assailant and the perpetrators responsible for the sudden spate of robberies in the town. As far as ET was concerned it was up to him to visit the home again.

Mrs Janes was surprised to see him as he entered her office once again. "Well I hope you're getting somewhere with this it's the third or fourth time you've been here. I thought you had interviewed all the girls the other day?"

"Well there are still the ones on night shift, we didn't get the chance to speak to them." said ET "But you told me they change over shifts today so I left a message for them to stay on for an hour this morning so I could have a word with them."

"Yes of course," said Mrs Janes "I'd forgotten about them, there's only three of them so it shouldn't take you too long. I remember one of them telling me but I must have forgotten about it, I wondered why I hadn't seen them leave at the usual time you'll probably find them in the rest room." The three ladies were not best pleased at having to stay on after what had already been a long hard shift. The electric had gone off during the night which had immediately activated the alarms. Some of the residents had got up to see what was happening and thought that the place was on fire. It had taken a few minutes to get the generator up and running and by that time all the residents were awake. Most of them were confused and frightened and it had taken the best part of an hour to get them settled down again.

ET could sense the mood of the women and thought it best to get the interviews over as quickly as possible. He didn't think it wise to interview them as a group, they may just decide to clam up and tell him nothing so they could get off home as quickly as possible. He took each one in turn, but it made no difference the answers from all three were the same. None of them could shed any light on the German visitor and none of them could remember anything unusual happening on the nights in question. All three assured him that no-one did, or could have entered the building after the doors had been locked. The three interviews were completed and the ladies gone in less than half an hour.

This was getting very tiresome, ET was convinced that someone in the home knew a lot more about this than they were admitting to, but who the hell was it and how on earth was he going to find out. He slowly made his way back to Mrs Janes office. "Well that's all the ladies seen and still no clue as to what's been happening here." He sat down heavily on a chair in front of Mrs Janes desk a figure of dejection. He hadn't a clue where to go next, who to ask or even what to ask. There had to be a way around it, there was something both Bene and he had been missing but what the blazes was it.

Bene meanwhile had not started his day yet. He was in Dot's kitchen having breakfast with Alex and waiting for ET to phone him, hopefully with some news, a lead maybe or a hunch, anything at all. Finally he could stand it no longer, maybe he should have gone with ET, but no, ET was entirely capable of conducting this type of interview himself and Bene knew nothing would be left out, if there was anything ET would find it. He took out his mobile and phoned. The news wasn't good.

"Nothing at all boss, there were only three women we hadn't seen before and none of them can help us at all. It's disappointing I know but I can't think where we go from here. I'm still convinced that one of them is involved but I've no idea how we're going to find who, it's got me beat."

Bene finished the call and sighing heavily he slumped forwards over the breakfast bar. Alex didn't like to see him like this. She knew how hard he worked on his cases, putting everything into them heart and soul. Even when things didn't work out for him he would stick at it until he made something happen. She remembered his last major case when he almost died trying to get to the truth, finally getting the evidence together to convict the people responsible for crimes that had shocked the whole town.

"Come on then Sherlock what's the problem?" Alex put her arm over his shoulder to comfort him. Bene wasn't frightened to tell Alex about the case. She had been a godsend on more than one occasion before. She had a habit of being able to see things that were blatantly obvious to her but completely oblivious to him. It was Alex who had been his rock, and whenever he had come up against a brick wall it was she who had helped him over it. She had the uncanny knack of knowing exactly what it was he was looking for but couldn't see, when he had been blind to the way forward it was Alex who was able to open his eyes and show him the way. Bene unburdened himself to her, telling her everything he knew about the deaths of the two men and the attempt on ET's life. Of ET's conviction that someone in the home was connected to, or working for the German visitor, and how both of them were convinced that the deaths were not natural.

"We've interviewed all the carers and even Mrs Janes herself, I honestly don't know what to do next. You can bet Sowerby won't be happy with this, he's expecting at least a good lead today and we can't even give him that."

Alex thought about it a moment then put a question to him. "Tell me again exactly who you've interviewed." Bene iterated the names of the carers and Mrs Janes. "There must be others there as well though," said Alex

"I mean there'll be a cook and a cleaner probably, the carers won't do all the work there. They might prepare the meals for eating and clean the rooms, but they won't do it all. Someone will have to cook the meals and someone will have to do the rest of the cleaning." Bene rose from the breakfast bar and gave Alex a huge kiss. "Yes we know about the cook, Mrs Janes told me she'd been with them for years, she's a local woman and married to one of the council workers. She doesn't think there's any way she could have been involved, but a cleaner, no I hadn't thought about that, I thought the girls would do it all but maybe there is someone else."

Luckily ET was still at the home when he took Bene's call. "OK boss I'll ask her." He asked Mrs Janes if there was a cleaner at the home."

"Well my girls usually do the residents rooms of course because it's part of their job, but I do have a girl who comes in three hours a day. She seems alright and she had good references from her last two employers, I like the girl."

"How long has she been with you?" asked ET

"Not long she came from a hospital down in Cheshire where they spoke very highly of her. Completely trustworthy they said and that's good enough for me."

"Could you let me see her references please just to satisfy myself."

"Yes I'll get them for you." She went over to her filing cabinet, unlocked it and drew out an A4 manila file with the girl's name on it, Anna Ferenc. She handed the file to ET.

"It's all in there and I've checked her references they're genuine enough."

"Does she have access to all the rooms?" asked ET.

"She does, but she only needs access to the residents' rooms if my girls are busy. she does everything else apart from the kitchen, cook doesn't like anyone messing around in there so she does it herself."

ET studied the file but could find nothing in it to cause any concern, all the papers and letters of reference seemed genuine enough and there was even a copy of her birth certificate which stated she was born in Camden Town, London on the 15th of May 1985. "She's not here at the moment then?" he asked.

"No she's on holiday just now but she's due back in again on Friday."

Everything looked to be in order according to the file yet ET had an uneasy feeling about the girl, something he couldn't quite explain. He couldn't put his finger on it but there was something about her that had started alarm bells ringing in his head. There was no reason why he should doubt her credentials, but nevertheless he needed to satisfy himself as to whether she was in any way implicated in the mystery. "If she has a locker here I think I'd like to have a look inside if that's possible." Mrs Janes had no objection and took out a bunch of keys which held amongst them the master key to all the staff lockers.

"I'll have to come with you and open it myself because I'm responsible for all the girls personal belongings. I need to make sure that if anything is taken out of the locker it's put back again in its proper place."

The locker was opened and ET started to empty it. A couple of house coats were all that were hanging up and after finding that nothing was concealed in them he left them undisturbed. He then removed a number of bottles from the shelf, mainly creams, a bottle of shampoo, a box of tissues and a small MP3 player. The box of tissues was barely half full and should have felt light but when ET balanced it in his hand he was surprised at the weight of the box. He placed it on the table, putting his hand inside he felt around until his fingers came into contact with something that definitely should not have been there. Withdrawing his hand he brought into view a set of shiny new keys. Mrs Janes was clearly taken aback, she had to reach out and steady herself against one of the lockers.

"Oh my God, I didn't expect you to find anything like that, she's such a lovely girl and we all took to her straight away when she came here. But unless I'm very much mistaken these keys are exactly like my own set of keys. I'll have to check of course but I'm sure I'll find that these ones are identical."

Chapter 20

More visiting

The North Lancashire men's prison is a category B prison which is situated on the outskirts of a large housing estate. Although a relatively new addition to Her Majesty's Prison Service it still exudes that forbidding aura of fear and hopelessness. The prison itself like many other similar ones is overcrowded and most of the cells which were originally designed for single purpose are now occupied by two prisoners. Visiting times are varied depending on whether the prisoner is on remand or convicted.

Sylvia was allowed two visits a month to her husband Ray but she was hoping on this visit to have it increased to a visit every week. Ray had been caught printing and dealing in forged Polish currency, along with his associate Karel Zajic. They had both been given sentence's of three years imprisonment. Ray had taken the news badly at first and it took him a while to adjust to prison life, but after the first few weeks he began to settle down to life inside and accepted the fact that he would lose at worst maybe two years of his freedom. He decided the best way of dealing with it was to keep his head down and make himself useful. If he could manage to see out the next twelve months he would be able to apply for parole, and if successful he could pick up the threads of his life and start living again.

In the few months Ray had been in prison he had put on a bit of weight around the midriff. Most people who have sampled prison food would say that it was not that good, but strangely enough Ray had found some of the dishes very much to his liking and this was the reason for his rather tubby appearance. Sylvia didn't like to see her husband piling on the pounds but thought better about saying so. If it helped in keeping him sane during his time inside then that was OK She was willing to let it happen so long as when he came out she could put him on a corrective course which would get him fit and healthy again.

She looked across the small table at her husband and found that she still liked what she saw. She watched him as he approached the table they were to share, she noticed the slight limp he still bore which was the result of a car accident way back in his youth. Also the slight disfigurement down the left side of his face which was virtually concealed under his large bushy sideburns. Put those to one side and it was clear he still retained his humour and charm. Leading up to his arrest both Ray and Sylvia had become greedy and that had probably been the reason he had been caught. The pain and humiliation of being dragged through the courts and the subsequent sentence had been traumatic for both of them. All they wanted now was to put this behind them and go back to living the life they had enjoyed before all that Polish business had started.

Ray greeted her with a wide smile "How's my best girl then?"

"I'm fine Ray but what about you, you look as if you're coping with this pretty well, I hope you don't get too used to this place I want you back home again as soon as possible."

"Well I'm doing OK, I've a new cell mate now, a guy from up north in Carlisle called Dave, he's good company and we get on OK together. It makes it a lot easier to deal with but I'm still lost without you to come home to every night. I try and look on the bright side, hopefully I'm into my last twelve months now and as long as I keep my nose clean I can look forward to being back home again in time to spend next summer with you."

"That's great Ray," she burst out "I can't wait." Then she leant forward and lowered her voice. "I do have some exciting news myself." she said quietly. Ray picked up his ears and leaned over the table to listen to what she had to say.

"I'm in a partnership to buy up some land that we're going to build on." Ray was curious.

"What land, where?" Sylvia explained the deal she was involved in with Alastair and Paul. Ray gasped.

"Paul? Paul Hanbury? so he's back in town is he."

Paul and Ray had been the best of pals since childhood and had been business partners for a number of years as well. In fact Paul had been in collusion with Karel and himself in the Polish currency scam but had disappeared over to France with his new wife Nicola just in time, leaving Ray and Karel to carry the can. "Are you sure you can trust him Sylvia, he left me with this lot remember." Sylvia assured him that she could handle Paul alright.

"Well I've put up three hundred thousand pounds for this deal but Paul's in it for a cool million. Don't worry I'll be watching him like a hawk, there's no way he'll con us again."

"Well be careful love it's a lot of money, are you sure we can afford it?"

"Yes I think we'll be alright. It's a good deal and certainly too good to miss out on, and I haven't borrowed any money to fund it either. I know the shop's not been doing too well recently but remember I did make a lot of money out of those clothes you brought in from abroad. Ray had to smile at this.

"Yes that was a nice little earner wasn't it."

The clothes in question had been brought in by Paul and Ray's Polish drivers from a warehouse near Krakow. They had been made in the Ukraine using top quality materials. Excellent copies of the latest Milan fashions that bore top designer labels which made them virtually indistinguishable from the real thing. Sylvia had been able to buy them in cheaply, and even with a high mark up she was still able to turn them over quickly. Her eager customers couldn't get enough of them, and of course Sylvia made a handsome profit out of it as well.

"It's a pity it came to such a sudden end," said Ray, "But then maybe that was our little bit of good fortune, if it had carried on for much longer you might have ended up in here with me." The thought of this made them both smile for fortune certainly had smiled on Sylvia back then. The regular stock she had been getting in each week had suddenly dried up, it was lucky for her that her shop Fellside Fashions had only recently sold the last of the faked items, just as the police were starting to become interested.

"I'm not sure about Paul though," said Sylvia, "A million is a lot of money even for him. I mean he's bought two new houses recently and their lifestyle isn't cheap you know. When he divorced Angie he thought he could buy her off cheaply by giving her his share of the house, but she wasn't going to let him off that lightly, not Angie. She'd been humiliated and wasn't going to settle for just the house, she wanted a lot more out of him and she got it. Poor Paul, he was so desperate to get rid of her so that he could be free to marry Nicola, he ended up handing over most of the profit he had made from that currency scam. I know he still has money from the sale of Esk Logistics and the inheritance from Matt Renwick's estate but his finances must have taken quite a hit."

She started to smile. "I hope he knows what he's doing because I think Alastair conned him into the deal. He gave him the chance to come in with us but in such a way that if Paul had refused he would have given the impression he couldn't afford it. So when he did accept he came up with the full million just to make himself look good."

"I don't blame Paul you know Sylvia, I know I got greedy and couldn't stop what we were doing, but I think Paul sensed that it had run its course and quit while we were well ahead. But we didn't lose all the profit we made out of it you know, I'm not that daft. I'll admit the police got a huge chunk of it but there was a lot they didn't get their hands on. I'll give you an internet bank access code and you can go on and have a look at it, I think you'll be surprised." Sylvia was more than surprised she was amazed, it was she who was the business brain in their partnership not him, but nevertheless she couldn't hide her delight at hearing his news.

Before he could say anymore the bell rang to signal that visiting time was over. "Now my love your time's up so get yourself away home. I'll send you the code in my next two letters, take the first letter in the first line, third in the third line, and so on down to the ninth letter in the ninth line in my first letter to you, then the second, fourth, sixth, eighth and tenth in the second one and you'll have it. The bank details will be in both letters as well, they'll all be in the last two sentences, use the same formula for those and convert the letters to numbers, A =1, B=2 etc and you'll have all you need to access the account."

"You clever so and so Ray Parrish I didn't know you could be so devious." Sylvia smiled.

"Why have you kept this to yourself all this time?"

"I wanted to keep it a secret until I got out, but I know the shop's not doing too well at the moment and I didn't want you to have any money worries while I'm locked up in here. I just want you to know that we'll be OK."

2

The currency scam had also claimed Karel Zajic who like Ray had fallen victim to its greed. Karel was also in prison, and at the same time Ray was enjoying the visit from Sylvia, Karel was welcoming his wife Eliska along with his brother Emil and his wife Agnieska.

Only a few months earlier Karel had been more than a little overweight, he was tall which did allow for some excess but his weight had increased to such an extent that his body proportions were no longer pleasing to the eye. During his time in prison where his favourite foods had been mostly denied him much of the excess fat that had built up over the years had now disappeared, this left him looking much the better for it. His rounded face was pale and bore all the signs of aging and lack of fresh air, and although he had lost most of his hair he still retained a little to each side of the head which was now grey, not the soft mousey brown of his earlier years.

He looked admiringly over to his wife Eliska, it always amazed him how she hardly seemed to have changed after all the years they had been together. Only a couple of inches shorter than him her figure was almost perfect. Her long oval face was surrounded by long tresses of beautiful hair, once a gorgeous golden colour but which over the years had gradually given way to a much lighter shade. She had the most attractive eyes of anyone he could ever remember, they simply sparkled. Although like him, she was approaching the latter part of her life, her eyes were still those of the sixteen year old girl he had met and fallen in love with all those years ago.

Karel rose to greet her, "So my darling and how are you?" His English was still not word perfect, a result of adjusting to the new language far too late in life.

Often when they had been at home together he would revert to his native language and speak to her in Polish. He smiled at his three visitors in turn. "Your visits are the only thing that keep me from going insane. This place is not a good place to be and I count the days until your next visit." Eliska had also been counting the days when she could see her husband again, she was finding it difficult being separated from him for such long intervals. Up until his imprisonment they had never had to spend more than a day apart and his confinement was affecting them both badly.

The conversation consisted mainly of normal day to day matters, Eliska's last week, Emil's work, and the weather of course. Karel would brighten up when he heard news of their two children back in Poland, he was longing to see them both again. There was nothing in the conversation that could cause any alarm to the supervising warden standing attentively alongside them. The three would dearly have liked to tell Karel about their night time exploits, but they couldn't. They would have liked to tell him about the plans they were making for when he was released, but again they couldn't. Neither could they tell him about the chance discovery that would provide them all with a much brighter future, again this would have to wait a little longer.

They wanted so much to give him something to look forward to for when he returned home again but it was still too soon for that, there was work still to be done on that score and Karel would have to wait a little longer.

Chapter 21

Some explaining is needed

Bene wasn't looking forward to going into the station that morning. The Chief would be looking to him for a result of some kind on the three cases he was working on. Bene knew he would have to work fast to give him something more tangible than what he had at the moment. The only new lead was the one ET had given him earlier, but leads were not much good unless they did actually lead to something meaningful, and this new lead was somewhat tenuous at best. But it was all he had to go on and he hoped it would keep Sowerby off his back until he could provide him with something a bit more substantial.

Heads were down when he entered the office and he could sense a general uneasiness in the atmosphere. Chief Inspector Sowerby's office door was closed and the silence was unnerving, it was clear that the chief was not going to be satisfied with the slow progress his team were making. Bene went over and knocked on the door and when summoned entered the Chiefs' office. Sowerby was on the phone and without looking up he motioned Bene to a seat opposite him. The call ended and the chief raised his head, without speaking he sat back, folded him arms and waited, looking intently at the CID officer facing him across the desk.

Bene tried to compose himself before speaking but was conscious of a growing sickness building up deep down in his stomach. Outwardly he was sweating up heavily and he couldn't disguise the fact that he was conscious of the rollicking he was about to get. He knew that whatever he was going to say to his superior, it wouldn't be good enough, he just wasn't able to tell the Chief what he wanted to hear.

With a nervousness that showed in his voice he began. "We're working on three different cases and we do have some leads on all three but nothing positive at the moment." The chief remained silent and waited for Bene to continue. "Firstly the two deaths up at the home. I'm pretty certain that neither of those men died from natural causes, they died through the influence of an outside agency, namely the German who visited each of them prior to their deaths. Nothing has shown up on the autopsies and there's no medical evidence to show that their deaths were unnatural, but we're both sure that he was responsible for them. But without any medical evidence to back it up we'll most likely never be able to prove it." OK so far he thought. "All the staff have been interviewed including the manageress and we do have a description of the man calling himself Huber, but why would he sign in under different names if not to hide his real identity. I got the address he had given the police in Preston and one of their officers called to see him, only to find out that the man had left and given no forwarding address or any indication of where he was going."

At this point Bene paused for breath and chanced a quick look at his chief to try and find out how his explanation was being received, seeing only a blank look he decided to push on. "At last though I think we have a good lead," Sowerby seemed to show some interest and leant forward to hear what Bene had to say. "The home employs a cleaner who comes in for a few hours each day. She's not at work this week, so with Mrs Janes permission ET took the liberty of looking in her locker. Hidden in a box of tissues he found a set of keys which had recently been cut and they matched exactly the set which is kept in a key case in Mrs Janes office. They were a full set and could open any door, cupboard or window in the home."

Sowerby was keen to know who this cleaner was and when she was going to be interviewed.

"We have an address in the town for her but Mrs Janes thinks she's gone off on holiday somewhere. None of the staff know where she is, it seems she was looking for a last minute deal somewhere. We're going to her digs as soon as ET gets back to see if any of her neighbours know where she's gone. Hopefully someone will be able to tell us, if not we'll check the travel agents in the town and track her down that way, it shouldn't be too difficult."

"What's her name then?" asked the chief.

"Anna Ferenc" replied Bene, "It's not a common name so that should help."

"OK" said the chief, "What about ET's assailant, any further forward on that score?"

"Nothing to add to what we had yesterday. There haven't been any further sightings of the man in the raincoat. It looks as though he entered the covered market and then left via another door, probably the exit onto Fisher Street where there aren't any CCTV cameras. We haven't been able to pick him up anywhere since he went into the market. We know that the briefcase contained maps as well as papers, ET had a look into it when he was in Preston station."

"Maps of what, or where?" asked the chief.

"ET didn't know, there were two of them, not real maps but hand drawn ones. One of them had symbols on, directions and distances and there were some buildings shown on them, also some writing underneath which he thought was French, but he had no idea what is said."

"And the other one?" asked the chief.

"The other one only showed what looked to be a wood or forest but there again it was vague, there was some writing on this one as well, also in French, possibly the name of the wood but ET couldn't tell what it was."

Sowerby was perplexed. "We really need to get that briefcase Bene, but where it is now and how the hell we get it is beyond me. You must concentrate all your efforts and those of ET into getting it back, it's the key to what this is all about. And find that bloody German Huber as well, he's up to his neck in all this, we need to speak to him before he disappears back to Germany."

"And the robberies" asked Bene "Do we need to spend time on those as well?"

"No leave the robberies to my men, if there are no more then that's OK. We'll catch them soon enough using our own resources, but if they do start up again then I'll draft in a couple of officers from division to help out. I have a strange feeling about them, there have only been two so far and both next door to each other. In my opinion they don't seem to fit into the general pattern you would expect from an experienced gang. I mean they wouldn't target houses so close together within a space of a few days, they would pick out houses in different areas and leave a time lapse between them. I'm fairly certain the burglaries here in Levensbridge aren't connected to the ones further south, there's something different about these ones. I'm sure there's a link between the two but what it is I can't fathom out just yet. I'll keep an open mind on it for the time being."

"So it's the briefcase we need to find and the German fellow?" said Bene,

"Yes" said the Chief, "And don't forget about Anna Ferenc, it looks like she's been working there under false pretences, she's involved with Huber alright and with a name like that she could even be related to him."

Bene rose to leave but was stopped by Sowerby who raised his hand. "By the way Bene that was division on the phone when you came in, they wanted to know if we would like to hand it all over to them. I told them I'd let them know after I had spoken to you. I think that with ET to help you the two of you can crack this case, and I'm prepared to let you carry on without interference from division for the time being. But they're watching us carefully and I won't be able to keep it local for much longer. We need a result Bene and quickly. So don't hang around, get out there and bring me back some good news."

Chapter 22

The hunt for Anna Ferenc

"At last we've got something to get our teeth into ET, let's see if we can track this girl down." They had an address from Mrs Janes where the girl was staying in town and the two detectives were on their way there in Bene's car.

"It might take a bit of doing though if she's gone off abroad like Mrs Janes said she had" chipped in ET.

"Yes I know, according to her she was looking for a last minute holiday somewhere in the Med. None of the girls at the home knew if she had managed to get one or not so we'll try her digs first and see if anyone there can tell us."

Bell pushes were fixed to the wall at the entrance of the building where Anna had a room, there were six of them. Bene tried the one which had the name Mrs Bowes (owner) shown alongside it. A lady's voice came through the speaker asking for their names and the nature of their business. Bene introduced the two of them and the lady invited them up to the second floor, a buzzing sound told them the door lock had been released. "So it's Anna you're looking for is it, she's a nice girl Anna no trouble at all, I wish all the others were as good as her. Anyway you won't find her here she's away on holiday, but you must have known that before you came here."

She looked worriedly at the two men. "You haven't come with bad news have you, I mean she's alright isn't she?"

"No it's nothing like that" said Bene calming her down, "Don't worry, as far as we know she's fine but we do need to speak to her urgently, have you any idea where she's gone?"

"I'm sorry but I haven't a clue, she shouted up to me that she was off and that she'd be back in a week's time. I looked out the window and saw her leaving. She had a bag with her and there were two people waiting for her outside. She looked up and gave me a wave and then she went off with them. I thought they must have been friends of hers and they were all going on holiday together, but it was a bit strange because they didn't seem to have any luggage with them. She'd been up in the town in the morning and I presumed she'd got fixed up with a holiday at short notice. She told me once before it's what she usually does, she said you can get them so much cheaper that way as long as you can leave right away. "

It was a bit of a blow not knowing where the girl had gone but there were other people with rooms in the same house, maybe one of them would know. "How many people have you got staying here," asked ET, "We'll need to know their names and when we can speak to them, Anna might have mentioned it to one of them. I presume she was on speaking terms with them."

"I have two other girls here and a single gentleman all with their own rooms, but you'll not find them here until after five o'clock they're all out working in the town. Anna was friendly with the two girls so I suppose she might have spoken to them before she went. The other man though, I don't think he'll be able to help you he keeps himself to himself does that one. He's alright mind don't get me wrong, he works up at the abattoir and doesn't go out very much. When he's not working he spends most of his time just sitting in his room watching television. I hear him going out sometimes late at night, I think he likes to go for a quiet walk when it's dark and there aren't many people about. I don't know where he goes to but sometimes he can be out for hours and it's almost light when he gets back in again. His wife left him about a year ago because of his job and I don't think he's fully come to terms with it yet."

"This couple she went off with," said Bene, "Have you seen them before?" Mrs Bowes shook her head.

"No never, she's a lovely girl Anna and she must have lots of friends but I've never seen her with either of those two. They looked older, quite a bit older I'd say judging by their clothes. I couldn't see them clearly because I was two floors higher than they were you see."

"Were they both men, women or a couple?" asked Bene.

"Hard to tell." Mrs Bowes was trying to remember. "Certainly not two women, they both had coats on but one was wearing a man's hat, the other was smaller so could have been a woman. If I had to guess I'd say they were a couple."

The two men left the house and went over to the cafe, they would have to spend an hour in there until they could return to the house and interview the two girls. ET was quick to volunteer buying the coffees again and when Bene looked over to the counter he could see why. ET's date was serving and he wanted to speak to her. When he finally came over with the drinks Bene asked him "I forgot all about you having a date with the girl there, how did you get on?"

"Oh brilliant," said a chuffed ET. "We got on like a house on fire it was just as if we'd known each other for ages, she's a rugby fan as well so that makes it perfect." Bene laughed.

"It's not a one night stand then, you'll be seeing her again will you?"

"Of course, we're going out tonight if I get finished in time, honest boss I can't get enough of her, she's fantastic. I can't see me going back down to Wales again if I can keep hold of her." Bene had been looking over to the girl behind the counter and noticed that she would often sneak a look over to their table.

"She's obviously just as keen on him." he thought.

Twenty minutes later Bene suddenly jumped up. "Come on we'll have to go, say a quick goodbye to your girl and we're off." He left his chair and made for the door. ET sensed that something important must happened to kick Bene into action like that, so after a quick farewell to his girlfriend he left the cafe to catch up with his boss.

"What is it boss we've still got half an hour before the girls get home." Bene was walking quickly up the high street and ET had to increase his pace to keep up with him.

"The travel agents ET, we need to catch them before they close, if we wait until we've spoken to the girls they'll be closed. I'm thinking that if they can't tell us anything then our only chance would be the travel agents. They would know where Anna's gone to, it's my own fault I should have thought about it earlier and we could have gone there first."

Levensbridge was not a large town and there were only two travel agents there. The largest one was on the High Street and a much smaller locally owned one two streets away. Checking his watch Bene thought they would be able to catch them both before closing time. "We'll go to the smaller one first just in case they close early, it won't get as much business as the one in the High Street so they might not stay open as late." They quickly reached the shop and found it open, although there were no customers in it, only one person was there and he was obviously the owner. It didn't take long to find out that wherever Anna had gone off on holiday she hadn't booked it through this agent.

A few minutes later they were in the larger shop and this was much busier. They were in no hurry now and could afford to wait until one of the three staff became available. ET was flicking through some of the literature which was displayed on the racks. "Are you looking for a holiday with this new girlfriend then, you realise it'll cost you twice as much now." Bene quipped. ET smiled.

"You've got to admit though boss she's worth it. But I couldn't ask her just yet anyway it's far too early, we've got to get to know each other a bit better first. I just hope it lasts and she doesn't just see me as someone to pass the time with until some other fellow comes along and snaps her up."

"My God," thought Bene, "He has got it bad, but from what I've seen I think she's just as keen on him. I hope it works out for them."

One of the customers rose and left the shop and this left one of the girls free to attend to them. When she heard what information they wanted she told them they would have to wait until she had spoken to the manager and got his authority. The manager came over to the desk and sat with the girl while she checked the computer records for Anna Ferenc. The name was checked and the dates she may have flown out on but in both cases the answer was the same. No-one of that name had booked a flight or a holiday with the company. When asked, the manager confirmed there were only the two shops in Levensbridge. He suggested she may have booked her holiday over the internet and if this were the case then it would take a lot longer to track her down.

The shop was about to close and there was nothing more the manager could do to help them. The two men left and returned to the house to interview the two girls. It was half past five now so they should both be in their rooms. They rang for Mrs Bowes again and she let them in. She came down to the hall and showed them the doors to the girls rooms. "I'll get them out here and introduce you, then you can speak to them separately or together just as you wish." Both girls answered their doors and came out into the hallway. ET spoke to them.

"Girls, we're trying to contact Anna and we need to speak to her urgently, we know she's gone on holiday somewhere but we don't know where, have either of you any idea where she went to?"

Both girls laughed, one of them said

"You tell them Jen." Obviously both girls knew where Anna was and this was a big relief to the two detectives. Jen told them the place where Anna had gone for her holiday.

"She's in Ibiza, she got a cut price holiday, you know one of those last minute things."

"That's great Jen, you see we need to contact her as soon as possible and it can't wait until she gets back on Friday. If you can tell us which company she booked it with we can get in touch with her through them."

"Yeah that's easy, she booked it through the travel agents in the High Street, she told me she'd got it in the morning and was leaving on a flight from Manchester later that night."

"Do you know if she was going with anyone else Jen, Mrs Bowes said she left with another couple and they might all be going away together?"

"No I'm sure she was just going by herself. She never mentioned going with anyone else I think she liked to go alone and do her own thing."

Hopes had been temporarily raised, but on hearing this they had sunk right back again. Both girls were thanked and allowed back into their respective rooms. Bene asked Mrs Bowes if they could check out Anna's room.

"As long as I can stay with you while you do it I've no objection." She went back upstairs to get the key, then when she came down with it she opened the door for them. The room was neat and tidy. "There I told you," said Mrs Bowes, "She's a good girl is Anna there's no mess in here, she looks after the place as if it were her own." The men had to agree it was certainly tidy, maybe a bit too tidy.

"There's not much in here is there?" suggested ET as he looked in the wardrobe and pulled out some of the drawers. "Just a few odd clothes, no personal bits and pieces or photos, in fact nothing much for her to come back to. She could have gone off for good and not missed any of this."

Chapter 23

Dinner at the Fox and Pheasant

"Fancy a meal down at the pub tonight?" Bene asked ET.

"Well it's kind of you to ask but I did tell you I was taking Sue out tonight didn't I and I don't want to let her down."

"Oh so that's her name is it, but the offer's open to both of you, Alex is coming with me and I thought it might lighten things up a bit if you had a bit of company. But if you'd rather be alone with her that's OK, it was just a thought." ET considered the invite.

"I'm picking her up at seven, but we haven't booked anything so I'll mention it to her and we'll do whatever she wants, if she wants to come we'll see you there, how's that?"

"Yeah that's fair enough, We'll probably be there about seven ourselves and we'll have a drink first before ordering. If you do decide to come we can order together, if not we'll wait until about seven thirty then we'll go ahead on our own."

Bene and Alex arrived at the Fox and Pheasant just after seven o'clock. Alex was keen to meet ET's girlfriend and was hoping that he would bring her in. The pub was fairly busy and most of the customers were enjoying their evening meal. "God I'm starving" said Alex. "The smells coming from the kitchen are really getting to me. I'll just have to eat soon, can't you hear my stomach rumbling?"

"Oh yes," said Bene unsympathetically "Well just remember how you make me wait when your mum's in the kitchen cooking for us and I've not eaten since breakfast, you enjoy watching me suffer so now it's your turn." Alex reached over and gave him a thump on the arm.

"You're a sadist you are, I hate you."

Each time the door opened Alex looked over expectantly, hoping it would be ET with his girlfriend, but when the clock showed seven thirty it looked like they would be eating alone. "Go on then Bene get the food ordered before I drop dead with hunger."

"Yeah that'll be the day when you go hungry, what are you going to have anyway?"

"Steak pie of course, I always have that, and tell Kris I want lots of gravy." Bene went over to the bar and was just on the point of ordering when in walked ET and Sue.

"Hold on to that for a moment Kris, there could be an extra two in with the order." Bene went back to the table to greet the couple, introductions were made and Bene suggested they join them for dinner.

"What do you recommend boss," asked ET "I've not been here before."

"Well they do a mean Steak pie it's a real favourite in here, Alex and me rarely have anything else."

"OK" said ET "That sounds good to me." After asking Sue what she would like four steak pies were ordered. When Kris had taken their order he beckoned Bene to the far end of the bar.

"See the two men over on the far table there?" Bene looked over and picked out the two men, one was Paul Hanbury the other man he didn't know.

"Yes I knew Paul was back in town but I don't know the other guy, who is he?"

"Well don't stare at them but you know I've joined the bowls club along with Adam." Bene hadn't known it was a complete surprise to him, nevertheless he let Kris continue. "That fellow Paul's talking to is one of the three remaining owners of the club, he's the one who has changed his mind and now wants to sell the land that the club is on. The other two owners are still opposed to the sale, but one of them is still in hospital and it doesn't look like he's coming out again. We're all worried, and if anything were to happen to the last one, the club would be finished."

Bene and Kris looked at each other, their thoughts going along the same lines. Bene spoke first. "If Paul Hanbury is involved I would be scared as well, he's been lucky so far with some of the things he's pulled off. I'm sure he's been up to his neck in a few incidents around here but I haven't been able to pin anything on him so far. To tell you the truth I wouldn't put murder past him if that's what it took to get what he wanted." Kris went on to tell him about the night Paul left Levensbridge immediately after his wedding a few months earlier.

"He gave me a mobile phone number to keep, one that no one else knew about, he said I was to phone him when something happened. Well I had no idea what he meant by that and told him so. All he would say was that

I would know when it happened and I was to phone him straight away." Bene became even more interested.

"So did you ever find out?"

"Oh yes" said Kris "I doubt if Paul had even reached his house in France before it happened. You must remember that as soon as Paul disappeared over the horizon that night Ray Parrish and Karel Zajic were arrested for that currency scam. You were there yourself when it happened, it was you who caught them wasn't it. Anyway I phoned Paul the very next day and told him the news and he didn't seem at all surprised. It must have been what he was expecting to hear because he told me to throw the mobile number away I wouldn't need it anymore."

Bene's face brightened up. "I bloody well knew he was involved in that, he got out just in time and fed Ray and the other fellow to the wolves. Thanks Kris that's good to know, I'm going to watch him a lot more closely now. If anything happens to either of those two owners at your club I'll make sure he doesn't get away with it."

"Come on Bene" shouted Alex "You should be over here with our guests not boring poor old Kris to death." Bene smiled at Kris

"That's my girl." and made his way back to join the company. ET and Sue were soon made to feel at ease with Bene and Alex, Alex was keen to get to know as much about Sue as she could. She was a good looking girl of about twenty two smartly dressed in an off white top with black slacks. She was two or three inches taller than Alex but did carry a little extra weight which helped to compliment her height. She had sensibly chosen shoes with low heels so as not to appear taller than her escort.

Her face was quite plain, an honest face with only a hint of makeup, it was surrounded by light brown hair which curled down around it in ringlets. She seemed happy in their company and it showed in her smile, when she spoke it was with a local accent which implied she hadn't spent much time away from her hometown.

The meals arrived and were quickly devoured by the four who had all worked up a healthy appetite. More drinks were ordered and the group sat back in their chairs to enjoy the rest of the evening. The girls were chatting away quite happily completely ignoring the two men. ET brought his chair a little closer to Bene and asked him about his conversation with Kris. Bene pointed out the two men at the far table and told him who they were. He told him about Paul's past history and his suspicions about him, then followed up with the story Kris had told him.

"I get the feeling there's a bit of history between Paul and you, you seem dead set on getting something on him." Bene didn't want to go into any details of the problems he had had with Paul over the past few years but did agree that there was no love lost between them. "That's another thing we'll have to keep a look out for," said ET "It looks like Paul is the one intent on buying up the land, and he knows he'll have to get rid of the two opposing owners before he can buy the other guy out. He must have made him a very generous offer."

"Jeez," said Bene "This is getting more and more like a thriller, there's too many suspicious deaths for my liking. Two up at the home and one at the bowls club, possibly another one any time soon, and maybe another one already being lined up, its bloody frightening."

"I don't want to make it appear even worse," said ET, "But we've these missing people as well. We've got to track down that guy Huber and his wife before they shoot off back to Germany, and that cleaner Anna Ferenc where the hell has she gone to and why did she lie about getting a cheap holiday. She didn't leave much in the room so it's possible she might have run off as well. It sure looks like all three are in it together doesn't it?" Bene had to agree.

"Yes it does. Then there's that briefcase one of them must have it. I've got a sinking feeling in my stomach that we may have seen the last of those three and the briefcase, and we'll never find out what it's all about."

Things were not looking good for the two detectives and it showed in their faces. Bene had been in the same position before and he knew that the answers wouldn't be found sitting around feeling sorry for themselves. "We need a breakthrough ET, we've got to work harder and make something happen. It's about time we had a bit of luck on our side, so far all the luck's been with the enemy. Let's be positive and go out there tomorrow and get some results."

Paul and his guest rose to leave the pub. The two had been so engrossed in their talks that when they passed Bene's table on the way out Paul never even noticed the four sitting there. Bene stared after them, his thoughts were not of a friendly nature. "I'll have you Paul, somewhere along the line you'll make a mistake and I'll be right there when you do."

Chapter 24

Secret agent at work

Ethan arrived at his Auntie's about mid morning, he went around the back of the house and propped his bike up against the garden shed. "I suppose I'd better tell her I'm here first before I go into town." He trudged into the house by the back door.

"Ethan, my you are keen aren't you and so early as well, your mam phoned and told me you were on your way over here and that you were going to help me in the garden. Oh I'm so pleased, I haven't been able to get in it much this last week or so and it's got into a bit of a state. But never mind now you're here to help me we'll soon have it knocked back into shape. Would you like a drink first before we start?"

Auntie didn't had time to draw breath during this cheerful welcome to her favourite nephew and the little secret agent never got the chance to get a word in himself. He could only stand with mouth agape waiting for a chance to tell her the real reason he was there. Gardening! he wasn't bothered about the garden, he had burglars to catch and he wasn't going to catch them in Auntie's garden was he. He wished he'd never mentioned the garden to his mam and dad, that was only to get him away from home so he would have all day to find out where the stolen furniture was hidden. Now he was sunk, he couldn't leave just now he would have to help her first. "Maybe there won't be much to do in the garden an' I'll get away after dinner, at least I'll have all afternoon to look for them."

"Right then Ethan let's get out there and make a start on it." Auntie led the not so willing little helper out into the large back garden. He looked around it glumly. The only interest he had in gardens was to play in them, run around on the grass and play hide and seek in the bushes, not to actually have to work in them, that's not what gardens were for. There was to be no escape though, auntie had made her plans which would keep them both busy for the next hour or two at least. The day which had begun with so much promise was now in danger of falling apart before he even had time to get started. Would he ever be able to get away from his auntie's to catch the robbers.

Auntie went over to the shed and wheeled out the new lawn mower she had recently bought. "There now Ethan what do you think of this?" she said proudly showing off the new machine. Ethan had to agree, it was a real beauty and much better than the old one he had been made to push around the last time he had been there. He didn't think he'd mind using this one it had an engine in it, he could just walk along behind it and it would do all the work for him, he wouldn't have to do anything just follow it around the garden.

"Well I expect I could do the grass for you but I don't think I could do much else 'cos my back's hurting something awful today" Ethan's face took on the most painful looking contortions as he rubbed his sore back, strangely enough the same back which two minutes ago was perfectly capable of weeding or doing many other things that needed doing in the garden.

"Ooh you poor little thing" said Auntie, sympathising with the boy. "Well I'll start up the lawn mower for you and you can cut the grass, it might be best if you leave the rest to me I don't want to make your back any worse than it is now."

Ethan's face returned to something resembling it's more normal features. "Great I'll soon have this lot done, then I'm off." The lawn mower was started and he proudly took charge of the large machine, this was going to be a doddle. He engaged the gear and was ready to speed around the lawn and get the job over as quickly as he could. The lawn mower was not one to be hurried though it only had one speed and that was nowhere near fast enough for the young boy. "Won't it go any faster Auntie?" he moaned.

"Oh heavens no Ethan, it's got to go at that speed so that it cuts the grass nice and even, you want to make a good job of it don't you?" This wasn't going to be as fast or as easy as he had first thought.

"I'll have to tell her I suppose. I don't want to be stuck here all day doing this."

"I'm a secret agent you know Auntie, I've got lots of other things to do today as well. I can't be here in the garden all day."

"Yes dear" said Auntie smiling, "Well you'll have plenty of time after dinner for that I'm sure." She didn't look up to see the scowl that had replaced the anguished look on his face a few minutes earlier.

An hour and a half later and the grass had all been cut, Ethan had also trimmed around the edges to give it a very professional finish. He had started out with the intention of getting it over with as quickly as possible, but coming to terms with the speed of the machine he decided that he may as well concentrate on doing the job well. That should please auntie and maybe she would let him go early so he could get on with his real work for the day, catching robbers.

He had to wait another half an hour for Auntie to finish her jobs then off they went into the house for dinner. "That's a good job you've done out there Ethan I'm really pleased with you, I hope your back's not too bad." Auntie was looking away so he wouldn't see her smiling, she had suspected the boy had been putting it on but didn't want to make it sound too obvious that she knew. Dinner was eaten and the dishes were cleared away, at last Ethan could escape.

"Right" said auntie "Off you go then and do your secret agent's work, have you got your book with you?"

"Yes Auntie I've got everything I need, I'll be back for tea later."

"Mind you don't get into any trouble now, don't go bothering people or upsetting them." she shouted after him as he rushed out of the house, Ethan jumped onto his bike and sped off down the road into town.

There were two or three shops and a few storage places in the town where he thought the stolen items would be found and he had all the addresses written down in his little book. He had no doubt at all that he would find the stolen furniture, it was just a matter of going around the different places until he came across it. "Now where should I start" he pondered, flicking through his book. "Right, I'll have a snoop round the shops first I think" and off he went to the first one.

Leaving his bike locked to a row of railings outside he went into a large furniture shop. Walking around he couldn't see anything that looked as if it had been stolen, it all looked very new to him. One of the sales assistants approached him. "Can I help you son, are your parents in here, maybe you're waiting for them is that it?" Ethan said nothing "Maybe you'd like to buy something yourself." the salesman added with a sneer. Ethan was not impressed, he didn't like the man.

"I'm not buying anything from you I'm looking for stolen stuff, have you got somewhere else where it could be hidden?" The salesman scowled at the young boy.

"Right off you go, we don't want cheeky little sods like you in here, go on now push off before I call the manager." The little secret agent was ushered unceremoniously out of the shop.

"I bet he's got stuff hidden somewhere an' he's trying' to stop me from finding it, I'm going to have a look round the back." Ethan left his bike where it was and walked around to the back of the shop to see if he could spot anything suspicious. Unfortunately there was a high brick wall all around the property and it was much too high for him to climb, he gave a snort of disgust and headed off to the next shop.

He had no luck with that one either. It wasn't as big as the first one and a quick look around satisfied him that there was nothing in there that wasn't new. The furniture in there was all nice and shiny with price tags that frightened him. "Blimey" he thought "I'd have to save my pocket money for years to buy anything in here." As one of the salesmen approached Ethan turned and walked out of the shop, he didn't want another encounter with these horrible sales people.

"How do they expect to sell anything if they're as nasty as they are, it's a wonder anyone comes in these shops at all." Ethan went back to his bike and crossed the name of the shop out of his book.

The only other places he had in his book were warehouses on an estate on the outskirts of the town. He cycled up the main street and headed out towards the Lower Kent Business Park, there were quite a few large buildings on that estate where stolen things could easily be hidden. Ethan cycled around them but found most of them locked. One or two of them had windows which he could see into but again with no success, no furniture could be seen. He tried the premises of Esk Logistics but that was closed as well. Standing on the seat of his bike he could just about see inside the building but all it seemed to contain were wagons and they were parked close together, he didn't think there was anything else in there.

The he moved on to the last one, Dunne's Warehousing and Storage Depot. This was also locked and the windows in the building were too high for him to see inside, even standing on his bike he still couldn't see in. "I bet the stuff's in there alright but I'll need a ladder so I'll be able to see in." The little lad set off to find a ladder. He didn't have any success with a ladder but did manage to find a large branch which had been blown off one of the trees that surrounded the estate. These had been planted years ago to shield the estate from the sight of passing motorists on the busy main road that passed close by.

Ethan dragged the branch over to the warehouse and placed it up against the wall as close to one of the windows as possible. He loved climbing trees so this was going to be easy. The branch was just about high enough to give him a view into the building. He wiped the dirty window to give him a better sight of what was inside, from his position high up he could see that the building was almost empty apart from a small office in one corner and another corner of the building which appeared to be sectioned off. He stretched as far as he could but it was no good he couldn't see into it. He would have to move the branch further down the wall to another window before he would be able to see what was in that corner.

He quickly climbed back down the branch and dragged it further along the building, he stood it up against the wall just below the window at the end of the warehouse and climbed up it. He had just reached the top and was in the act of cleaning this new window when a loud shout from below stopped him from any further activity.

"OK sonny come on down!" Ethan hesitated, although shocked by this intrusion he couldn't get down just yet, this was the last place he had to look to find the stolen furniture.

"It must be in here 'cos I've looked everywhere else, I'll just have to have a look into that corner." He was shaking with fright and knew he was in big trouble, but he really needed to have a quick look into that part of the warehouse before climbing down again, he wouldn't get another chance. He quickly rubbed the window with his sleeve and pressed his face up against the window, a quick glance inside told him there was nothing to see, the corner was completely empty.

"Come on sonny, don't keep me waiting or you'll be in even more trouble, do you want me to call the police?"

A subdued and frightened little boy climbed back down the branch to face his captor. "Like to tell me what you're doing up there sonny, I hope you haven't been up to any mischief, breaking things or worse." Ethan looked up into the face of the man who had caught him out.

"Honest mister I haven't been doing anything bad, I'm a secret agent see and I'm looking for all that stolen furniture that the police can't find, I'm helping them see." The man was a little taken aback, maybe the lad wasn't too bad after all.

"Well I suppose you're on your own, you're not in a gang or anything like that so I might just believe you, but you'll have to give me some proof that you're not lying?" Ethan took out his book which had Secret Agent's Book written across the front and showed the man the names of the shops and buildings he thought the stolen goods might be found in.

"Have you been round all these places then?" he asked the boy.

"Yes of course I have but I can't find the stuff anywhere, I don't know where it is, I'll have to have another think." The man handed the book back and looked hard at the little boy.

"OK then I think you're probably telling me the truth, but you get off home now and if you take my advice you'll leave all this to the proper people, the police right?"

There was nothing more Ethan could say so he agreed that he wouldn't carry on with the search. The man smiled down at him, let him get on his bike and watched as he rode off out of the estate.

"Well that's rotten that is, don't know where I'm going to go now, the stuffs got to be somewhere." The little lad was muttering to himself as he rode back into the town. He didn't want to go back down the main street in case he bumped into any of those nasty salesmen so he took the street that ran parallel with it behind all the main shops. When he thought he was past the furniture shops he turned into a road which led back to the main street, he needed to be back there so he'd be able to find his way back to auntie's house.

This road was a lot narrower and as he rode along he could see quite clearly into the little windows of the terraced houses. He was passing a small shop with a bow fronted window and saw inside it some old furniture. He braked suddenly. "Maybe the stuff's in there," he thought. "I bet it is." He got off his bike and went over to have a closer look. "Yeah I bet that's it, no wonder the police couldn't find it, I bet they didn't even come down here, in fact probably never knew there was a shop here at all."

There were no lights on in the shop and the door was locked. “Must have closed early I suppose ‘cos it’s nearly tea time. Can’t see anything in there though and it’s not that big, I’ll have a look round the back.” Ethan wheeled his bike round to the back of the shop and this time there was no high wall, there was a wall but only about six feet high. Standing on his bike he could easily see over it and what he did see brought a huge grin to his face, for there sitting behind the wall at the back of the shop was a large metal container, at least twenty feet long.

“That’s where it is then,” he had known he would find it. He ducked down as two men came out from the back of the shop and walked over to the container. One of them spoke. “I’ve not much more to go in so I’ll finish off loading tomorrow morning, if you bring the wagon round about lunch time we’ll get it loaded and you can take it away. They’ll be some happy faces in America when they see what’s inside this one.”

Ethan heard one of the men lock the container and then listened as they walked back to the shop, when he thought they were safely out of sight he stood up and looked over the wall. Now that he had found the stolen goods he didn’t know what to do about it. He pondered his next move. “I’ll have to come back tomorrow an’ have a look inside just to make sure.” Then there was a long pause while he thought of what to do after that. It wasn’t going to be easy as he hadn’t got that far with his plans, all he had been thinking about was finding the goods, not what to do when he did find them.

Then the secret agent in him came up with the answer. "It's got a number on, I'll write it down and give it to ET, his house is on the way back to Auntie's, then when they arrest them they'll know it was me 'cos I've written the number down for them." Ethan took out his little book and wrote in it.

stolen stuffs in this big metal thing at the back of little shop with funny window
I got the number for you   OSQU4064718   22VH
                                                        Jurgen Drenthe

Then on the bottom he wrote "from little et." There was nothing else he could do now so he got back on his bike and headed for ET's flat. He knocked on the door and when no one came he knocked again, still there was no answer. "I've got to get back to Auntie's she'll be mad if I'm late for tea." He tore the page from the book and stuffed it into ET's letter box. "There that'll have to do, he'll get it when he comes back later." The little secret agent had done his bit now it was up to ET and Bene to do the easy bit. He peddled as fast as he could back to Auntie's house whistling loudly and happily along the way.

Chapter 25

The hunt for Anna continues

It was Sunday morning and Bene was still in a deep asleep when he was rudely awakened by his mobile phone ringing. It took him a few seconds to realise what it was and by that time Alex was awake as well. "For God's sake Bene answer it I want to get back to sleep again." He reached over to pick up the phone and was surprised to hear the Chief's voice at the other end.

"Bene I've just had a call from Manchester airport, Anna Ferenc is booked on a flight from Corfu to Manchester arriving there later this morning. I want you to get down to the airport and bring her back here as soon as the plane gets in."

Chief Inspector Sowerby was taking no chances and had contacted customs and immigration. They had been on the lookout for anyone with the name Anna Ferenc who was flying into or out of the country. There was a possibility of course that she had already left the country and may not return, but he was hoping that there was still a chance they would find her.

"What time does her flight get in?" Bene asked.

"It's due in at ten thirty so you'd better get a move on. When you get there ask for the Chief Customs Officer. He's going to meet her off the plane and escort her to his office, he'll hold her there until you arrive."

"What was all that about?" said Alex, yawning noisily beside him.

"Nothing for you to worry about just go back to sleep again." Now he was wide awake he looked over at her with envy, she looked so warm and cosy lying there beside him. Surely if he was going to be deprived of his sleep then in all fairness she should lose some as well. He picked up a glass of water from the bedside table and carefully spilled a few drops down the back of her neck. Alex jumped up at once and scolded him

"You utter beast," she yelled as she grabbed a pillow and threw it at him, "Get out of here and leave me in peace," then sank back down into the bed again. Bene laughed as he hopped off the bed to find his clothes.

Looking at his watch he saw it was only half past seven. He thought he had plenty of time to have breakfast before leaving and he could still be at the airport in time for the plane landing. Living with Alex and her mam he hadn't needed to do any cooking himself Dot did all that for them. His mind went back to when he was living alone in the flat before he met Alex, he had quite enjoyed making his favourite scrambled eggs and bacon for breakfast. He looked around the kitchen and found all the ingredients he needed and started to make the meal. The lovely smells that drifted up to their bedroom wouldn't allow Alex to get off to sleep again. She groaned and swore under the bedclothes, finally she couldn't stand it anymore and dragged herself out of bed and went downstairs into the kitchen.

"You absolute rotter, you're only doing this to annoy me, you know I can't resist a good fry up. Now I'm awake and down here you'd jolly well better make me some as well." Of course all this noise and commotion brought Dot down to the kitchen as well, so it was breakfast for three. An hour later Bene left the house for the airport.

Although it was Sunday there were still a lot of flights coming in and out of the busy airport. On his arrival Bene was shown into the customs office The Chief Officer was outside waiting for the plane to arrive and Bene was to remain in his office until he brought the girl back with him. It was almost an hour later when they entered the office, the Chief Customs Officer came in first with the girl following behind. Bene didn't know exactly what he expected the girl to look like, by all accounts she was a bubbly twenty five year old with brown hair.

The person who came into the office was not at all like that, Bene took her age to be somewhere between thirty and forty, well built and dressed in dull looking clothes, she had black dank unkempt hair and wore a sullen expression on her face. "Well here she is sergeant I'll leave her in here with you and you can interview her. When you've finished come and let me know what you're going to do with her; there'll be some paperwork to prepare if you're going to take her back with you."

The woman took a seat when offered and pulled her suitcase towards her feet. "I don't know why you want to see me I have done nothing wrong, my passport is in order and I have had British citizenship for the last ten years. I have only been out of the country for one week visiting my parents back home in Warsaw." She spoke in clear and concise English but with a distinct eastern European accent. She handed Bene her passport which showed her address to be in Salford.

"This address is up-to-date then" he asked, "You're still living in Salford?"

"Of course, I have lived in Salford ever since I came to this country fifteen years ago, it is my home." Bene had to make sure she was telling the truth.

"Can you tell me who you work for and where."

"I'm employed by the council as a cleaner, here you can see my card." She took out her plastic ID card and handed it to him, it confirmed she was telling the truth, it even had her photo on it. Bene took the card from her and studied it before handing it back.

"And have you ever lived or worked in Levensbridge?"

"Levensbridge, I don't know that name where is it?" Bene explained the whereabouts of Levensbridge to her.

"No I have never been to that place."

There was nothing else for it but to let the woman go, she was not the Anna Ferenc he was looking for. "Another bloody wasted journey." he thought. He thanked the woman and apologised for keeping her back. The two of them left the office and Bene showed her how to get back to the airport arrivals area. He had a brief word with the Chief Officer and left the airport himself for the drive back to Levensbridge. "Damn it, another blind alley, Sowerby won't take much more of this, I'll have to find the right Anna soon or he'll be forced to hand it all over to division."

He had travelled about ten miles up the motorway when his mobile rang. He accepted the call but had to place it on hands free before answering.

"Bene, are you there Bene?" the familiar voice of Chief Inspector Sowerby came over the airwaves.

"Yes I'm on my way back sir, I'm afraid it was a bit of a wild goose chase, the woman who came in on that flight wasn't the Anna Ferenc we're looking for."

"Never mind about that," said the Chief. "Just get back here as fast as you can. They've just pulled a woman's body out of the river, mid twenties, medium height with light brown hair. I think we've found her."

Chapter 26

A troubled meeting

The committee meeting for the Kent Park lawn bowls club was scheduled for seven thirty that night. The committee consisted of twelve members which included the owners. Kris was one of the members, and being one of the youngest he had been voted onto the committee on the death of one of the owners for a particular reason. His mandate was to encourage more young people of his own age to join. The club membership had been in a slow decline over the years and this trend had only been stemmed at the beginning of the last season when a neighbouring club had closed down, the remaining members had come over and joined Kent Park.

Kris had gone to the meeting with grave misgivings over the future of the club. Together with Adam Firth he had drawn up a list of concerns which he intended to bring before the committee, and he intended to get answers for these. The chairman opened the meeting with the sad news of the death of one of the owners. "Unfortunately Harold never regained consciousness after being admitted to hospital, I received a phone call earlier this morning to say he had passed away peacefully. Our condolences go out to his family at this sad time and I think it would be appropriate if we could all stand and observe a minute's silence for him. We can reflect on his life and what his friendship meant to each of us, and of course all the good work he did here at the club."

When the members resumed their seats the Chairman gave out apologies for absence, one from a member who was recovering from a knee operation and one from Derek Cooper one of the two remaining owners.

"What's wrong with Derek then, we were expecting him here tonight?" voiced one of the members. Another chipped in

"We were hoping to get some assurances from him tonight regarding the future of the club." The chairman acknowledged the questions but could offer no explanation for the owner's decision not to attend.

"All I know is that my wife took a call from him this morning when I was out, all he said was that he wasn't able to attend the meeting tonight but gave no reason for it."

The members were not happy. There were various criticisms thrown towards the chairman and none of them complimentary. The general feeling of the committee was that it didn't look good for the future of their club. They had all heard rumours about a possible sell out and the non appearance of one of the owners at the meeting did nothing to dispel that. The other owner George Wheeler stood up, he needed to try and calm the members down. "Mr Chairman I would like to address the meeting if I may." The chairman gave his consent.

"Now you all know me and you know that my heart and soul is in this club. I want to assure you that there's no reason at all why you should be worried about these rumours flying around about the club being sold. The club can only be sold with the permission of all the owners, one man alone cannot sell it. I don't know why Derek has suddenly decided he doesn't want the club to continue, maybe his business isn't doing too well and he needs the money. I honestly don't know because he hasn't spoken to me for the past month, I've tried to contact him about it but he's become rather evasive."

Kris decided it was time to speak. "We all know that you would never sell George but look at it from our point of view. A month ago there were four owners and all four of you were keen members and it looked very promising for the future of the club. Then about that time Derek stopped coming, and on more than one occasion since then he's been seen in the company of men who we all know are keen to buy up any prime land in the town. If it were sold, this plot of land we're sitting on would be worth a fortune." George was keen to reaffirm his commitment to the club.

"Yes Kris I appreciate what you're saying but I did tell you that I wouldn't agree to sell under any circumstances, you have my word on that."

Kris wasn't finished though. "In the last month two of the owners have died so their shares in the club have gone to Derek and to you George. Don't you think it's a bit odd the way those two have died, a nasty accident, that nothing or nobody could prove otherwise. Then this latest one, a result of food poisoning. Both of them during the last few weeks when these rumours have been circulating. Is it just coincidence or is there something sinister behind it all? I don't want to frighten you George but what if anything should happen to you, that's the real reason we're worried." The meeting went very quiet as everyone took in the enormity of what had just been said. Kris had expressed the thoughts and fears of every one of them, it was something that had to be said and he had put it over expertly. George was worried now, he hadn't thought about his own life being in danger. Health-wise he'd always been fit and well and had never had any reason to think that anything untoward would happen to him.

No one wanted to speak because Kris was still standing, he hadn't finished and they were all waiting for more. "I know I was elected onto the committee to try and bring some new blood into the club but here again I have to say that despite my efforts no progress has been made. I went round the local schools and at two of them I got a few of the lads interested. I arranged for them to come down and have a go at it, I told them we had spare shoes and bowls and they could use those for practice. I arranged a time for them to come with the green keeper and they were looking forward to it. When we got here he had just started to cut the grass something he always did in the mornings, so the lads couldn't get on the green. I arranged another time and the same thing happened. He had just spiked the green and gone home before rolling it so again the lads couldn't play."

The members listened intently, they couldn't understand what the green keeper was playing at. Kris continued.

"To cap it all when I brought them here again the green keeper wasn't here and all the spare bowls and shoes had been locked away, and of course I don't have a key to the store. Well that was it, the lads got fed up and I couldn't ask them again as I had already let them down three times." The committee were disappointed, these lads were just the type they wanted in the club so why were they being discouraged from trying it out. Kris had one final comment to make to them.

"As you can imagine I was upset and bloody annoyed, and when I got back to the pub who do you think was there, Ron the green keeper and Derek sitting smugly over in a corner of the bar. Well I tackled him of course and he gave some sort of explanation which to me didn't disguise the fact that it was deliberate, but why I asked myself. Then when these rumours started I began to think that it was Derek who was behind it all."

One of the members came to life. "I suppose that if the membership continues to decline then Derek could have a good reason for closing down the club, but if you'd been successful in getting a few new members to join, especially younger ones then it would have been difficult for him to close it, it would have given the club a bit of new blood. I think he's right George, you'd better look after yourself we don't want anything to happen to you."

There were a few other items on the agenda. A friendly had been arranged and the catering for that had to be ordered. Transport needed to be worked out for the next away game and some funding found for repairing one of the old walls at the south side of the club.

The meeting was closed at nine o'clock and the members went home feeling a lot worse than when they had arrived. It was getting a bit dark outside and as George left the club he checked over both shoulders on the way to his car. He'd been thinking a lot about what Kris had said and was worried by it. Was there something lying in wait for him, an accident maybe. Should he be taking extra care, and how would he know, it could be at any time and in any place, he would have no idea. He had a nasty feeling that it wouldn't be long before he found out.

Chapter 27

Dreams and nightmares

The little secret agent was fast asleep in bed with wonderful dreams swimming around inside his head. In one of them he was in London helping the police to round up a gang of criminals who had been threatening to blow up the Bank of England. The Chief of Police had personally thanked him for playing a crucial role in their arrest and Ethan was basking in the praise and glowing with pride. If auntie had looked in on him just then she would have seen his little face beaming with happiness.

The dreams continued. In the next one he was hiding in a cave on a rocky coastline, he was working for the coastguards this time. They were waiting for smugglers to land their boat so they could jump out and catch them. Everything was going exactly to plan when he heard the boat arrive and being dragged up high onto the pebbled beach. He peered out from his hiding place and saw two huge rough looking men pulling up the boat. These men were much too big for him to tackle on his own so he would leave it to the coastguards to arrest them. He withdrew back into the cave and looked behind him for the coastguards who he was expecting to run out and capture the smugglers at any moment. To his horror he couldn't see any of them the cave was completely empty, they had all disappeared and left him on his own.

He was feeling a bit scared now, where had they gone? surely they didn't expect him to arrest them all on his own. These men looked really mean and he didn't think they'd be very happy if they found out he was there, they might want to capture him and take him away in their boat. He looked around the cave frantically trying to find some means of escape, but there was none. The only way out was onto the beach, he couldn't get out that way because the men would see him and it would be him who was captured not them. There was only one place he could see, a little crevice set further back in the cave wall. He ran over and tried to squeeze into it, it wasn't deep enough to keep him completely out of sight and no matter how hard he tried he couldn't quite fit into it. He was only partly hidden but it was the best he could do, maybe in the dark the men wouldn't see him.

He stood very still and quiet as he heard the men approach the cave, his little heart was pounding. Shaking with fright his eyes were tightly closed, too scared to look. One of the men spoke in a gruff voice. "Let's hide the stuff in here then we'll go back to the island and get the rest of it." The little secret agent relaxed a little maybe they wouldn't spot him after all. He would have to wait until they went back out in the boat again then he would be able to escape. Until then he would keep his eyes closed, he didn't dare to look at what was happening. He heard the two men come into the cave and drop something heavy on the floor. Two more trips were made and more things were brought in, then it went quiet and Ethan thought they must have left. He remained in his hiding place for another minute then thought it would be safe to open his eyes and prepare to make his escape.

Slowly he opened his eyes, it was dark inside the cave and there was only a small shaft of moonlight coming in through the entrance to show him where it was. He decided he would make a run for it because he didn't want to be found in there when the men returned. He made a dash towards the light but forgot about the heavy objects on the cave floor. He stumbled over a large wooden box and let out a cry as he fell over it. He cursed as he struggled to get back onto his feet but then froze as a bright light was shone into his eyes blinding him, someone was standing over him shining a torch into his face. Ethan screamed.

"Hey" said Auntie jumping back from the window where she had just drawn back the curtains to let in the sunshine. "What was all that about, have you been dreaming again?" Ethan looked up at his Auntie with a startled expression on his face and in a frightened little voice he said.

"Some big men were after me Auntie and I tripped up and they caught me."

"Well they're not here now so you can relax, anyway it's time you were up it's nearly ten o'clock, I thought you said you wanted to be off somewhere this morning."

Ethan was still in shock after his last dream which had turned into a bit of a nightmare. Slowly coming around, the memory of his exploits the day before gradually came back to him. "Blimey I'll have to get a move on or that crate thing will have gone before I get the chance to have a look inside it." He dressed quickly and ran downstairs with the intention of going back to the shop again as quickly as he could. Auntie was having none of it though. "Not until you've had your breakfast young man, now eat your boiled egg and toast and then you can go and not before." Ethan gobbled down his breakfast and went out for his bike. "Are you coming back here before you go home tonight?" Auntie asked.

"I might come back if I get finished early, but if I'm a bit late I expect I'll just go home."

"OK Ethan, if I don't see you again this afternoon thanks for helping me in the garden yesterday, and I'll see you next weekend maybe." Ethan didn't hear the last part as he was already peddling as fast as he could down the road to get back to see what was inside that crate. The nightmare he had had only an hour ago was now just a distant memory.

He arrived at the back of the little shop and placed his bike against the same wall he had used the day before. Standing on the seat he looked over the wall and was relieved to see the container was still there, again the door was open so the man must have been loading more stolen furniture into it. He looked all around but there was no-one else in sight. There was no movement around the container or the back of the shop either, this might be the best time to creep round and have a peep inside. If he left it much longer the man might come out and shut the door then he would have lost his chance of finding out exactly what was in it.

The little secret agent left his bike in the lane and walked round to the back of the property, the gate was open and he waited just for a moment to check there was still no one around who would see him going into the container. When he felt it was all clear he made his move, eyes flicking from side to side, checking all the time for anyone coming around the corner he made his way to the open door. "Now or never." he thought as he slipped inside. The large container looked almost full and everything inside was covered up in sheets and tied up. "Wonder what all this stuff is?" he thought. "I'll loosen off one or two of the ties and have a look." The nearest ones were too tight and he couldn't undo them. Moving a little further back he crept into a space behind one large piece where he found he could work away undoing the ties and be out of view from anyone looking in. Slowly he managed to free one of the ties and started on the next one, soon he would have that off as well then he would be able to see if the furniture was the same as the ones which had been stolen. His little fingers were working hard to undo the tie which had been pulled much tighter than the first one. Concentrating on what he was doing he didn't at first hear the footsteps of the two men approaching, when he did he froze.

"OK Peter, that's the lot then is it?"

"That's all for this trip anyway, I've got some more coming in over the next few weeks so I'll need you again then, I'll let you know when I've got enough for another load." The large door slammed shut with a deafening crash and the little secret agent clamped his hands to his ears to try and shut out the noise.

It was completely dark inside the container but he knew he would have to stay where he was until the men left before he could chance leaving. He settled down on some of the large wrapping sheets piled up on the floor, at least these were warm and comfy. After a few minutes he thought it was time to leave, he didn't want to stay in there any longer. If the men were still there he would just say he had thrown a ball over and thought it might have rolled inside the container so he had gone to have a look for it.

"Yeah that sounds alright, they'll believe that, anyway maybe they'll have gone back in the shop again so I won't have to make an excuse."

Ethan made his way quietly back to the doors of the container, cautiously he pushed the door which minutes earlier had been wide open. The door didn't move, he pushed harder the next time but still the door didn't open, he pushed again as hard as he could but the door refused to move even a fraction. He tried several more times without any success before finally giving up.

"There's got to be a handle somewhere I'll just have to feel around till I find it." He ran his hands all over the door as far as he could reach but no handle could be found.

"Maybe it's at the top, I'll push one of these things over and stand on that."

With the help of something to stand on the little lad managed to reach the full extent of the door but there was no handle to be found inside the container at all, the only way was for someone to open it from the outside.

"I'll have to shout and one of the men will come back and let me out, then I'll tell him about losing my ball and he'll let me go home."

Suddenly there was a loud roar, the wagon driver had started up his engine, Ethan shouted as loud as he could but the noise of the engine was louder, it drowned out any noise coming from inside the container. Ethan was desperate now, why was he revving up the engine so loud. On the outside the shop owner was putting chains onto the four lugs of the container. When he had done this the wagon engine roared even louder as the huge container was slowly lifted off the ground and placed onto the back of the wagon. The little secret agent was shaking with fright. He realised now that he shouldn't have gone in there in the first place, but now he was in there how was he going to get out again, what if nobody came to open the crate. He knew the furniture was going to America but he didn't know where America was, he only knew it must be a long way away. He could be locked in there for weeks if no-one rescued him, he could be left in there to die.

It was completely dark inside and he had brought no food or drink to sustain him, all he had eaten was his boiled egg, toast and a cup of tea. He started to shout again and banged and kicked the big metal doors, still no-one heard him. He banged and banged on the metal door until his hands and feet hurt him, then when he was too sore and exhausted he gave up and slumped down onto the sheets. He hadn't told anyone where he was going and no-one had seen him go into the container. Nobody at all knew where the little secret agent was. He curled up on the floor with the few blankets wrapped around him to keep him warm and sobbed his little heart out.

Chapter 28

Secret agent – missing in action

It had been purely by chance that the body of Anna Ferenc had been discovered at all. A local fisherman had been trying his luck downstream on a private stretch of the water and his line had become entangled under an overhanging tree. The last heavy rainfall had eroded the river bank at that point and exposed the tree roots which were now hanging down into the water, the tree was barely clinging on to solid ground and would certainly collapse into the river with the next flood. The fisherman had waded across the river to free his line and came across the body which was caught up in the roots. The pathologist who examined the body estimated it had been in the river for five or six days. There were no noticeable signs to show how she had died but he would carry out a full post mortem when she was taken back to the Path Lab.

There was nothing further to be done until the pathologist had completed his examination so Bene left the scene and went home. He would have to try and contact the next of kin who would need to be informed about the death, and of course the body would have to be formally identified.

But in all the conversations he had had with people about the girl there had never been mention of any family. In any case it would have to wait until the morning.

It hadn't been a good day for Bene. It had started out with at least the promise of getting a bit nearer the truth as to what had happened up at the residential home, but now the day was almost over and he was still no nearer to finding out. Maybe the post mortem would be able to tell him something but he wasn't too confident of that either. Everything seemed to be conspiring against him, it was someone else who was in control, someone else pulling all the strings, not him.

The rain which had been threatening to come all day suddenly arrived, the sky had been growing ever darker over the past hour and now the heavy clouds began to release the huge volumes of water they had been carrying across the North Atlantic. The Lakeland hills were the first obstacle in their path and as the clouds struggled to rise above them the rainwater poured out drenching everything on the ground below.

A tired and dejected Bene arrived home, at least here he was assured of a nice warm welcome. He drove the car as near to the front door as possible so he could make a quick dash into the house. Alex and Dot must have known he was about to arrive as the front door was open. He ran into the hallway and took off his jacket to shake the rain from it. Alex and Dot were both there to meet him but a quick look at their faces told him that all was not well. It was Dot who spoke. "Bene something terrible has happened."

"Good God, what is it?" He couldn't imagine what was wrong but by the look on their faces it was obvious something serious had happened. And it must have happened in the last few minutes otherwise one of them would have phoned him, and he knew he hadn't missed a call.

"It's little Ethan next door," said Dot, "He hasn't come home. He stayed at his Auntie's last night because Ken and Maggie were away at a wedding yesterday and stayed the night in York. Well, Ethan was supposed to come back this afternoon but he never came."

"I suppose they've checked with his Auntie then?" asked Bene.

"Yes of course but he left there before dinner and she hasn't seen him since. He raced off somewhere and said he might go back to her house if he got finished whatever it was he was going to do, if not he would just go home."

"So what was it he was going to do that was so important?"

"His auntie doesn't know, he never said but he was in a hurry. He had slept quite late and when he got up it seemed as though he was late for something, he gobbled his breakfast down as fast as he could and shot off on his bike."

"Bene they're really worried about him," said Alex "You have to do something." Bene was still trying to take it all in, he hoped he hadn't led the boy on too much knowing that the lad thought he was going to help them solve some cases. But surely that had just been talk, the little lad couldn't have gone out looking for the robbers. He hadn't told him where the robberies had taken place, who they had suspected or where they thought the stolen items could be.

"No I've told him nothing about any of the cases," he thought, "There's no way he could be involved in anything we're working on." He remembered bumping into Ethan the morning before, the lad had told him then he was on a case and would catch the robbers and hand them over to him. But Ethan didn't know anything about the burglaries, how could he? Even though Bene couldn't believe that the little lad knew anything that could get him into trouble he still felt uneasy about it.

"Have they phoned the station do you know?" Bene asked.

"Yes of course" said Dot "about half an hour ago, they rang up Maggie's sister who Ethan was staying with and she told them she hadn't seen him since about eleven o'clock when he rushed off. She wasn't worried because she thought he had just gone home afterwards, she was only half expecting him back at her house anyway but she wasn't surprised when he didn't come back."

"I'll have to go to the station and see what they're doing about it, I'll give ET a ring first in case he hasn't heard."

ET arrived at the station the same time as Bene where they found Chief Inspector Sowerby in the act of organising a search party for the boy. The men had their instructions and were about to leave the station, Bene approached the Chief and told him about the boy's interest in police work and helping them to catch burglars.

"You know the lad then?" the Chief asked as he led the men outside, Bene and ET walked with him.

"Yes he lives next door to Dot's house where I'm living, he sees himself as a bit of a secret agent and he's always telling me that he'll catch all the villains for me, but honestly sir I haven't told him anything about what we're doing or the cases we're working on, I wouldn't be that stupid."

ET chipped in with his little bit of information. "I saw the lad yesterday as well he nearly knocked me over with his bike he was in such a hurry. He told me he was going to help us catch the criminals, or in his words "robbers and murderer's". Well I didn't think much about it at the time it's what lots of lads of his age dream about, they imagine they're policemen and go and act out their little fantasies, I was just the same myself at that age there's no harm in it."

"OK then you two, you'd better join in the search, we need as many men as we can muster for this and we have to move quickly. It's going to be dark pretty soon and if this rain doesn't ease off a bit it's going to make it even more difficult, we've got to find him quickly before it gets too dark. I don't want him spending the night out there in this weather. If he's injured or trapped somewhere he might not survive and one body in the river today is quite enough. I don't think I could cope with another tragedy."

The Chief had given the men their orders and split them up into three groups of twos and threes. It was all the resource he could call upon at such short notice, everything else had to take second place until the boy was found.

"The problem is we've no idea where to look, he didn't tell anyone where he was going or what he was going to do or look for. I've had to spread the men out thinly to cover as much of the town as we can, but we won't be able to cover everywhere, it's possible we could still miss him." The Chief sent Bene and ET back up to the Teasdale's house to see if they could remember anything else about the little boy's plans or where he might have gone.

Ken and Maggie were distraught and Maggie was in such a state that she would be no help to them at all. Dot and Alex had gone round to try and comfort the couple and they stayed with Maggie in the lounge while Bene and ET talked to Ken in the kitchen.

"I've told the police all I know" he said. "I've got a few friends coming round to help me look for him. Ethan was up early yesterday and Maggie and me both laughed about it because he usually stayed in bed until much later on Saturday mornings. He said he was in a hurry and had lots of jobs to do, when I asked him what he said he was going to cut the grass for his auntie. Well he's never been in a rush to do that before so I didn't really believe him but I didn't press him on it, we just laughed it off."

"So you've no idea what his intentions really were for yesterday and today?" asked Bene.

"No I'm afraid not." said Ken the tears starting to well up in his eyes.

"You know what he's like Bene he fantasises a lot and thinks he's a secret agent. Well we know he plays at it but we've never thought there was any danger in it. It kept him occupied and amused and we thought it was just natural, it was his way of expressing himself and living out his dream of becoming the real thing."

"Did he take anything with him?" asked ET. "Not really, it was fine yesterday so he didn't take a coat, I didn't see him with anything else but then I didn't take much notice either, he was in such a rush to get away and we were getting ready to leave ourselves. Him leaving earlier just made it a bit easier for us, one less thing to worry about before we left."

The two detectives left just as Ken's friends were arriving at the house. Bene told them where they'd be able to find the Chief Inspector who would assign them an area where they could help search for the boy. Bene and ET went back into the town centre. The rain continued to pour down and this was going to make the search even more difficult. They went to the area the Chief had allocated them to search and over the next two hours checked out every possible place they came across where the boy could have got lost or trapped in. No trace could be found of the little boy or his bike, if he had been there at any time in the last twenty four hours he was certainly not there now.

Darkness and the driving rain combined to bring the search for the boy to an end for the night. With heavy hearts the policemen and civilians who had volunteered for the search dragged themselves wearily back to the station and then home. Chief Inspector Sowerby ordered the search to be resumed at daybreak the next day and asked the men to report to the station just before dawn to ensure they would be in place to start again as soon as it was light enough.

Bene and ET returned to their respective homes each with their own thoughts on what could have happened to the little boy. The murders, the robberies and everything else had paled into insignificance when put alongside the boy's disappearance. Dot was staying the night with Maggie next door but Alex was at home waiting up for Bene when he arrived home, miserable and soaked to the skin. He fell into her arms and both of them broke down in tears, neither knowing what to do or to say. Bene undressed and had a quick shower, he hadn't eaten since earlier that day but had no appetite for food anyway. He set the alarm for five o'clock, turned out the lights and tried to sleep, neither of them were in the mood for romance that night.

He lay there trying to get off to sleep, but sleep wouldn't come. His mind was full of events and questions which were spinning around in his head like a continually changing kaleidoscope, they formed patterns which he couldn't understand and threw up questions to which he had no answers for. At every turn he was being frustrated, making no progress at all in any of his cases. Instead of making progress the problems just kept piling up and were threatening to engulf him completely. He felt empty inside, utterly devoid of any hope or expectation, worst of all he had that sickening feeling that in some way he was responsible for the little boy's disappearance. He curled himself up into a little ball feeling miserable and sorry for himself. This had been a bad day, the darkest day he could remember.

2

The rain had eased through the night and at five o'clock the sky was still dark but clear, the forecast said dry but with some cloud. Bene rose and went down for breakfast feeling no better for the few hours sleep he had managed to get. At the station the men were again gathered ready to resume the search for Ethan. The Chief was addressing them and preparing them to leave. The strain was showing on the serious faces of the Chief and his men. It had been a bad night for anyone to be out in never mind a little boy. Most of them thought that the search last night would have ended in a good result, but now they feared the worst. It might be a body they were looking for now not a cheerful young lad of tender years.

ET hadn't slept well either he had only seen the lad a couple of times and spoken to him just the once but he had taken a liking to the little fellow. He felt they had formed a sort of friendship which had come through their shared initials ET. The two detectives were asked to extend their search to the estate on the outskirts of the town, maybe for some reason the boy had visited there.

"I suppose he could have gone up there," said ET as they drove up in Bene's car. "He did say he was looking for robbers and murderers, so in his mind they could just as well be up there as anywhere else." They drove into the estate, got out of the car and looked around at all the different buildings.

"OK" said Bene "It's Monday and still early so there won't be anyone starting work just yet, we'll split up and start at opposite ends then we'll work our way back and meet up somewhere in the middle, that OK with you?"

The pair separated and walked to the furthest buildings on each side before making their way slowly back towards each other. The search was thorough and nowhere or nothing was left out, all the buildings that they could look into were checked. The ground around the buildings was also combed through in case the lad had got trapped in some of the tangled undergrowth which lay on the outer fringes of the estate. An hour later they met up again, the search had drawn a blank, there had been no sign of the boy or his bike. ET had a suggestion.

"Most of the estate would be closed yesterday but it's possible one or two of the firms might have been open, and some of them are bound to be open on Saturdays. I think we should track down the owners and see which ones were open, the lad might have gone inside and been accidently locked in."

"Yes that's a good idea ET, I'll go back to the station and get in touch with them, you can stay up here if you like and when the workers start coming in you can search the rest of the buildings and ask around to see if anyone might have seen him up here over the weekend."

Bene got into the car and left the estate. ET looked at his watch it was nearly seven thirty, some of the businesses would be opening shortly so he sat down and prepared to wait. The first of the workers came in and ET stopped and questioned the man, but he could tell him nothing as he hadn't been on the estate since Friday. Shortly afterwards others began drifting in, he didn't have time to speak to all of them, just catching the ones on bikes or who had walked there. At eight thirty most of the buildings were open and it seemed that most if not all the staff were now in their place of work. He would have to go round them individually, speak to the people and check the buildings at the same time.

He had no success at the first two buildings but at the third one he came across the man who had accosted Ethan on Saturday on the estate.

"Is it the young lad you're looking for?" he asked ET.

"Yes we think he might have been up here yesterday or the day before, he's gone missing you see and his parents are beside themselves with worry." The man described the boy to ET and at once he knew it was the right one. The man went on to tell him everything that had happened. ET wanted as much information as he could get and grilled the man thoroughly.

"So he told you he was up here to find stolen furniture, is that right?"

"That's it, and he showed me his little book, Secret Agents Notebook I think it was. He had names and addresses written down in it of shops in the town and some of the firms up here, he said he'd already been in the shops and didn't find anything so he was trying up here." At last ET thought he was getting somewhere.

"So did he stay here or did he leave after you caught him looking in the windows?"

"Oh he left alright I made sure of that, he said he didn't know where to look next, and I told him to leave it all to you fellows. I didn't think anymore about it, I mean he didn't look a bad lad just a bit fanciful I thought."

"And that's the last you saw of him was it, what time did he leave here?" The man thought a moment

"It must have been about three o'clock I think, I was going to head off home myself about then to make the tea."

ET rang Bene from his mobile and repeated everything the man had told him. Bene told him a car would pick him up and bring him back to the station and he would meet him there. Bene immediately phoned the Chief to give him the news.

The Chief had just taken a call from the boy's father who had found the telephone book in Ethan's bedroom, he had read out the shops and businesses that Ethan had marked and these seemed to confirm what the man had seen in Ethan's book. It was now mid morning and the shops in the town were all open. The Chief wanted Bene and ET to go round to the ones on Ethan's list and quiz the staff to see if they could remember seeing the boy in the shops on Saturday. Ethan had been remembered in most of them, a little boy in a furniture shop on his own without an adult would always draw attention to himself. Bene and ET listened to the salesmen who had either seen him or spoken to him. One of them telling them about the boy looking for stolen furniture before being chased out of the shop.

There seemed little else they could do for the moment so they decided to break for lunch. ET wasn't far from his flat so he walked over there to grab a sandwich, pity his girlfriend wasn't working or he could have gone over to the shop to see her. He let himself in and trampled over the mail lying inside the door,

"Not more junk, pity the last fellow didn't put a change of address in at the post office because most of this lot will be for him." He switched on the TV in the lounge then went into the kitchen and made a coffee and a sandwich, he took them through to the lounge and sat down to watch the news. The local news carried a picture of little Ethan and the story of his disappearance, ET went over and switched the TV off.

He hadn't enjoyed his break, the TV had spoiled it. On his way out he bent over and collected all the bits and pieces of mail lying on the floor. Just as he thought most of it was junk mail, but there were two for him, one from the local gym club he had applied for membership for and another from one of the utility companies. Between these two a scrap of notepaper, he pulled it out intending to screw it up but the childish writing and a long line of numbers caught his attention. He straightened it out and read the message.

stolen stuffs in this big metal thing at the back
of little shop with funny window
I got the number for you OSQU4064718 22VH
Jurgen Drenthe

from little ET

Chapter 29

Rebuilding old friendships

Monday morning arrived and the three jubilant investors were due to meet at eleven thirty in the Fox & Pheasant public house. Paul and Sylvia were early and decided to have a pre celebratory drink while they waited for Alastair to arrive. Both were finding it a little difficult without Alastair in the company, when there were three of them it eased the tension between the two old friends. Sylvia had never forgiven Paul for deserting her husband and his best friend Ray when suddenly and without warning he had left Levensbridge earlier that year.

The atmosphere between them was not good and it badly needed to improve if they were going to be partners in a successful business. Paul decided to take the bull by the horns and try to sort out their differences before they deteriorated any further. "This isn't a good start to our partnership Sylvia we have to talk. If we're going to be working together on this deal we need to come to some sort of agreement where we can work together without any bad feelings coming between us and spoiling the success of this scheme." Sylvia remained silent, she wasn't going to forgive him that easily, he had opened up and that was a start but as far as she was concerned it was him who was going to have to apologise and if any concessions were to be made they had to come from him. She was prepared to let him continue and see exactly what he was expecting from her. Paul seemed to understand and took the hint.

"I realise that you blame me for selling up the business and leaving you and Ray behind here to face the music, but let's look at some of the facts. Believe me, if I had any idea that the police knew anything at all about our little scam and were getting ready to pounce and arrest Ray and Karel I would have stayed and helped them get rid of the stuff first. To tell you the truth we'd all made a lot of money out of it and I for one was happy with what I'd got out of it. But all good things come to an end and I decided the time was right for me to pack it in." He took a little breather at this point to try and judge if Sylvia was showing any interest in what he was saying.

She wasn't showing any signs to either encourage or discourage him from continuing, she remained silent. Nevertheless he decided to press on, there were things that had to be said and facts that had to be faced. "I know you're hurting with Ray locked up in prison and I know it could be another year before he's back home again. But look to the future, when we've both made a fortune out of this deal and Ray's back home again you can both look forward to a very comfortable retirement." Sylvia still didn't think it was time to speak she wanted more from him, she looked directly into his eyes and waited.

"Let's face it Sylvia, Ray did get greedy. When I gave over my share of Dunne's to him it was a gift, simple as that. I just wanted to get away from Dunne's and Esk Logistics, and when I got a good offer right out of the blue for Esk I took it as an omen to completely rid myself of everything connected to the business including the Polish scam. The difference was, Ray was happy with being the sole owner of Dunne's and happy to carry on with the scam." Paul paused for a moment to get Sylvia's full attention then shrugged his shoulders and spread his arms out in front of her. "You have to agree with me Sylvia, Ray would never have given it up if he hadn't been caught red handed." Sylvia looked down at the table lifted her glass and took a long slow drink from it.

Paul continued. "Remember all the good years we had together the four of us, we had some great times and both Nicola and me want them to be great again. Can't we put all this behind us and get back to the way we were before this damned Polish venture came along and all but destroyed us. Let's face it we're going to be working closely together over the next few months at least, and if we can get through that then let's get back to when we were the best of friends." He took another pause and in a very serious and sincere voice appealed to her.

"I've meant everything I've said Sylvia and I'm sorry if I've upset you with what I've said about Ray but I've been completely truthful with you. Honestly we've missed the two of you dreadfully, I mean France is a great place but it was very dull without you and Ray there with us. I'd love to go and visit him in prison if he'll agree to see me he's always been my best mate and I'd like to help him in any way I can. Nicola and I both want our friendship with you to continue and we want it to start again right now, if you'll agree of course. If you still feel bitter about it I'm sorry, but believe me I never betrayed Ray or you. I wouldn't hurt either of you, you're the best friends we've ever had and always will be."

Sylvia was in deep thought. She had listened to everything Paul had said, and to her amazement found that she couldn't disagree with any of it. The last time she had visited Ray in prison even he had told her that he didn't lay any of the blame on Paul for his own misfortune. He had admitted the fact that he had become too greedy and couldn't force himself to give it up. Of course Ray and Paul had been best friends since schooldays, Nicola and she had also been good friends. The four of them had had some fantastic times together and if Ray could forgive, then why could she not do the same. Paul had done his bit now it was up to her.

"Well I suppose if we're going to be working together we should at least be civil. Let's start with that and see how it goes eh?" At least she did have a faint smile on her face when facing him so it looked as though it might still be possible to build bridges and re-establish their friendship.

Paul looked at his watch. "It's gone twelve o'clock, where the hell is Alastair he should have been here half an hour ago." They had spent the last forty minutes trying to reassure each other that they were still capable of being good business partners, now it was Alastair who was letting the side down. "We don't want to be hanging around here much longer Sylvia we need to be on our way to Preston to get the copies of the deeds and the maps. I've made us an appointment with the architect for four o'clock, I think we'll give him another ten minutes and if he's not here by then we'll have to go without him."

Ten minutes later and Alastair had still not arrived. "OK" said Paul "Luckily I've only had a couple of glasses of wine so I'll drive us there." The two left the pub and set off for Preston in Paul's car. Using the same car park in Preston they left on foot for the office of Mr Ogilvy. On their arrival there Mr. Ogilvy welcomed them into his office.

"Good to see you both again but where is Mr McKay, was he not coming with you?"

Paul explained that Alastair for whatever reason had failed to meet them at the appointed time so they had come alone.

"That's not a problem" said Mr Ogilvy "I have everything you need here and there's no need for all three of you to be here. The cheques were all in order and the owner has given me instructions to send off the original deeds to the land registry office for change of ownership. I should have them back in about ten days time but the copies will suffice until the originals are returned to me, I'll let you know as soon as I have them. In the meantime the copies will do for the architect to work from and to apply for outline planning permission of course. They're all you'll need to get you through the initial stages of your plans."

Mr. Ogilvy reached into one of the drawers in his desk and brought out a large brown envelope. It was sealed, and without opening it he handed it to Paul.

"I think you'll find everything you need in here, so if you'll excuse me I have another client coming in shortly and I need to prepare a few things before he gets here." Paul and Sylvia took this as a sign that their meeting with Mr Ogilvy was over and rose from their chairs to leave. Goodbyes were exchanged and the two left Mr Ogilvy's office with the envelope still sealed.

They started the journey back to Levensbridge in a happy mood, up until Paul had a sudden thought that worried him. "What about Alastair, what if he's not at the Fox and Pheasant, do you know where he lives?" Sylvia had no idea, the first time she had met him was in the pub, and all their meetings since then had also been there. "Well I've no idea where he lives either I think we'll have to go back and ask Mr Ogilvy he seems to know him quite well." They came off at the next motorway exit and drove back to Preston.

"I don't think we'll get back in time to keep our appointment with the architect Paul, we'll have to make another one with him tomorrow or the day after maybe. It's a pity but we can't do anything without Alastair so it's important that we know where we can get hold of him." It had taken them less than an hour from leaving the office of Mr Ogilvy until their return there. Climbing the stairs up to the office Paul reached for the door handle and turned it. The door didn't open, it was locked, he stood back surprised.

"Well he can't have gone far, I mean he had another appointment and work to do before it so he must be coming back fairly soon, he wouldn't have got all that done in the time we've been away." They waited patiently at the top of the stairs for almost an hour but Mr Ogilvy didn't return. Paul tried the door again but it was definitely locked, he peered in through the partially frosted glass door but could see little. The desk was still there and everything else seemed to be as it had been when they had left earlier.

"It's funny though Sylvia, Mr Ogilvy was on his own when we were here before so where was his secretary, surely she should have been here as well I mean she was here when we came the other day." Sylvia could offer little in the way of explanation.

"No idea, maybe he's given her the day off or maybe she's on holiday, I don't know. Anyway let's get back to Levensbridge I'm sick of waiting around here. When we get back to the pub I expect Alastair will be there and all this will have been a waste of time."

"Yes you're right of course we shouldn't have bothered coming back at all, even if he's not there someone will know where he lives." Sylvia had a thought.

"I can always ask Mr Rawlings, it was him who introduced Alastair to the club so he must know where he lives." With this comforting thought the two resumed their journey back to Levensbridge.

Chapter 30

George gets angry

The morning had not started out with much promise, dark clouds had been hanging ominously over the town for much of the early part of the day. After lunch the sky had brightened up and things were looking much better. Kris took a call from Adam Firth and arranged to go to the bowls club with him for a roll-up. "Not sure how many will turn up," said Adam "But there should be enough for a couple of triples I would think. I'll phone around and try to get a few others to come down with us."

At two thirty Kris left the pub which by now was almost empty, Ebony would chase the remaining punters out and close at three. It would give her a couple of hours before opening again at five o'clock when customers would start coming in for evening meals. Fourteen members turned up for a three o'clock start which made a rink and a triple. Kris and Adam were on different sides in the rink and George Wheeler was playing third for Adam's team. No-one seemed keen on being skip so it was left to Kris and Adam to do the job, it was an opportunity for them to talk in private as they walked up to the far end of the green together.

Adam opened the conversation,

"Good speech you made at the meeting the other night, I think you shook poor old George up a bit. It certainly made him see just how serious this is, and with two of the other owners dying I think you've scared him as well."

Kris laughed "Well it needed to be said, things have been happening here which the members needed to know about. I mean it can't be coincidence that I've been thwarted every time I've tried to get new members in. If you ask me the green keeper's in on it as well, all of a sudden he's best pals with Derek Cooper. Both of them are not only trying to prevent the club from expanding but seem hell bent on getting it closed down altogether."

"Yes" agreed Adam, "Somewhere along the line there's a lot of money involved in this, any idea who's behind it?"

"Well nothing I could prove Adam, but you know as well as I do that Paul Hanbury has been sniffing around and he's been seen in Derek's company a few times recently. He's obviously got a stack of money burning a hole in his pocket so it doesn't take an Einstein to work it out does it."

Play had started and the two skips were giving instructions to their respective teams. When the number threes had bowled they changed ends and went down to deliver the final bowls in that end. Play continued for an hour with the scores fluctuating. The only chance they had of talking to George was on the exchange as they crossed the green. Half an hour later and with only two ends to play Adam caught his attention as they crossed.

"We'd like to have a little chat after the game George if that's OK?" George nodded and when the game finished the three men went back to the men's locker room to change. One or two new members had started to arrive and Kris thought it might be best if thcy left.

"I think we should go back to the pub, that way we can talk more privately."

Kris brought over drinks from the bar and they sat down at a table well away from the other customers, it was still early and only another two tables were occupied. Adam opened up the conversation

"So have you given any more thought to what was said at the meeting George?"

George had given it a lot of thought, what he had heard at the meeting had upset and frightened him.

"I must admit I've been witness to some of the things that Kris talked about at the meeting and heard about most of the others, but I never realised just how bad things had got." Confronted by the two committee members facing him he was feeling rather ashamed of himself. "I'm really sorry fellows I've been guilty of not doing more to protect the club, not only that I've been naive in not recognising the real reason behind it all. Like everyone else I was saddened by the deaths of two of our joint owners but I never thought there was any malice involved. Now I'm looking at it with my eyes wide open and I can see that there is evil at work here. To tell you the honest truth I'm bloody scared."

Adam and Kris could see that George was in danger of breaking down. Adam tried to reassure him by saying there may be a way in which they could find out exactly what was going on behind the scenes. They needed to work together and put some pressure on Derek, if necessary force him to come clean with any plans he might have for pushing through a sale of the club.

"The question is George what are we going to do about it? I think we should tackle both Derek and Ron the green keeper and get them to explain what the hell is going on. If we can get Ron on his own first and get him to admit how deep he's involved in it, he might just crack. He has a lot of explaining to do because what he's been doing is deliberate sabotage and we can just about prove it. With all the evidence Kris came up with at the meeting he would be foolish to deny it. Maybe you could threaten him with the sack, I mean you could do that on your own without Derek's agreement couldn't you?"

"Yes I could," agreed George. "He might think he's bullet proof as he's got so pally with Derek, but I could confront him with the evidence and he wouldn't be able to defend himself against it. He's got a good job with us and if he lost it he'd find it difficult to get another, he might just crack and tell us what Derek's up to."

Just then the door opened and in walked Derek Cooper, Paul Hanbury and Ron the green keeper. They all smiled and acknowledged the three as they passed on their way to the bar.

"Well this might be a chance," said Kris. "It might not be a good idea to tackle Ron while he's in their company but it might be a good idea to approach Derek and see if you can tie him down to a meeting, seeing that he's been so evasive lately." George was less frightened now, as they had been talking the fear was being replaced by anger which had been slowly building up inside him. He would go over to Derek and tell him he needed to speak to him urgently, there were things which couldn't be put off any longer. Derek couldn't very well deny him a meeting not when there were so many others around him.

The newcomers left the bar and sat down at a table on the far side of the room. George took the opportunity and walked over to Derek's table.

"Well you've been a hard man to track down lately Derek, I need to speak to you pretty soon about a private matter, when can we meet?" Derek didn't offer any excuse.

"Well not just now George you can see I'm busy here, but how about you come down to the yard later on we can have a chat about it then." George was surprised but pleased that at last he would get the chance to find out what Derek's plans were.

"Yes that would suit me fine Derek, what time should we say?"

"I'll be here until about seven then I'll have to eat, how about half past eight will that be OK?" The meeting had been arranged and George went back to his two friends.

"Well that was a lot easier than I thought, no trouble at all. I'm seeing him later so if we can all meet here again tomorrow I should have some news for you." The three thought they had at last achieved something, George had got his dander up and hopefully he would be able to bring them some news the next day. Adam and George left together. Kris went back behind the bar to help Ebony who had been giving him some dirty looks, while he had been sitting with his friends she had been left to manage the bar on her own.

George was feeling a lot better on his way home, in a couple of hours he would be meeting Derek and he was not going to accept anything other than the truth from him, if necessary he would badger and bully him to get the answers he wanted. He took his time over dinner and sat down to watch some TV, outside it was starting to get dark. At a quarter past eight he left the house, it was a lot darker now as he drove down to Derek's yard. He hadn't stopped to think why Derek should want to meet him at the yard and not at his house, maybe he had some paperwork to catch up on in his office down there, yes that would be it. He swung the big car into the builders yard and parked it up near the office. It was all in darkness, only a dim light was showing from the office window in the raised port cabin. "Does he always work in such a badly lit place, he'll not get much done in there."

He walked up the steps to the cabin and tried the door handle, but it didn't move, he knocked hard but still there was no response from inside. He gave it one last try but obviously Derek was not in there. He checked his watch and found it was still only twenty five past eight, "Maybe I'm a bit early, I'll hang around for a bit and wait until he comes."

Fifteen minutes later he got fed up waiting and walked back to his car, he was angry now, once again Derek had fobbed him off, how the hell was he ever going to get to speak to the man. As he reached the car a voice suddenly called out, "Over here man, where the hell have you been?" George thought.

"So the bugger is here after all, how come he didn't see me come into the yard or hear me knocking, he must be losing it."

He walked over to where the voice had come from and found himself looking up to the next level where there was a pallet jutting out. "Is that you up there Derek?" he shouted. There was no answer but as he continued to look up it seemed the pallet had moved slightly. "That's odd what on earth is he doing up there at this time of night." He shouted up again. "Come on down then, I can't talk to you when you're up there." Still there was no reply. Held in that position his neck was getting stiff so he bent forward and rubbed it to ease the muscles. It was a big mistake for he didn't see or hear the pallet which had silently moved forward again, it rested precariously on the edge just for a moment before tipping over and spilling out its contents. Heavy objects poured out from the upper floor and poor George had no chance as the wall of bricks crashed down and pummelled him to the ground.

Chapter 31

The number of missing people is rising

The post mortem on Anna Ferenc's body had been carried out and Bene was looking at the results in the presence of the pathologist who had completed the report.

"So in plain English what was the cause of death?" he asked.

"Well the body didn't go into the river where it was eventually found, at a guess I'd say it entered the water much further upstream, possibly somewhere in the town itself. It reminds me of that poor postman we pulled out of the river a few months ago. The body was badly bruised from the battering it must have taken on its way down the river and it wasn't easy at first to see exactly how she had died."

"Yes" said Bene we can imagine all that but was it an accident or was she killed?"

"Oh she was killed alright no doubt about that. Strangled with some sort of ligature, something very strong."

"You mean a rope?" asked Bene.

"No not a rope, more like a piece of strong material, a man's tie maybe or something like that."

Bene left the pathologist with mixed feelings. Up until now all the deaths he was looking into had been classed merely as suspicious, there had been no hard evidence to say that any of them had been murdered. The deaths of the two elderly Germans at the residential home and two of the co-owners at the golf club had been suspicious, that was all. If somehow they had been murdered it was going to be very difficult to prove the case in any one of them.

The two men whose bodies had been exhumed from the woods after sixty odd years in the ground had certainly been shot by someone, but it would never be known exactly when they had been shot or by whom, it was another case which would probably never be solved. Then there was the attempt on ET's life which would have been murder if it had been successful, but it wasn't, so that remains a case of attempted murder only.

But Anna Ferenc had certainly been murdered and that changed everything. Chief Inspector Sowerby was going to be looking for an arrest for her murder and he wouldn't be satisfied with anything less, and he would want someone apprehended for it damned quickly as well. No more robberies had been reported since the one at Paul Hanbury's house and that was the only good news there was. But the priority now was to find the missing boy Ethan, if he could be found safe and well it would go a long way to taking some of the pressure off him and his Chief. He had to remain positive on this, but the fact that the lad had been missing for twenty four hours didn't look good. Bene was worried.

He went home to an empty house for lunch, Dot was still with Maggie next door and Ken was out with some of their friends and neighbours helping in the search for Ethan. Bene was fearful of what might had happened to the little lad he desperately wanted him to be found safe and well. But if it was anyone else, some other boy he didn't personally know then he knew what the outcome was more likely to be. That after twenty four hours it was doubtful that the youngster would be found alive, most likely it would be a body they were looking for.

A sandwich and a cup of coffee was all he could be bothered to make, and that was only because his stomach was beginning to rumble, he sat down and ate and drank in silence. When he had finished he stood up and looked at his face in the mirror, a face which reflected the tremendous strain he was under. He slapped his hands angrily onto the sides of his face and shouted at the image he was looking at. "Oh God if ever I needed help it's now, this is too bloody much, give me a break for Christ's sake."

His mobile rang, it was the Chief. "Bene we've found his bike"

"Where was it?" Bene asked.

"A young lad brought it in, he found it down at the bottom of Regents Lane yesterday and took it home. He said he was going to return it but to be truthful I think he was looking at keeping it himself. Anyway he heard about the missing boy and thought the bike might have been his so it pricked his conscience and he decided to bring it in to us. It's the lad's bike alright his dad's just been in to confirm it."

"Well we searched that area thoroughly last night and we didn't see any sign of him." said Bene.

"I know" said the Chief.

"It's worrying, it looks as though he may have been abducted and that makes the whole thing that much worse. If that's the case then he could be anywhere by now, anywhere in the country, we may never find him."

He ended the call and left the house to return to the station. Chief Inspector Sowerby would have to go public with this now, there was no way it could be kept local. Division were already aware of the boy's disappearance and now it would go national, soon the police forces up and down the country would be on the lookout for the boy. The Chief would have to call a press conference in front of the media and by tomorrow morning the boy's photo would be splashed across the front pages of all the national newspapers. He hadn't the courage or the inclination to go next door to face the boy's parents, a uniformed policeman was already stationed there and he would inform Maggie and Ken that the boy's bike had been found.

He got into his car but found he was physically and mentally unable to operate any of the controls, never mind drive the damned thing. He just sat there rigidly for what seemed like hours but in actual fact was probably only a few minutes. His eyes stared blankly through the windscreen his mind screaming in turmoil. Suddenly he jolted back to the present and to the reality of it all. His normally impassive face screwed up and took on an ugly and contorted look as he smashed his fists down hard repeatedly on the dashboard of the car, he didn't stop until they started to bleed.

"This wasn't the break I wanted," he sobbed

"This only makes it bloody worse, is there no sodding justice in this world. For Christ's sake the lad is just a kid living out his dreams, he doesn't deserve this. Why the hell can't he just walk around the corner and come home."

Finally he calmed down sufficiently for him to drive down to the police station where he found the entrance blocked with reporters and cameramen. He felt like attacking the whole bunch of them. "Bloody vultures hanging around and waiting for the kill." He was so angry when he got out of the car that when his mobile rang again he barely heard it. "Yes what is it?" he snapped. It was ET on the other end. ET explained to Bene about the note which Ethan had posted through his letter box.

"I almost missed it boss, he must have shoved it through sometime on Saturday afternoon or maybe yesterday and it got stuck in between the flaps on the box, it only came through this morning when the postman came. He always makes sure the mail is pushed right through and it must have come through together with his mail.

"So he's given you the number of a container is that it?"

"Looks like it boss, but whether he got caught looking into it or he went inside and got trapped in there I don't know."

"Well that fits in with what the Chief's just told me because they've found his bike which had been left in Regents lane, one of the places we searched last night."

"But we didn't see any bike when we were there." said ET. Bene explained about the bike being taken away earlier and returned that morning to the police station.

"He mentions a shop with a funny window" said Bene "That would be Peter Hoffmann's shop wouldn't it. If the container was at his place yesterday where is it now, we need to get hold of him and find out where he's sent it."

"I wonder" said ET "Do you think Peter Hoffmann is behind those robberies, we didn't really suspect him but it looks that way now doesn't it?" Bene had to agree.

"If the lad's locked up inside that thing he could suffocate, I mean they're airtight those things aren't they. Get in touch with Peter Hoffmann right away and see what he knows about it. I don't care how you do it but you have to find out where that container's going to. If he denies it tell him he'll be on a murder charge if the lad's inside and we don't get to him in time."

Bene had been walking over to the station as he was speaking to ET. Ignoring the crowd around the entrance he pushed them aside and stormed right through into the station, he headed straight for the Chiefs office to give him the news. ET arrived only a minute behind Bene and was right behind him as they approached the office, without waiting for an invitation they marched straight in. The Chief had his Divisional Super at the desk with him and was not best pleased with the intrusion.

"Out you two" he shouted at them, "I'll see you when I'm ready and not before." This was no time for niceties though and Bene and ET stood their ground refusing to move until they had been heard.

"I'm sorry sir but this is too important to put off, we believe we know where the boy could be." The Chief relaxed a little.

"Go on then tell me." "Well we're not sure of course but something has come to light which we think is a definite clue as to what's happened to him." Bene looked at ET and gave him the nod to explain to the two senior officers the note which had been put through his door.

"We think the boy has somehow got trapped in one of these containers and is in transit, probably to a distribution centre somewhere or to one of the ports maybe." ET and Bene looked for a reaction from the two men.

"Right" said the Chief "Get onto it right away, find the shop owner and find out where he's sent the container, then follow it up and get the damned thing opened. I don't know how long anyone can last in one of those things without a supply of fresh air, but if he's been in there for this length of time we probably haven't got much time left in which to find him and get him out." The Chief was already waving them out as he shouted after them.

"I'll get onto whoever controls or records the movement of these things and see if we can find out that way, when I get anything useful I'll phone you. Now get going I don't want to see you back here again until you have that little lad with you." He dismissed them again and immediately picked up the phone to start his own enquiries.

The two detectives dashed out of the station and made straight for Bene's car. Bene took the wheel and as they drove out of the station car park. ET got out his mobile and phoned Peter Hoffmann's shop, the phone rang several times without reply.

"I suppose we should call round there first just in case he's in." said ET. "I'll give his house number a ring while we're on our way there." There was no answer on Peter's house phone either and when they arrived at the small shop a few minutes later they found it locked up securely and there were no lights showing.

"Well there's definitely no-one here" said ET "We'll have to get over to his house in Preston, it shouldn't take us long. Stick that blue lamp on the roof and we'll be there in half an hour." The two left Levensbridge and sped off down the motorway to Preston. ET was pleased he wasn't going there on his own, the memory of his last visit and his lucky escape from Peter's wife was still very fresh in his mind.

Their arrival at the house met with the same result as the shop in Levensbridge. No answer at the door and no sign that there was anyone in the house. The neighbours were questioned but none of them had seen the couple at all over the weekend.

"Maybe they've gone away for a few days," one of them suggested, "Although they don't seem to do that very often I must admit." she added "They live pretty much separate lives if you ask me, they don't seem to do much together. It's a pity because they don't have any family that I know of, well I've never seen anyone visiting them anyway. Very private they are, not unfriendly you understand but a good morning or a remark about the weather is about all you'll get out of them, not what you would call real conversation. But then they're no trouble so I can't complain."

The two men left the house and returned to the car, they were just getting into it when the woman called them over again. "I've just remembered something, when I said they didn't have any visitors I was wrong. I did see a chap here a couple of times recently I'd almost forgotten about him."

"Who was it do you know?" asked Bene

"No I've no idea but the first time I saw him was about two or three weeks ago, then he came back again last week, I saw him go into the house but didn't notice him leaving. I'm not nosey you know I just happened to be cleaning the front window when he came to the house, when I'd finished the cleaning I went back into the kitchen and forgot all about him."

Then she smiled at ET "Then of course you were here yourself a few days ago weren't you, you didn't stop long after her husband left though." she laughed. "Give you a bit of a fright did she, If you ask me I think she had her sights set firmly on you, you had a lucky escape you did." The woman was clearly enjoying herself as she watched ET's face which was starting to blush.

The woman couldn't give a good description of the man as she hadn't seen his face, she could only tell them that although it was a warm day the man was of average size and wore a coat and a trilby style hat. They took their leave and went to the address of Peter's shop in the town. Here again the shop was locked up and clearly no-one was inside. The only other alternative was Peter's wife's shop. They got the address and found it tucked away in a narrow street not too distant from the main shopping area. As with the other premises this was also closed. Enquiries at neighbouring shops brought no news either, as to where the owner was or when she was likely to be back again. They decided it would be fruitless to remain in Preston much longer, clearly they were not going to find out where either of the couple were so there was little else they could do if they stayed.

Then Bene had an idea "Peter won't be the only antique dealer in a place this size there must be others as well, maybe one of them can throw some light on where he is." Further enquiries took them to another and much larger shop in the town centre. Here the proprietor was at least able to give them some information.

"Well I do know the fellow of course and we do a little business together occasionally, but I can't tell you where he is I've no idea at all about his private life. We don't tend to keep in touch you understand, we're not friends as such, we have a business arrangement and we keep it at that."

"We believe he may ship some of his stock out of the country have you any idea if he has any customers abroad?" The proprietor smiled at Bene

"As a matter of fact he does, he has a few collectors over in the States. He buys odd pieces from me and from some of my colleagues as well, he sends them over there when he has sufficient to fill a container. I think that's where most of his business is done." Bene was trying to seek some clarity over this.

"The States then, is that where you think most of his items are heading, he doesn't send containers anywhere else that you know of?" The proprietor thought about this but shook his head

"No, it's just the States as far as I know, that's where the money is, he wouldn't be interested in sending it anywhere else I'm sure of that."

Bene thanked the man and the two detectives left the shop and went back to the car. Bene phoned the Chief and told him the likely destination of the container. The Chief had also been able to find out a few details about it.

"The number of the container registers alright and we know it's a standard size for transit by wagon, rail or ship. Also a bit of good news, the fact that the V in the 22-VH that comes after the number means the container is ventilated."

"Wow, that's a relief then" said Bene. "Let's just hope we can find the container and he's in it."

The two men were on their way back to Levensbridge when Bene's mobile rang again. Again it was the Chief who was calling.

"Where are you now Bene?"

"On our way back from Preston, we're about half way." was his reply. The Chief had instructions for them.

"Right turn around as soon as you can and get yourselves over to Liverpool docks, that container is due to leave on a boat for America, it arrived there on Sunday and will be stacked along with the others. I've phoned ahead and they're expecting you."

The news was the first piece of good news they had had so far, as long as Ethan was in the container everything would turn out well. Feeling a whole lot better the two detectives drove over to Liverpool and reported to the official in charge of the cargo operation for that vessel. "You the guy's looking for this container are you?" said the official. He was a rather short stout fellow with a strong scouse accent, not well dressed but he had the air of being respected and probably feared by his team of dock workers.

"OK," said Bene "So which one is it?" asking in such a way to which he fully expected the man to point over in one direction or another and say "That's it over there." He should have known it wouldn't be that easy.

Although all credit to the man he did spread out him arms in the direction of the dock forecourt and told him.

"That's the shipment over there, your container will be somewhere among that lot." This was not the answer Bene wanted as he looked over to where a stack of containers were sitting.

"Well it's a relief the ship's not been loaded yet, when does it sail?"

"It's not due to leave for a couple of days yet, my lads will be starting to load it tomorrow. The ship's captain and crew won't be here until later tomorrow night and the master won't let it go until he's checked with the captain that all the papers are in order."

"Oh well" said Bene "As long as we can get cracking it shouldn't take us long to find it. Can we make a start?" he asked the official.

"I'll have one of my men take you over, he'll show you how far the line of containers stretch along the dock, but you must be finished before midnight tomorrow, the captain won't wait any longer for you.

The ship's got a timetable to keep to and if he's late it costs him a lot of money."

Bene laughed "I don't think that will happen there can't be that many containers to go on." The official was unimpressed

"You think not then, you think these ships sail all over the world with just a few dozen containers on, they wouldn't make much money out of it if they did that my friend."

"Go on then, how many are we talking about?"

"Well," said the man "I'll give you the bad news first shall I, the largest of the new fleet will carry over sixteen thousand of these on each trip." Bene gasped, he had no idea that there were ships big enough to carry such a huge amount of containers.

"And the good news?" he asked in a much quieter voice.

"The good news my friend is that this one has nowhere near as many on it, eight thousand four hundred and twenty at the moment but we could get another hundred or so in today so it will be nearer to nine thousand when it's ready to leave. The line of containers we're talking about stretches a quarter of a mile down the dock, I think you'd better be making a start, don't you?" This was going to be a much bigger job that the two detectives had even dreamt about.

"I'm phoning Sowerby, we need a lot more men for this."

"By the way" said the official "They're stacked up to four high you know, you'll need help from us as well. I'll get someone to move them for you so you can check out the ID's on them."

Chapter 32

A visit to the architect

Paul was making a phone call to Sylvia. It had been twenty four hours since they had taken possession of the copies of the deeds and maps to their new acquisition and Paul was surprised that Alastair hadn't contacted them.

"I'll see you down at the coffee shop Sylvia and we'll find out where he lives or where he's staying. Failing that I think you should go and see Andrew Rawlings, he must have an address for him."

Sylvia wasn't too worried, if Alastair wanted to leave all the planning to them that was OK. Paul and her had decided that they could utilise the land a lot better without his involvement, there was more money to be made from having more link houses on the site. Detached houses with large gardens were fine but the large gardens Alastair had been talking about would mean lots of land being taken up which could be put to much better use for building more houses on, they could still have gardens, but smaller ones.

The two met as arranged, and over coffee started to prepare for an initial meeting with a local architect.

"I don't know if you have anyone in mind Sylvia, if not I can recommend someone I'm already using for another little venture I'm in the course of developing." Sylvia was aware there were at least two or three architects in the town but had no experience of any of them. "Who is it you're using then?" she asked.

"A fellow called Stuart McKendrick, he has an office in Micklegate, he's been here for about five years and I've found him very helpful."

"OK if you think he's alright we'll use him, it doesn't matter to me who we use. What's this other bit of business you're working on with him, is it as big as this?"

"No nowhere near as big as this and it's nowhere near finalised either, it's still in the early stages. Things have been progressing quite well but there's still one obstacle in the way and we may have to wait until that's been resolved before we can press ahead with it."

Thankfully for Paul, Sylvia didn't seem too interested in his other venture, and anyway he didn't want to have to discuss it with anyone else, it was much too sensitive.

"So have you arranged a time with this fellow?" She asked.

"Well I had an appointment with him yesterday about another matter and he said we could call in and see him sometime today. He wouldn't be able to do anything about it right away because he's much too busy. He said we could drop off the map and he would have a look at it later in the day if he had time, then we could arrange a proper meeting with him to discuss the plans in a bit more detail."

"Well that's a start then," said Sylvia, "I suppose these things take time and if he's as good as you say he is, it'll be well worth waiting until he's had a good look at it first. We need to emphasise the fact that he needs to maximise the number of houses that can be built on it. This is a much better opportunity than those other schemes we were involved in, this one's legal and completely above board. It's the big chance we've been waiting for to make a killing, and if it all goes well Ray and me intend to pack up work altogether and have a very comfortable retirement."

The two finished off their coffees and left for the office of Stuart McKendrick. It was only a short walk to the office in Micklegate and barely five minutes had passed before they arrived there. Paul knocked on the glass fronted door and they went straight in. Sylvia was impressed, the office was buzzing with activity. Stuart had two other men working with him and three girls who all appeared to be busy either on the phone or working on their computers. None of the girls as much as glanced over in their direction, seemingly unaware of their presence in the office.

A smart young man of about thirty in grey slacks and open necked white shirt with a slight check came over to them hand outstretched in welcome. He had a broad grin on his well tanned face and spectacles hung down on a rope from his neck. His hair was more silver than grey and kept falling forward over his forehead covering his eyes, he was continually sweeping it back with his hand. His build was slim and wiry as a result of his favourite weekend pastime rock climbing in the local hills.

"Good to see you again Paul, no progress yet on the matter we were talking about yesterday?"

"No, not just yet but I'm expecting some news shortly which will speed things up a bit. But anyway let me introduce you, this is Sylvia my partner in the other enterprise I mentioned yesterday." Sylvia took the hand offered by Stuart and shook it warmly.

"As you can see Paul we're extremely busy and I've another client to see in an hour's time. Do you want to leave your bits and pieces with me and I'll have a look at them later, although to be honest with you it's more likely to be tomorrow." He looked quizzically at Paul who looked in turn at Sylvia to see if that arrangement suited her. She had taken a liking to Stuart who she thought was not only a very pleasant man but also gave the impression of a first class professional as well, he seemed to have plenty of clients and the office was certainly busy.

"Yes" she thought, "This guy's good." She smiled at Paul and then Stuart. "Yes I'm happy with that, as long as when you've had a good look at them we can arrange a proper meeting soon afterwards. We'd both like to get things moving along as quickly as possible, can we agree on that?" Stuart smiled back.

"Yes of course Sylvia, give me a day or two and I'll get back to you with a meeting hopefully before the end of the week, is that OK with you both?" Paul and Sylvia were both happy to leave it at that for the time being.

The three exchanged goodbyes and Paul and Sylvia left the office.

"I like that fellow Paul I feel confident in him I think he'll do a good job for us."

"Yes" agreed Paul "I think we're lucky to have him, he certainly knows what he's doing and I'm sure we're in good hands. I wonder where on earth Alastair is we'd better start asking around, it's odd that he hasn't been in touch, I mean he's got a lot of money invested in this, I hope he's not ill or had an accident of some kind."

Much to the contrary Alastair was in perfect health. His wife came into the lounge with tea and cakes on a tray.

"Only tea my dear?" said Alastair "I thought champagne would be in order today."

"Not at this time of day surely, that can wait until tonight."

"Ah yes tonight," said Alastair "Donald's coming over with Grace isn't he and we're going down to the Midland to celebrate." Although the town was a little run down there were still some nice places in Morecambe where you could enjoy a good meal with first class evening entertainment. Alastair was looking forward to it.

Chapter 33

A severe bout of amnesia

George Wheeler woke up but was still half dazed, his tired eyes slowly taking in the unfamiliar surroundings he found himself in. It was a place he couldn't remember ever being in before. The walls were white and everything else in the room also looked white. He tried hard to think, but no, he was sure he had never been in this room before. But then why was he here, he didn't live here did he. His mind was struggling with the problem and the problem was he couldn't remember where he did live, maybe he did live here, maybe this was his home after all. He didn't care much for the decor of the place, if it was his home then he would have to see about getting the decorators in, he couldn't live here with all this white. And why have all these bright lights, they were hurting his eyes, he would have to have them changed as well. His mind gave up, his eyes closed and he slipped back into a comatose state.

When he awoke a few hours later he found nothing much had changed, except now it was not only his eyes which were hurting it was his whole body, he had pains in his head, in both arms and legs and his stomach felt sore as well. “What’s happened to me?” he thought. He couldn’t remember doing anything to warrant the pains he was feeling. “Was I drunk maybe, yes that would be it, I got drunk and fell down the stairs and that’s what it’s all about. I’ll ask ....” He was thinking he would ask his wife, but he couldn’t remember her name, “Oh, maybe I’m not married I can’t remember getting married anyway, Ah well never mind I’ll sort it all out tomorrow, I’ll go back to sleep again and then the pains will go.”

Kris picked up the phone in the bar of the Fox and Pheasant and was at first puzzled by the voice on the other end of the line, a voice he barely recognised, it took a little while before he realised it was Adam Firth who was speaking to him.

“Adam is that you, calm down a bit mate I can hardly make out what you’re trying to tell me.” Eventually Adam told him about George Wheeler being taken into hospital after some sort of accident in Derek Cooper’s yard.

“I don’t know any details yet but he did say he was meeting Derek last night and was going to get some answers from him.”

“Yes I know that,” said Kris “But why was he in Derek’s yard, surely he would have arranged to meet him at his house not in the yard, unless Derek was working late of course.”

“I know” said Adam “but there it is, he’s in hospital and lucky to be alive by all accounts. His wife’s been down to see him but she said he’s been unconscious most of the time. Some of his injuries are pretty bad so it’s probably best he stays that way for a while. It appears a pallet of bricks fell on top of him and ...." he left the sentence unfinished.

"Do you think we should go and see him Adam?" Adam couldn't see why not.

"Well his wife said she wouldn't mind, it would give her a bit of a break because they've no family to speak of, no-one close anyway. If he does come round when we're there he might be able to tell us something. I mean a pallet of bricks just doesn't fall like that they would have to be pushed over. It looks to me as if all our fears are coming true, if we lose George that's our last hope of saving the club from being sold for development, and I for one don't fancy joining that other damned club it's much too bloody snobbish for me."

The two met at the pub and went to the local hospital to see their friend. George's wife was pleased to see them and asked if they could stay a couple of hours or so just to give her time to go home and freshen up. They pulled up two chairs one on either side of George's bed and waited hopefully for George to regain consciousness. They hadn't been there long when the nurse came in to check on him.

"What do you think nurse." Kris asked. "How bad are his injuries?" The nurse didn't take her eyes off her patient but answered him without seeming to acknowledge him or his question.

"He should be OK, he's a strong fellow physically and he seems to have looked after himself. But he was very lucky that most of the bricks appear to have landed on his body and limbs and not his head. He must have reacted quickly when he realised what was happening and brought his arms up to protect his head, doing that probably saved his life."

"So do you think he'll recover alright then?" "The nurse adjusted the drip and checked the monitor beside the bed.

"Physically I'd say he should be OK, but he's going to find he's in quite a bit of pain for the next week or so. He does have a few bruises around the head and we won't know if there's any damage there until he regains consciousness, we'll just have to wait and see." It didn't look as if there was anything else she wanted to add and after watching the monitor carefully for a few moments she left the room.

Adam and Kris remained by the bedside for another two hours quietly discussing the possible causes of how George's visit to Derek Cooper's yard could have led to his accident. Did Derek, or Paul, or the two of them acting together have something to do with it. Was the land the club was on so valuable that they would go so far as to murder for it. Both men were shaken by the thought.

With just the three of them in the room and only two who could converse Adam leaned over the bed and spoke quietly to Kris.

"A month or so ago we had four seemingly very happy owners. Now one accident I can believe and two is stretching it a bit, but three, no way, the odds on that happening in such a short space of time is far too great. This has all been planned I'm sure of it. I'm going to the police with it and put the facts to them, they can't dismiss it they'll have to investigate. And when they do they'll have to investigate all the deaths whether it turns out they were just accidents or not, but they'll have to look into them."

George's wife returned and the two men left, during their time with George there had been no change in his condition. Kris was going to be busy in the pub that night but Adam said he would come back for an hour or so later and give her another break. She was glad of his offer and thanked him for it.

"Well you never know Kris he might come round sooner rather than later, and if possible I'd like to be there when he does."

"Yes, sorry I can't come back myself but it's going to be busy tonight and I can't keep leaving Ebony on her own. She'll be busy in the kitchen for most of the night, the barmaid's good but she'll still need some help behind the bar, it's not fair on either of them if I'm not there." "Don't worry Kris if there's any change I'll phone you, I'll only be there a couple of hours myself so it's more than likely nothing will happen anyway, you get off back to the pub and make yourself useful."

Adam left it late to return to the hospital, if George's wife was going to stay with him through the night then she needed to get a little sleep herself. He went back just after seven o'clock and told her not to come back until midnight, if there was any change he would phone her straight away. Pulling up the two chairs he made himself comfortable on one and placed the other where he could rest his legs. He had brought a book to read and some Sudoku puzzles to keep him awake and occupied, he settled down prepared for a long wait.

He looked over occasionally to check if there were any signs of movement or change in George's breathing pattern but over the next four hours nothing altered at all. He was well into his last hour of patient watching when suddenly a grunt from the bed drew his attention. George had started to make deep guttural noises in his throat. Adam put down his book and watched as first his eyelids moved slightly and then began to flicker wildly. George was beginning to come out of his inert state and return to consciousness.

Adam went to the door and attracted the attention of the night nurse on duty at the base outside. She came in and looked at the monitor, the red LED numbers were changing constantly and she immediately rang for a doctor. At that moment George opened his eyes and looked at the two people standing over him.

"What the hell are you two doing in my house" he mouthed gruffly. "You're not burglars are you?" He then looked intently at the nurse and said "Are you my wife, I don't recognise you what's your name, and who's that with you I've never seen him before either. I think I'd like you both to leave, I'm a bit tired you know I need my sleep." With that he closed his eyes and returned to his previous quiet and relaxed state.

The doctor arrived and adjusted the settings on the monitor and altered the drip. He looked at Adam and smiled. "Don't worry if he didn't seem normal to you, it's the medication he's on. We have to keep him on a high level to lessen the pain from his injuries. We'll reduce it a bit at a time as his wounds begin to heal and in a few days he'll be able to come off it altogether, but until then you'll just have to be patient."

"And his memory, will that come back as well?" asked Adam.

"That's something I can't tell you, certainly some of it will return but whether it all comes back depends. There may be parts of it that he would not want to remember. If he's had a bad experience and subconsciously wants to wipe it from his memory then his brain will protect him and prevent it from coming back."

Adam waited until George's wife arrived and told her of George's short spell of waking. He added that it looked as though he had a temporary loss of memory which would come back in time, also the effects the medication was having on him and what she might expect when he came to again. With that he left her at her husband's bedside and went home, no wiser at all as to what had happened to his friend.

"At least he's safe in there, no-one is going to take a chance of harming him while he's in hospital, I think it's best if he stays in there as long as possible." Even so, as he drove back home he didn't feel fully confident, he still had an uneasy feeling about it. The slight doubt he was harbouring at the back of his mind was going to prove well founded, for someone at that very moment was also thinking about George in hospital, someone with evil thoughts. Someone who cared nothing about George's well being only the rewards that would be his if George were not to survive his stay in hospital.

Chapter 34

A cry for help

Twelve more officers had been drafted in from the Liverpool police force to help in the search for Ethan Teasdale. The task had all the hallmarks of being a long and arduous one, many of the containers were stacked so close together that the identification numbers couldn't be seen. The dock workers were helping with this problem by using the large mobile cranes to move the containers aside just far enough for the police to check the ID's on them. Although the container was known to be somewhere in among the thousands stacked along the dock side there was no order to which they were stacked, the one they wanted could be anywhere.

Bene was working alongside ET "I hope this isn't another wild goose chase, I don't think I could stand it if we found the right container and the boy wasn't inside it. The only clue we have as to where he could be is the number he wrote down and put through your door."

"I know," said ET "I just hope he got the number right, I mean he might be bright in some ways but his written English isn't too good is it. What are the chances he got the numbers mixed up or missed one off like he does with his written English, if only one number is wrong or missing we'd never find the right container, there must be millions of them up and down the country."

This scenario was just too horrifying to even contemplate so it was quickly dismissed from their minds. The search continued with more fervour than ever. It was starting to get dark now and they were barely a quarter of the way through the huge stack of containers. The foreman approached them.

"I've been given authority to bring in some extra staff by the gaffer, some of them are paid staff but most are volunteers who have heard about the little fellow and are keen to give up their time to come and help look for him. I'll have extra lighting put up as well which will help when it becomes really dark. The problem is the time, it's cold in those things and if he has to spend another night in there it might just be too much for him."

The search intensified with the men working as quietly as possible in case the boy could be heard calling out for help, the only sounds were those of the huge cranes which were constantly moving the containers around. Bene and ET were getting worried, they now had an army of paid men and volunteers all working furiously to find the elusive container.

Finally just after two o'clock in the morning a loud shout from one of the dock workers brought everything to a standstill, the container had been found. Bene, ET and the rest of the men ran over to where the call had come from and looked expectantly at the worker who had revealed it.

"Up there lads, the third one up on that stack there." The dock foreman waved over one of the cranes and as it lumbered down the dockside towards the stack of containers the crowd of men gathered around waiting anxiously for it to arrive. An ambulance drew up alongside and two uniformed men stepped out from the vehicle and joined the waiting crowd.

The crane driver manoeuvred the machine into a position where he was able to lift off the top container and place it on the ground. Then he locked onto the container which was the one everyone was interested in and brought it down to ground level. The foreman arrived with cutters to break the seal and unlock the large swing doors, only one of the doors was opened but it was sufficient for light from the portable light tower to illuminate the inside of the container.

No noise came from the inside and no young boy came running out, had this been another kick in the teeth for the two detectives. The men stood back silently and waited for the two detectives to enter the huge container. Bene went in first and could see at once that it was filled almost to capacity. There was a narrow gap which he could squeeze through between the furniture and he forced himself to go in as far as he could. He shone his torch along to the furthest point where he could see right to the end but there was no sign of the boy at all.

ET followed Bene in but remained at the front of the container waiting for news from his boss. Bene had nothing to report, he had not seen or found any sign of the boy and his face couldn't disguise his huge disappointment. ET turned to leave and in his frustration inadvertently kicked the loose wrappers which were piled on the floor just inside the door which was closed. His foot stubbed against a hard object and a cry of pain came from inside the wrappers. ET quickly pulled them away and uncovered the little boy who was curled up in a ball underneath. He picked him up and held him close to his chest, the frightened little boy clung onto him tightly, sobbing quietly.

The three came out from the container to huge cheers from the crowd who were overcome with relief that the boy had been found alive. The little lad wouldn't let go his grip on ET and clung to him all the way to the ambulance where he was taken in by the crew. He insisted ET came with him in the ambulance, so after looking for permission from his boss ET climbed into the back of the vehicle, closed the doors and went off to the hospital with the little secret agent.

Bene thanked the extra police who had been drafted in to help with the search and also the foreman of the dock workers. He then turned to all the volunteers who had worked diligently through most of the night until the boy had been found and thanked them all generously. He rang Chief Inspector Sowerby to give him the good news and was relieved when the Chief assured him that the boy's parents were already on their way to Liverpool and would be told their son had been found safe and well, they would soon be reunited with their young adventurer.

There was nothing else to do that night so Bene walked back to his car and settled into the driving seat. All the mobile lighting had been switched off and the place was in semi darkness. Bene placed his still bruised hands on the steering wheel and rested his weary head upon them. At last he could relax and release some of the pent up emotion that had built up inside him. The tears flowed copiously down both cheeks and through his fingers as he sobbed uncontrollably. Not with anger this time but with a mixture of joy and sheer relief that at last something had gone right for him. It had resulted in a happy ending for Ethan, his parents and family and almost everyone in the town of Levensbridge.

Chapter 35

Back to reality

After only a few hours sleep Bene walked back into Levensbridge police station to find ET had just beaten him in. The atmosphere in there was much more relaxed now that the search for Ethan had ended successfully, and without any harm or lasting injury to the boy. The staff were all smiling and busy congratulating themselves on a good result.

Bene got the call from the Chief and went in to see him. Even he looked years younger, much of the strain he had been under over the last few days had all but gone.

"That's a relief I can tell you, and thank God all those media folk have gone I couldn't have kept them at bay for much longer. It's a good result Bene and it's one that could have ended a whole lot worse than it did. A good job your colleague found that note. If the postman hadn't called at his place yesterday and pushed the lad's note through his letter box it could have been stuck in there for days, and that could have meant the difference between finding him alive or dead. Thank the Lord we got lucky for once."

Bene allowed himself a little smile but knew that this short happy interlude would not last too long. There was still a lot of work waiting for him on his return to the station. All the cases he had been working on before the search for Ethan had taken priority now needed his urgent attention.

The Chief was thinking along exactly the same lines. "So with that little episode behind us you can go back and concentrate your efforts on finding out who killed that girl from the residential home. We need that cleared up quickly Bene, I know there've been a few suspicious deaths in the town recently but without any concrete evidence to prove otherwise that's all they are. But Anna Ferenc that's different, she was murdered alright no doubt about it, and in her case we badly need an arrest. And don't forget the attack on your colleague either, we have to get to the bottom of that one as well. I don't have to tell you that there's not much doubt the two crimes are linked."

Bene and ET left the station and worked tirelessly during the rest of the day trying to find something that would give them a breakthrough into the death of Anna Ferenc. Another visit to the home and Mrs Janes only resulted in idle speculation from some of her staff. It appeared that Anna had not been quite as popular as first thought. She had been a good worker and cheerful enough but had not made any firm friendships during her stay there. Anna had always kept herself a little remote from the rest of the staff and some of the girls were a little wary of her. She had been interested and would listen to them talking about their personal lives, but gave little away about her own.

The girls had found her chatty enough, but even so Anna never talked about her private life. When asked about her they were surprised how little they actually knew about the girl. No-one seemed to know where she came from originally or what she did when she wasn't at work, neither did they know if she had any family or close friends for she never talked about any. She had seemed like a very normal girl to them at the time, but when they looked back they realised she had been more like a stranger amongst them.

There was nothing more to keep them at the home so they left Mrs Janes and her staff and drove down into the town to the house where Anna had been renting a room. Mrs Bowes came down this time to let them in, her manner was a lot more subdued than on their previous visit there. "That poor girl, I heard what happened to her but I still can't believe it. I keep expecting her to walk back in through the door telling me what a good holiday she's had. I haven't had the heart to go up to her room yet, it's still just as she left it. I suppose I'll have to clear it out soon so I can let it out again but I can't bring myself to do it just yet."

Anna had obviously been a good tenant and even though she didn't seem to have any real friends where she worked she had certainly been on good terms with her landlady. Mrs Bowes was concerned about Anna's family and what to do with the items she had left behind. "I know there can't be much left in the room, I mean she never had a lot of clothes, I think she took most of them with her when she left. Have you been able to find any of her family, I'd like to send Anna's things to them if you can give me an address."

Bene told her he would give her the address when they had traced her next of kin, at the moment they were still trying to find them. "Have you thought of anything else that might help us track down the couple who came for her the day she left for her holiday. Is there anything else you remember about them, any detail however small could be helpful?" Mrs Bowes thought hard but there was nothing she could add to what she had already told them on their first visit. It was proving to be very difficult to unearth any personal information on Anna Ferenc. Everyone knew a little something about the girl but she had been careful not to give anything away about her personal life or family history.

The two men went back to the station where Bene was told by the desk sergeant he had a visitor waiting in the interview room. He grabbed a coffee first then opened the door to find Paul Hanbury waiting there. Paul immediately jumped up and it was clear he was in no mood to be fobbed off with excuses, he was irate and it showed in his face and his raised voice. "Right Bene lad you've found that young boy now so that's finished with, so what the hell are you doing about the robbery up at our place. I've not seen any of your lot around and I need that desk back, like yesterday. I told you it's important to me it has business papers and contracts in it that could cost me thousands if they end up in the wrong hands."

Bene tried to calm him down. "We're working hard on it Paul I can assure you of that, and of course you're right, now that the search for the boy has finished we can get back to looking for whoever stole your desk. There's not been any more burglaries since then and we think it's been a one off, when I say one off I mean your house and the one next door. We've got one or two leads to follow up on and have checked all the CCTV cameras. We've narrowed it down to an area where we are looking but obviously I can't tell you where that is. But I don't think it will be long before we arrest someone and I'm pretty sure we'll have it all sorted in a day or two. In the meantime just try to be patient and I give you my word it won't be long before we've got it back for you."

Paul wasn't entirely happy with what he had heard, he felt Bene was trying to over elaborate the efforts he was making in tracking down his stolen desk. But of course he couldn't prove it and had to accept what Bene had told him at face value. Bene continued.

"In fact the container we found the little boy in was full of furniture which had all come from Levensbridge, we had all the contents checked out but it was all legitimate stuff. It was all antique furniture for export to America, but neither your desk or the stolen furniture from your next door neighbour was in there."

Paul had relaxed a little and calmly re-iterated his initial offer to Bene that he would be reimbursed generously if he were to return the desk to him complete with all the contents intact. Bene waved this offer aside.

"I'll pretend I didn't hear that Paul, you go off home and leave it to us, believe me we'll get it back for you, just give us another day or two." With that he stood up and opened the door as an indication the interview was over. Paul looked directly into Bene's eyes and waved his finger as he passed on the way out.

"You just make sure you do that Bene."

Bene returned to his desk and was told by Val to phone Dot. "Yes Dot, what's wrong?"

"Well I don't know about you but nothing's wrong here. I just wanted to say that Ken and Maggie are throwing a bit of a party next door tonight and they want us all to go round, can you get away on time for once?" Bene smiled

"Yes I should be able to I have a few phone calls to make first but I'm sure I can make it, what time do they want us there?"

"Well it won't be late, about six I would think, it's a welcome home party for Ethan so they don't want to keep him up too late. They didn't get him back home until six this morning, they had to wait until he'd been checked over at the hospital first and the little lad's slept most of the day since."

"I'll look forward to it then I should be back in an hour or so." Dot suddenly butted in

"Is your colleague ET with you?"

"Yes he's still here" Bene glanced over at ET who had looked up when he realised they were talking about him.

"Ethan is insistent that he comes as well, he's the lad's new hero now, not you. Tell him to bring his new girlfriend along as well, what's her name, Sue isn't it?"

"Yes I'll tell him." With that he replaced the receiver.

ET was waiting to hear what it was all about.

"Looks like you're the flavour of the month mate, there's a party next door tonight and you're the one everyone wants to be there. The little secret agent has insisted you must be there and you're to bring Sue along with you as well. You'd better get on the phone to her and arrange it right away, and remember this isn't a request it's an order."

ET picked up his phone and called the cafe to speak to his girlfriend Sue. Two minutes later the invitation had been accepted and both were looking forward to the party. "Before you go," said Bene "I want you to phone the hospital in Cheshire where Anna had been employed before she came to Greenacres. Try and speak to someone who remembers her and see what you can find out."

"OK boss, and if there's no-one on duty who remembers her, what then?"

"Then try again first thing in the morning, we have to find out a lot more about her than what little we know so far. Somewhere along the line she must have been close to somebody, built up some sort of relationship, or at least confided in someone."

Bene rang Mrs Janes and asked her to give him the details on Anna's file, he remembered that she had been born in London but couldn't remember exactly where or the date she was born. Mrs Janes read out the details.

"St James Hospital, Camden Town, London and the date was 15th May 1985." Bene jotted it down on a post it note and handed it to the civilian admin girl.

"Can I leave this with you Val, I need a copy of her birth certificate so we can trace any family members she may have."

Val was pleased to be given something to do that didn't just involve typing or answering the phone she would start on it right away. She looked up at the clock

"It might be too late for the records office they're probably closed for the day but I'll give them a try. It's more likely I'll have to leave it until tomorrow and catch them during office hours."

"OK, let me have it as soon as you can. As far as I know no next of kin has been found yet but if she did have someone out there we need to inform them of her death as soon as possible."

It didn't look as if there was anything else to do so Bene told ET to get off home, he could meet him at Dot's house at six o'clock. Both men had put in a full day's work after only a few hours sleep the night before and they needed a good night's sleep tonight to make sure their minds were fresh and alert the next morning. Bene was pleased that the party was an early one for he could see himself being in bed long before midnight.

At six o'clock on the dot ET arrived with Sue and together the five of them went next door to be welcomed by a very joyful Ken and Maggie. It wasn't a big party there were only family members and a few close friends invited, Bene estimated there were no more than twenty people there altogether. Maggie grabbed ET by the hand and took him through to the conservatory at the back of the house where most of the guests were gathered.

"Look who's here Ethan." The little lad ran over to ET and gave him a big hug.

"I knew you'd come to my party" and turning to his mother "Didn't I tell you he'd come mum." Everyone congratulated the two detectives on finding Ethan and the smiles on the faces of his parents and the rest of the guests was sufficient reward for both of them.

Ethan spent most of the evening with ET and kept bombarding him with lots of questions about police work, how many crimes had he solved and how many crooks had he arrested.

"I thought you were a secret agent?" said ET.

"Not anymore" yelled Ethan, he wanted everybody to know that he had changed his mind "I'm going to be a great detective like you two, you said I could didn't you dad?"

Ken smiled at the boy, he didn't want to spoil the lad's party but neither did he want his son wandering off again and ending up goodness knows where. "You've got to listen to these two men Ethan, police work has to be left to them. It can be really dangerous sometimes and we don't want you having another escapade like you've had over the last few days now do we. You can be a detective when you're a bit older but for the time being leave it to the experts."

When the buffet was served Ethan left ET and went over to the table to help himself to a mountain of his favourite foods. Ken went and sat next to ET and asked him to have a quiet word with Ethan. "I don't want to put the lad off or destroy his dreams of becoming a policeman, but if you can persuade him to leave it to the two of you in the meantime and maybe promise him that in a few years time when he's a bit older and has been good you'll do what you can to get him into the force. Hopefully that will bring him down to earth a bit and we can all stop worrying so much."

ET was sympathetic to Ken's worries about his son and promised that he would spend time with the boy and make sure that he didn't go off on his own detecting again. Their conversation finished just in time as Ethan had returned with a plateful and plonked himself down next to ET and Sue. At least they were spared more questions for the next few minutes as Ethan gorged down his sandwiches and coke. Ten minutes later the little lad had fallen asleep and had to be taken to bed. Not much later Bene and Alex left the party, Bene couldn't stop himself yawning. Alex dragged him off the sofa, "Come on Sherlock let's get you back home." they made their excuses to the hosts and left. Bene was so tired that Alex had to support him all the way down the path and into their own house next door. Ten minutes later he too was fast asleep.

Chapter 36

Sylvia turns detective

It was one thirty in the coffee shop and two of the three investors were enjoying their lunchtime coffees. "Any luck in tracking Alastair down yet Sylvia?" Sylvia was a little puzzled by Alastair's non appearance but not worried.

"No not yet, I asked Kris and Ebony in the pub but neither of them have seen him, not since our last meeting with him there anyhow. It's only been a couple of days though and I expect he has other business to attend to as well as ours."

"Yes that'll be it I suppose," said Paul "But this is a big one even for him. I'm getting a little bit concerned and I think we should make a real effort today to get hold of him. He's got a lot of his money invested in this, and although we have our own ideas as to how we would like the plans to be developed for the estate I think it's important that we take into consideration his views as well." Sylvia agreed.

"Yes OK, I'll call round and see Andrew Rawlings before we go to the architect's I'll get Alastair's address from him, it was Andrew who met him first and introduced him to our club. In fact I'll go round there now and meet you back here in say.... umm, an hour is that OK?"

The two separated and Sylvia drove over to see Andrew the investment club chairman. "Come on in Sylvia," Andrew welcomed her and ushered her into the lounge. "It's good of you to come and see me." The room was sparsely furnished, it didn't look as if he had changed anything since the death of his wife. The couple had enjoyed many happy years together until her untimely death from leukaemia some twenty years ago. Never blessed with children the two had been devoted to each other, their lives revolved very much around their work and their combined hobby of walking in the fells.

He offered her a drink which she thanked him for but waved aside. "No thanks Andrew I've just come from the coffee shop." He led her over to a comfortable chair before settling down into his own favourite.

"So what brings you here then, nothing wrong with the club is there?"

"No of course not Andrew, Pat and you are working hard on behalf of all of us at the club I think you take care of just about everything. In fact I feel a bit guilty myself for not contributing as much as I should towards it. But the shop takes up a lot of my time, and with Ray where he is at the moment the house takes up much of the time I have left. I'll be pleased when he's home and we can get our lives back to normal again."

She didn't want to make her visit to Andrew too short for that would be unsociable, and she knew that he was unlikely to get many visitors so he would enjoy her company, it would be nice for him to have someone to talk to. Normally they would never meet socially, their only contact with each other was at the investment club meetings and there all the talk was wrapped up in financial issues. But neither did she want to stay too long either, there was still the appointment with the architect later in the afternoon and she didn't want to miss that.

After a brief chat about their personal situations and the weather she decided to broach the subject of Alastair.

"You remember introducing us to Alastair McKay at one of our meetings Andrew?"

"Yes I remember him, I believe he scared a few of our members off didn't he. If I remember correctly he had some rather large proposition to put before us. I think it was quite a substantial amount he was looking for wasn't it? I don't know if anyone took up his offer but no-one's mentioned it to me since then. I'd all but forgotten about it, were you interested Sylvia?" Sylvia didn't want to say how much she was already involved in it, and she certainly wasn't going to divulge how much she had actually put into the scheme.

"I was rather interested I must admit, to be honest it sounded like quite a good opportunity, I was wondering if you know where he lives?"

Andrew couldn't provide her with an address and Sylvia's face dropped ever so slightly. "I don't think he lives in Levensbridge, in fact I'm pretty sure he doesn't. It's not a big town and if he did live here I'm sure we would have seen much more of him." Sylvia was now feeling rather twitchy.

"So you've no idea where he lives then, he never gave you an address, how about a phone number he must have contacted you somehow?" Andrew shook his head.

"No, no phone number either. I wouldn't know how to contact him." Sylvia's face slipped further. "But I can tell you how you can find out." Sylvia lightened up a little.

"How's that then?"

"Well I met the fellow at the Graham Arms in Lonsdale Street. I meet up with some of my former colleagues there on a Friday afternoon and we spend a couple of hours in there each week, just to keep in touch you know. Well one Friday when I arrived there Mr McKay was already talking to some of them. I went over to join them and he was introduced to me. Evidently he had been asking around to see if there would be anyone interested in a good investment. They said to hang around until I came in as I was the Chairman of the local investment club. Well we had a little chat but I told him it wouldn't be appropriate to discuss that type of subject matter in the present company, I suggested he come along to one of our meetings and I would introduce him to the rest of you. And that's about it really, I wasn't interested myself but I felt it only fair to leave it up to the other members to listen to what the man had to say and then decide for yourselves if you were interested or not."

"So how will that help me to find him?" asked Sylvia.

"Well he told me he was staying at the hotel so if you go along there you'll be able to see him. Or if not they'll be able to give you an address or a contact number for him, they're bound to have that at least.

Everyone has to leave those details when they book into a hotel don't they?"

Sylvia felt a lot happier, of course Alastair had told them when he came to the first meeting that he was new in the town, so it was only logical he would stay in a hotel or rent somewhere first before committing to buying a house. She would go along to the Graham Arms and find him there. She rose to leave. "I'd better get back to the shop Andrew I've left my young assistant in charge and she'll be needing a break. Thanks for the chat and letting me know where I can find Mr McKay, I'll come back again soon and we can talk again." Andrew rose as well and followed her to the door.

"Make sure you do Sylvia, I've enjoyed our little chat."

The drive down to the Graham Arms was only a short one and Sylvia parked her car in the little car park at the rear of the hotel. She went in and made straight for the reception desk. She had to wait for a moment while the receptionist explained to some of the guests where to find the local museum and one or two other attractions they might be interested to see in the town. The guests left and the smiling girl looked towards Sylvia. Sylvia explained the nature of her visit and the girl's smile increased. "Oh yes I remember Mr McKay alright, a lovely gentlemen he was and he tipped the girls very generously. But I'm afraid you've missed him he's no longer with us, he checked out a few days ago."

"Can you let me have an address for him?" asked Sylvia "I need to contact him quite urgently." The girl's smile faded.

"I'm sorry but we're not at liberty to give out that kind of information. It's the data protection act you see we must protect our clients details, I'm sure you appreciate that." This was a blow, but Sylvia was not to be put off legally or otherwise. This was far too important for a small detail like the data protection act to prevent her from getting the information she wanted.

"If someone important like the police for instance came in looking for him you'd have to give them his details, right?"

"Yes of course," said the girl "But you're not the police are you?"

"No," agreed Sylvia "But just supposing you were not actually to tell me?"

"What do you mean" said the girl looking puzzled. Sylvia continued,

"All your guests have to sign in when they arrive here, in the book you have on the desk in front of you there?" the girl nodded, still not knowing where this was going. "And all their details are on your computer over there,"

"Yes" agreed the girl again. "But that information is confidential, it's for the hotel staff only no-one else is allowed access to it."

"No of course not, but the computer is always switched on isn't it and someone's details will always be showing even though it's only you who can see them, right?" Another nod.

"So what are you getting at?" said the girl.

"What I'm getting at is this, this is a small hotel and you're the only person at the desk. Now you can't be expected to be here all the time can you, I mean you must have other duties to do when there are no guests around.

And there must be times when you have to go to the rest room or for a coffee maybe, and obviously you don't switch off the computer every time you leave the desk do you?"

"No of course not" she replied "It takes too long to start up again. I need it on all the time, you never know when someone might come in or want to check out in a hurry."

"And sometimes when you come back there could be someone waiting to see you, yes?"

"Yes occasionally someone may come in when I'm not here, but they can ring the bell and I'm never far away, they'd only have to wait a few seconds no longer."

"Well that's good service isn't it?" Sylvia leaned over the desk to be nearer the girl. The hotel lobby was empty apart from the two of them. Sylvia spoke quietly to the girl. "Now this is what I suggest happens."

The receptionist looked a little wary but listened to what she was being offered. "If you just happened to have Mr McKay's details up on your computer over there and the monitor was turned around ever so slightly you might want to go and wash your hands and bring a coffee back. Now I'm going to leave now but I'll come back in a minute or two, If you're not here I'll ring the bell and when you come back I'll ask you for directions to the local library. Then when you've given me that information I'll smile say thank you and leave a little tip for you, and after that you'll never see me again OK."

The receptionist wasn't keen on any of this, she didn't like what the woman was suggesting. Not only was it illegal, she could get into big trouble with her employers if they were to find out and most likely end up getting the sack. "I think it's best if you leave madam." she told Sylvia.

"By the way," said Sylvia completely unmoved by the girl's reaction. "Do you have an envelope I could borrow?" The receptionist reached under the counter and brought out an envelope with the hotel's name printed on.

Sylvia took the envelope from her and opened her purse, she extracted two hundred pounds in twenty pound notes, counted them out in front of the girl and placed them in the envelope. "What's your first name by the way?"

"Alison" said the girl.

Sylvia wrote the name on the front of the envelope and sealed it. Five minutes later a smiling Sylvia left the hotel for the second time, this time with the information she needed.

Chapter 37

Some success at last

It was mid morning and progress was still slow in the hunt for the killer of Anna Ferenc. getting any information at all about the girl had been like pulling teeth. It seemed that no-one could be found who had been close to her at all. The hospital where she had worked previously could give them nothing more than they knew already which was precious little. Then at last there was some news. Val had eventually managed to get a copy of a birth certificate, but like everything else concerning Anna Ferenc it wasn't straightforward. The Anna Ferenc who had been born in the hospital that day had died only a few hours later. There had been complications with the birth and when given the choice of saving his wife or the child the father had opted to save his wife, hoping they could try for another child sometime in the future.

Val persevered with the search and came across a record of another birth on the same day which attracted her attention. She called Bene and ET over to her desk. She explained the records she had found on Anna Ferenc and then asked them to look at the other one she had dug out.

"See this one here." she put the image of the birth certificate up on her monitor. "Now that's what I call creepy." The name on the certificate was Anna Bauer with the parents names shown as Otto and Esther.

"Didn't you say there was an Otto Bauer who died about a year ago and was a friend of Dr Kohler and Dieter Hoffmann, by her age I think she must have been his granddaughter." Bene recalled the name.

"That's right I remember now there were three of them weren't there, what a coincidence well done Val keep looking."

"Well I've seen a copy of her birth certificate at the home" said ET, "And she's definitely Anna Ferenc on that. She must have got hold of a copy of the birth certificate for the girl who died in hospital and she's been using it to pass herself off as her. Can you press on with this Val and see if you can find any trace of her actual parents, they must still be alive I would think, I mean they can't be that old. For some reason I think she'd got herself involved with this Huber lot. Maybe they found out her real name and as they seem to have been trying to wipe out anyone with the name of Bauer, Kohler or Hoffmann maybe they're the ones who killed her."

"Yes I'm sure she was helping them in some way," agreed Bene, "Or why else did she have a set of keys cut for the residential home and keep them hidden in her locker. She certainly didn't come up here just to work in the home she had an ulterior motive alright. It makes it even more imperative that we track down this Alois Huber and his wife as soon as possible before they kill again."

The team in the station worked tirelessly on the case of Anna Bauer, (aka Ferenc). Val managed to track down Anna's father in London and gave Bene a contact number for him. Bene phoned Otto and asked him when he had last seen his daughter. "Oh it's a long time now," was the reply "She had a big falling out with her mother and me a few years ago and she left home, I'm afraid neither of us have seen her for the last four years. We knew she had been working in hospitals and she did move around quite a lot, but unfortunately we lost track of her when she moved away from London."

There was no easy way to do this, Bene had to tell him. "I'm afraid I may have some bad news for you." There was a silence at the other end of the line, Otto was waiting to hear it. "We recovered the body of a young woman about your daughter's age from a river up here at the weekend and we believe it might be her. We think she was using a different name, can you think of any reason why she should do that?" There was another short silence before the man answered.

"It could be possible, what name was she using?"

"Ferenc," said Bene "does that name mean anything to you.

"Yes it does," said Otto "It goes back to when she was born. There were two girls born in the next beds to each other in the hospital and one of them died. At the time there was a terrible mix up and for some reason the staff weren't sure which girl had died, whether it was the daughter of the Ferenc's or it was our daughter. We had a long wait until it was finally proven that our daughter Anna was not the one who died."

"So because of that" said Bene "it was a name you would always remember."

"Well yes of course, the uncertainty at the time left us with a lot of bad memories. And there were more things that happened at the time which came back to haunt us."

"Go on." said Bene.

"The Ferenc family are related to a family we have some bad history with and they came to the hospital and accused us of stealing the daughter of the Ferenc's. They wouldn't believe that the girl who died was theirs, they insisted it was our daughter who had died. They even made an attempt to steal her, we had to move away because of it."

"Was that an end to it then?" asked Bene.

"No, if anything it got worse, a few years ago we told Anna the story and she seemed to dwell on it rather a lot after that. She got it into her mind that she wasn't our real daughter, she kept pointing out little differences between her and her mother and me, just small things you know nothing major. We knew of course that she was our natural child but for the last year she was at home with us she became more and more certain she was the daughter of the Ferenc's and not ours. Nothing we could do or say would convince her otherwise. By the time she left home she was like a stranger to us, thankfully we have two other children who are loving and normal but we do miss Anna."

"We can't be positive that it is Anna's body we've found," said Bene "But from what you've just told me it looks very likely. I'm going to need someone to come and formally identify her. Would you be prepared to do that?"

"Yes of course I'll come up tomorrow if that's alright. If it is her I don't think her mother would be up to it, I'll come alone."

Bene was ready to end the call but something was niggling away at the back of his mind, something he didn't think was of any relevance to the case but nevertheless he felt he needed to know. "Mr Bauer, you mentioned some relations of the Ferenc family who tried to steal Anna away from you, who were they?"

"Oh those people, well as you probably guessed my father settled here after the war and started a family and he was very happy here. However another family from our homeland came over to this country they were looking into the past, stirring up trouble and making outrageous accusations against my family. I don't know what they were after but they were a bad lot. After the incident where they tried to steal Anna we moved away and thankfully we never saw them again."

"What was their name then?" There was a slight pause before Otto answered, Bene had brought back some bad memories to him, at last he replied

"Huber."

Bene replaced the receiver and related the conversation he had just had with the father of Anna to ET. He quickly summed it up.

"So it looks as if we could be right about her, she thought she was really part of the Huber family and has been working for them up at the home. She's either let them into the home and they've killed those two men, or she's done it herself."

A loud shout came from the Chief's office "Bene!" Bene jumped, it was a summons from the Chief.

"Right bring me up to date with this girl, what do we know?" Bene gave him the news which fifteen minutes ago he hadn't been privy to. "So this Huber family seem to have spread their roots everywhere" The Chief took a moment to reflect. "I know we haven't had much luck so far Bene but I've got division on my back again, they're pressurising me into letting them take over. What's our chances of finding this couple before the whole thing blows up in our faces."

Bene was trying to think of an answer which might give the Chief reason to keep division at bay for a little longer. The Chief was not waiting though. "Finding that lad has been our only saving grace in this whole sad affair so far, but nothing short of an arrest will satisfy division now. Twenty four hours Bene, that's all I can give you. Bring me that couple by tomorrow night or I'll have to take ET and you off the case and hand it over to them." He didn't wait for a response from Bene, instead he picked up his phone and waved Bene out.

Bene went back to his desk and told ET the Chief's ultimatum, They continued with their deliberations over Anna's connection with the Huber family. "But if she's been helping them," said Bene "Why kill her?"

"Well" said ET "It's maybe just as we thought earlier, they found out her real name and decided to do away with her, who knows. But I'm sure they did kill her and we need to find them. The trouble is they could be anywhere now, out of the country even."

After what the Chief had told him only minutes earlier Bene was feeling rather at a loss as to what to do next.

There was one piece of good news had he but known it. Alois Huber was not out of the country, in fact at the very same time the detectives were pondering his whereabouts he was less than half a mile away from where they stood.

Chapter 38

Investments can go down as well as up

"Where have you been Sylvia you've been gone ages, I thought I'd have to go and see Stuart on my own." Sylvia gave out a huge sigh and plonked her enormous handbag down on the floor before joining Paul at the table.

"Oh get me a coffee Paul I'm gasping, you wouldn't believe what an afternoon I've had." Paul went over to the counter and asked for two more coffees to be brought over to their table.

"Go on then tell me, did you manage to find out where Alastair is?"

"Well yes and no."

"What do you mean yes and no, you either did find out or you didn't." Sylvia explained her visit to Andrew and what he had told her about meeting Alastair in the hotel.

"Alastair had been staying at the Graham Arms but he's not there now he's left, it's cost me two hundred pounds to find out where he lives."

"So where does he live?" asked Paul.

"Morecambe." replied Sylvia

"Morecambe, you got the address though didn't you?"

"Yes I've got that, but there was no phone number just an address."

"Well it doesn't look as though he's going to be with us today does it, we'll go over to Morecambe in the morning and find out what's been holding him back. Bloody hell if I had half a million invested in something I'd want to follow it every step of the way." Paul looked at his watch. "Come on then finish off that coffee and let's go, we're late already and we don't want to keep Stuart waiting any longer for us. If we don't get there soon we'll have missed our appointment altogether, and if we have to make another one it'll set us back another day at least, maybe more."

They arrived at Stuart's office a few minutes later but were still more than fifteen minutes late for their meeting. Paul offered their apologies and waited for Stuart who was making finishing adjustments to a design one of his team was working on. Stuart was not smiling but Paul didn't know if it was because they were late or that something in the office had gone badly wrong. Finally Stuart was free and came over to meet them, he held out his hand to greet them but the welcoming smile was not there. Paul reckoned he would have to do a bit of grovelling to get back into Stuart's good books.

Stuart led them over to his office and when all three were inside he closed the door behind them. He looked serious and seemed a bit unsure as to how to start the conversation. Paul didn't think he should be the one to start it either so a silence followed in which all three felt a little uncomfortable. Eventually Stuart opened up.

"That map you brought in the other day Paul, where did it come from?" Paul hesitated before replying, he was wondering why this should be of any importance to Stuart. He went on to explain about the investment with Alastair and the visit they had made to the solicitor in Preston where they had paid for the deeds to the land and the map detailing the actual plot.

"It's all legit Stuart, the deeds are correct and the map fits in with them, what's the problem?

Stuart pulled open a drawer from his desk and took out the map Paul had left with him, he laid it out on the desk. Then from another drawer he pulled out what looked like an identical map and laid this alongside it. He waited for a response from Paul or Sylvia, but nothing was coming. "Look at them Paul and tell me what you see?" Paul looked at the two maps and had to admit that they did look very similar, almost identical in fact.

"So why have you got a map the same as ours, have you had it copied or something?"

"No Paul, this is the one you brought in and I put it away in the desk here, then another customer came in this morning and brought this one in." Stuart pointed to the second map. "Well there must be some mistake then, how would someone else get a copy of the same map, this one must be a forgery, whoever it was is trying to con you." Stuart didn't seem to think so.

"The person who brought the second one in is from the housing department at the council, and I don't see them making a mistake with something like this do you? Now come over here there's something I think you should have a look at."

He invited Paul and Sylvia to take their time looking over the two maps. "Now do you see any difference between them?" Paul and Sylvia both looked at the maps and could see some slight differences. Paul said

"Oh I see now because they're not exactly the same are they, one side of this one is slightly longer and the right hand side is more rounded where it comes up to the road. So they're not the same map at all are they." Paul heaved a sigh of relief, but it was short lived as Stuart went on to show them another point where the maps differed.

"OK now don't look at the maps themselves but look at what else is different about them." The two bent over the desk and looked again but neither could see what it was that Stuart was driving at.

"I can't see anything else." said Paul and Sylvia agreed with him. Stuart was not enjoying this, he knew the big disappointment that was waiting for them both when he explained what it was they should have noticed.

He put his finger on the second map over the compass sign. "You know about these I suppose?"

"Yes" said Paul, "They point North."

"That's right and this one is pointing North. Now have a look at your map, someone has written French's Field along the top to indicate that the map is meant to look as if it's the right way up and facing North. But the compass sign is on the bottom and North is actually pointing South, you'd have to turn the map around to make it face North." Paul still didn't understand.

"So what are you saying Stuart?"

"What I'm saying Paul is that these are two very similar maps but for different parcels of land. As you know French's Field is split down the middle with the road running through the centre of it and the flood bank running alongside it. Well both sides are called French's Field but the actual field is in two halves. You've bought one half and the council have bought the other half."

"Yes" said Paul "so what on earth do the council want buying land on the wrong side of the road?" Still the penny hadn't dropped with him, but the inference of what Stuart was saying hadn't escaped Sylvia.

She dropped the bombshell. "What he's trying to tell us Paul is that we've bought the wrong bloody piece of land. the land that we've bought isn't protected by the new flood barrier and we won't get planning permission to build on it. That's why Alastair hasn't been in contact with us, the bastard's stitched us up good and proper and left us with a white elephant."

Paul was in a state of shock, his mind had ceased to work and his whole body had gone numb. He stood there with his mouth half open but no words were coming out. Stuart could see the effect it had on him, he had known it was going to be hard news for him to break to them. He took hold of Paul's arm and led him over to a chair and sat him down.

Sylvia on the other hand was fully aware of what had happened and she was fuelled with rage. She knew that there were steps to be taken and must be taken quickly if they were going to have any chance of salvaging anything out of this debacle. She shook Paul by the shoulder vigorously. "Come on Paul snap out of it, we have to get hold of Alastair and that solicitor of his, Ogilvy, and see what we can do to get our money back."

Getting no response from Paul she turned her attention to Stuart instead. "I suppose extending the flood barrier to cover this part of the field would be expensive would it?" Stuart nodded his head.

"Far too expensive to make it worth your while I'm afraid, it's not just the barrier which would need extending it would also involve raising the level of the road which would have to cross over it. You're talking a lot of money for that Sylvia and even then the council wouldn't consent to any building on the land, not until the new defences had fully settled in and proved themselves. That would normally be around twenty years, and I don't think you'd want to wait around that long would you."

"What's the value of the land as it stands now then?" Stuart took a moment or two to consider the question.

"Well you have to understand how the land can be best utilised, but to be honest with you I don't think there's much chance of it been used for anything other than grazing. That would give it an agricultural value of around two thousand pounds an acre maybe a little more, but it is only a few acres we're talking about. Your best bet would be to sell it or let it out to a local farmer. I'm sorry to have been the one to break the bad news to you, but surely your solicitor should have pointed all this out when you were in the process of buying it."

Sylvia didn't want to disclose any details of how Paul and her had been duped, she was too ashamed to admit it. "Well thanks for spelling it out for us Stuart, it looks like we've been wasting your time as well as ours over this." Stuart felt sorry for the couple and hoped they would be able to get over the shock.

"I hope you didn't pay too much over the odds for it, it looks as though you'll just have to put it down to experience, anyway I hope you can find another piece of land and maybe we can do some real business."

Sylvia led a still shocked Paul out of the office and back to the coffee shop. They ordered coffees, sat down and tried to come to terms with the realisation that they'd been the victims of a very elaborate scam. The coffee was helping and Paul was starting to recover, he began to reiterate the facts with Sylvia.

"So what do we do now I mean most of my money is tied up in this, I can't just walk away without doing something to try and get it back."

Sylvia had a list of things in her mind which she put to Paul. "It's too late to go to Preston because the solicitor's office will be closed, and the banks are closed as well, but it's not too late to go to Morecambe. We can't take a chance on leaving it until tomorrow we'll have to get over there right away and see Alastair. I have the address so we should be able to track him down quite easily. We know the money has left our bank accounts and we need to get it back somehow. I don't know how we'll do that yet, but whether we have to threaten Alastair physically or through the courts it doesn't matter we'll do whatever it takes. Then tomorrow morning we'll go to the banks and see if there's anything they can do. After that the solicitor in Preston, and after that I don't know, the police maybe. Now come on let's get going."

The journey didn't take too long and as they drew near the address which Sylvia had obtained from the Graham

Arms Hotel it was starting to get dark. They pulled up outside the semi detached property but remained seating in the car for a minute or so before getting out. "Right," said Paul "he won't be expecting us so as soon as he opens the door we're going in, we're not going to give him a chance to shut the door in our faces." The two approached the house and Paul knocked on the door preparing to stick his foot inside as soon as the door opened. But no-one did come to open it, he knocked again but with the same result. "Damn it he must be out, I don't see any lights on anywhere I suppose we'll just have to hang around until he comes back. I'll check round the back first just in case there is someone in and hasn't heard us."

He walked around to the back of the house but there was no sign of anyone in the back rooms either. Sylvia meanwhile went to the house next door where there were lights on in the front room. A small lady came to the door and told her that Alastair, his wife and another couple had gone out for the evening.

"They're not usually out late, if you want to wait for them I expect they'll be back around eleven, every where's closed by then anyway." Sylvia thanked her and went back to the car where Paul was waiting.

Paul moved the car a little way from the house to a position where they would still be able to see the four when they returned home but far enough away as not to give cause to scare them off. Eleven o'clock came and went and still no-one came back to the house. "Surely they can't be much longer," said Paul "They're not youngsters anymore, they won't have gone onto a nightclub or anywhere like that."

Neither of them were aware that Alastair and Donald had returned to the house. They had parked their car in the back lane which had given them access to the rear of the house well out of sight of the two people waiting in the car on the front.

"It's lucky you have a conscientious neighbour Alastair."

"Yes I agree it's a lucky escape, we could have been caught out if my neighbour hadn't phoned me in the hotel."

"What did she say exactly?"

"She said a man and a woman had come to the house and were obviously looking for me. When no-one answered the door the woman came to her house and asked where we were. Our neighbour didn't know who they were and was a bit worried so she kept an eye on them. Well, instead of waiting outside the house which you would expect them to do they moved the car further down the street and were watching the house from there. She couldn't understand why they would do that and it aroused her suspicions, she thought she'd better phone and warn me. By the way she described the couple and the car I've no doubt it's Paul and Sylvia, although how they should have got hold of this address is beyond me, obviously I haven't covered my tracks well enough."

The two men moved silently around the house in the semi darkness picking up personal items and a few clothes. "Well it's probably just as well," said Donald, "We weren't planning on staying around here for much longer were we. I've got my house sold and you're just renting this one so we won't be leaving much behind, nothing that we'll miss anyway."

"No that's right," said Alastair. "we'll leave with this lot and head off down to London for a few days, you've got the passports haven't you because we're going to need them. I think we'll leave those two to stew in the car for the night."

Donald chuckled. "I wonder what they'll do next, probably go down to Preston looking for the elusive Mr Ogilvy."

"Yes you took a good part there Donald, I was finding it hard to keep a straight face, it's a good thing they don't know our real names." The two had a final look around the house and left quietly by the back door. They went down the garden and out into the lane where their wives were waiting in the car. After loading the suitcases Alastair started the engine.

"Shall we bid them a final farewell." he giggled. He drove the car down the lane and out onto the street, as they turned the corner the four could see the car with Paul and Sylvia inside, it was parked about a hundred yards further up the street. Alastair headed towards it. As they approached he switched the headlights on to full beam, and on passing the car he blew loudly on the horn several times. The four inside were beside themselves with laughter.

"What the hell was all that about" said Sylvia

"I don't know, bloody hooligans I expect." snapped Paul who was now getting very irate with the long wait.

He opened the car window and put his head out. " I hope you get caught for drink driving you inconsiderate bastards." he shouted after the car.

It was after midnight now, the two didn't realise it but they were in for a long and fruitless wait. They had been outmanoeuvred by two very slippery customers and a well meaning neighbour. If only they hadn't moved the car so far away their trip to Morecambe might have had a very different outcome.

Chapter 39

A small matter of revenge

"Right" said Bene "that's enough for today we've done as much as we can, I'll see you all back here tomorrow. But before you go I must warn you that we'll not be going home tomorrow night until we've arrested someone for this murder. How we do it will be entirely down to our own efforts but somehow we have to crack it by tomorrow night. Chief Inspector Sowerby badly wants us to succeed, but division have given him that deadline and if we don't make an arrest by then they'll take the case off us. Now none of us want that to happen so I need all of you to go home and get an early night tonight and come in tomorrow with your minds clear and fresh."

Everyone involved in the case with Bene wanted the same result. He continued. "I want you to try hard and think of anything that we can do or anything we haven't done, are there any new lines we can follow up. Try to think of anything we might have missed, some little detail that may have been overlooked or seemed insignificant at the time. We desperately need a breakthrough in this case, but if it's any help I have a gut feeling that we're very close to making one. So off you go." He waved them all away except one. "Everyone except you ET. Do you have your car outside?"

"Yes, sure boss."

"OK then I want you to follow me back to Dot's house, I want to run a few ideas over with you, we'll consider them over night and see if any of them can help us make that breakthrough tomorrow."

The two detectives left in their separate cars and headed through the town. It was rush hour and the town at that time of day was busy with traffic. Bene pulled up at the lights and sat patiently waiting for them to change colour. He was fourth in the line of cars waiting to move off when he saw a white van coming from the opposite direction and make a left turn at the lights. It didn't register for a moment but something about it caught his eye as it disappeared up the street which led directly onto the road out of town on the east side of Levensbridge.

He was too close to the car in front to pull out so he jumped out and ran back to ET's car. "Quick as you can, turn around and get up to the top of the main road out east, and if you see a white transit van pull him in, go! go! go!" ET spun the car around and sped off up the next street where he could hopefully reach the top of the town before the van. The lights had changed and the cars behind Bene were tooting their horns. Bene flew back to his car and set off up the street where the white van had disappeared a minute earlier. It was just his luck that several other cars were travelling up the same street and it was too narrow to allow him to pass, he had to sit behind and hope that some of them would turn off into the side streets.

He was making slow progress and rued the fact he didn't have the blue lamp and siren with him. He eventually reached the outer limits of the town and found ET waiting for him, but there was no white van to be seen. He pulled alongside ET's car and wound his window down. "No luck then, did you see him at all?"

"No nothing at all, I've been here a while and I'm sure I would have beaten him here if he did come up this way. There were no cars in front of me and I literally flew up the hill. When I turned onto this street at the top I would have seen him coming along, but he never appeared. I'm sure I wouldn't have missed him boss I don't think he can have come up this far."

Bene was thinking furiously. "So if he didn't get up to this point he must have turned off onto one of the side streets somewhere up the hill. This isn't a big estate so he must be somewhere on it. At least he doesn't know we're looking for him so we might be lucky and find him."

"What do you think boss should we split up, drive around and see if we can spot him?"

"Yes" said Bene "That's exactly what we'll do, you take the top three streets and I'll have a go further down, it'll probably take us no longer than half an hour to cover the lot."

"Tell me about the van so I know what I'm looking for." ET knew it was a transit but wanted a more detailed description if possible.

"I only noticed it because I spotted the large S on the side as it went round the corner that's all, I didn't catch the name or anything just the large letter S."

The two went in search of the white van both hoping the owner hadn't already garaged the vehicle, if so it would take them that much longer to track it down. Luckily the van hadn't been put away and ET spotted it on the second street he was driving along. He pulled over to the pavement a few doors from where the van was parked and phoned Bene. When Bene joined him the two officers left their vehicles and walked over to the house that had the van parked in the driveway. The name of the side of the vehicle was Superdecking which advertised branches in Manchester, Leeds, Preston and Newcastle upon Tyne. They were suppliers and fitters of outside decking and patios and could be contacted via an 0800 number. The registration plate bore the letters SD followed by four numbers.

Bene asked ET to go to the rear of the house before ringing the bell just in case the owner decided to make a run for it. However the owner didn't seem to be alarmed at all and answered the door quite naturally. Bene showed the man his warrant card and told him who he was. "I'd like to ask you a few questions, firstly can you tell me your name?" The man answered

"My name is Emile, why do you want to know?"

"One thing at a time sir, Emile what?"

"Emil Zajic if you must know."

The name sounded familiar to Bene. "Are you related to Karel Zajic?"

"Yes he's my brother, he's alright isn't he?"

"Yes as far as I know," said Bene "He's still in prison isn't he, he went down with Ray Parrish?"

"That's right, he was foolish and now he is paying the price for it, but what has this got to do with him?"

"Oh I'm sorry it's nothing to do with your brother it's you I need to talk to, shall we go inside?"

ET had come back to the front of the house and all three went into the home of Emile Zajic. "Do you live alone?" Bene asked.

"No, my wife will be home shortly why are you asking me?" Bene continued.

"That's your van outside is it?"

"Well it belongs to the firm I work for, it's not mine personally you understand." Bene asked him where he was on the two nights the burglaries had been committed. The three men had been standing, but when Bene mentioned the two dates Emile turned white, sighed heavily and sat down on the settee.

He didn't answer right away it was as if he'd been dealt a heavy blow to the solar plexus. Bene repeated the question. Finally Emile looked up and spoke quietly.

"You know don't you, you know where I was and what I was doing. But I have to tell you I had a good reason to do what I did. It was to get back at that monster who led my poor brother astray and then left him and the other man to get arrested and sent to jail, I tell you that man is evil."

Bene stood back. "You mean Paul Hanbury?"

"Yes that man, he was the one who started it all and he got away with all the money. My poor brother lost everything, his money, his freedom and most of all his good name. When I heard he was coming back to the town I wanted to get back at him, steal something from him so that he would know what it was like to lose something you love."

Bene still couldn't fully understand. "But why steal from Mr Taylor next door, he hadn't done you or your brother any harm."

"I know" said Emile "I got the wrong house at first, when I realised it wasn't Paul's house I had to go back and do a second robbery. Believe me I hated it, it's not like me at all, I have never ever done anything so bad. I was just so mad and I wanted Paul Hanbury to suffer a little bit like he made us suffer. I was sorry about the first robbery but I couldn't do anything to make it right. I mean I couldn't take a chance on taking the things back I would probably have been caught, so I just had to keep them. I wasn't going to do anything with them, sell them or anything like that, I just couldn't think of a way to get the things back to him without getting into more trouble myself."

Bene continued with the questioning. "But you only took one piece from Paul's house."

"I know" said Emile, "And he almost caught me, but when I got away in the van I laughed because I had got his favourite piece of furniture and I wasn't going to let him have it back." "So where is the furniture now, what have you done with it?" asked ET.

"It's in the garage, that's why I can't use it for the van, the garage is full of furniture."

The three left the house and Emile opened the garage doors to reveal the stolen items. "Right," said ET "You'd better lock it up so it doesn't get stolen again. I'll have to take you down to the station where you'll be charged with burglary." ET took the man back to the house where he let Emile write a note to leave for his wife.

"I won't be locked up tonight will I?"

"No" said ET "You'll be formally charged at the station and you can phone your solicitor from there, when he comes down he should be able to get you released on bail and you can come back home. Then from tomorrow you'll have to report daily to the police station until your trial comes up."

ET led the man away and arranged to meet Bene at his house later in the evening. Bene pulled out his mobile and phoned the Chief, he sounded relieved that at least one crime had been cleared up. "I thought this case was just an isolated one I don't know why, I just had a feeling about it. Anyway well done and I'm pleased I was right and it wasn't connected to all those other burglaries in the area. Give me more good news tomorrow." The call ended sharply.

Bene rang Mr. Taylor to give him the good news. He was delighted and eager to get his furniture back as soon as possible. "We'll get you to come down and make sure it's yours first, when you've confirmed that we can arrange to have it delivered back to you. In the meantime it's in a safe place and I can tell you that the man who stole it has been arrested."

"It isn't damaged is it?" asked a concerned Mr Taylor

"No I didn't see any marks on it, but you'll be able to see for yourself. I'll let you know when and where you can see it, probably sometime tomorrow."

His next call was to Paul Hanbury, secretly he had wished the desk would never be found but now that it had been at least it would keep him off his back. The phone was ringing but there was no answer at Paul's house. "Oh well I'll try him again in the morning, one more day won't make any difference."

Chapter 40

The hunter and the hunted

It was Thursday afternoon in the library and only an hour until closing time, Pat was looking forward to the weekly investment club meeting. She had not gone home for lunch as she had much to do before the evening meeting started. Instead she had used the time to prepare a rather promising report on a company she had been following in the Daily Telegraph over the last few days. “I think Andrew will like this one, even Agnes and Harriet will be keen for us to buy some shares in it. It’s not too risky and I think we can all make a little money out of it.” She rubbed her hands together and smiled to herself as she thought how pleased Andrew would be with her.

Her assistant glanced over and shook her head “I swear she’s getting worse, her mind’s just not on her work on Thursdays. I wonder what they do down at that club of hers, whatever or whoever it is that gets her so excited must be really special. Anyway she’ll not have much longer to wait it’s four o’clock already, she’ll have the door shut at five on the dot so I can get away on time too.”

Just at that moment the door opened and in walked Alois Huber and his wife. "Oh I hope they don't want to stay long or ask for anything else out of that box in the cellar." Pat was clearly not happy at seeing the two Germans in her library again. However they didn't ask for any assistance but instead went over to the local history section and removed one or two books from the shelves. They took the books to a table and sat down to study them. Pat watched them carefully.

She remembered about the visit she'd had from the police and how interested they had been in the two people, they had asked her to let them know if they came in again. One of them had left his card with her and asked her to phone him immediately. "Well I suppose I should ring him," she thought. "It must be important, I wonder if it's to do with that little boy who went missing. I hate anyone who would want to hurt a poor innocent child, I'll get that policeman to come around straight away."

Pat went into her office and sat down where she could still keep an eye on the two people at the table. She found the card Bene had left her and using her office phone she called the number on the card. No-one answered the phone, the voice told her that the person she was calling could not take the call and would she leave a message. She was annoyed, she didn't like leaving messages, she wanted to speak to real people not to one of those infernal machines. She waited a few more minutes then called again, but still she was diverted to the messaging service. "I'll give it another minute or so then I suppose I'll have to leave a message, why on earth can't he answer the phone, if it was so urgent he should make sure he's available at all times."

It was half past four and the two people stood up and went over to replace the books on the shelf. In desperation Pat phoned again and this time she forced herself into leaving a message. She told Bene that the two Germans were in the library but were on the point of leaving and she didn't know where they would be going. She was feeling rather guilty, she was looking forward to her meeting at the Fox and Pheasant with Andrew, but here were these two Germans the police wanted to talk to urgently. She fretted and fretted, her mind in torment. She had never missed a Thursday night with Andrew at the Fox and Pheasant and she didn't want to miss this one either. But could she in all honesty let these two people just walk out and do nothing about it. Finally her mind was made up.

With a bit of luck they wouldn't go far and she could phone the policeman again and tell him where he could find them. Then she could carry on to the Fox and Pheasant and still be in time to attend the meeting with the investment club. That way nothing would be lost.

The two Germans were ready to leave, the man thanked Pat and her assistant and walked over to the door. Pat picked up her coat and handbag and went over to speak to her assistant. "Those were the two Germans the police were interested in. I can't get in touch with the policeman on the number he gave me. Maybe you can try and phone him again after I've gone, his card's on my desk.

Try and get hold of him and tell him I'm following them and I'll let him know where they go. Now I'll have to get a move on or I'll have lost them before I've even started. I've left my keys on the desk if you'll lock up for me." She pulled on her coat as she was leaving and dashed out of the library as fast as she could in hot pursuit of the two Germans.

The Germans hadn't gone very far and Pat almost ran into them as she rushed through the outer door of the building onto the busy street. The couple were only a matter of yards away and Pat was still in the process of pulling on her coat, it was that action which brought her to the attention of the woman. Pat was flustered and didn't know what she should do, in an attempt to make her exit more natural she rushed over the street and into a newsagent's shop. "There, that was quick thinking," she was pleased with herself. "They'll just think I've dashed over here to get the late edition of the evening news."

She bought a paper even though the paper boy would have pushed one through her own front door earlier. "Well I couldn't do anything else I suppose," she thought. "I don't want to give them any reason to suspect that I'm following them." She remained in the shop where she could watch the couple without being seen herself. The two Germans eventually seemed to decide where they would go and started walking along the street away from the town centre, Pat left the paper shop and looked along the street after them. She would not follow too closely but keep well back so as not to draw any more attention to herself.

She followed them for about two hundred yards and not once did either of the two look back. “Well this is easy,” she thought. “I just hope they don’t go much further, I’ve got better things to do than follow them around.” After another hundred yards she realised they were heading towards the railway station. “Oh I hope not, if they get on a train I’ll just have to let them go I couldn’t possibly follow them on that, I mean they could be going to London or anywhere. Why didn’t that stupid policeman answer his phone, I’m having to do his job for him.”

The couple arrived at the station and went inside only a minute before Pat got there. She waited a few moments before looking cautiously around the entrance, she didn’t want to be caught out again if they were waiting just inside the station. That certainly would give the game away and she would have no answer if they confronted her and asked why she was following them. She couldn’t see either of them at first so slowly she edged her way into the main building, her eyes flashed first one way then the other but she couldn’t see them. She felt a little panicky her heart began beating faster. Where were they, they hadn’t had time to board a train so they must be somewhere near.

It was the man she spotted first, he was standing with his back to her, there was no doubt it was him because she recognised the long coat and the hat. But where was the woman she was nowhere to be seen. Pat stood motionless not wanting to look conspicuous, her eyes scanned over the people in the station which was now beginning to fill up with commuters going home from work. Suddenly the woman appeared from behind her, she walked briskly past her waving a newspaper, seemingly oblivious of Pat's presence.

"I managed to get one Alois." she shouted over to her husband.

Pat froze. The man looked around and smiled at his wife.

"That's good Sabine, is there any news in it for us?" Pat didn't dare move an inch, so far neither of the two had seen her and she badly wanted it to stay that way. The woman shouted over the crowd of people to her husband again.

"You should go and get the tickets and then we can go home, it's a fast train so we'll be there in half an hour, and then we can start planning our next move."

The man walked over to the ticket office and Pat watched as he bought the tickets and walked back over to where his wife was waiting. What should she do she couldn't leave now, she had to find out where home was for this couple, at least then she could tell the police where they could find them. She went over to the ticket office and spoke to the man behind the window. "Can you tell me where the man bought tickets for please, the man who was at the window here a minute ago?" The ticket office clerk was not helpful.

"I'm sorry madam but we can't give out that kind of information, you'll have to go and ask him yourself."

This was no good, how was she going to find out where they lived now, what the clerk had suggested was completely out of the question. She had a difficult decision to make. "I've already come this far so I'll have to carry on until I find out where this couple can be found by the police." She looked at her watch and remembered the woman saying home was only half an hour away. If that was as long as it would take she could easily get a ticket herself and follow them home returning to Levensbridge by the next train. She might miss the start of the meeting but she would still have time to impress them with her new investment proposition.

Her mind was made up, she went to the ticket office and asked for a return to Preston. The London train was the next one to arrive and that must be the train the couple would travel on. If they only lived half an hour away they must live somewhere between here and Preston, there was no need for her to buy a ticket for anywhere further than that. The train arrived on time and she watched as people started to get on it. She kept her eyes on the German couple and when she saw them get on she boarded herself on the next carriage.

The train made two stops but the German couple remained on the train. Pat was getting anxious, they had already been on the train more than half an hour and the next stop was Preston. If the couple didn't get off there she would have to leave the train as her ticket only allowed her to travel that far. Ten minutes later the train pulled into Preston station and Pat looked out of the window to see if the couple would get off. Thankfully they did, she waited until they were walking down the platform before alighting herself, keeping a safe distance between the couple and herself she followed them out of the station.

An uncomfortable thought occurred to her, what if they got into a taxi. Would she have to grab the next one like they did in the movies and say "Follow that cab." The couple obviously didn't live too far from the station as they continued walking, but it was a lot longer than she thought and before long she was tiring, "How much further?" she thought. "I don't want to lose them but I can't go on like this for more than another five minutes, If they don't stop soon I'll just have to let them go. Anyways I can give the police directions to here so it shouldn't take too long to find them."

Pat continued to trudge along behind them but set herself a target of one more street, if they went past that point she would give up and go back to the station. She watched as the couple reached the next corner and heaved a sigh of relief as she saw them turn into the side street. "Aha" she said to herself. "I must get up there quickly and see where they go." Her legs were very tired now but she forced herself to walk as fast as she could to the street the couple had turned into. Seriously out of breath she made the street corner, easing off gradually she walked a little way around it to see if she could still see the couple. Just in time she saw them going through a gate and walk up to the door, the man took out a key and opened the door and they both went inside. Pat counted out the house number from the ones facing her, "2, 4, 6, 8 so it's number 10 is it, thank goodness for that."

She walked back from the street a little way and stopped for a while to get her breath back. She glanced at her watch and sighed, it had taken much longer than she had planned and it was much too late now for her to get back to Levensbridge in time for the meeting. She sighed again, it would be the first one she had missed. Even so she felt a deep sense of pride in what she had achieved. When she got back home she could phone the police and they could come over here and pick up the two Germans. She would probably get a personal thank you from the Chief Superintendant, and when Andrew found out about her exploits he would be so proud of her.

When at last her breathing had returned to normal she started to make her way back to the railway station. It was dark now and the street lights were not too bright in this part of the town. Fortunately she remembered the way quite well but even so she was making slow progress. She was tired and her legs were hurting her, she thought with dismay that it was unlikely there would be any taxis passing by, she would have given a week's salary just to be able to sit down in the back seat and be driven back to the station.

At the end of the next street she had to stop again, her legs were aching dreadfully now and she thought she would sit for a while on a low wall in front of one of the bungalows. Some car lights were coming her way but she took no notice of them it certainly wasn't a taxi. However the car drew up alongside her and a voice beckoned her. "You look tired, can I offer you a lift?" The voice sounded vaguely familiar but she was so tired she couldn't remember where she had heard it before. But the offer was too good to refuse and after thanking the driver profusely she climbed into the back of the vehicle and settled down thankfully on the seat.

"Are you going anywhere near the railway station?" she enquired of the driver.

"I can take you there but I have another call to make first, but that won't take long."

Pat slumped back in the seat and relaxed, she closed her eyes and was enjoying the warmth and comfort of the car and the pleasurable effect it was having on her aching limbs. She was so tired now she was on the point of dozing off when the car swung off the road and headed off down a narrow lane. "I wonder where he's taking me first," she thought. "It doesn't matter as long as we get to the station in time for the next train." She dozed again.

When she woke again the car had stopped. She looked up but there was no-one in the driver's seat, "I suppose he's making his call." She yawned. Looking out through the front windscreen she couldn't at first make out what it was she was looking at, she forced herself into a more wakened state and tried to focus on it. Then it dawned on her, it was water and the moonlight shining on it was making it shimmer, it was that which had attracted her eyes towards it. She looked around but could see no houses or lights anywhere and wondered where the driver had gone. Maybe the car had broken down and he had gone for help.

Then suddenly and without warning the car started to move forward. If she had been more alert she would have realised that a driverless car moving downhill towards water meant danger and she should jump out. But she was too tired and sleepy and her aching body was reluctant to leave the warmth of the car, so instead of taking any action which might have saved her she just sat there and closed her eyes. Her mind was bewildered and her body and limbs were still very sore. "It must be a dream," she thought "I'll go back to sleep and when I wake up everything will be back to normal again."

In the Fox and Pheasant the chairman was bringing the meeting of the investment club to a close. Rising from his chair he apologised to the members for the lack of input which had been promised by Pat.

"She's never missed a meeting in her life Andrew." said Agnes and Harriet together.

"No that's true and I really can't think what has happened to her, she would have phoned me if she wasn't going to be here. I do know she was rather excited about a new investment she wanted us to look at so it must be something serious which has prevented her from coming along tonight and sharing it with us." Andrew checked the time on his watch. "It's a bit late now but maybe I'll pop round to the library in the morning and make sure she's alright."

But Pat was not alright she was still very tired from her exertions over the last few hours. The car was gathering pace as it made its way down the hillside and she was only half conscious when it reached the bottom and rolled off the edge, the car plunged into the water at the deepest end of the reservoir. It didn't sink immediately but settled for a while on the surface looking as if it may just sit there floating around. Pat opened her eyes, she didn't know why the car had gone into the water she just seemed to accept the fact that it had, her mind was confused. "I'm floating on the top it must be a boat I'm in not a car, it's very strange I don't understand it at all." Then she felt her feet getting wet. "But the boat's letting in water that can't be right, why doesn't the man come and get me out of here, I'm getting really wet now, and it's so cold."

Then gradually the water started to fill up the interior of the car and ever so slowly it began to sink below the surface. As the car was sinking the water rushed in at a much faster rate and it was icy cold. Within a few moments the shock of it overtook her completely. Thankfully her mind shut down and as the car drifted down into the depths of the reservoir she felt no pain or discomfort as her body succumbed to the inevitable. It was just as well she hadn't known that the club meeting she attended last week was to be her last one. If she had known it would have finished her off just as surely.

Alois Huber stood and watched until the car had disappeared below the water completely then he made his way back up to the road where another car was waiting to pick him up. "So, she was not so clever that one was she?" he smirked.

"No, but we really must leave this place now, I don't like it here anymore." his partner replied.

Chapter 41

A case of two solicitors

The street in Morecambe where Paul and Sylvia had been parked was beginning to get busy with the morning traffic, it was a passing car horn that brought the sleeping couple back to life again.

"Bloody hell Paul what time is it?" Sylvia stretched her aching arms which had been pressed against the car door as she had slept. Paul looked at his watch

"Quarter past eight," he yawned "Christ we've been asleep for hours let's get over to the house before they go out again." The two brushed down their crumpled clothes and walked over to Alastair's house. Paul knocked on the door but with the same result as the night before, there was no answer. He looked through the front window and could see the room was furnished but there was no-one to be seen.

"I'll go next door again and ask the woman there, she seems to know them pretty well." Sylvia went to the neighbour's house and knocked on the door. The same small woman came to the door and gave Sylvia a rather quizzical look.

"You were here last night weren't you looking for the folk next door?" Sylvia nodded. "Yes we really do need to see them did they come back do you know?" The woman smiled. "Oh they came back alright didn't you see them?"

"No" said Sylvia "what time did they get back, it must have been very late because we waited for hours for them." The woman smiled.

"But you were parked up the road there weren't you, you must have seen them as they drove past you. To tell you the truth I was a bit suspicious about you when you moved your car up there so I phoned him to let him know. I think they came back soon after that, I was keeping a look out but I didn't see them go into the house. They must have left the car in the lane and gone in through the back door because when I went into the kitchen I saw him and his brother leaving that way. I came back into the lounge and saw the car as it came round the corner onto the street and I watched it as they drove past the house. They blew loudly on the horn as they went by you, you must have seen them."

Sylvia remembered the incident the night before. "So that was him was it?"

"There'd be four of them," said the woman. "Him, his brother and their two wives. I was just being a good neighbour when I phoned him because I didn't know who you were. But to tell you the truth Alf and me have never got on with them I've always thought they were a bit too smart those two, I hope they haven't taken advantage of you. They were only renting that house anyway so I don't think we'll see them back here again."

Sylvia thanked the woman, she went back to meet Paul and tell him her worst fears. "Let's go to Preston and see what we can find out there." she suggested. Paul had long since got over the shock of what was happening to him and his money, he was angry now very angry indeed. The two set off to Preston in the car to see if they could find any clues there which would lead them to the two men.

They arrived at the building which had housed Mr Ogilvy's office and found it closed even the brass plate which had proudly displayed the name of the solicitors had been removed. They went into the premises on the ground floor to make enquiries about the solicitor. The answer was not what they wanted to hear but again neither was it totally unexpected. It was just another nasty surprise to add to all the others that were stacking up against them. Mr Ogilvy or whoever it was who had been using that name had only taken the office for a month. The rent had been paid in advance and the tenant had only occupied it over the last ten days or so. As far as the owner knew he had not been seen for the last two days and was not expected to return.

The two left the premises more dismayed and angry than ever. "I think we need some professional advice on this Sylvia, we'll go back to Levensbridge and have a word with the solicitors there and see if they can help us."

The offices of Lattimer, Metcalfe & Grainger were easily found, the firm had never moved from the original building in which Gerald Lattimer had started his business in the town over a hundred years ago. The last Lattimer had retired and had passed over control of the firm to his two junior partners Tom Metcalfe and Ellis Grainger. The secretary Sarah Bentley welcomed them into the office. "Would you like to make an appointment with one of the partners?" Both Paul and Sylvia were well known to her as the firm had represented their interests over a number of years.

"No" said Paul we really need to speak to someone today. We're not bothered which one of them it is Tom or Ellis, but this is too important for us to leave without seeing one of them." Sarah hesitated for a moment, this was a little irregular as neither of the partners liked to speak to a client without at least some prior notice as to the nature of their business. But they were both good clients and she didn't want to take a chance of upsetting them and losing their custom, Ellis wouldn't be happy if that were to happen. She thought she could handle it.

"Can I ask what it's about, maybe I can have a word with Mr Metcalfe and see if he can squeeze you in?"

"I'm sorry I can't tell you, it's a very private matter it will have to be Tom, if he is free we'd be grateful if he could spare us a few minutes." Sarah smiled.

"Alright Paul I'll have a word with him and see what I can do." She knocked on Tom Metcalfe's door and entered. Tom was sitting at his desk doing the Telegraph crossword. "Yes Sarah what is it?" Sarah told him the names of the two people who wished to see him. Tom raised his head from the paper but didn't speak immediately, eventually he nodded his head.

"Well I suppose I've nothing on at the moment and if I put them off I might have a problem fitting them in tomorrow, yes send them in Sarah I'll see them now."

Paul and Sylvia were shown into the office, they were both well acquainted with Tom Metcalfe who looked every inch a solicitor. He was one of the old school, dressed in a tweed jacket which had seen better days, a checked country style shirt with club tie and dark green trousers. They say that a man looks very much like the dog he owns, if that were true then Tom's dog would be a bloodhound. His long face, sad looking eyes and drooping cheeks certainly matched the characteristics of that animal.

"Take a seat" he offered them. "Now tell me what's so important that it can't wait until tomorrow?" Paul had wanted to speak to Tom urgently, but now as he was sitting in his office and Tom was giving him the chance to explain he seemed reluctant to do so. As well as being angry he was also feeling ashamed of himself for falling under the influence of a run of the mill conman who had cheated him out of a lot of money. Sylvia on the other hand had no qualms about it and readily spoke up. Over the next few minutes she related to Tom everything that had happened, right from their first meeting with Alastair up until their search for him in Morecambe and the empty office in Preston.

Tom listened with interest to what she had to say and didn't attempt to interrupt until it was clear she had finished. He sat back in his chair emitting a series of small sigh's as he mulled over his response. At last he was ready to speak. "Well I have to say it's certainly been a well organised scam. This fellow Alastair McKay, do you think that's his real name?" Sylvia didn't know but admitted that it probably wasn't.

"We never thought much about it, but come to think of it I don't expect he would have used his real name would he. Whatever he is he's not stupid he wouldn't want to leave anything behind that we could trace him by."

"Have you brought any of the paperwork with you, the deeds perhaps?" Paul took out a large envelope and handed it over to Tom. He pulled out the deeds and looked at them closely. "These are not the originals then?" Paul explained that they were copies and the originals had been sent to the land registry for transferring the ownership. "Hmm, I suppose he could have sent them off." said Tom flicking through the papers. "In any case it doesn't matter they look OK and I think you'll find that you've purchased this piece of land quite legally. To be honest I don't think there's much you can do about it. This fellow's sold you land, just not the piece you thought you were buying. If you had come to me with it before making the purchase I would have seen through it and advised you not to go ahead with it." He replaced the deeds in the envelope and handed it back to Paul.

"So is there nothing we can do about it?" said Sylvia.

"Not as far as I can see," replied Tom. "A court would look at it this way, in their view you bought a piece of land quite legally. It would be almost impossible to prove that this Mr McKay or whoever he is cheated you into thinking it was something other than what it actually was. You'll just have to put it down to a bad experience I'm afraid, there's nothing I can do to help you." He relaxed back into the comfort of his old leather chair.

The two were stunned, this had been their last chance. They had felt sure that a real solicitor would have found something to give them hope of recouping at least some of their losses, now it seemed there was no chance of getting anything back. They rose, thanked Tom for hearing them out and left his office quietly. Sarah looked up as they came out, but recognising the look on their faces she wisely averted her eyes and opened a file on her desk.

Sylvia had her own thoughts on the scam.

"Thank the Lord Ray told me about the money he has stashed away in that offshore account, at least we'll still have plenty for our retirement. I told him I could afford to lose that much, I wonder if Paul can say the same."

Paul was not so happy

"This has been a complete bloody disaster it's almost wiped me out. I shouldn't have got involved with Sylvia and that other bastard, I don't know how I'm going to survive on what's left of Matt's money, I'll have to sell that house in France for a start."

Tom had also been thinking. Seeing Paul again had brought back memories of his good friend Matt Renwick and his wife Cathy. "That fellow Paul did well out of his Transport business when he sold it, not to mention the money he inherited from Matt's estate when he died. I'm sure he had something to do with Matt and Cathy's deaths but I don't suppose I'll ever be able to prove it. I've never been convinced they gassed themselves. I think I'll pay another visit to the police station and see if they're still looking into it. That young CID fellow seemed to have some doubts about it the same as me, maybe I'll have a word with him."

Chapter 42

Danger beware

Bene had been experiencing problems with his mobile phone, it had been playing up over the last twenty four hours and was getting worse. It was an essential part of his kit and he would have to replace it first thing that morning. It was via the house phone that ET eventually reached him.

"Bene, at last" said his DC.

"Yes I know" said Bene "My mobile's gone wonky, what's the problem?" ET had some interesting news.

"I've had a call from the library, the assistant there is worried about her boss Pat Latham. It seems that those two Germans were in the library yesterday afternoon and she was trying to get hold of you to go over there and see them. When she couldn't contact you she decided to follow them herself to see where they went to." ET had Bene's full attention.

"And did she find out where they went?"

"The assistant doesn't know because she left her to lock up. Her boss left the library just after half past four to follow the two Germans, but she hasn't turned up for work this morning and evidently she's never late so the assistant thought she's better let us know." Bene was trying to make some sense out of it.

"Well it's not much to go on is it, I mean those two could have gone anywhere and she could be anywhere as well, has the assistant tried to contact her boss at home?"

"Yes of course that's the first thing she did, but she's not there and hasn't been seen since yesterday. The chairman of the investment club also went to the library this morning to see what had happened to her, evidently she didn't turn up for their meeting last night."

Bene's hopes had been raised initially at the start of ET's call he thought they could be onto something, but now it was beginning to look less promising. "Well is that it, is there nothing more to go on?"

"Well there could be," said ET "Because later that night one of the librarians from the Preston branch who knows Ms Latham quite well was walking home, she thought she saw her in Preston walking up through the Newfield housing estate. She was pretty sure it was her but although she called out the woman ignored her. Anyway she phoned the library here this morning to ask if she had been in Preston the evening before and was worried when the assistant told her she hadn't come in." ET continued. "Now we know that Peter Hoffmann lives up there so I thought I should go over and ask him if he's seen them around, it's not a big estate and if those two are staying there we should be able to track them down."

"Good," said Bene "Call round here first and I'll come with you."

Ten minutes later ET arrived and parked his hatchback outside Dot's house, Bene came down the path to meet him. "It could rain so I've brought a couple of brollies we might need them, I'll throw them in the back." As he was doing that the house phone rang again, Dot called down the path to him.

"It's for you again Bene, for goodness sake go down and get a new phone this morning. Sowerby will kill you if he can't get in touch with you, especially at a time like this. You know fine well he needs to know exactly where you are and what you're doing. It's no good you looking for assistance if your phone isn't working, those two you're after are dangerous and have already killed people. I'm sure if they knew you were on to them they wouldn't hesitate to bump the two of you off as well." She wagged her finger at him.

"In the same situation you wouldn't let Alex or me go off without some means of contacting you so don't you dare let us be worrying about you, so make sure you go and get a new one before you go to Preston."

Bene went back into the house to take the call, It was Emile Zajic. He listened to what Emile had to say and thought it was important enough to call and see him before he went to Preston. He left the house again and spoke to ET. "Something else has just cropped up, I'm not going to be able to come with you right now. I've just had a call which could have a bearing on a case I was working on a few months ago. I'll take Dot's advice and get a new phone first then I'll have to go and see this chap. He's the one who was responsible for those two burglaries by the way and he might have some information which could be important."

"That's OK boss, I'll get away now and you can catch up with me later. I'll go to Peter's first and see what I can find out there, if he can't tell me anything I'll let you know and I'll start cruising around and see if I can spot them anywhere." Bene could see that ET sounded a little apprehensive and he knew it wasn't because of the danger he could find himself in, he laughed.

"Yes I know what you're thinking, it's about the last time you went there isn't it. Well if she answers the door keep a safe distance between her and yourself and whatever you do don't go into the house."

Next door Ethan had left the house and was on his way to school. Hearing the voices on the path next door he stopped and listened to what was being said. "Dangerous criminals eh, murderer's even, ET won't be able to capture them on his own he'll need a hand." He went down the path and saw the hatchback still open. "He won't let me come if I ask him so I'll jump in here and then I can jump out at the other end and we'll capture them together." He looked all around, and seeing there was no-one else about he climbed into the back of the vehicle and pulled the hatch down. He couldn't quite close it so he held it down as best as he could so that it wouldn't spring open.

The two men had finished making their plans for the day so ET left and walked back towards his car, leaving Bene to get his own car out. "It shouldn't take me more than an hour or so." Bene shouted as he turned to the garage. "I'll call you nearer the time and arrange a place to meet, OK?" ET waved acknowledgement as he reached his car parked on the roadside, slamming the hatch shut as he walked past he didn't hear the little cry of pain from inside. He started the engine and moved away not knowing he had a stowaway on board.

Bene, as he had promised Dot made the phone shop his first call, he purchased a new phone but transferred the number from the old one to the new. This done he made his way up to Emile's house to see for himself exactly what had been found. Emile let him in and showed him through into the conservatory at the back of the house. He pointed over to a roll top desk sitting against the far wall. "A van came yesterday to take away all the furniture from the garage, and everything was in there except this piece, Paul Hanbury's desk."

"So why didn't they take this with all the other stuff?" Bene asked. "Well my wife and I were both out at work when they came so my daughter let them into the garage, she didn't know about the desk so they left without it."

Bene went over to the desk. "So this is the only piece you stole from Paul is it?"

"Yes just that." said Emile. But it must be important to him because I've heard he's put out a reward to get it back. Now I'm no expert in the value of furniture but I don't think the desk itself is worth very much, so I thought there must be something inside it which could be valuable." Bene looked warily at him

"So you've had a look inside then?"

"Yes I have and at first I couldn't see anything significant. There were lots of books and papers of course, but nothing which looked to be important, mostly to do with when he owned his own company, but of course he doesn't have that anymore. There was no money or jewellery or anything like that in there. So I was thinking, what was in the desk which was so valuable to him but which would have no value to anyone else. So I looked more closely at everything that was in there."

Bene looked at his watch, he wasn't sure if this was going to lead anywhere or not, he was worried that it would turn out to be something so trivial that his journey up there would turn out to be a complete waste of time. He had a much greater demand on his time than to spend it here listening to this tedious monologue. He pressed Emile to get to the point quickly. Emile obliged, he pulled on a pair of gloves. "Well I was looking carefully through the contents until I came upon this envelope addressed to Paul." He took out the envelope and handed it to Bene. "Have a look at this and tell me if you see what I see." Bene began to show a little more interest. He pulled on his own gloves opened the letter carefully and read the contents.

"Well it's a letter from Matt Renwick to Paul. It doesn't give any details but it looks as though Matt had caught Paul out doing something he shouldn't have been doing. It must have been serious if Matt was going to the police about it but it doesn't say exactly what it was. Well maybe Paul had been up to something illegal but there's nothing in here that would incriminate him."

Emil smiled he was pleased with himself, he had seen something in the letter that Bene hadn't. Bene waited for him to point out what it was in the letter that had got Emile to bring him up there. "Well at the time those two people died in their bungalow from gas poisoning there was talk of a note being left, a kind of suicide note, you must have seen it." Bene nodded but didn't admit the fact. Emile went on "Well a few people did see it and it seemed to be common knowledge at the time exactly what it did say. I also heard from someone who did see the note and he said it looked as if it could have been cut or torn from something else. It was Matt's handwriting alright but it just didn't look or read like a suicide note should."

Bene could remember exactly how the note was worded and picked up the letter again. He came to the part which said.

"You've been warned. I've had enough and I'm going to put an end to it."

Again he didn't admit that it did look like the note which had been found in the bungalow. "Yes it was probably something along those lines, but the letter's here and the line which says this is intact so it's of no consequence."

Emile brought out another sheet of paper from the desk and handed it do Bene. It appeared to be a copy of the same letter written by Matt Renwick to Paul. It had been enlarged a little but nevertheless it was the same letter. Bene stared hard at it and couldn't believe what he was seeing. It was an exact copy of the original letter word for word, up until it reached the point where the line

"You've been warned. I've had enough and I'm going to put an end to it." should have been. This line was missing from the copy, it had been carefully cut out. At last he began to understand the reason why Matt and Cathy had to die. He had suspected at the time that it wasn't suicide, and his suspicions were backed up by

Tom Metcalfe a good friend of the family who hadn't been convinced either. He would go back to the station and look in the file containing all the information they had about Matt and Cathy's deaths. The alleged suicide note would be in there and when he placed that on the missing part of the copy letter he had no doubt it would fit perfectly.

He was ecstatic but trying hard not to let his emotions show. Two robberies by this fairly unassuming little man which had irked him somewhat at the time had given him the chance to arrest someone for two murders, two murders which at the time had been believed to be suicides. "At last," he thought "I knew I would get something on that sod in the end, I didn't know how, where or when, but I think I've got the bugger now."

Emile had been waiting patiently for Bene's reaction and he wasn't kept waiting long. "Well you've proved to be a bit of a detective yourself haven't you. Did you wear your gloves when you were searching through the desk?"

"Yes, I knew I was in trouble for stealing it but I didn't want to face any other charges so I made sure no-one would find my fingerprints on anything in the desk."

"Good," said Bene. "Well I'll have to take both pieces with me and have them checked over for prints, but yours won't be on them, right?"

"No you won't find my fingerprints on either of them."

Bene needed the desk as well.

"I'll have someone come and collect the desk this afternoon can I rely on you to be here when they come?"

"Yes I'm not working today I'll be at home." Emile thought he would ask if helping the police would go in his favour at his trial. "When I go to court do you think this will help me if it turns out that you can arrest someone as a result of me finding this evidence?"

Bene couldn't make any promises although he wished that he could. "I think that if you get yourself a good lawyer and he convinced the jury that the robberies were just done as a means of getting a bit of justice for your brother and not for any financial gain it would help. He could also say that you have an unblemished record and character witnesses could be brought to court to confirm that, that would help as well. And if there is a conviction as the result of this evidence that would go very much in your favour. I can't promise anything of course but if all these are taken into consideration I'd be fairly confident you won't be facing a prison sentence, more likely a fine and some form of community service." Emile was looking much more cheerful.

Bene phoned the Chief and briefly gave him the news of what he had discovered in Paul Hanbury's desk.

"OK Bene you'd better bring it down here and we'll get it checked over for prints. And now that you're back on that case as well I think you should get over to the bungalow and see if you can find anything that we may have missed earlier, we'll probably need something else to go with the letter before we can make an arrest, I doubt if we'll get a conviction on the strength of the letter alone."

ET meanwhile had arrived at Peter Hoffmann's house in Preston and was hoping he would find him home, he didn't fancy another encounter with Claire after his last visit there. He sat for a while taking in deep breaths as he prepared himself for the possibility of another tricky situation. Eventually he left the car and approached the house.

Ethan thought it was time to get out of the car and help his rescuer "This must be the house of the murderers, I'll get out and have a quick look." He felt around for a handle or switch to open the back of the car but he couldn't find one. It was dark inside and though he tried hard to find some means of escape he was having no success.

ET rang the bell and his heart sank a little when it was Claire who came to answer the door. She smiled when she saw who it was. "I knew you'd be back didn't I say so, come on in." She stood aside to let him into the house. ET didn't move.

"It was Peter I really came to see is he in?" Claire's smile was spreading.

"No of course not silly, remember I told you to come back when he wasn't in, and here you are." ET was finding it very difficult but stuck to his task manfully.

"No I'm sorry but I do need to speak to Peter urgently, where can I find him?" Claire's smile faded.

"What do you want to speak to him about?" ET explained about the German couple who had been seen on the estate and wondered if either her or Peter had seen them or knew where they were staying.

Claire shook her head.

"No I can't help you but maybe Peter can he's down at my shop doing a few jobs for me, would you like me to take you down there?" Claire had dropped her seductive tone and ET was thankful for it, he said they could use his car. Claire collected a coat and the two of them went down to ET's car. Ethan heard them approaching and thought he had better keep quiet.

It was only a few minutes' drive to the shop and Claire got out first and unlocked the door. "Does he lock himself in?" ET asked.

"Well he's working in the cellar on the electrics and he wouldn't know if someone just walked in, we have to keep it locked when the shop's not open for business." The two of them walked into the little shop and Claire switched on a light. She walked over to the far side behind the small counter beckoning ET to follow her. She opened a door which led down into the cellar and stood aside to allow him to go down.

ET looked down into the cellar which was in darkness, only the steps leading down into it were in light. Then just inside the door he saw something which took him completely by surprise. For there, stood up against the wall at the top of the steps was the same briefcase that had been snatched from him at the railway station. He gasped in astonishment what a lucky find, and boy would Bene be pleased that he'd got it back again. With a big grin on his face he turned around to face Claire. As he was doing so something else caught his eye, hanging from a peg on the opposite wall was a dark blue raincoat with light yellow patches on the sleeves.

"So," he thought. "It was Peter all along I should have known." His eyes were transfixed on the raincoat and his body rooted to the spot. But that was soon to change, for at that moment a long hard cardboard roll was being thrust towards his back with considerable force. When it came into contact with his lower body he blacked out with the pain as it pitched him forwards and headlong down the steep steps into the cellar.

Chapter 43

Secret agent in action

Bene rushed back to the police station with the two pieces of evidence he hoped would lead to an arrest in the deaths of Matt and Cathy Renwick. He left them with the Chief who would have someone check them over for fingerprints. "You sure no-one has touched them Bene?"

"No, both Emile and I used gloves when we handled them, so if you do find any prints on them they'll be the prints of the person who left the note."

He left as quickly as he could, if the deadline for making an arrest in the case of the murdered girl was to be met then he had much to do. He sped off to the bungalow which had been the Renwick's home, he hadn't been back there since checking over the place in the days following their deaths. He pulled on his gloves. The bungalow hadn't been occupied since that time and as he entered the house he thought that as far as he could see everything appeared to be exactly the same as it had been then.

"Well where do I start," he muttered. "We went over everything at the time and found nothing, just the note on the worktop and the towels which had been put down at each of the doors confining the gas to the kitchen and the bedroom where the couple had slept." He wandered aimlessly around the bungalow for a few minutes to see if anything different jumped out at him, but there was nothing. "No I think we covered everything at the time, there's nothing new in here." He opened the side door and went outside. "Well if I'm going to find anything it must be out here somewhere." He opened the garage and went inside, he spent a good fifteen minutes looking around but he couldn't see anything unusual among the few items which were in there. The garage had been used for its intended purpose of garaging the car not as a storeroom, so there was little space for anything else when the car had been in there.

He locked the garage behind him and looked down the path towards the back garden, he couldn't see it but remembered there was a small shed tucked away behind the garage where Matt had kept the lawn mower and his garden tools. Bene walked around the back of the garage to the shed and opened it, it wasn't locked. Matt hadn't seen the need for padlocks as there was no access from the private wood at the bottom of the garden to the house. The shed was only medium sized, about eight feet by six feet and everything in there was clean and tidy and in good order. He could see almost everything without going in too far. The lawn mower of course was on one side and a few garden tools hanging up on the opposite wall. At the far end Matt had built a work bench across the width of the shed, but the only items on it were a few cans of paint. A framework was fitted to one wall and had on it small plastic clip-on boxes with a variety of nails and screws. Various other tools were hanging from nails or clips on the far wall. As far as he could see there was nothing unusual about the shed. He stood there for a few moments with his mind beginning to lose interest in what was proving to be a pointless exercise. He should leave and catch up with ET, his time would be far better spent with him in Preston.

For no apparent reason he walked over to the bench and looked more closely at the items on it, he lifted up the tins of paint to see if there was anything underneath but there was nothing. As he pulled one of the boxes of nails from the rack it slipped from his hand and spilled its contents out onto the floor. Cursing to himself he bent down to pick them up and found his eyes attracted to a shiny object hanging on a cup hook behind the far supporting post, it was almost hidden from view against the back wall. It was a house key. "Now why would Matt want to keep a spare key in here, he'd have to get down on his hands and knees to reach it. Tom Metcalfe had told him that Matt kept a spare door key in a key coded box on the side of the house and that had been checked at the time. The only prints on it were Matt's, so why have a key in here as well?"

He still had his gloves on so he reached under the bench and removed the key. He closed the shed door behind him and walked up the path to the back door of the bungalow. Trying the key in the lock he found it opened the door easily so he placed it in a plastic bag and took it away with him. "Might be something in it." he thought. "I don't think this key belonged to Matt, I think someone else has had it cut for their own purposes.

I'll get the Chief to check this for prints as well, you never know someone might have been foolish enough to have left them on."

He called back at the station and handed the key to the Chief who held it up to the light.

"I won't know until it's been checked of course but if there are any prints on it and none of them belong to Matt or Cathy then it could be just what we need." He put the key down and looked down at his watch, "Are you still here?" Bene took the hint and left. On his way out he phoned ET, the message he heard was.

"The person you are calling is unable to take your call at the moment, please leave a message after the tone." He threw the phone down on the passenger seat of the car and set off to Preston. "I'll give him another call when I'm nearly there."

2

Ethan meanwhile was trying in vain to open the hatchback which had him locked inside. "I've got to get out of here, ET's been gone ages and something must have happened to him." He gave up struggling with the hatch and felt around to see if there was any other way he could get out. Pushing upwards he felt the cover which was clipped onto the back of the rear seats. "Ah now that's better." He pushed hard and one of the clips released itself, pushing hard on the other side another clip sprung away and the cover shot back. Now he could see light, he pulled the ring on the top of the seat and it sprung forward giving him room to crawl into the back seat of the car. He opened the door and stepped out onto the pavement, his little eyes peered up and down the street. "Right where did you go?"

ET was coming around very slowly his body was aching like mad. It was dark and he didn't know where he was or why he felt so bad, his mind took him back a few days. Was he on the railway line, he remembered standing on the platform and someone had pushed him off. If he was on the track it would be too dark for him to see the train when it came along, he felt around for a rail but couldn't find one, he was confused. He opened and closed his eyes but it made no difference it was dark either way so he curled up and went back to sleep.

When he came around again he could remember exactly what had happened, his body was still very sore but feeling around he didn't think anything was broken. He thought he would try and move but as he reached out with his arm to find something to support him he touched something that sent a shockwave right through him. Someone else was down in the cellar lying right beside him. "Who the hell are you, have you been thrown down here as well?" A man's voice answered him.

"Oh so you've come round at last have you, I recognise the voice now you're the policeman aren't you, the one who came to our house."

"Peter is that you?" ET asked, also recognising the voice of the man who had spoken to him. "What on earth are you doing down here. A few minutes ago I was about to start looking for you and arrest you for murder, now you've saved me the trouble I've got you."

"Don't be stupid man why would I want to murder anybody?" ET laughed even though he was still in considerable pain.

"Well that briefcase up there by the door and the raincoat you wore when you pushed me off the platform it's obvious isn't it, Christ man you could have killed me."

"Bloody hell man haven't you got it yet, I only saw the briefcase as I was being pushed down here myself and the raincoat isn't mine its Claire's." ET was finding it difficult to understand.

"Why would Claire do that, she seems so ...." He left the sentence unfinished, he didn't want to embarrass Peter by telling him she was a vamp. There was a short silence before Peter spoke again.

"Well I think it's best that I tell you everything then you'll understand. When Claire and I got married Claire wasn't her real name, she just thought that name would go down better if we were living in England."

"Why" asked ET, "What's her real name?" Peter explained.

"I met her when I went over to Germany, I knew her as Sabine and we fell in love and got married within a few short weeks, I didn't tell her that I had lied about my name. You have to understand that Maierhofen the town where we lived, was and still is very sympathetic to the Nazi cause. My family were not welcome there after the war so I took on the surname Neumann so as not to reopen any old sores or make life difficult for me."

Peter took a short breather before continuing. "It was when I persuaded her to come back with me to England that she discovered my real name. If she had known at the time I'm sure she would never have agreed to marry me. Now you know that my real name is Peter Hoffmann but what you didn't know was that Claire's real name is Sabine Huber. We come from two very different backgrounds and when she found out my real name was Hoffmann her love for me disappeared pretty fast. We've lived together for two years over here but we're no longer in what you would call a relationship. She's been saving up her money to open a shop in Maierhofen so she can go back there to live. Anyway when those two bodies were discovered in the woods she found out that they were ancestors of hers and she became even more hostile towards me. Then her brother came over and when they met up the situation went from bad to worse."

Peter was tired and his speech was getting slower. "When I brought my father's briefcase home Claire must have looked into it and found something that was important to her and her brother. I hadn't looked in it before I gave it to you so I had no idea what it contained. I think that when you took it she must have followed you and it was her who pushed you onto the track and stole the briefcase from you. I didn't know of course, I only suspected, but when her brother kept coming here I knew something was going on. They were so close and I was afraid, not only of him but of Claire as well, she had become very animated and I knew I had to be careful. I've heard them discussing some place in France and I think that's where they're heading for. Just like you she lured me here on a false pretence and locked me in. I think they'll be making their way out of the country now, so unless you can get out of here quickly I think you'll be too late to stop them getting away."

ET spoke "What about that girl Anna Ferenc do you think they killed her?" Peter thought they had done.

"They used her, and although she thought she was one of them they knew her real name and they didn't accept her. I overheard the two of them talking one day and Alois said she had to go, he said they would offer to take her with them when they left but would make sure she never left the country. When she was working at the home she was useful to them but when she had served her purpose I think they did away with her."

A short silence followed, ET thought that Peter had told him all he knew.

"So is there no other way out of here?" he asked. Peter replied

"No, just that door and its locked and bolted on the other side we won't be able to break it down from in here." ET looked up and saw a dim light coming in through a small window higher up the wall.

"What about that then, where does that come out?"

"It's on the rough ground at the side of the shop at ground level, but there are bars across on the outside so that's no good either."

ET got up tentatively and went over to the wall, there was a makeshift wooden bench which he dragged over to the wall. He was able to stand on this and look out. The window was dirty so he took out a hankie and wiped some of the dirt and cobwebs away. It still didn't let in much light so he spit on the hankie a few times and wiped it again, this time it was much clearer and he pushed his face up nearer to it. What he saw next almost sent him crashing back to the floor. Through the window and only inches from his face a pair of small eyes peering through rounded spectacles were looking at him. He recognised them immediately, they belonged to Ethan.

Bene had arrived in Preston an hour ago but hadn't been able to contact ET or find out where he had gone. He had gone to Peter Hoffmann's house first and found no-one in, none of the neighbours had seen him or had any idea where he might be. He decided to have a trawl around the streets on the estate while he waited for ET to phone. "Maybe there's no reception where he is, I expect I'll get a call from him shortly."

Five minutes later he did get a call, but it wasn't from ET it was from Chief Inspector Sowerby. "Bene I've had a 999 call come through. I can't tell if it's genuine or a hoax but you'd better get down to Sampson Street and find out. The caller was phoning on behalf of someone else who told him a policeman has been locked up in a building there and he needs rescuing." Bene switched off the phone.

"Is that why I can't get hold of you ET, if it is you of course, boy you do get into some scrapes." He shot off down to Sampson Street as fast as he could.

He had no idea whereabouts on Sampson Street he was supposed to look but remembered that Claire's shop was in the same street. He stopped the car half way down, got out and started walking. Before he had gone very far a small voice rang out.

"Bene, over here."

"Bloody hell it can't be." thought Bene, but the voice did sound familiar. He was right, little Ethan was further down the street and waving to him enthusiastically.

"Come on Bene quick, he's in here." Bene ran down to meet him and together they went around the shop, Ethan showed him the small window near the ground.

"He's down in there." Ethan pointed to the window.

Bene called for reinforcements and when they arrived they broke into the shop, smashed their way into the cellar and brought out the two men who had been held captive. Both were bruised and sore but neither of them required hospital treatment. The briefcase was brought out along with the raincoat and both would be taken back to Levensbridge police station.

Peter came back with them to help with the enquiries into where his wife and her brother might be going. Ethan came back as well, his head swelling with pride at being able to help in ET's rescue. He was dropped off at home and Ken and Maggie could only shake their heads in disbelief when Bene told them what had happened. The two detectives and Peter continued on to the police station.

"Well" said the Chief "They have a good start on us and I doubt we'll be able to cover all the ports and airports at such short notice, but I'll put out a general call and we can only hope for the best, they might be using false passports of course. Where do you think they're headed?" He was addressing Peter who told him he thought they were going to somewhere in France first then back to Maierhofen in Germany. "Right then, they might slip through the net here so I'll alert Interpol and hopefully they can pick them up in France, if not they'll get them when they go back to Germany."

The Chief wanted to know if the couple could be charged. "Do you think they're responsible for the murder of Anna Ferenc?"

"Absolutely," said Bene. "And Sabine was the one who pushed ET off the platform so that's another charge against her of attempted murder."

"And the deaths up at the home, can we do anything about those?" asked the Chief. Bene didn't think so.

"We think Anna was involved along with them and I'm sure that together the three of them were in some way responsible for them dying, but I doubt we'll ever be able to prove it."

"OK" said the Chief "That will do for me, I've no doubt we'll see them again soon once Interpol have picked them up." Bene remembered about the librarian.

"I think Patricia Latham might be a victim in this as well, she hasn't been seen since she was in Preston and I think we might have another body on our hands before too long, when she shows up we'll charge them with that as well."

The Chief went back to the briefcase. "Let's have a look in the briefcase then and see if there are any clues in there." The briefcase was opened and all the contents laid out on the table in front of them. ET was the only one in the room who had seen any of them before so the Chief asked him to look through what was there and see if anything was missing. ET sifted through the papers and agreed that it was more or less what he had seen. He picked up the diary and remembered seeing that as well.

"Most of it seems to be here except the maps, they're missing."

They looked at each piece of paper separately but all they could see were records of who was in the camp and when. Some of the lists were names of the POW's only, others had names and home addresses and included and a few personal details. There were other pieces of general information amongst the lists but none of it was of any relevance. The Chief picked up the diary.

Chapter 44

The diary of Dieter Hoffmann

The Chief opened the diary and began to look through it. "Of course it's written in German and I only learned French at school, here Peter you read it for us." The office was silent as Peter read quietly for almost five minutes without lifting his head. The three men sitting beside him waited in anticipation for him to share the contents with them. When he did look up he told them what he had read so far.

"Well I've gone through about half of it and there's nothing interesting up to now, it's not a diary as such it's just a book that he carried around with him jotting down events and dates as they happened. It starts from when my father and his two friends joined the army and it goes on to describe their experiences as they went into France and onto the northern coast where they were based."

He had almost brought them up to date with what he had read. "It seems as though they had a pretty awful time over there, but nothing I've read up to now looks to have any bearing on what is so important to warrant murdering anyone for." He bent over the book again and began reading the second half. Another minute or so passed until he raised his head again. "I think I'm at the part now which is the reason for my wife and her brother's interest in it. I'll read it out exactly as he has written it in the book, so it's his words you will hear not mine." The three men listened intently as he began.

"Saturday 15th January 1944. Today we are to accompany Franz and Karl Huber to a place somewhere south of here. We have not been told the reason why but it must be important to them. I do not know if the journey has been authorised.

Sunday 16th January. Yesterday was the worst day of our lives and the horror of it will live with us forever. The place we went to is one that none of us want to return to in our lifetime. But if any of our descendants want to go there after we have departed from this life then I have drawn maps which will lead them to the exact location. It will be up to them as to what they do with the incredible secret we discovered there.

I will explain exactly what took place while it is still vivid in my mind. We travelled for about an hour, I do not remember exactly how far but you can use the map to trace our journey. We arrived at a farmhouse but only Franz and Karl went in, my friends and I stayed in the truck. The farmer and his daughter came out with the brothers and were taken into a barn and we feared the worst for them. However nothing happened and the brothers and the farmer came out but without the girl. They brought him to our truck and we all left the farm. We drove for about another ten minutes and pulled up at the edge of what appeared to be either a large wood or forest. "We have to walk now" said the farmer, so we left the truck and entered the forest on foot. He led us along a track through the trees.

Franz was laughing and I asked him where we were going and why, and why had we gone to the farm in the first place. Evidently the last weekend the daughter had rejected Karl's advances so they had gone back to the farm with the intention of raping her. The farmer begged them not to and told them he could make them rich men if they left his family alone. Franz told me the story that the farmer had told him.

He said he had a nephew who worked in one of the central banks in Paris. His nephew said that a few days before our army entered the city panic was breaking out. The banks in particular were worried that all their assets would be stripped and taken to Germany. The finance minister and the major bankers took the decision to remove all the gold bullion and other valuables from their vaults, they would store it in selected places across the country where it would remain hidden until France was a free country again. The nephew was there when the gold was taken away, it seems that the gold bullion from his bank and all the others left Paris on the same day, all bound for different places.

On that evening the farmer saw lights from three vehicles moving up this way but had no idea where they came from, where they were going or what they were carrying. The next day he followed the tracks they had left and found they led into the forest. He followed up through the woods and came across an old disused Special Services training camp which had been built after the First World War. He had known about the camp and knew there were underground cellars in it which were encased in concrete, about as secure as you could get I suppose. He is sure that this is one of the places where gold bullion from one of the banks is hidden.

We reached a point in the forest where the tracks appeared to veer off the main path but a fallen tree was blocking the way. "See," said the farmer, "This tree has been cut down to prevent anyone from getting to the camp, we can get around it from up there," he pointed to a spot a little further along. We soon found our way around the obstacle and after little more than a hundred metres we came upon the old camp.

The only entrance to the main block was through a large door which was securely locked and there were no proper windows as such in the building, only narrow slits in the walls. It was possible to shine a torch inside but there was no obvious entry to the underground cellars that we could see. The farmer assured us that there were cellars there and the brothers seemed satisfied he was telling the truth. They seemed happy with what they had seen and together we returned to the truck and drove back to the farmhouse.

I asked Franz if we would be able to get the gold out but he said

"Not yet, even if we could get it out we couldn't do anything with it until after the war, I just wanted to satisfy myself that it was one of the chosen sites. We will leave it here until the war is over then we can take it back to Germany and we will all be very rich." Then I asked him.

"What if the bank people come back for it after the war?" But he just laughed and said.

"Well that's the best part, because when the vehicles left the banks the only people who knew where they were going were the men in the wagons, the bank manager, three of his staff who drove out here to store it and an armed escort. When the wagons left here to return to Paris one of our planes spotted them and gunned the vehicles down, the wagons were badly burned and all the people inside were killed, none of them made it back to Paris. So you see no one but the farmer knew that the gold was here."

We drove back to the farm and were feeling a little happier thinking that no harm would now come to the farmer or his daughter, but how wrong we were. When we arrived back at the farm Franz, Karl and the farmer went back into to barn but we stayed in the truck. We heard a shot ring out and a scream, the screaming went on for a long time before another shot was fired and then it all went quiet. We sat in the truck trembling, we were too afraid of the two brothers to do anything to help the poor family.

Franz and Karl came out laughing and we were very frightened. They took some fuel from the truck and set fire to the barn and the farmhouse. We cried as we listened to the screams coming from the house. The rest of the family were trapped upstairs and there was no escape for them, the brothers were firing their guns at the windows and didn't stop until the screams had died down. We were not allowed to leave until the whole place was burned to the ground.

Tuesday 18th January. We have been so lucky. Last night we got the chance to leave all this horror behind us. We were taken across the channel to England by a fisherman and his family. Otto, Lukas and myself are now safe in England.

Peter looked up to see the reaction. "Phew," said the Chief. "that's some story. It will have been hard for you to read it Peter, your father's own words about what he had been through all those years ago."

"Yes, the war was a very bad time for everyone, but even though he deserted I'm still very proud of what he did, and more importantly what he didn't do, especially at that farm."

"Is there more?" asked the Chief. Peter flicked through the pages until he came to the part where the Huber brothers came to the POW camp.

"Nothing much until after the invasion and then it seems that the Huber brothers were taken to the same camp and caused a lot of trouble." He read further.

"I think you should hear what he says in this piece. It's from sometime in mid August." Peter read out the entry.

"Today the three of us were called into the Camp Commander's office. He told us that the Huber brothers were proving too hard to keep under control and he didn't have sufficient staff to guarantee our safety for much longer. They had made no secret of the fact they would kill us if the chance arose and he was gravely concerned not only for our safety but that of the other inmates. He made a suggestion which would give us the chance to do them all a favour and get rid of the two men once and for all.

Yesterday we took up his suggestion and finding the three rifles and the tools which had been left out for us we went into the woods just after the brothers had left with the guard. We followed at a safe distance until we came to the place where they were supposed to be working. We hid behind trees until the guard had gone back to the camp then watched to see what they were doing. We were just in time as they had already started to run away, they were trying to escape. Luckily they were coming our way so when they were close enough we stepped out from behind the trees and shot them dead. We were all shaking but we still managed to dig two graves with the tools we had brought with us. We buried them alongside each other making sure the ground was put back to its original state. When that was done we walked slowly back to the camp leaving the guns and tools in the agreed place on the way. We were all feeling bad about what we had done and we went straight to our hut and stayed there until the next morning.

Another entry in the book at a later date said. "Since that time the camp became a good place to be again, no-one talked about Franz and Karl Huber anymore, they were forgotten."

Peter looked up. "There's more but nothing of any importance, I think the book just about explains everything." There was a minute or two of silence as the four men took it all in. It was the Chief who spoke first.

"Well to take the last part first it explains who killed the two Huber brothers and why. But as the three men who shot them are all dead we can't bring any charges against them, then there's the Camp Commander, he seems to have been involved as well but he's also dead. Anyway at least I can hand the diary over to division and they can close the case."

The other three were more interested in the gold bullion. "It's a pity we don't have that map," said Bene. "I expect Alois and your wife have it Peter."

"Yes" said the Chief. "We should get it back when Interpol catch up with them. Until then I don't think anyone will be able to find out where this place is." He questioned ET about the map again.

"Is there nothing more you can tell us about it, a name or something to give us a clue. It must be in a wood somewhere." ET had been thinking a lot about the map.

"There was something but it didn't mean anything to me."

"Go on then" said the Chief "let's have it."

"It was a name something like Foret Shousas." The Chief thought about it.

"Well Foret is French for wood, but I can't make out the other word, are you sure it was Shousas, it couldn't have been Choucas could it?" ET grinned.

"That's it, yes that's exactly what it was, Foret Choucas, what does it mean?"

"It means" said the Chief "Jackdaw's Wood" "So we're looking for a place called Foret Choucas somewhere in France, I expect there are hundreds of them, but at least it's something."

Chapter 45

A job nearly done

George Wheeler awoke to find his bed surrounded by people sitting around looking at him. Adam Firth and Kris were on one side, two members of the bowls club and his wife on the other side. "What the hell are all you lot doing here, I'm not sure I want any witness' to my heavy snoring and my funny night time habits, Norah plays war with me don't you dear." His wife smiled.

"Well it's just nice to know that you remember who I am at last, yesterday you hadn't a clue had you?" Everyone laughed, it was good to see George a bit more like to his old self again.

"Can you remember what happened yet?" asked Adam. "Not a damned thing, I remember going down to the yard to see Derek but I can't remember what happened after I got there, by the way has anyone seen him?" They all shook their heads, no-one it seemed had seen Derek for the last day or so. There was a longish pause as none of them knew just what to say after that. They had all been worried about George, especially after the deaths of the two other owners. They all at one time or another wondered if Derek was behind it all, he had changed so much over the last month and had become very secretive and elusive. His father had been one of the founding members of the club and Derek had always been a keen bowler himself. Now it seemed that all he wanted to do was sell the ground for a quick profit.

During this lull in conversation the door opened and in walked the devil himself. "George old chap I've just heard what happened, how are you?" Derek Cooper came to the bedside and placed a concerned hand on top of George's. "I've been away and I only got back a couple of hours ago, my neighbour told me you were in here." George looked a little bemused.

"But you asked me to come down to the yard didn't you, I remember going there but I can't remember anything after that, were you there?" Derek kept his hand on top of George's.

"No you cancelled our meeting don't you remember, I got home after I'd seen you in the pub and my son said there was a message from you to say you couldn't make it, don't you remember?" There were a few things George couldn't remember too clearly but up until he went out that night he knew he hadn't made that call to Derek.

"Well blow me" said Derek "I wonder who it was, someone's been playing tricks on us, but why would anyone do that."

Derek didn't dwell on it though, he stroked George's hand and smiled. "Anyway never mind about that you're going to be alright aren't you, and listen I've got some news for you." He looked around and smiled at the others, he wanted them all to hear what he had to say.

"You'll all want to hear this because things have changed, I'm no longer interested in selling the ground." He checked himself at that point to see the reaction on their faces, most of them were blank. "Yes I can see you're surprised but I've been thinking a lot about it lately. Believe me with what's happened to our two other co-owners and what's just happened to poor old George here it got me worried, I was pretty frightened I can tell you. I was beginning to think something sinister was going on and it could be me next, and that really did scare me."

Adam wanted to make sure that Derek was serious about not wanting to sell. "Are you sure you really mean this Derek, you won't suddenly change your mind again?"

"Not a chance Adam, I must admit the offer was tempting, but I've made my mind up not to go any further with it, especially after what's happened to old George here. In any case I'm not sure if the offer is still on the table, the chap who was interested seems to have fallen on hard times so maybe it's just as well." Derek looked around the bedside to see the reaction.

"So I hope that's a bit of good news for you all." The bedside congregation were now nodding and smiling. "Oh," he continued "I've just remembered, I've been out and bought some new club shirts for next season. I think you'll like them, they're green and purple and you'll look good in them." He waved his finger at them. "And I expect you to win the league for us next year, I think those colours could be lucky, you never know we might even do the double."

Derek rose and shook George warmly by the hand. "Now you make sure you're out of here as soon as possible and then we can all get back to doing what we likc best, bowling." He said his goodbyes and left the room. Some around the bed still had their mouths halſ open, Derek had given them quite a shock.

2

Bene and ET were in Chief Inspector Sowerby's office, the Chief was summarising the events of the last twenty four hours. "Right then let's have a look at what we've got. We can't bring charges against anyone for the two German POW's whose bodies were found in the wood, because everyone who was involved in any way is now dead, but at least the case can now be closed. Neither can we pin the deaths of the two residents up at the home on anyone. They may have looked suspicious, but as you say there's no evidence and we've got nothing else to go on. The pathologist found nothing so it's possible that after all their deaths were natural and could have been expected of people their age. So again we can close those."

He folded the two files, set them aside and replaced them with others. "Now let's concentrate on what we can act on. The first one is the murder of Anna Bauer/Ferenc. Now we're sure that we can charge Alois and Sabine for this one and we will do as soon as they're picked up by Interpol." He looked up at Bene. "And you think they may be responsible for another murder as well?"

"That's right, Patricia Latham hasn't been seen since she was spotted near their place in Preston and it's just not like her to go off without telling anyone. I think her body will turn up sooner or later and we'll find that she was another of their victims."

Another two files were put aside and the Chief opened the next one. "Now we come to Emile Zajic, he'll be charged with robbery and he'll plead guilty is that right?" Bene agreed.

"Yes but with the help he's given us I expect the judge will let him off lightly." The Chief seemed satisfied with that and put that file along with the others.

The Chief opened the last file. "This is the one that's going to give you the most satisfaction Bene. The pieces of evidence Emile found have been checked and both are positive, we already had the fellow's prints on file for a motor accident he was involved in a few years earlier. We couldn't prove anything at the time but his details remained on our records. The prints match up alright so all we need now is for him to identify the desk and we've got him. It turns out that he's the one who left the alleged suicide note inside the bungalow, we thought it was strange at the time when we didn't find any prints on it, not even Matt's. He entered the house using the key that he kept in the shed, he must have borrowed one at some time and had a copy cut. I don't know why he put it back in the shed he should have taken it with him or just thrown it away, maybe he thought he might need it again if the gas didn't kill them." The Chief was smiling broadly. "Anyway those were his two mistakes, keeping hold of that copy which had his prints on and leaving the key in the shed. He should have worn gloves when he handled those, I mean he was careful to wear them when he was in the house."

The Chief was enjoying himself now. "Well we did alright, and we didn't have to hand any of it over to division. And look at what else we've achieved. I had Tom Metcalfe in this morning, I told him to get tomorrow's evening paper. Matt and Cathy were good friends of his and I think he'll be pleased to find out that his doubts about their suicide have proved to be true. He'll be a lot happier when he sees an arrest for their murder in tomorrow's paper. Well it's time to go, the van's waiting outside. But just before we go I haven't thanked you both sufficiently for everything you've done over the last week or so. It's been a hellish time for all of us but especially you two, but I think we're almost there now. Just this one little piece to finish off and I want you to do it Bene."

The three went up to the house of Paul Hanbury in the van containing Paul's desk. Bene approached the house and rang the bell. The door was answered by Paul and when Bene told him the desk had been recovered he was over the moon. "Great, is it in the van?"

"Yes" said Bene "I just need you to confirm that it's yours and that's it." Bene took him over to the back of the van which was open and let Paul look inside.

"That's the one alright, let's get it back in the house." He started to climb into the back of the van but Bene held him back.

"You are sure it is yours Paul?"

"Absolutely mate no doubt about it."

Bene had waited a long time for this moment. "Paul Hanbury I'm arresting you for the murders of Matthew and Cathleen Renwick." He proceeded to read him his rights. Paul just laughed at him and looked at the other two officers.

"Who the hell is this clown, come on Bene boy you can't pin that on me you big jerk." A big smile broke out across Bene's face.

"Just four things Paul, Shed! House Key! Desk! Photocopy!" The smirk on Paul's face was instantly replaced with a look of disbelief and then fear, he seemed to visibly shrink at hearing those few words. ET came round and put the handcuffs on him and he was led over to a waiting police car which took him and ET down to the police station.

3

It was party time at Dot's house and everyone was there. ET was still a little sore from his unpleasant incident in the cellar but he was being comforted by his girlfriend Sue who was holding onto his arm and stroking his head, ET was milking it for all it was worth. Ethan was crawling around the floor. "I'm chasing a spider and I think it went under your chair." Ken and Maggie just laughed. Ken shrugged "Well what else can we do."

Adam came over to sit beside Bene bringing two cans of beer with him. "Here get this down you, you look as if you need it."

"Thanks Adam I do need it, for a long time there I didn't think we'd get anywhere with this lot. The minute you retired everything started to happen and it just kept piling up until we were overwhelmed by it all, it was too much." Adam smiled.

"Yes but you got there in the end didn't you?"

"Yes with some help from ET and little ET over there and a bit of good fortune thrown in as well. But it could all have turned out very differently."

"Yes but it didn't did it." said Adam. "When Interpol pick up those two you'll have cleared up all the crimes on your desk. And if another body does turn up I'm sure you'll find some piece of evidence to connect the two of them with that as well. But Paul Hanbury, that was the most rewarding one wasn't it, we both wanted something that would tie him in to those two deaths, and you got that as well didn't you?"

"Well I needed a bit of luck and a slip up from him to clinch it. But yes I have to agree with you that was the best."

Alex cuddled up to him on the sofa. "So have I got you to myself now, you won't go chasing after anyone else for a while. We need to spend a bit more time on our own without all these people here, not to mention half the police force in the house." Bene laughed.

"Yes I must admit I do feel a bit more relaxed now it's almost over, how about a couple of weeks away and you can choose."

"Then when we come back, what happens then?" She looked up expectantly.

"When we come back we get married." Alex cuddled in closer.

There was a knock on the door and a policeman handed over a packet addressed to Chief Inspector Sowerby, he opened it and read the letter inside. It had come from Peter Hoffmann and it was a little thank you for Ethan. Everyone watched as the Chief took the box over and handed it to him. Ethan opened it and pulled out a magnifying glass, it was just like the one Sherlock Holmes would use. “It’s a little reward for you Ethan, and if you want to use it to find that spider here’s a clue, it’s running up your leg.”

“Yikes” shouted Ethan as he jumped to his feet and shook himself vigorously to shrieks of laughter from the room.

Chapter 46

The secret of Jackdaw's Wood

Alois and Sabine were approaching a small hamlet about fifty kilometres south west of Etaples in northern France. They had used false passports to escape England and had wasted no time in using the map to direct them to the forest where the treasure would be found. "Have we got all the tools we need Alois?" Alois laughed.

"We've got enough dynamite to blow the whole forest up, and this truck will be big enough to take as much gold out as we are likely to find there. I've put a couple of shovels in, some rope and a few other tools as well. The only thing I'm bothered about is the noise, we don't want to draw attention to the wood when we're blasting the concrete away."

"It's a chance we'll just have to take" she replied. "But hopefully we won't be disturbed." They were both conscious of the weather which was changing for the worse, dark clouds were creeping closer and the wind speed was increasing.

They continued along the road until they came to the ruins of the farm where they stopped to check the map. "This must be where they started out from." said Alois

"The map says it's up that way along the rough track." They moved away and followed the track until they came to the forest.

"Well it's certainly isolated," said Sabine. "it doesn't look as though many people will bother to come all the way up here, I don't think we'll have any problems."

Alois brought out the map showing directions into the forest. "It looks fairly straightforward we should be able to follow it alright. When we come to the part where it's blocked off we just have to work our way around it, we'll be nearly there then." The couple left the truck behind and carried on up the track on foot. It took them about thirty minutes to reach the old camp and they had seen no evidence along the way to show that anyone else had been there. The only witnesses to their presence in the wood were the noisy Jackdaws.

They unloaded the tools and went over to see the old building. "Well it still looks intact," said Alois. "It doesn't look like anyone has tried to get into it, the door's still secure and the walls and roof show no sign of damage." The first sound of thunder was heard and when they looked up they could sense that rain was not far away.

"OK" said Alois. "let's get started, this weather will help us. If people hear us blasting away they'll just think it's thunder." He laughed out loud. "Even the weather is helping us, I can't believe the luck we're having." They took all the equipment over to the building, Alois looked for a good place where he could put the explosives to blast the heavy door away. When this was done he wired it up and they stood well back behind the trees as he pushed the handle down.

The forest erupted when the explosives went off, it not only blew the door away it also took out part of the wall surrounding it, even the heavy concrete on the roof above was cracked and distorted. The Jackdaws had flown off in fright. Alois laughed out raucously. "That shook the old place up a bit didn't it, and I got rid of those cackling birds as well."

"You used too much Alois I hope we can still get into the cellars." They waited until the dust had settled then went into the building. Bits of the wall and a few pieces off the roof had fallen in but the cellar entrance which was sealed was in view and looked to be undamaged.

The storm was getting worse, the loud claps of thunder deafened the air and the rain began to come down. "Quick get this thing open and at least we can get inside and keep dry." Sabine hurried Alois into setting another charge of explosive. "But don't use too much this time or you'll have the whole place down and we'll be here for ages trying to clear it away." Alois quickly set everything up and took the equipment back behind the cover of the trees which would protect them when the sealed entrance was blown away. "Come on then," she urged. "This rain's getting worse, we don't want to be caught in the woods if lightning strikes."

The explosives did the trick and the entrance was blown open. Debris was scattered everywhere but they quickly cleared enough away to make it easy for them to go down into the cellar and claim their reward. "I think you've used too much again Alois, look at the walls and the roof they don't look very safe to me."

"You worry too much Sabine, come on let's get down there out of this horrible weather." The two walked down into the cellar and looked around in the semi darkness, only a faint light was coming in through the opening two metres above them. Sabine brought out a torch and when she switched it on they both took a step back in amazement. Dozens of gold ingots were stacked uniform along large wooden posts laid out on the floor.

The pair of them fell silent for several moments taking in the enormity of the wealth which was spread out before them. Sabine spoke first. "My God I didn't expect as much as this it's a fortune, much more than I ever imagined." Alois laughed again.

"We'll stay down here until the storm blows over then we'll start taking it up. Let's just sit down and relax and have a little celebration." He took his backpack off and brought out a bottle of champagne and two mugs. They sat and drank the champagne as the intensity of the storm above them increased. The thunder was now directly overhead and the heavy clouds were releasing huge volumes of rainwater that poured down onto the forest below. The building above them which had been seriously weakened by the explosives was starting to yield to the strong winds and heavy rain that battered down onto it. The cracks in the roof were getting bigger and the whole building looked in danger of collapsing.

Suddenly there was a huge crash and the dim light which had been coming into the cellar was extinguished, the place was in complete darkness. The mugs were thrown down and both of them ran over to the steps leading out of the cellar. A large concrete slab was blocking the exit. Pushing and heaving with all the muscle they could muster was having no effect on the huge block of concrete above them, it wouldn't move an inch. Unbeknown to them it was not just one slab which had fallen but several, if they had known just how much concrete was blocking the entrance they wouldn't even have bothered to attempt to move it.

Two hours later the batteries in the torch ran out. There was to be no escape for the brother and sister who had stopped at nothing, even murder to get their hands on the treasure. Alois took out a box of matches and struck one, then several more until finally he was holding the last one. As the light from that began to flicker out brother and sister looked at each other for the last time. Neither Interpol or the British police would ever arrest them for the murders they had committed.

Outside the storm had abated, the Jackdaws slowly began to return to their roosts where they would continue to guard the secret. It would be months later when the French authorities found the elusive Jackdaw's Wood. And when they removed all the debris in the old camp and uncovered the entrance to the cellar, they would find two well preserved bodies surrounded by a fortune in gold bullion.

Lightning Source UK Ltd.
Milton Keynes UK
UKOW04f1806131213

222965UK00001B/3/P